THE WORKS OF

WILLIAM MAKEPEACE THACKERAY

KENSINGTON EDITION

VOLUME XXIX

C. M.

Thackeray
at Jack Bell's
July 1853.

Thackeray Speaking

Drawing by C. Martin

CATHERINE: A STORY

THE FITZ-BOODLE PAPERS

TALES

BY

WILLIAM MAKEPEACE THACKERAY

WITH THE AUTHOR'S ILLUSTRATIONS

NEW YORK
CHARLES SCRIBNER'S SONS
1904

THE DE VINNE PRESS

NOTE TO THE
KENSINGTON EDITION

CATHERINE was written in 1839, in Great Coram
Street, and published in the same year and the beginning of the next in *Fraser's Magazine,* over the signature of "Ikey Solomons, jun." It did not appear in book form until the collected edition of 1869.
Its motive, as a satire on the favourite highwayman-
literature of the time, clearly seems from contemporary comment not to have been accepted as Thackeray had hoped and intended; and in spite of individual
appreciation of its strength, on the whole it cannot be
said to have helped the growing interest in his work.
His heroine had been suggested to him by the career of
a historic murderess of a century before, Catherine
Hayes; and one rather timeworn incident in the history
of the story is the anger called down upon Thackeray,
some years after its publication, when a misunderstood
allusion to this fact caused the absurd idea to become
prevalent that Thackeray had cast some slur upon Catherine Hayes, a very popular Irish singer of his own
day. Mrs. Ritchie, Mr. Crowe (in his "Haunts and
Homes"), Trollope (in his Life), and Sir Leslie

Stephen (in the National Biography) have all told the story of the little tempest that this caused, and of the Irish gentleman who hired rooms opposite Thackeray's house with the intention of avenging the lady, but was happily dissuaded. A letter written by Thackeray to the *Morning Chronicle,* under the title "Capers and Anchovies," referred to the incident.

THE FITZ-BOODLE PAPERS were published in *Fraser's Magazine* in 1842, but did not make their appearance in book form until the issue of Bradbury and Evans's series of Miscellanies, in which they were published as one of the later volumes in 1857. Of the little tales here included, "Miss Löwe" appeared with "The Fitz-Boodle Confessions" in 1842; and "Bluebeard's Ghost" also in *Fraser* the next year. "The Professor" was first published in *Bentley's Miscellany,* and afterward included in the two volumes of "Comic Tales and Sketches" already referred to in these notes as published in 1841.

The frontispiece of this volume is from a pencil drawing of Thackeray speaking at dinner, by C. Martin. It is a recent addition to the British Museum's collection, and is believed not to have been before reproduced. The original bears the note in the artist's hand: "Thackeray at Frank Bell's," and the date "July, 1853."

CONTENTS

CATHERINE: A STORY

CONTENTS

THE FITZ-BOODLE PAPERS

TALES

LIST OF ILLUSTRATIONS

CATHERINE

A STORY

CATHERINE

A STORY

CHAPTER I

INTRODUCING TO THE READER THE CHIEF PERSONAGES
OF THIS NARRATIVE

AT that famous period of history, when the seventeenth
century (after a deal of quarrelling, king-killing,
reforming, republicanizing, restoring, re-restoring,
play-writing, sermon-writing, Oliver-Cromwellizing,
Stuartizing, and Orangizing, to be sure) had sunk
into its grave, giving place to the lusty eighteenth;
when Mr. Isaac Newton was a tutor of Trinity,
and Mr. Joseph Addison Commissioner of Appeals;
when the presiding genius that watched over the
destinies of the French nation had played out all the
best cards in his hand, and his adversaries began to pour
in their trumps; when there were two kings in Spain
employed perpetually in running away from one another; when there was a queen in England, with such
rogues for Ministers as have never been seen, no, not in
our own day; and a General, of whom it may be severely
argued, whether he was the meanest miser or the greatest
hero in the world; when Mrs. Masham had not yet put
Madam Marlborough's nose out of joint; when people
had their ears cut off for writing very meek political

pamphlets; and very large full-bottomed wigs were just beginning to be worn with powder; and the face of Louis the Great, as his was handed in to him behind the bed-curtains, was, when issuing thence, observed to look longer, older, and more dismal daily. . . .

About the year One thousand seven hundred and five, that is, in the glorious reign of Queen Anne, there existed certain characters, and befell a series of adventures, which, since they are strictly in accordance with the present fashionable style and taste; since they have been already partly described in the "Newgate Calendar;" since they are (as shall be seen anon) agreeably low, delightfully disgusting, and at the same time eminently pleasing and pathetic, may properly be set down here.

And though it may be said, with some considerable show of reason, that agreeably low and delightfully disgusting characters have already been treated, both copiously and ably, by some eminent writers of the present (and, indeed, of future) ages; though to tread in the footsteps of the immortal FAGIN requires a genius of inordinate stride, and to go a-robbing after the late though deathless TURPIN, the renowned JACK SHEPPARD, or the embryo DUVAL, may be impossible, and not an infringement, but a wasteful indication of ill-will towards the eighth commandment; though it may, on the one hand, be asserted that only vain coxcombs would dare to write on subjects already described by men really and deservedly eminent; on the other hand, that these subjects have been described so fully, that nothing more can be said about them; on the third hand (allowing, for the sake of argument, three hands to one figure of speech), that the public has heard so much of them, as to be quite tired of rogues, thieves, cut-throats, and Newgate altogether;—though all these objections may be urged, and each is excellent, yet we intend to take a few more pages from the " Old Bailey Calendar," to bless the public with one more draught from the Stone Jug: [1]— yet awhile to listen, hurdle-mounted, and riding down the Oxford Road, to the bland conversation of Jack Ketch, and to hang with him round the neck of his patient, at the end of our and his history. We give the reader fair notice, that we shall tickle him with a few such scenes of villainy, throat-cutting, and bodily suffering in general, as are not to be found, no, not in ——; never mind comparisons, for such are odious.

In the year 1705, then, whether it was that the Queen of England did feel seriously alarmed at the notice that a French prince should occupy the Spanish throne; or whether she was tenderly attached to the Emperor of Germany; or whether she was obliged to fight out the quarrel of William of Orange, who made us pay and fight for his Dutch provinces; or whether poor old Louis Quatorze did really frighten her; or whether Sarah Jennings and her husband wanted to make a fight, knowing how much they should gain by it;—whatever the reason was, it was evident that the war was to continue, and there was almost as much soldiering and recruiting, parading, pike and gun-exercising, flag-flying, drum-beating, powder-blazing, and military enthusiasm, as we can all remember in the year 1801, what time the Corsican upstart menaced our shores. A recruiting-party and captain of Cutts's regiment (which had been so mangled at Blenheim the year before,) were now in Warwickshire; and having their depot at Warwick, the captain

[1] This, as your ladyship is aware, is the polite name for her Majesty's prison of Newgate.

and his attendant, the corporal, were used to travel through the country, seeking for heroes to fill up the gaps in Cutts's corps,—and for adventures to pass away the weary time of a country life.

Our Captain Plume and Sergeant Kite (it was at this time, by the way, that those famous recruiting-officers were playing their pranks in Shrewsbury,) were occupied very much in the same manner with Farquhar's heroes. They roamed from Warwick to Stratford, and from Stratford to Birmingham, persuading the swains of Warwickshire to leave the plough for the pike, and despatching, from time to time, small detachments of recruits to extend Marlborough's lines, and to act as food for the hungry cannon at Ramillies and Malplaquet.

Of those two gentlemen who are about to act a very important part in our history, one only was probably a native of Britain,—we say probably, because the individual in question was himself quite uncertain, and, it must be added, entirely indifferent about his birthplace; but speaking the English language, and having been during the course of his life pretty generally engaged in the British service, he had a tolerably fair claim to the majestic title of Briton. His name was Peter Brock, otherwise Corporal Brock, of Lord Cutts's regiment of dragoons; he was of age about fifty-seven (even that point has never been ascertained); in height, about five feet six inches; in weight, nearly thirteen stone; with a chest that the celebrated Leitch himself might envy; an arm, that was like an opera-dancer's leg; a stomach so elastic that it would accommodate itself to any given or stolen quantity of food; a great aptitude for strong liquors; a considerable skill in singing *chansons de table* of not the most delicate kind; he was a lover of jokes, of which he made many, and passably bad; when pleased, simply coarse, boisterous, and jovial; when angry, a perfect demon: bullying, cursing, storming, fighting, as is sometimes the wont with gentlemen of his cloth and education.

Mr. Brock was strictly, what the Marquis of Rodil styled himself in a proclamation to his soldiers after running away, a *hijo de la guerra*—a child of war. Not seven cities, but one or two regiments, might contend for the honour of giving him birth: for his mother, whose name he took, had acted as camp-follower to a Royalist regiment; had then obeyed the Parliamentarians; died in Scotland when Monk was commanding in that country; and the first appearance of Mr. Brock in a public capacity displayed him as a fifer in the General's own regiment of Coldstreamers, when they marched from Scotland to London, and from a republic at once into a monarchy. Since that period, Brock had been always with the army; he had had, too, some promotion, for he spake of having a command at the battle of the Boyne; though probably (as he never mentioned the fact) upon the losing side. The very year before this narrative commences, he had been one of Mordaunt's forlorn hope at Schellenberg, for which service he was promised a pair of colours; he lost them, however, and was almost shot (but fate did not ordain that his career should close in that way) for drunkenness and insubordination immediately after the battle; but having in some measure reinstated himself by a display of much gallantry at Blenheim, it was found advisable to send him to England for the purpose of recruiting, and remove him altogether from the regiment, where his gallantry only rendered the example of his riot more dangerous.

Mr. Brock's commander was a slim young gentleman of twenty-six, about whom there was likewise a history, if one would take the trouble to inquire. He was a Bavarian by birth (his mother being an English lady), and enjoyed along with a dozen other brothers the title of count: eleven of these, of course, were penniless; one or two were priests, one a monk, six or seven in various military services, and the elder at home at Schloss Galgenstein breeding horses, hunting wild boars, swindling tenants, living in a great house with small means; obliged to be sordid at home all the year, to be splendid for a month at the capital, as is the way with many other noblemen. Our young count, Count Gustavus Adolphus Maximilian von Galgenstein, had been in the service of the French, as page to a nobleman; then of his Majesty's *gardes du corps;* then a lieutenant and captain in the Bavarian service; and when, after the battle of Blenheim, two regiments of Germans came over to the winning side, Gustavus Adolphus Maximilian found himself among them; and at the epoch when this story commences, had enjoyed English pay for a year or more. It is unnecessary to say how he exchanged into his present regiment; how it appeared that, before her marriage, handsome John Churchill had known the young gentleman's mother, when they were both penniless hangers-on at Charles the Second's court;—it is, we say, quite useless to repeat all the scandal of which we are perfectly masters, and to trace step by step the events of his history. Here, however, was Gustavus Adolphus, in a small inn, in a small village of Warwickshire, on an autumn evening in the year 1705; and at the very moment when this history begins, he and Mr. Brock, his corporal and friend, were seated at a round table before the kitchen-fire, while a small groom of the establishment was leading up and down on the village green, before the inn door, two black, glossy, long-tailed, barrel-bellied, thick-flanked, arched-necked, Roman-nosed Flanders horses, which were the property of the two gentlemen now taking their ease at the "Bugle Inn." The two gentlemen were seated at their ease at the inn table, drinking mountain-wine; and if the reader fancies from the sketch which we have given of their lives, or from his own blindness and belief in the perfectibility of human nature, that the sun of that autumn evening shone upon any two men in county or city, at desk or harvest, at court or at Newgate, drunk or sober, who were greater rascals than Count Gustavus Galgenstein and Corporal Peter Brock, he is egregiously mistaken, and his knowledge of human nature is not worth a fig. If they had not been two prominent scoundrels, what earthly business should we have in detailing their histories? What would the public care for them? Who would meddle with dull virtue, humdrum sentiment, or stupid innocence, when vice, agreeable vice, is the only thing which the readers of romances care to hear?

The little horse-boy, who was leading the two black Flanders horses up and down the green, might have put them in the stable for any good that the horses got by the gentle exercise which they were now taking in the cool evening air, as their owners had not ridden very far or very hard, and there was not a hair turned of their sleek shining coats; but the lad had been especially ordered so to walk the horses about until he received further commands from the gentlemen reposing in the "Bugle" kitchen; and the idlers of the village seemed so pleased with the beasts, and their smart saddles and shining bridles, that it would have been a pity to deprive them of the pleasure of contemplating such an innocent spectacle. Over the Count's horse was thrown a fine red cloth, richly embroidered in yellow worsted, a very large count's coronet and a cipher at the four corners of the covering; and under this might be seen a pair of gorgeous silver stirrups, and above it, a couple of silver-mounted pistols reposing in bearskin holsters; the bit was silver too, and the horse's head was decorated with many smart ribbons. Of the Corporal's steed, suffice it to say, that the ornaments were in brass, as bright, though not perhaps so valuable, as those which decorated the Captain's animal. The boys, who had been at play on the green, first paused and entered into conversation with the horse-boy; then the village matrons followed; and afterwards, sauntering by ones and twos, came the village maidens, who love soldiers as flies love treacle; presently the males began to arrive, and lo! the parson of the parish, taking his evening walk with Mrs. Dobbs, and the four children his offspring, at length joined himself to his flock.

To this audience the little ostler explained that the animals belonged to two gentlemen now reposing at the "Bugle:" one young with gold hair, the other old with grizzled locks; both in red coats; both in jack-boots; putting the house into a bustle, and calling for the best. He then discoursed to some of his own companions regarding the merits of the horses; and the parson, a learned man, explained to the villagers, that one of the travellers must be a count, or at least had a count's horse-cloth; pronounced that the stirrups were of real silver, and checked the impetuosity of his son, William Nassau Dobbs, who was for mounting the animals, and who expressed a longing to fire off one of the pistols in the holsters.

As this family discussion was taking place, the gentlemen whose appearance had created so much attention came to the door of the inn, and the elder and stouter was seen to smile at his companion; after which he strolled leisurely over the green, and seemed to examine with much benevolent satisfaction the assemblage of villagers who were staring at him and the quadrupeds.

Mr. Brock, when he saw the parson's band and cassock, took off his beaver reverently, and saluted the divine: "I hope your reverence won't baulk the little fellow," said he; "I think I heard him calling out for a ride, and whether he should like my horse, or his lordship's horse, I am sure it is all one. Don't be afraid, sir! the horses are not tired; we have only come seventy mile to-day, and Prince Eugene once rode a matter of fifty-two leagues (a hundred and fifty miles), sir, upon that horse, between sunrise and sunset."

"Gracious powers! on which horse?" said Doctor Dobbs, very solemnly.

"On *this*, sir,—on mine, Corporal Brock of Cutts's black gelding, 'William of Nassau.' The Prince, sir, gave it me after Blenheim fight, for I had my own legs carried away by a cannon-ball, just as I cut down two of Sauerkrauter's regiment, who had made the Prince prisoner."

"Your own legs, sir!" said the Doctor. "Gracious goodness! this is more and more astonishing!"

"No, no, not my own legs, my horse's I mean, sir; and the Prince gave me 'William of Nassau' that very day."

To this no direct reply was made; but the Doctor

looked at Mrs. Dobbs, and Mrs. Dobbs and the rest of the children at her eldest son, who grinned and said, "Isn't it wonderful?" The Corporal to this answered nothing, but, resuming his account, pointed to the other horse and said, "*That* horse, sir—good as mine is—that horse, with the silver stirrups, is his Excellency's horse, Captain Count Maximilian Gustavus Adolphus von Galgenstein, captain of horse and of the Holy Roman empire" (he lifted here his hat with much gravity, and all the crowd, even to the parson, did likewise). "We call him ' George of Denmark,' sir, in compliment to her Majesty's husband: he is Blenheim too, sir: Marshal Tallard rode him on that day, and you know how *he* was taken prisoner by the Count."

"George of Denmark, Marshal Tallard, William of Nassau! this is strange indeed, most wonderful! Why, sir, little are you aware that there are before you, *at this moment,* two other living beings who bear these venerated names! My boys, stand forward! Look here, sir: these children have been respectively named after our late sovereign and the husband of our present Queen."

"And very good names too, sir; ay, and very noble little fellows too; and I propose that, with your reverence and your ladyship's leave, William Nassau here shall ride on George of Denmark, and George of Denmark shall ride on William of Nassau."

When this speech of the Corporal's was made, the whole crowd set up a loyal hurrah; and, with much gravity, the two little boys were lifted up into the saddles; and the Corporal leading one, entrusted the other to the horse-boy, and so together marched stately up and down the green.

The popularity which Mr. Brock gained by this manœuvre was very great; but with regard to the names
of the horses and children, which coincided so extraordinarily, it is but fair to state, that the christening of the
quadrupeds had only taken place about two minutes
before the dragoon's appearance on the green. For if
the fact must be confessed, he, while seated near the inn
window, had kept a pretty wistful eye upon all going
on without; and the horses marching thus to and fro for
the wonderment of the village, were only placards or
advertisements for the riders.

There was, besides the boy now occupied with the
horses, and the landlord and landlady of the "Bugle
Inn," another person connected with that establishment
—a very smart, handsome, vain, giggling servant-girl,
about the age of sixteen, who went by the familiar name
of Cat, and attended upon the gentlemen in the parlour,
while the landlady was employed in cooking their supper
in the kitchen. This young person had been educated in
the village poor-house, and having been pronounced by
Doctor Dobbs and the schoolmaster the idlest, dirtiest,
and most passionate little minx with whom either had
ever had to do, she was, after receiving a very small portion of literary instruction (indeed it must be stated that
the young lady did not know her letters), bound apprentice at the age of nine years to Mrs. Score, her relative,
and landlady of the "Bugle Inn."

If Miss Cat, or Catherine Hall, was a slattern and a
minx, Mrs. Score was a far superior shrew; and for the
seven years of her apprenticeship, the girl was completely at her mistress's mercy. Yet though wondrously
stingy, jealous, and violent, while her maid was idle and
extravagant, and her husband seemed to abet the girl,

Mrs. Score put up with the wench's airs, idleness, and
caprices, without ever wishing to dismiss her from the
"Bugle." The fact is, that Miss Catherine was a great
beauty; and for about two years, since her fame had
begun to spread, the custom of the inn had also increased
vastly. When there was a debate whether the farmers,
on their way from market, would take t'other pot, Catherine, by appearing with it, would straightway cause the
liquor to be swallowed and paid for; and when the traveller who proposed riding that night and sleeping at
Coventry or Birmingham, was asked by Miss Catherine
whether he would like a fire in his bedroom, he generally
was induced to occupy it, although he might before have
vowed to Mrs. Score that he would not for a thousand
guineas be absent from home that night. The girl had,
too, half-a-dozen lovers in the village; and these were
bound in honour to spend their pence at the alehouse she
inhabited. O woman, lovely woman! what strong resolves canst thou twist round thy little finger! what gunpowder passions canst thou kindle with a single sparkle
of thine eye! what lies and fribble nonsense canst thou
make us listen to, as they were gospel truth or splendid
wit! above all, what bad liquor canst thou make us swallow when thou puttest a kiss within the cup—and we are
content to call the poison wine!

The mountain-wine at the "Bugle" was, in fact, ex-
ecrable; but Mrs. Cat, who served it to the two soldiers,
made it so agreeable to them, that they found it a pass-
able, even a pleasant task, to swallow the contents of a
second bottle. The miracle had been wrought instan-
taneously on her appearance: for whereas at that very
moment the Count was employed in cursing the wine,
the landlady, the wine-grower, and the English nation

Mrs. Catherine's
Temptation

generally, when the young woman entered and (choosing so to interpret the oaths) said, " Coming, your honour; I think your honour called "—Gustavus Adolphus whistled, stared at her very hard, and seeming quite dumb-stricken by her appearance, contented himself by swallowing a whole glass of mountain by way of reply.

Mr. Brock was, however, by no means so confounded as his captain: he was thirty years older than the latter, and in the course of fifty years of military life had learned to look on the most dangerous enemy, or the most beautiful woman, with the like daring, devil-may-care determination to conquer.

" My dear Mary," then said that gentleman, " his honour is a lord; as good as a lord, that is; for all he allows such humble fellows as I am to drink with him."

Catherine dropped a low curtsey, and said, " Well, I don't know if you are joking a poor country girl, as all you soldier gentlemen do; but his honour *looks* like a lord: though I never see one, to be sure."

" Then," said the Captain, gathering courage, " how do you know I look like one, pretty Mary? "

" Pretty Catherine: I mean Catherine, if you please, sir."

Here Mr. Brock burst into a roar of laughter, and shouting with many oaths that she was right at first, invited her to give him what he called a buss.

Pretty Catherine turned away from him at this request, and muttered something about "Keep your distance, low fellow! buss indeed! poor country girl," &c. &c., placing herself, as if for protection, on the side of the Captain. That gentleman looked also very angry; but whether at the sight of innocence so outraged, or the insolence of the Corporal for daring to help himself first, we cannot say. "Hark ye, Mr. Brock," he cried very fiercely, "I will suffer no such liberties in my presence: remember, it is only my condescension which permits you to share my bottle in this way; take care I don't give you instead a taste of my cane." So saying, he, in a protecting manner, placed one hand round Mrs. Catherine's waist, holding the other clenched very near to the Corporal's nose.

Mrs. Catherine, for *her* share of this action of the Count's, dropped another curtsey, and said, "Thank you, my lord." But Galgenstein's threat did not appear to make any impression on Mr. Brock, as indeed there was no reason that it should; for the Corporal, at a combat of fisticuffs, could have pounded his commander into a jelly in ten minutes: so he contented himself by saying, "Well, noble Captain, there's no harm done; it *is* an honour for poor old Peter Brock to be at table with you, and I *am* sorry sure enough."

"In truth, Peter, I believe thou art; thou hast good reason, eh, Peter? But never fear, man; had I struck thee, I never would have hurt thee."

"I *know* you would not," replied Brock, laying his hand on his heart with much gravity; and so peace was made, and healths were drank. Miss Catherine condescended to put her lips to the Captain's glass; who swore that the wine was thus converted into nectar; and although the girl had not previously heard of that liquor, she received the compliment as a compliment, and smiled and simpered in return.

The poor thing had never before seen anybody so handsome, or so finely dressed as the Count; and, in the simplicity of her coquetry, allowed her satisfaction to be quite visible. Nothing could be more clumsy than the gentleman's mode of complimenting her; but for this, perhaps, his speeches were more effective than others more delicate would have been; and though she said to each, "Oh, now, my lord," and "La, Captain, how can you flatter one so?" and "Your honour's laughing at me," and made such polite speeches as are used on these occasions, it was manifest from the flutter and blush, and the grin of satisfaction which lighted up the buxom features of the little country beauty, that the Count's first operations had been highly successful. When following up his attack, he produced from his neck a small locket (which had been given him by a Dutch lady at the Brill), and begged Miss Catherine to wear it for his sake, and chucked her under the chin and called her his little rosebud, it was pretty clear how things would go: anybody who could see the expression of Mr. Brock's countenance at this event might judge of the progress of the irresistible High-Dutch conqueror.

Being of a very vain, communicative turn, our fair barmaid gave her two companions not only a pretty long account of herself, but of many other persons in the village, whom she could perceive from the window opposite to which she stood. "Yes, your honour," said she—"my lord, I mean; sixteen last March, though there's a many girl in the village that at my age is quite chits. There's Polly Randall now, that red-haired girl along with Thomas Curtis: she's seventeen if she's a day, though he is the very first sweetheart she has had. Well, as I am saying, I was bred up here in the village—father and mother died very young, and I was left a poor orphan— well, bless us! if Thomas haven't kissed her!—to the care of Mrs. Score, my aunt, who has been a mother to me—a stepmother, you know;—and I've been to Stratford fair, and to Warwick many a time; and there's two people who have offered to marry me, and ever so many who want to, and I won't have none—only a gentleman, as I've always said; not a poor clodpole, like Tom there with the red waistcoat (he was one that asked me), nor a drunken fellow like Sam Blacksmith yonder, him whose wife has got the black eye, but a real gentleman, like—"

"Like whom, my dear?" said the Captain, encouraged.

"La, sir, how can you? why, like our squire, Sir John, who rides in such a mortal fine gold coach; or, at least, like the parson, Doctor Dobbs—that's he in the black gown, walking with Madam Dobbs in red."

"And are those his children?"

"Yes: two girls and two boys; and only think, he calls one William Nassau, and one George Denmark—isn't it odd?" And from the parson, Mrs. Catherine went on to speak of several humble personages of the village community, who, as they are not necessary to our story, need not be described at full length. It was when, from the window, Corporal Brock saw the altercation between the worthy divine and his son, respecting the latter's ride, that he judged it a fitting time to step out on the green, and to bestow on the two horses those famous historical names which we have just heard applied to them.

Mr. Brock's diplomacy was, as we have stated, quite successful; for, when the parson's boys had ridden and retired along with their mamma and papa, other young gentlemen of humbler rank in the village were placed upon "George of Denmark" and "William of Nassau;" the Corporal joking and laughing with all the grown-up people. The women, in spite of Mr. Brock's age, his red nose, and a certain squint of his eye, vowed the Corporal was a jewel of a man; and among the men his popularity was equally great.

"How much dost thee get, Thomas Clodpole?" said Mr. Brock to a countryman (he was the man whom Mrs. Catherine had described as her suitor), who had laughed loudest at some of his jokes: "how much dost thee get for a week's work, now?"

Mr. Clodpole, whose name was really Bullock, stated that his wages amounted to "three shillings and a puddn."

"Three shillings and a puddn!—monstrous!—and for this you toil like a galley-slave, as I have seen them in Turkey and America,—ay, gentlemen, and in the country of Prester John! You shiver out of bed on icy winter mornings, to break the ice for Ball and Dapple to drink."

"Yes, indeed," said the person addressed, who seemed astounded at the extent of the Corporal's information.

"Or you clean pigsty, and take dung down to meadow; or you act watchdog and tend sheep; or you sweep a scythe over a great field of grass; and when the sun has scorched the eyes out of your head, and sweated the flesh out of your bones, and well-nigh fried the soul out of your body, you go home, to what?—three shillings a week and a puddn! Do you get pudding every day?"

"No; only Sundays."

"Do you get money enough?"

"No, sure."

"Do you get beer enough?"

"Oh no, NEVER!" said Mr. Bullock quite resolutely.

"Worthy Clodpole, give us thy hand: it shall have beer enough this day, or my name's not Corporal Brock. Here's the money, boy! there are twenty pieces in this purse: and how do you think I got em? and how do you think I shall get others when these are gone?—by serving her sacred Majesty to be sure: long life to her, and down with the French King!"

Bullock, a few of the men, and two or three of the boys, piped out an hurrah, in compliment to this speech of the Corporal's: but it was remarked that the greater part of the crowd drew back—the women whispering ominously to them and looking at the Corporal.

"I see, ladies, what it is," said he. "You are frightened, and think I am a crimp come to steal your sweethearts away. What! call Peter Brock a double-dealer? I tell you what, boys, Jack Churchill himself has shaken this hand, and drunk a pot with me: do you think he'd shake hands with a rogue? Here's Tummas Clodpole has never had beer enough, and here am I will stand treat to him and any other gentleman; am I good enough company for him? I have money, look you, and like to spend it: what should *I* be doing dirty actions for—hay, Tummas?"

A satisfactory reply to this query was not, of course, expected by the Corporal nor uttered by Mr. Bullock; and the end of the dispute was, that he and three or four of the rustic bystanders were quite convinced of the good intentions of their new friend, and accompanied him back to the "Bugle," to regale upon the promised beer. Among the Corporal's guests was one young fellow whose dress would show that he was somewhat better to do in the world than Clodpole and the rest of the sunburnt ragged troop, who were marching towards the alehouse. This man was the only one of his hearers who, perhaps, was sceptical as to the truth of his stories; but as soon as Bullock accepted the invitation to drink, John

Hayes, the carpenter (for such was his name and profession), said, "Well, Thomas, if thou goest, I will go too."

"I know thee wilt," said Thomas: "thou'lt goo anywhere Catty Hall is, provided thou canst goo for nothing."

"Nay, I have a penny to spend as good as the Corporal here."

"A penny to *keep,* you mean: for all your love for the lass at the 'Bugle,' did thee ever spend a shilling in the house? Thee wouldn't go now, but that I am going too, and the Captain here stands treat."

"Come, come, gentlemen, no quarrelling," said Mr. Brock. "If this pretty fellow will join us, amen say I: there's lots of liquor, and plenty of money to pay the score. Comrade Tummas, give us thy arm. Mr. Hayes, you're a hearty cock, I make no doubt, and all such are welcome. Come along, my gentleman farmers, Mr. Brock shall have the honour to pay for you all." And with this, Corporal Brock, accompanied by Messrs. Hayes, Bullock, Blacksmith, Baker's-boy, Butcher, and one or two others, adjourned to the inn; the horses being, at the same time, conducted to the stable.

Although we have, in this quiet way, and without any flourishing of trumpets, or beginning of chapters, introduced Mr. Hayes to the public; and although, at first sight, a sneaking carpenter's boy may seem hardly worthy of the notice of an intelligent reader, who looks for a good cut-throat or highwayman for a hero, or a pickpocket at the very least: this gentleman's words and actions should be carefully studied by the public, as he is destined to appear before them under very polite and curious circumstances during the course of this history.

The speech of the rustic Juvenal, Mr. Clodpole, had seemed to infer that Hayes was at once careful of his money and a warm admirer of Mrs. Catherine of the "Bugle:" and both the charges were perfectly true. Hayes's father was reported to be a man of some substance; and young John, who was performing his apprenticeship in the village, did not fail to talk very big of his pretensions to fortune—of his entering, at the close of his indentures, into partnership with his father—and of the comfortable farm and house over which Mrs. John Hayes, whoever she might be, would one day preside. Thus, next to the barber and butcher, and above even his own master, Mr. Hayes took rank in the village: and it must not be concealed that his representation of wealth had made some impression upon Mrs. Hall, towards whom the young gentleman had cast the eyes of affection. If he had been tolerably well-looking, and not pale, rickety, and feeble as he was; if even he had been ugly, but withal a man of spirit, it is probable the girl's kindness for him would have been much more decided. But he was a poor weak creature, not to compare with honest Thomas Bullock, by at least nine inches; and so notoriously timid, selfish, and stingy, that there was a kind of shame in receiving his addresses openly; and what encouragement Mrs. Catherine gave him could only be in secret.

But no mortal is wise at all times: and the fact was, that Hayes, who cared for himself intensely, had set his heart upon winning Catherine; and loved her with a desperate, greedy eagerness and desire of possession, which makes passions for women often so fierce and unreasonable among very cold and selfish men. His parents (whose frugality he had inherited) had tried in vain to

wean him from this passion, and had made many fruitless
attempts to engage him with women who possessed
money and desired husbands: but Hayes was, for a wonder, quite proof against their attractions; and, though
quite ready to acknowledge the absurdity of his love for
a penniless alehouse servant-girl, nevertheless persisted
in it doggedly. "I know I'm a fool," said he; "and
what's more, the girl does not care for me; but marry
her I must, or I think I shall just die: and marry her I
will." For very much to the credit of Miss Catherine's
modesty, she had declared that marriage was with her a
sine quâ non, and had dismissed, with the loudest scorn
and indignation, all propositions of a less proper nature.

Poor Thomas Bullock was another of her admirers,
and had offered to marry her; but three shillings a week
and a puddn was not to the girl's taste, and Thomas had
been scornfully rejected. Hayes had also made her a
direct proposal. Catherine did not say no: she was too
prudent: but she was young and could wait; she did not
care for Mr. Hayes *yet* enough to marry him— (it did
not seem, indeed, in the young woman's nature to care
for anybody) —and she gave her adorer flatteringly to
understand that, if nobody better appeared in the course
of a few years, she might be induced to become Mrs.
Hayes. It was a dismal prospect for the poor fellow to
live upon the hope of being one day Mrs. Catherine's
pis-aller.

In the meantime she considered herself free as the
wind, and permitted herself all the innocent gaieties which
that "chartered libertine," a coquette, can take. She
flirted with all the bachelors, widowers, and married men,
in a manner which did extraordinary credit to her years:
and let not the reader fancy such pastimes unnatural at

her early age. The ladies—heaven bless them!—are, as
a general rule, coquettes from babyhood upwards. Little
she's of three years old play little airs and graces upon
small heroes of five; simpering misses of nine make attacks upon young gentlemen of twelve; and at sixteen,
a well-grown girl, under encouraging circumstances,—
say, she is pretty, in a family of ugly elder sisters, or an
only child and heiress, or an humble wench at a country
inn, like our fair Catherine—is at the very pink and
prime of her coquetry: they will jilt you at that age with
an ease and arch infantine simplicity that never can be
surpassed in maturer years.

Miss Catherine, then, was a *franche coquette,* and Mr.
John Hayes was miserable. His life was passed in a
storm of mean passions and bitter jealousies, and desperate attacks upon the indifference-rock of Mrs. Catherine's heart, which not all his tempest of love could beat
down. O cruel, cruel pangs of love unrequited! Mean
rogues feel them as well as great heroes. Lives there the
man in Europe who has not felt them many times?—who
has not knelt, and fawned, and supplicated, and wept,
and cursed, and raved, all in vain; and passed long wakeful nights with ghosts of dead hopes for company;
shadows of buried remembrances that glide out of their
graves of nights, and whisper, "We are dead now, but
we *were* once; and we made you happy, and we come
now to mock you:—despair, O lover, despair, and die?"
—O cruel pangs! dismal nights!—Now a sly demon
creeps under your nightcap, and drops into your ear
those soft, hope-breathing, sweet words, uttered on the
well-remembered evening: there, in the drawer of your
dressing-table (along with the razors, and Macassar oil),
lies the dead flower that Lady Amelia Wilhelmina wore

in her bosom on the night of a certain ball—the corpse
of a glorious hope that seemed once as if it would live for
ever, so strong was it, so full of joy and sunshine: there,
in your writing-desk, among a crowd of unpaid bills, is
the dirty scrap of paper, thimble-sealed, which came in
company with a pair of muffetees of her knitting (she
was a butcher's daughter, and did all she could, poor
thing!), begging "you would ware them at collidge, and
think of her who"—married a public-house three weeks
afterwards, and cares for you no more now than she does
for the pot-boy. But why multiply instances, or seek to
depict the agony of poor, mean-spirited John Hayes?
No mistake can be greater than that of fancying such
great emotions of love are only felt by virtuous or exalted men: depend upon it, Love, like Death, plays
havoc among the *pauperum tabernas,* and sports with
rich and poor, wicked and virtuous, alike. I have often
fancied, for instance, on seeing the haggard, pale young
old-clothesman, who wakes the echoes of our street with
his nasal cry of "Clo'!"—I have often, I said, fancied
that, besides the load of exuvial coats and breeches under
which he staggers, there is another weight on him—an
atrior cura at his tail—and while his unshorn lips and
nose together are performing that mocking, boisterous,
Jack-indifferent cry of "Clo', clo'!" who knows what
woful utterances are crying from the heart within?
There he is chaffering with the footman at No. 7, about
an old dressing-gown; you think his whole soul is bent
only on the contest about the garment. Psha! there is,
perhaps, some faithless girl in Holywell Street who fills
up his heart; and that desultory Jew-boy is a peripatetic
hell! Take another instance:—take the man in the beef-
shop in Saint Martin's Court. There he is, to all ap-

pearances quite calm: before the same round of beef—
from morning till sundown—for hundreds of years very
likely. Perhaps when the shutters are closed, and all the
world tired and silent, there is HE silent, but untired—
cutting, cutting, cutting. You enter, you get your meat
to your liking, you depart; and, quite unmoved, on, on he
goes, reaping ceaselessly the Great Harvest of Beef.
You would fancy that if Passion ever failed to conquer,
it had in vain assailed the calm bosom of THAT MAN. I
doubt it, and would give much to know his history. Who
knows what furious Ætna-flames are raging underneath
the surface of that calm flesh-mountain—who can tell
me that that calmness itself is not DESPAIR?

＊   ＊   ＊   ＊   ＊

The reader, if he does not now understand why it was
that Mr. Hayes agreed to drink the Corporal's proffered
beer, had better just read the foregoing remarks over
again, and if he does not understand *then,* why, small
praise to his brains. Hayes could not bear that Mr.
Bullock should have a chance of seeing, and perhaps
making love to Mrs. Catherine in his absence; and
though the young woman never diminished her coquetries, but, on the contrary, rather increased them in his
presence, it was still a kind of dismal satisfaction to be
miserable in her company.

On this occasion, the disconsolate lover could be
wretched to his heart's content; for Catherine had not
a word or a look for him, but bestowed all her smiles
upon the handsome stranger who owned the black horse.
As for poor Tummas Bullock, his passion was never
violent; and he was content in the present instance to
sigh and drink beer. He sighed and drank, sighed and
drank, and drank again, until he had swallowed so much

of the Corporal's liquor, as to be induced to accept a
guinea from his purse also; and found himself, on returning to reason and sobriety, a soldier of Queen
Anne's.

But oh! fancy the agonies of Mr. Hayes when, seated
with the Corporal's friends at one end of the kitchen,
he saw the Captain at the place of honour, and the smiles
which the fair maid bestowed upon him; when, as she
lightly whisked past him with the Captain's supper, she,
pointing to the locket that once reposed on the breast
of the Dutch lady at the Brill, looked archly on Hayes
and said, " See, John, what his lordship has given me;"
and when John's face became green and purple with
rage and jealousy, Mrs. Catherine laughed ten times
louder, and cried, " Coming, my lord," in a voice of
shrill triumph, that bored through the soul of Mr. John
Hayes and left him gasping for breath.

On Catherine's other lover, Mr. Thomas, this coquetry
had no effect: he, and two comrades of his, had by this
time quite fallen under the spell of the Corporal; and
hope, glory, strong beer, Prince Eugene, pairs of
colours, more strong beer, her blessed Majesty, plenty
more strong beer, and such subjects, martial and bac-
chic, whirled through their dizzy brains at a railroad
pace.

And now, if there had been a couple of experienced
reporters present at the " Bugle Inn," they might have
taken down a conversation on love and war—the two
themes discussed by the two parties occupying the
kitchen—which, as the parts were sung together, duet-
wise, formed together some very curious harmonies.
Thus, while the Captain was whispering the softest no-
things the Corporal was shouting the fiercest combats of

the war; and, like the gentleman at Penelope's table, on
it *exiguo pinxit prælia tota* bero.   For example:—

Captain.—"What do you say to a silver trimming,
pretty Catherine?   Don't you think a scarlet riding-
cloak, handsomely laced, would become you wonderfully
well?—and a grey hat with a blue feather—and a pretty
nag to ride on—and all the soldiers to present arms as
you pass, and say, There goes the Captain's lady?
What do you think of a side-box at 'Lincoln's Inn'
playhouse, or of standing up to a minuet with my Lord
Marquis at—?"

Corporal.—"The ball, sir, ran right up his elbow, and
was found the next day by Surgeon Splinter of ours,—
where do you think, sir?—upon my honour as a gentleman it came out of the nape of his—"

Captain.—"Necklace—and a sweet pair of diamond
earrings, mayhap—and a little shower of patches, which
ornament a lady's face wondrously—and a leetle rouge
—though, egad! such peach-cheeks as yours don't want
it;—fie! Mrs. Catherine, I should think the birds must
come and peck at them as if they were fruit—"

Corporal.—"Over the wall; and three-and-twenty of
our fellows jumped after me.   By the Pope of Rome,
friend Tummas, that was a day!—Had you seen how
the Mounseers looked when four-and-twenty rampag-
ing he-devils, sword and pistol, cut and thrust, pell-mell
came tumbling into the redoubt!   Why, sir, we left in
three minutes as many artillerymen's heads as there were
cannon-balls.   It was, 'Ah sacré!' 'D—— you, take
that!' 'O mon Dieu!' run him through. 'Ventrebleu!' and it *was* ventrebleu with him, I warrant you:
for *bleu,* in the French language, means 'through;' and
ventre—why, you see, ventre means—"

Captain.—"Waists, which are worn now excessive long;—and for the hoops, if you *could* but see them— stap my vitals, my dear, but there was a lady at War- wick's Assembly (she came in one of my lord's coaches) who had a hoop as big as a tent: you might have dined under it comfortably;—ha! ha! 'pon my faith, now—"

Corporal.—"And there we found the Duke of Marl- borough seated along with Marshal Tallard, who was endeavouring to drown his sorrow over a cup of Johan- nisberger wine; and a good drink too, my lads, only not to compare to Warwick beer. 'Who was the man who has done this?' said our noble General. I stepped up. 'How many heads was it,' says he, 'that you cut off?' 'Nineteen,' says I, 'besides wounding several.' When he heard it (Mr. Hayes, you don't drink) I'm blest if he didn't burst into tears! 'Noble, noble fellow,' says he. 'Marshal, you must excuse me, if I am pleased to hear of the destruction of your countrymen. Noble, noble fellow!—here's a hundred guineas for you.' Which sum he placed in my hand. 'Nay,' says the Marshal, 'the man has done his duty:' and, pulling out a magnificent gold diamond-hilted snuff-box, he gave me—"

Mr. Bullock.—"What, a goold snuff-box? Wauns, but thee *wast* in luck, Corporal!"—

Corporal.—"No, not the snuff-box, but—*a pinch of snuff,*—ha! ha!—run me through the body if he didn't! Could you but have seen the smile on Jack Churchill's grave face at this piece of generosity! So, beckoning Colonel Cadogan up to him, he pinched his ear and whispered—"

Captain.—"'May I have the honour to dance a min- uet with your ladyship?' The whole room was in titters

at Jack's blunder; for, as you know very well, poor
Lady Susan *has a wooden leg.* Ha! ha! fancy a minuet and a wooden leg, hey, my dear?—"
     Mrs. Catherine.—" Giggle—giggle—giggle: he! he!
he! Oh, Captain, you rogue, you—"
     Second table.—" Haw! haw! haw! Well, you *be* a
foony mon, sergeant, zure enoff."

       *   *   *   *   *

This little specimen of the conversation must be sufficient. It will show pretty clearly that each of the two
military commanders was conducting his operations with
perfect success. Three of the detachment of five attacked by the Corporal surrendered to him: Mr. Bullock, namely, who gave in at a very early stage of the
evening, and ignominiously laid down his arms under
the table, after standing not more than a dozen volleys
of beer; Mr. Blacksmith's boy, and a labourer whose
name we have not been able to learn. Mr. Butcher himself was on the point of yielding, when he was rescued
by the furious charge of a detachment that marched to
his relief: his wife namely, who, with two squalling children, rushed into the "Bugle," boxed Butcher's ears,
and kept up such a tremendous fire of oaths and screams
upon the Corporal, that he was obliged to retreat. Fix-
ing then her claws into Mr. Butcher's hair, she proceeded
to drag him out of the premises; and thus Mr. Brock
was overcome. His attack upon John Hayes was a still
greater failure; for that young man seemed to be in-
vincible by drink, if not by love: and at the end of the
drinking-bout was a great deal more cool than the Corporal himself; to whom he wished a very polite good-
evening, as calmly he took his hat to depart. He turned
to look at Catherine, to be sure, and then he was not quite

so calm: but Catherine did not give any reply to his good-night. She was seated at the Captain's table playing at cribbage with him; and though Count Gustavus Maximilian lost every game, he won more than he lost, —sly fellow!—and Mrs. Catherine was no match for him.

It is to be presumed that Hayes gave some information to Mrs. Score, the landlady: for, on leaving the kitchen, he was seen to linger for a moment in the bar; and very soon after Mrs. Catherine was called away from her attendance on the Count, who, when he asked for a sack and toast, was furnished with those articles by the landlady herself: and, during the half-hour in which he was employed in consuming this drink, Monsieur de Galgenstein looked very much disturbed and out of humour, and cast his eyes to the door perpetually; but no Catherine came. At last, very sulkily, he desired to be shown to bed, and walked as well as he could (for, to say truth, the noble Count was by this time somewhat unsteady on his legs) to his chamber. It was Mrs. Score who showed him to it, and closed the curtains, and pointed triumphantly to the whiteness of the sheets.

"It's a very comfortable room," said she, "though not the best in the house; which belong of right to your lordship's worship; but our best room has two beds, and Mr. Corporal is in that, locked and double-locked, with his three tipsy recruits. But your honour will find this here bed comfortable and well-aired; I've slept in it myself this eighteen years."

"What, my good woman, you are going to sit up, eh? It's cruel hard on you, madam."

"Sit up, my lord? bless you, no! I shall have half of

our Cat's bed; as I always do when there's company."
And with this Mrs. Score curtseyed and retired.

*　　*　　*　　*　　*

Very early the next morning the active landlady and
her bustling attendant had prepared the ale and bacon
for the Corporal and his three converts, and had set a
nice white cloth for the Captain's breakfast. The young
blacksmith did not eat with much satisfaction; but Mr.
Bullock and his friend betrayed no sign of discontent,
except such as may be consequent upon an evening's
carouse. They walked very contentedly to be registered
before Doctor Dobbs, who was also justice of the peace,
and went in search of their slender bundles, and took
leave of their few acquaintances without much regret:
for the gentlemen had been bred in the workhouse, and
had not, therefore, a large circle of friends.

It wanted only an hour of noon, and the noble Count
had not descended. The men were waiting for him, and
spent much of the Queen's money (earned by the sale
of their bodies overnight) while thus expecting him.
Perhaps Mrs. Catherine expected him too, for she had
offered many times to run up—with my lord's boots—
with the hot water—to show Mr. Brock the way; who
sometimes condescended to officiate as barber. But on
all these occasions Mrs. Score had prevented her; not
scolding, but with much gentleness and smiling. At
last, more gentle and smiling than ever, she came downstairs and said, " Catherine darling, his honour the Count
is mighty hungry this morning, and vows he could pick
the wing of a fowl. Run down, child, to Farmer Brigg's
and get one: pluck it before you bring it, you know, and
we will make his lordship a pretty breakfast."

Catherine took up her basket, and away she went

by the back-yard, through the stables.   There she heard the little horse-boy whistling and hissing after the manner of horse-boys; and there she learned that Mrs. Score had been inventing an ingenious story to have her out of the way.   The ostler said he was just going to lead the two horses round to the door.   The Corporal had been, and they were about to start on the instant for Stratford.

The fact was that Count Gustavus Adolphus, far from wishing to pick the wing of a fowl, had risen with a horror and loathing for everything in the shape of food, and for any liquor stronger than small beer.   Of this he had drunk a cup, and said he should ride immediately to Stratford; and when, on ordering his horses, he had asked politely of the landlady "why the d——— *she* always came up, and why she did not send the girl," Mrs. Score informed the Count that her Catherine was gone out for a walk along with the young man to whom she was to be married, and would not be visible that day. On hearing this the Captain ordered his horses that moment, and abused the wine, the bed, the house, the landlady, and everything connected with the "Bugle Inn."

Out the horses came: the little boys of the village gathered round; the recruits, with bunches of ribands in their beavers, appeared presently; Corporal Brock came swaggering out, and, slapping the pleased blacksmith on the back, bade him mount his horse; while the boys hurrah'd.   Then the Captain came out, gloomy and majestic; to him Mr. Brock made a military salute, which clumsily, and with much grinning, the recruits imitated.   "I shall walk on with these brave fellows, your honour, and meet you at Stratford," said the Corporal.   "Good," said the Captain, as he mounted.   The landlady curtseyed; the children hurrah'd more; the little horse-boy, who held the bridle with one hand and the stirrup with the other, and expected a crown-piece from such a noble gentleman, got only a kick and a curse, as Count von Galgenstein shouted, "D— you all, get out of the way!" and galloped off; and John Hayes, who had been sneaking about the inn all the morning, felt a weight off his heart when he saw the Captain ride off alone.

*   *   *   *   *

O foolish Mrs. Score! O dolt of a John Hayes! If the landlady had allowed the Captain and the maid to have their way, and meet but for a minute before recruits, sergeant, and all, it is probable that no harm would have been done, and that this history would never have been written.

When Count von Galgenstein had ridden half a mile on the Stratford road, looking as black and dismal as Napoleon galloping from the romantic village of Waterloo, he espied, a few score yards onwards, at the turn of the road, a certain object which caused him to check his horse suddenly, brought a tingling red into his cheeks, and made his heart to go thump—thump! against his side. A young lass was sauntering slowly along the footpath, with a basket swinging from one hand, and a bunch of hedge-flowers in the other. She stopped once or twice to add a fresh one to her nosegay, and might have seen him, the Captain thought; but no, she never looked directly towards him, and still walked on. Sweet innocent! she was singing as if none were near; her voice went soaring up to the clear sky, and the Captain put his horse on the grass, that the sound of the hoofs might not disturb the music.

"When the kine had given a pailful"—sang she,
  "And the sheep came bleating home,
Poll, who knew it would be healthful,
  Went a-walking out with Tom.
Hand in hand, sir, on the land, sir,
  As they walked to and fro,
Tom made jolly love to Polly,
  But was answered no, no, no."

The Captain had put his horse on the grass, that the sound of his hoofs might not disturb the music; and now he pushed its head on to the bank, where straightway "George of Denmark" began chewing of such a salad as grew there. And now the Captain slid off stealthily; and smiling comically, and hitching up his great jackboots, and moving forward with a jerking tiptoe step, he, just as she was trilling the last *o-o-o* of the last *no* in the above poem of Tom D'Urfey, came up to her, and touching her lightly on the waist, said,

"My dear, your very humble servant."

Mrs. Catherine (you know you have found her out long ago!) gave a scream and a start, and would have turned pale if she could. As it was, she only shook all over, and said,

"Oh, sir, how you *did* frighten me!"

"Frighten you, my rosebud! why, run me through, I'd die rather than frighten you. Gad, child, tell me now, am I so *very* frightful?"

"Oh, no, your honour, I didn't mean that; only I wasn't thinking to meet you here, or that you would ride so early at all: for, if you please, sir, I was going to fetch a chicken for your lordship's breakfast, as my mistress said you would like one; and I thought, instead of going to Farmer Brigg's, down Birmingham way, as she told me, I'd go to Farmer Bird's, where the chickens is better, sir—my lord, I mean."

"Said I'd like a chicken for breakfast, the old cat! why, I told her I would not eat a morsel to save me— I was so dru—, I mean I ate such a good supper last night—and I bade her to send me a pot of small beer, and to tell you to bring it; and the wretch said you were gone out with your sweetheart—"

"What! John Hayes, the creature? Oh, what a naughty story-telling woman!"

"—You had walked out with your sweetheart, and I was not to see you any more; and I was mad with rage, and ready to kill myself; I was, my dear."

"Oh, sir! pray, *pray* don't."

"For your sake, my sweet angel?"

"Yes, for my sake, if such a poor girl as me can persuade noble gentlemen."

"Well, then, for *your* sake, I won't: no, I'll live; but why live? Hell and fury, if I do live I'm miserable without you; I am,—you know I am,—you adorable, beautiful, cruel, wicked Catherine!"

Catherine's reply to this was "La, bless me! I do believe your horse is running away." And so he was; for having finished his meal in the hedge, he first looked towards his master and paused, as it were, irresolutely; then, by a sudden impulse, flinging up his tail and his hind legs, he scampered down the road.

Mrs. Hall ran lightly after the horse, and the Captain after Mrs. Hall; and the horse ran quicker and quicker every moment, and might have led them a long chase— when lo! debouching from a twist in the road, came the detachment of cavalry and infantry under Mr. Brock. The moment he was out of sight of the village, that gentleman had desired the blacksmith to dismount, and had himself jumped into the saddle, maintaining the subordination of his army by drawing a pistol and swearing that he would blow out the brains of any person who attempted to run. When the Captain's horse came near the detachment he paused, and suffered himself to be caught by Tummas Bullock, who held him until the owner and Mrs. Catherine came up.

Mr. Bullock looked comically grave when he saw the pair; but the Corporal graciously saluted Mrs. Catherine, and said it was a fine day for walking.

"La, sir, and so it is," said she, panting in a very pretty and distressing way, "but not for *running*. I do protest—ha!—and vow that I really can scarcely stand. I'm so tired of running after that naughty, naughty horse!"

"How do, Cattern?" said Thomas. "Zee, I be going a zouldiering because thee wouldn't have me." And here Mr. Bullock grinned. Mrs. Catherine made no sort of reply, but protested once more she should die of running. If the truth were told, she was somewhat vexed at the arrival of the Corporal's detachment, and had had very serious thoughts of finding herself quite tired just as he came in sight.

A sudden thought brought a smile of bright satisfaction in the Captain's eyes. He mounted the horse which Tummas still held. "*Tired,* Mrs. Catherine," said he, "and for my sake? By heavens, you shan't walk a step farther! No, you shall ride back with a guard of honour! Back to the village, gentlemen!—rightabout face! Show those fellows, Corporal, how to rightabout face. Now, my dear, mount behind me on Snowball, he's easy as a sedan. Put your dear little foot on the toe of my boot. There now,—up!—jump! hurrah!"

"*That's* not the way, Captain," shouted out Thomas, still holding on to the rein as the horse began to move. "Thee woan't goo with him, will thee, Catty?"

But Mrs. Catherine, though she turned away her head, never let go her hold round the Captain's waist; and he, swearing a dreadful oath at Thomas, struck him across the face and hands with his riding-whip. The poor fellow, who at the first cut still held on to the rein, dropped it at the second, and as the pair galloped off, sat down on the roadside and fairly began to weep.

"*March,* you dog!" shouted out the Corporal a minute after. And so he did: and when next he saw Mrs. Catherine she *was* the Captain's lady sure enough, and wore a grey hat with a blue feather, and red riding-coat trimmed with silver-lace. But Thomas was then on a bare-backed horse, which Corporal Brock was flanking round a ring, and he was so occupied looking between his horse's ears that he had no time to cry then, and at length got the better of his attachment.

This being a good opportunity for closing Chapter I., we ought, perhaps, to make some apologies to the public for introducing them to characters that are so utterly worthless; as we confess all our heroes, with the exception of Mr. Bullock, to be. In this we have consulted nature and history, rather than the prevailing taste and the general manner of authors. The amusing novel of "Ernest Maltravers," for instance, opens with a seduction; but then it is performed by people of the strictest virtue on both sides: and there is so much religion and philosophy in the heart of the seducer, so much tender innocence in the soul of the seduced, that—bless the little dears!—their very peccadilloes make one interested in them; and their naughtiness becomes quite sacred, so deliciously is it described. Now, if we *are* to be interested by rascally actions, let us have them with plain faces, and let them be performed, not by virtuous philosophers, but by rascals. Another clever class of novelists adopt the contrary system, and create interest by making their rascals perform virtuous actions. Against these popular plans we here solemnly appeal. We say, let your rogues in novels act like rogues, and your honest men like honest men; don't let us have any juggling and thimblerigging with virtue and vice, so that, at the end of three volumes, the bewildered reader shall not know which is which; don't let us find ourselves kindling at the generous qualities of thieves, and sympathizing with the rascalities of noble hearts. For our own part, we know what the public likes, and have chosen rogues for our characters, and have taken a story from the "Newgate Calendar," which we hope to follow out to edification. Among the rogues, at least, we will have nothing that shall be mistaken for virtues. And if the British public (after calling for three or four editions) shall give up, not only our rascals, but the rascals of all other authors, we shall be content:—we shall apply to Government for a pension, and think that our duty is done.

CHAPTER II

IT will not be necessary, for the purpose of this history, to follow out very closely all the adventures
which occurred to Mrs. Catherine from the period when
she quitted the "Bugle" and became the Captain's lady;
for, although it would be just as easy to show as not,
that the young woman, by following the man of her
heart, had only yielded to an innocent impulse, and by
remaining with him for a certain period, had proved the
depth and strength of her affection for him,—although
we might make very tender and eloquent apologies for
the error of both parties, the reader might possibly be
disgusted at such descriptions and such arguments:
which, besides, are already done to his hand in the novel
of "Ernest Maltravers" before mentioned.

From the gentleman's manner towards Mrs. Catherine, and from his brilliant and immediate success, the
reader will doubtless have concluded, in the first place,
that Gustavus Adolphus had not a very violent affection
for Mrs. Cat; in the second place, that he was a professional lady-killer, and therefore likely at some period to
resume his profession; thirdly, and to conclude, that a
connection so begun, must, in the nature of things, be
likely to end speedily.

And so, to do the Count justice, it would, if he had

been allowed to follow his own inclination entirely; for (as many young gentlemen will, and yet no praise to them) in about a week he began to be indifferent, in a month to be weary, in two months to be angry, in three to proceed to blows and curses;. and, in short, to repent most bitterly the hour when he had ever been induced to present Mrs. Catherine the toe of his boot, for the purpose of lifting her on to his horse.

"Egad!" said he to the Corporal one day, when confiding his griefs to Mr. Brock, "I wish my toe had been cut off before ever it served as a ladder to this little vixen."

"Or perhaps your honour would wish to kick her downstairs with it?" delicately suggested Mr. Brock.

"Kick her! why, the wench would hold so fast by the banisters that I *could* not kick her down, Mr. Brock. To tell you a bit of a secret, I *have* tried as much—not to kick her—no, no, not kick her, certainly; that's ungentlemanly—but to *induce* her to go back to that cursed pot-house where we fell in with her. I have given her many hints—"

"Oh, yes, I saw your honour give her one yesterday— with a mug of beer. By the laws, as the ale run all down her face, and she clutched a knife to run at you, I don't think I ever saw such a she-devil! That woman will do for your honour some day, if you provoke her."

"Do for *me?* No, hang it, Mr. Brock, never! She loves every hair of my head, sir: she worships me, Corporal. Egad, yes! she worships me; and would much sooner apply a knife to her own weasand than scratch my little finger!"

"I think she does," said Mr. Brock.

"I'm sure of it," said the Captain. "Women, look

you, are like dogs, they like to be ill-treated: they like it, sir; I know they do. I never had anything to do with a woman in my life but I ill-treated her, and she liked me the better."

"Mrs. Hall ought to be *very* fond of you then, sure enough!" said Mr. Corporal.

"Very fond;—ha, ha! Corporal, you wag you—and so she *is* very fond. Yesterday, after the knife-and-beer scene—no wonder I threw the liquor in her face: it was so dev'lish flat that no gentleman could drink it: and I told her never to draw it till dinner-time—"

"Oh, it was enough to put an angel in a fury!" said Brock.

" —Well, yesterday, after the knife business, when you had got the carver out of her hand, off she flings to her bedroom, will not eat a bit of dinner forsooth, and remains locked up for a couple of hours. At two o'clock afternoon (I was over a tankard), out comes the little she-devil, her face pale, her eyes bleared, and the tip of her nose as red as fire with sniffling and weeping. Making for my hand, 'Max,' says she, 'will you forgive me?' 'What!' says I. 'Forgive a murderess?' says I. 'No, curse me, never!' 'Your cruelty will kill me,' sobbed she. 'Cruelty be hanged!' says I; 'didn't you draw that beer an hour before dinner?' She could say nothing to *this,* you know, and I swore that every time she did so, I would fling it into her face again. Whereupon back she flounced to her chamber, where she wept and stormed until night-time."

"When you forgave her?"

"I *did* forgive her, that's positive. You see I had supped at the 'Rose' along with Tom Trippet and half-a-dozen pretty fellows; and I had eased a great fat-

headed Warwickshire land-junker—what d'ye call him?
—squire, of forty pieces; and I'm dev'lish good-
humoured when I've won, and so Cat and I made it up:
but I've taught her never to bring me stale beer again—
ha, ha!"

This conversation will explain, a great deal better
than any description of ours, however eloquent, the state
of things as between Count Maximilian and Mrs. Catherine, and the feelings which they entertained for each
other.   The woman loved him, that was the fact.   And,
as we have shown in the previous chapter how John
Hayes, a mean-spirited fellow as ever breathed, in respect of all other passions a pigmy, was in the passion
of love a giant, and followed Mrs. Catherine with a
furious longing which might seem at the first to be foreign to his nature; in the like manner, and playing at
cross-purposes, Mrs. Hall had become smitten of the
Captain; and, as he said truly, only liked him the better
for the brutality which she received at his hands.   For
it is my opinion, Madam, that love is a bodily infirmity,
from which humankind can no more escape than from
small-pox; and which attacks every one of us, from the
first duke in the Peerage down to Jack Ketch inclusive;
which has no respect for rank, virtue, or roguery in man,
but sets each in his turn in a fever; which breaks out the
deuce knows how or why, and, raging its appointed time,
fills each individual of the one sex with a blind fury and
longing for some one of the other (who may be pure,
gentle, blue-eyed, beautiful, and good; or vile, shrewish,
squinting, hunchbacked, and hideous, according to circumstances and luck); which dies away, perhaps in the
natural course, if left to have its way, but which contradiction causes to rage more furiously than ever.   Is not

history, from the Trojan war upwards and downwards, full of instances of such strange inexplicable passions? Was not Helen, by the most moderate calculation, ninety years of age when she went off with his Royal Highness Prince Paris of Troy? Was not Madame La Vallière ill-made, blear-eyed, tallow-complexioned, scraggy, and with hair like tow? Was not Wilkes the ugliest, charmingest, most successful man in the world? Such instances might be carried out so as to fill a volume; but *cui bono?* Love is fate, and not will; its origin not to be explained, its progress irresistible: and the best proof of this may be had at Bow Street any day, where, if you ask any officer of the establishment how they take most thieves, he will tell you at the houses of the women. They must see the dear creatures though they hang for it; they will love, though they have their necks in the halter. And with regard to the other position, that ill-usage on the part of the man does not destroy the affection of the woman, have we not numberless police-reports showing how, when a bystander would beat a husband for beating his wife, man and wife fall together on the interloper and punish him for his meddling?

These points, then, being settled to the satisfaction of all parties, the reader will not be disposed to question the assertion that Mrs. Hall had a real affection for the gallant Count, and grew, as Mr. Brock was pleased to say, like a beefsteak, more tender as she was thumped. Poor thing, poor thing! his flashy airs and smart looks had overcome her in a single hour; and no more is wanted to plunge into love over head and ears; no more is wanted to make a first love with—and a woman's first love lasts *for ever* (a man's twenty-fourth or twenty-fifth is perhaps the best): you can't kill it, do what you

will; it takes root, and lives and even grows, never mind
what the soil may be in which it is planted, or the bitter
weather it must bear—often as one has seen a wall-flower
grow—out of a stone.

In the first weeks of their union, the Count had at
least been liberal to her: she had a horse and fine clothes,
and received abroad some of those flattering attentions
which she held at such high price. He had, however,
some ill-luck at play, or had been forced to pay some
bills, or had some other satisfactory reason for being
poor, and his establishment was very speedily diminished. He argued that, as Mrs. Catherine had been
accustomed to wait on others all her life, she might now
wait upon herself and him; and when the incident of
the beer arose, she had been for some time employed as
the Count's housekeeper, with unlimited superintend-
ence over his comfort, his cellar, his linen, and such
matters as bachelors are delighted to make over to active
female hands. To do the poor wretch justice, she actually kept the man's *ménage* in the best order; nor was
there any point of extravagance with which she could
be charged, except a little extravagance of dress displayed on the very few occasions when he condescended
to walk abroad with her, and extravagance of language
and passion in the frequent quarrels they had together.
Perhaps in such a connection as subsisted between this
precious couple, these faults are inevitable on the part of
the woman. She must be silly and vain, and will pretty
surely therefore be fond of dress; and she must, disguise it as she will, be perpetually miserable and brood-
ing over her fall, which will cause her to be violent and
quarrelsome.

Such, at least, was Mrs. Hall; and very early did the

poor vain, misguided wretch begin to reap what she had sown.

For a man, remorse under these circumstances is perhaps uncommon. No stigma affixes on *him* for betraying a woman: no bitter pangs of mortified vanity; no insulting looks of superiority from his neighbour, and no sentence of contemptuous banishment is read against him; these all fall on the tempted, and not on the tempter, who is permitted to go free. The chief thing that a man learns after having successfully practised on a woman is to despise the poor wretch whom he has won. The game, in fact, and the glory, such as it is, is all his, and the punishment alone falls upon her. Consider this, ladies, when charming young gentlemen come to woo you with soft speeches. You have nothing to win, except wretchedness, and scorn, and desertion. Consider this, and be thankful to your Solomons for telling it.

It came to pass, then, that the Count had come to have a perfect contempt and indifference for Mrs. Hall;— how should he not for a young person who had given herself up to him so easily?—and would have been quite glad of any opportunity of parting with her. But there was a certain lingering shame about the man, which prevented him from saying at once and abruptly, "Go!" and the poor thing did not choose to take such hints as fell out in the course of their conversation and quarrels. And so they kept on together, he treating her with simple insult, and she hanging on desperately, by whatever feeble twig she could find, to the rock beyond which all was naught, or death, to her.

Well, after the night with Tom Trippet and the pretty fellows at the "Rose," to which we have heard the Count allude in the conversation just recorded, For-

tune smiled on him a good deal; for the Warwickshire
Squire, who had lost forty pieces on that occasion, insisted on having his revenge the night after; when,
strange to say, a hundred and fifty more found their
way into the pouch of his Excellency the Count. Such
a sum as this quite set the young nobleman afloat again,
and brought back a pleasing equanimity to his mind,
which had been a good deal disturbed in the former difficult circumstances; and in this, for a little and to a certain extent, poor Cat had the happiness to share. He
did not alter the style of his establishment, which consisted, as before, of herself and a small person who acted
as scourer, kitchen-wench, and scullion; Mrs. Catherine
always putting her hand to the principal pieces of the
dinner; but he treated his mistress with tolerable good-
humour; or, to speak more correctly, with such bearable
brutality as might be expected from a man like him to a
woman in her condition. Besides, a certain event was
about to take place, which not unusually occurs in circumstances of this nature, and Mrs. Catherine was expecting soon to lie in.

The Captain, distrusting naturally the strength of his
own paternal feelings, had kindly endeavoured to provide a parent for the coming infant; and to this end had
opened a negotiation with our friend Mr. Thomas Bullock, declaring that Mrs. Cat should have a fortune of
twenty guineas, and reminding Tummas of his ancient
flame for her: but Mr. Tummas, when this proposition
was made to him, declined it, with many oaths, and vowed
that he was perfectly satisfied with his present bachelor
condition. In this dilemma, Mr. Brock stepped forward,
who declared himself very ready to accept Mrs. Catherine and her fortune; and might possibly have become the

possessor of both, had not Mrs. Cat, the moment she heard of the proposed arrangement, with fire in her eyes, and rage—oh, how bitter!—in her heart, prevented the success of the measure by proceeding incontinently to the first justice of the peace, and there swearing before his worship who was the father of the coming child.

This proceeding, which she had expected would cause not a little indignation on the part of her lord and master, was received by him, strangely enough, with considerable good-humour: he swore that the wench had served him a good trick, and was rather amused at the anger, the outbreak of fierce rage and contumely, and the wretched, wretched tears of heart-sick desperation, which followed her announcement of this step to him. For Mr. Brock, she repelled his offer with scorn and loathing, and treated the notion of a union with Mr. Bullock with yet fiercer contempt. Marry him indeed! a workhouse pauper carrying a brown-bess! She would have died sooner, she said, or robbed on the highway. And so, to do her justice, she would: for the little minx was one of the vainest creatures in existence, and vanity (as I presume everybody knows) becomes *the* principle in certain women's hearts—their moral spectacles, their conscience, their meat and drink, their only rule of right and wrong.

As for Mr. Tummas, he, as we have seen, was quite as unfriendly to the proposition as she could be; and the Corporal, with a good deal of comical gravity, vowed that, as he could not be satisfied in his dearest wishes, he would take to drinking for a consolation: which he straightway did.

"Come, Tummas," said he to Mr. Bullock, "since we *can't* have the girl of our hearts, why, hang it, Tummas, let's drink her health!" To which Bullock had no objection. And so strongly did the disapointment weigh upon honest Corporal Brock that even when, after unheard-of quantities of beer, he could scarcely utter a word, he was seen absolutely to weep, and, in accents almost unintelligible, to curse his confounded ill-luck, at being deprived, not of a wife, but of a child: he wanted one so, he said, to comfort him in his old age.

The time of Mrs. Catherine's *couche* drew near, arrived, and was gone through safely. She presented to the world a chopping boy, who might use, if he liked, the Galgenstein arms with a bar-sinister; and in her new cares and duties had not so many opportunities as usual of quarrelling with the Count: who, perhaps, respected her situation, or, at least, was so properly aware of the necessity of quiet to her, that he absented himself from home morning, noon, and night.

The Captain had, it must be confessed, turned these continued absences to a considerable worldly profit, for he played incessantly; and, since his first victory over the Warwickshire Squire, Fortune had been so favourable to him, that he had at various intervals amassed a sum of nearly a thousand pounds, which he used to bring home as he won; and which he deposited in a strong iron chest, cunningly screwed down by himself under his own bed. This Mrs. Catherine regularly made, and the treasure underneath it could be no secret to her. However, the noble Count kept the key, and bound her by many solemn oaths (that he discharged at her himself) not to reveal to any other person the existence of the chest and its contents.

But it is not in a woman's nature to keep such secrets; and the Captain, who left her for days and days, did not reflect that she would seek for confidants elsewhere. For want of a female companion, she was compelled to bestow her sympathies upon Mr. Brock; who, as the Count's corporal, was much in his lodgings, and who did manage to survive the disappointment which he had experienced by Mrs. Catherine's refusal of him.

About two months after the infant's birth, the Captain, who was annoyed by its squalling, put it abroad to nurse, and dismissed its attendant. Mrs. Catherine now resumed her household duties, and was, as before, at once mistress and servant of the establishment. As such, she had the keys of the beer, and was pretty sure of the attentions of the Corporal; who became, as we have said, in the Count's absence, his lady's chief friend and companion. After the manner of ladies, she very speedily confided to him all her domestic secrets: the causes of her former discontent; the Count's ill-treatment of her; the wicked names he called her; the prices that all her gowns had cost her; how he beat her; how much money he won and lost at play; how she had once pawned a coat for him; how he had four new ones, laced, and paid for; what was the best way of cleaning and keeping gold-lace, of making cherry-brandy, pickling salmon, &c. &c. Her *confidences* upon all these subjects used to follow each other in rapid succession; and Mr. Brock became, ere long, quite as well acquainted with the Captain's history for the last year as the Count himself:—for he was careless, and forgot things; women never do. They chronicle all the lover's small actions, his words, his headaches, the dresses he has worn, the things he has liked for dinner on certain days;—all which circumstances commonly are expunged from the male brain immediately after they have occurred, but remain fixed with the female.

To Brock, then, and to Brock only (for she knew no

other soul), Mrs. Cat breathed, in strictest confidence, the history of the Count's winnings, and his way of disposing of them; how he kept his money screwed down in an iron chest in their room: and a very lucky fellow did Brock consider his officer for having such a large sum. He and Cat looked at the chest; it was small, but mighty strong, sure enough, and would defy picklocks and thieves. Well, if any man deserved money, the Captain did ("though he might buy me a few yards of that lace I love so," interrupted Cat),—if any man deserved money, he did, for he spent it like a prince, and his hand was always in his pocket.

It must now be stated that Monsieur de Galgenstein had, during Cat's seclusion, cast his eyes upon a young lady of good fortune, who frequented the Assembly at Birmingham, and who was not a little smitten by his title and person. The "four new coats, laced, and paid for," as Cat said, had been purchased, most probably, by his Excellency for the purpose of dazzling the heiress; and he and the coats had succeeded so far as to win from the young woman an actual profession of love, and a promise of marriage provided Pa would consent. This was obtained,—for Pa was a tradesman; and I suppose every one of my readers has remarked how great an effect a title has on the lower classes. Yes, thank heaven! there is about a free-born Briton a cringing baseness, and lickspittle awe of rank, which does not exist under any tyranny in Europe, and is only to be found here and in America.

All these negotiations had been going on quite unknown to Cat; and, as the Captain had determined, before two months were out, to fling that young woman on the *pavé,* he was kind to her in the meanwhile: people always are when they are swindling you, or meditating an injury against you.

The poor girl had much too high an opinion of her own charms to suspect that the Count could be unfaithful to them, and had no notion of the plot that was formed against her. But Mr. Brock had: for he had seen many times a gilt coach with a pair of fat white horses ambling in the neighbourhood of the town, and the Captain on his black steed caracolling majestically by its side; and he had remarked a fat, pudgy, palehaired woman treading heavily down the stairs of the Assembly, leaning on the Captain's arm: all these Mr. Brock had seen, not without reflection. Indeed, the Count one day, in great good-humour, had slapped him on the shoulder and told him that he was about speedily to purchase a regiment; when, by his great gods, Mr. Brock should have a pair of colours. Perhaps this promise occasioned his silence to Mrs. Catherine hitherto; perhaps he never would have peached at all; and perhaps, therefore, this history would never have been written, but for a small circumstance which occurred at this period.

"What can you want with that drunken old Corporal always about your quarters?" said Mr. Trippet to the Count one day, as they sat over their wine, in the midst of a merry company, at the Captain's rooms.

"What!" said he. "Old Brock? The old thief has been more useful to me than many a better man. He is brave in a row as a lion, as cunning in intrigue as a fox; he can nose a dun at an inconceivable distance, and scent out a pretty woman be she behind ever so many stone walls. If a gentleman wants a good rascal now, I can recommend him. I am going to reform, you know, and must turn him out of my service."

" And pretty Mrs. Cat?"

" Oh, curse pretty Mrs. Cat! she may go too."

" And the brat?"

" Why, you have parishes, and what not, here in England. Egad! if a gentleman were called upon to keep all his children, there would be no living: no, stap my vitals! Crœsus couldn't stand it."

" No, indeed," said Mr. Trippet: "you are right; and when a gentleman marries, he is bound in honour to give up such low connections as are useful when he is a bachelor."

" Of course; and give them up I will, when the sweet Mrs. Dripping is mine. As for the girl, you can have her, Tom Trippet, if you take a fancy to her; and as for the Corporal, he may be handed over to my successor in Cutts's:—for I will have a regiment to myself, that's poz; and to take with me such a swindling, pimping, thieving, brandy-faced rascal as this Brock will never do. Egad! he's a disgrace to the service. As it is, I've often a mind to have the superannuated vagabond drummed out of the corps."

Although this *résumé* of Mr. Brock's character and accomplishments was very just, it came perhaps with an ill grace from Count Gustavus Adolphus Maximilian, who had profited by all his qualities, and who certainly would never have given this opinion of them had he known that the door of his dining-parlour was open, and that the gallant Corporal, who was in the passage, could hear every syllable that fell from the lips of his commanding officer. We shall not say, after the fashion of the story-books, that Mr. Brock listened with a flashing eye and a distended nostril; that his chest heaved tumultuously, and that his hand fell down mechanically to his side, where it played with the brass handle of his sword. Mr. Kean would have gone through most of these bodily exercises had he been acting the part of a villain enraged and disappointed like Corporal Brock; but that gentleman walked away without any gestures of any kind, and as gently as possible. "He'll turn me out of the regiment, will he?" says he, quite *piano;* and then added (*con molta espressione*), "I'll do for him."

And it is to be remarked how generally, in cases of this nature, gentlemen stick to their word.

CHAPTER III

IN WHICH A NARCOTIC IS ADMINISTERED, AND A GREAT
DEAL OF GENTEEL SOCIETY DEPICTED

WHEN the Corporal, who had retreated to the
street-door immediately on hearing the above
conversation, returned to the Captain's lodgings and
paid his respects to Mrs. Catherine, he found that lady
in high good-humour. The Count had been with her,
she said, along with a friend of his, Mr. Trippet; had
promised her twelve yards of the lace she coveted so
much; had vowed that the child should have as much
more for a cloak; and had not left her until he had sat
with her for an hour, or more, over a bowl of punch,
which he made on purpose for her. Mr. Trippet stayed
too. "A mighty pleasant man," said she; "only not very
wise, and seemingly a good deal in liquor."

"A good deal indeed!" said the Corporal. "He was
so tipsy just now, that he could hardly stand. He and
his honour were talking to Nan Fantail in the market-
place; and she pulled Trippet's wig off, for wanting to
kiss her."

"The nasty fellow!" said Mrs. Cat, "to demean himself with such low people as Nan Fantail, indeed! Why,
upon my conscience now, Corporal, it was but an hour
ago that Mr. Trippet swore he never saw such a pair of
eyes as mine, and would like to cut the Captain's throat
for the love of me. Nan Fantail indeed!"

"Nan's an honest girl, Madam Catherine, and was a great favourite of the Captain's before some one else came in his way. No one can say a word against her—not a word."

"And pray, Corporal, who ever did?" said Mrs. Cat, rather offended. "A nasty, angry slut! I wonder what the men can see in her?"

"She has got a smart way with her, sure enough; it's what amuses the men, and—"

"And what? You don't mean to say that my Max is fond of her *now?*" said Mrs. Catherine, looking very fierce.

"Oh, no; not at all: not of *her;*—that is—"

"Not of *her!*" screamed she. "Of whom, then?"

"Oh, psha! nonsense! Of you, my dear, to be sure: who else should he care for? And, besides, what business is it of mine?" And herewith the Corporal began whistling, as if he would have no more of the conversation. But Mrs. Cat was not to be satisfied,—not she, and carried on her cross-questions.

"Why, look you," said the Corporal, after parrying many of these,—"Why, look you, I'm an old fool, Catherine, and I *must* blab. That man has been the best friend I ever had, and so I was quiet; but I can't keep it in any longer,—no, hang me if I can! It's my belief he's acting like a rascal by you: he deceives you, Catherine; he's a scoundrel, Mrs. Hall, that's the truth on't."

Catherine prayed him to tell all he knew; and he resumed.

"He wants you off his hands; he's sick of you, and so brought here that fool Tom Trippet, who has taken a fancy to you. He has not the courage to turn you out of doors like a man; though in-doors he can treat you like a beast. But I'll tell you what he'll do. In a month he will go to Coventry, or pretend to go there, on recruiting business. No such thing, Mrs. Hall: he's going on *marriage* business; and he'll leave you without a farthing, to starve or to rot, for him. It's all arranged, I tell you: in a month, you are to be starved into becoming Tom Trippet's mistress; and his honour is to marry rich Miss Dripping, the twenty-thousand-pounder from London; and to purchase a regiment;—and to get old Brock drummed out of Cutts's too," said the Corporal, under his breath. But he might have spoken out, if he chose; for the poor young woman had sunk on the ground in a real honest fit.

"I thought I should give it her," said Mr. Brock, as he procured a glass of water; and, lifting her on to a sofa, sprinkled the same over her. "Hang it! how pretty she is."

*   *   *   *   *

When Mrs. Catherine came to herself again, Brock's tone with her was kind, and almost feeling. Nor did the poor wench herself indulge in any subsequent shiverings and hysterics, such as usually follow the fainting-fits of persons of higher degree. She pressed him for further explanations, which he gave, and to which she listened with a great deal of calmness; nor did many tears, sobs, sighs, or exclamations of sorrow or anger escape from her: only when the Corporal was taking his leave, and said to her point-blank,—"Well, Mrs. Catherine, and what do you intend to do?" she did not reply a word; but gave a look which made him exclaim, on leaving the room,—

"By heavens! the woman means murder! I would not be the Holofernes to lie by the side of such a Judith as that—not I!" And he went his way, immersed in deep thought. When the Captain returned at night, she did not speak to him; and when he swore at her for being sulky, she only said she had a headache, and was dreadfully ill: with which excuse Gustavus Adolphus seemed satisfied, and left her to herself.

He saw her the next morning for a moment: he was going a-shooting.

Catherine had no friend, as is usual in tragedies and romances,—no mysterious sorceress of her acquaintance to whom she could apply for poison,—so she went simply to the apothecaries, pretending at each that she had a dreadful toothache, and procuring from them as much laudanum as she thought would suit her purpose.

When she went home again, she seemed almost gay. Mr. Brock complimented her upon the alteration in her appearance; and she was enabled to receive the Captain at his return from shooting in such a manner as made him remark that she had got rid of her sulks of the morning, and might sup with them, if she chose to keep her good-humour. The supper was got ready, and the gentlemen had the punch-bowl when the cloth was cleared,—Mrs. Catherine, with her delicate hands, preparing the liquor.

It is useless to describe the conversation that took place, or to reckon the number of bowls that were emptied; or to tell how Mr. Trippet, who was one of the guests, and declined to play at cards when some of the others began, chose to remain by Mrs. Catherine's side, and make violent love to her. All this might be told, and the account, however faithful, would not be very pleasing. No, indeed! And here, though we are only in the third chapter of this history, we feel almost sick of the characters that appear in it, and the adventures which they are called upon to go through. But how can we help ourselves? The public will hear of nothing but rogues; and the only way in which poor authors, who must live, can act honestly by the public and themselves, is to paint such thieves as they are: not dandy, poetical, rose-water thieves; but real downright scoundrels, leading scoundrelly lives, drunken, profligate, dissolute, low; as scoundrels will be. They don't quote Plato, like Eugene Aram; or live like gentlemen, and sing the pleasantest ballads in the world, like jolly Dick Turpin; or prate eternally about τὸ καλὸν, like that precious canting Maltravers, whom we all of us have read about and pitied; or die whitewashed saints, like poor "Biss Dadsy" in "Oliver Twist." No, my dear Madam, you and your daughters have no right to admire and sympa-thize with any such persons, fictitious or real: you ought to be made cordially to detest, scorn, loathe, abhor, and abominate all people of this kidney. Men of genius like those whose works we have above alluded to, have no business to make these characters interesting or agree-able; to be feeding your morbid fancies, or indulging their own, with such monstrous food. For our parts, young ladies, we beg you to bottle up your tears, and not waste a single drop of them on any one of the heroes or heroines in this history: they are all rascals, every soul of them, and behave "as sich." Keep your sympathy for those who deserve it: don't carry it, for preference, to the Old Bailey, and grow maudlin over the company assem-bled there.

Just, then, have the kindness to fancy that the conver-sation which took place over the bowls of punch which Mrs. Catherine prepared, was such as might be expected to take place where the host was a dissolute, dare-devil, libertine captain of dragoons, the guests for the most part of the same class, and the hostess a young woman originally from a country alehouse, and for the present mistress to the entertainer of the society. They talked, and they drank, and they grew tipsy; and very little worth hearing occurred during the course of the whole evening. Mr. Brock officiated, half as the servant, half as the companion of the society. Mr. Thomas Trippet made violent love to Mrs. Catherine, while her lord and master was playing at dice with the other gentlemen: and on this night, strange to say, the Captain's fortune seemed to desert him. The Warwickshire Squire, from whom he had won so much, had an amazing run of good luck. The Captain called perpetually for more drink, and higher stakes, and lost almost every throw. Three hundred, four hundred, six hundred—all his winnings of the previous months were swallowed up in the course of a few hours. The Corporal looked on; and, to do him justice, seemed very grave, as, sum by sum, the Squire scored down the Count's losses on the paper before him.

Most of the company had taken their hats and staggered off. The Squire and Mr. Trippet were the only two that remained, the latter still lingering by Mrs. Catherine's sofa and table; and as she, as we have stated, had been employed all the evening in mixing the liquor for the gamesters, he was at the head-quarters of love and drink, and had swallowed so much of each as hardly to be able to speak.

The dice went rattling on; the candles were burning dim, with great long wicks. Mr. Trippet could hardly see the Captain, and thought, as far as his muzzy reason would let him, that the Captain could not see him: so he rose from his chair as well as he could, and fell down on

Mrs. Catherine's sofa. His eyes were fixed, his face was pale, his jaw hung down; and he flung out his arms and said, in a maudlin voice, "Oh, you byoo-oo-oo-tiffle Cathrine, I must have a kick-kick-iss."

"Beast!" said Mrs. Catherine, and pushed him away. The drunken wretch fell off the sofa, and on to the floor, where he stayed; and, after snorting out some unintelligible sounds, went to sleep.

The dice went rattling on; the candles were burning dim, with great long wicks.

"Seven's the main," cried the Count. "Four. Three to two against the caster."

"Ponies," said the Warwickshire Squire.

Rattle, rattle, rattle, rattle, clatter, *nine.* Clap, clap, clap, clap, *eleven.* Clutter, clutter, clutter, clutter: "Seven it is," says the Warwickshire Squire. "That makes eight hundred, Count."

"One throw for two hundred," said the Count. "But stop! Cat, give us some more punch."

Mrs. Cat came forward; she looked a little pale, and her hand trembled somewhat. "Here is the punch, Max," said she. It was steaming hot, in a large glass. "Don't drink it all," said she; "leave me some."

"How dark it is!" said the Count, eyeing it.

"It's the brandy," says Cat.

"Well, here goes! Squire, curse you! here's your health, and bad luck to you!" and he gulped off more than half the liquor at a draught. But presently he put down the glass and cried, "What infernal poison is this, Cat?"

"Poison!" said she. "It's no poison. Give me the glass." And she pledged Max, and drank a little of it. "'Tis good punch, Max, and of my brewing; I don't think you will ever get any better." And she went back to the sofa again, and sat down, and looked at the players.

Mr. Brock looked at her white face and fixed eyes with a grim kind of curiosity. The Count sputtered, and cursed the horrid taste of the punch still; but he presently took the box, and made his threatened throw.

As before, the Squire beat him; and having booked his winnings, rose from table as well as he might, and besought Corporal Brock to lead him downstairs; which Mr. Brock did.

Liquor had evidently stupefied the Count: he sat with his head between his hands, muttering wildly about ill-luck, seven's the main, bad punch, and so on. The street-door banged to; and the steps of Brock and the Squire were heard, until they could be heard no more.

"Max," said she; but he did not answer. "Max," said she again, laying her hand on his shoulder.

"Curse you," said that gentleman, "keep off, and don't be laying your paws upon me. Go to bed, you jade, or to ——, for what I care; and give me first some more punch—a gallon more punch, do you hear?"

The gentleman, by the curses at the commencement of this little speech, and the request contained at the end of it, showed that his losses vexed him, and that he was anxious to forget them temporarily.

"Oh, Max!" whimpered Mrs. Cat, "you—don't—want—any more punch?"

"Don't! Shan't I be drunk in my own house, you cursed whimpering jade you? Get out!" And with this the Captain proceeded to administer a blow upon Mrs. Catherine's cheek.

Contrary to her custom, she did not avenge it, or seek to do so, as on the many former occasions when disputes of this nature had arisen between the Count and her; but now Mrs. Catherine fell on her knees, and clasping her hands, and looking pitifully in the Count's face, cried, " Oh, Count, forgive me, forgive me! "

" Forgive you! What for? Because I slapped your face? Ha, ha! I'll forgive you again, if you don't mind."

" Oh, no, no, no! " said she, wringing her hands. " It isn't that. Max, dear Max, will you forgive me? It isn't the blow—I don't mind that; it's—"

" It's what, you—maudlin fool? "

" *It's the punch!* "

The Count, who was more than half-seas-over, here assumed an air of much tipsy gravity. " The punch! No, I never will forgive you that last glass of punch. Of all the foul, beastly drinks I ever tasted, that was the worst. No, I never will forgive you that punch."

" Oh, it isn't that, it isn't that! " said she.

" I tell you it is that,——you! That punch, I say that punch was no better than paw—aw—oison." And here the Count's head sank back, and he fell to snore.

" *It was poison!* " said she.

" *What!* " screamed he, waking up at once, and spurning her away from him. " What, you infernal murderess, have you killed me? "

" Oh, Max!—don't kill me, Max! It was laudanum— indeed it was. You were going to be married, and I was furious, and I went and got—"

" Hold your tongue, you fiend," roared out the Count; and with more presence of mind than politeness, he flung the remainder of the liquor (and, indeed, the glass with it) at the head of Mrs. Catherine. But the poisoned chalice missed its mark, and fell right on the nose of Mr.

Tom Trippet, who was left asleep and unobserved under the table.

Bleeding, staggering, swearing, indeed a ghastly sight, up sprung Mr. Trippet, and drew his rapier. "Come on," says he; "never say die! What's the row? I'm ready for a dozen of you." And he made many blind and furious passes about the room.

"Curse you, we'll die together!" shouted the Count, as he too pulled out his toledo, and sprung at Mrs. Catherine.

"Help! murder! thieves!" shrieked she. "Save me, Mr. Trippet, save me!" and she placed that gentleman between herself and the Count, and then made for the door of the bedroom, and gained it, and bolted it.

"Out of the way, Trippet," roared the Count—"out of the way, you drunken beast! I'll murder her, I will—I'll have the devil's life." And here he gave a swinging cut at Mr. Trippet's sword: it sent the weapon whirling clean out of his hand, and through a window into the street.

"Take my life, then," said Mr. Trippet: "I'm drunk, but I'm a man, and, damme! will never say die."

"I don't want your life, you stupid fool. Hark you, Trippet, wake and be sober, if you can. That woman has heard of my marriage with Miss Dripping."

"Twenty thousand pound," ejaculated Trippet.

"She has been jealous, I tell you, and *poisoned* us. She has put laudanum into the punch."

"What, in *my* punch?" said Trippet, growing quite sober, and losing his courage. "O Lord! O Lord!"

"Don't stand howling there, but run for a doctor; 'tis our only chance." And away ran Mr. Trippet, as if the deuce were at his heels.

The Count had forgotten his murderous intentions regarding his mistress, or had deferred them at least, under the consciousness of his own pressing danger. And it must be said, in the praise of a man who had fought for and against Marlborough and Tallard, that his courage in this trying and novel predicament never for a moment deserted him, but that he showed the greatest daring, as well as ingenuity, in meeting and averting the danger. He flew to the sideboard, where were the relics of a supper, and seizing the mustard and salt pots, and a bottle of oil, he emptied them all into a jug, into which he further poured a vast quantity of hot water. This pleasing mixture he then, without a moment's hesitation, placed to his lips, and swallowed as much of it as nature would allow him. But when he had imbibed about a quart, the anticipated effect was produced, and he was enabled, by the power of this ingenious extemporaneous emetic, to get rid of much of the poison which Mrs. Catherine had administered to him.

He was employed in these efforts when the doctor entered, along with Mr. Brock and Mr. Trippet; who was not a little pleased to hear that the poisoned punch had not in all probability been given to him. He was recommended to take some of the Count's mixture, as a precautionary measure; but this he refused, and retired home, leaving the Count under charge of the physician and his faithful corporal.

It is not necessary to say what further remedies were employed by them to restore the Captain to health; but after some time the doctor, pronouncing that the danger was, he hoped, averted, recommended that his patient should be put to bed, and that somebody should sit by him; which Brock promised to do.

"That she-devil will murder me, if you don't," gasped the poor Count. "You must turn her out of the bed-room; or break open the door, if she refuses to let you in."

And this step was found to be necessary; for, after shouting many times, and in vain, Mr. Brock found a small iron bar (indeed he had the instrument for many days in his pocket), and forced the lock. The room was empty, the window was open: the pretty barmaid of the "Bugle" had fled.

"The chest," said the Count—"is the chest safe?"

The Corporal flew to the bed, under which it was screwed, and looked, and said, "It *is* safe, thank heaven!" The window was closed. The Captain, who was too weak to stand without help, was undressed and put to bed. The Corporal sat down by his side; slumber stole over the eyes of the patient; and his wakeful nurse marked with satisfaction the progress of the beneficent restorer of health.

*   *   *   *   *

When the Captain awoke, as he did some time after-wards, he found, very much to his surprise, that a gag had been placed in his mouth, and that the Corporal was in the act of wheeling his bed to another part of the room. He attempted to move, and gave utterance to such unintelligible sounds as could issue through a silk handkerchief.

"If your honour stirs or cries out in the least, I will cut your honour's throat," said the Corporal.

And then, having recourse to his iron bar (the reader will now see why he was provided with such an imple-ment, for he had been meditating this *coup* for some days), he proceeded first to attempt to burst the lock of the little iron chest in which the Count kept his treasure, and failing in this, to unscrew it from the ground; which operation he performed satisfactorily.

"You see, Count," said he, calmly, "when rogues fall out, there's the deuce to pay. You'll have me drummed out of the regiment, will you? I'm going to leave it of my own accord, look you, and to live like a gentleman for the rest of my days. *Schlafen sie wohl,* noble Captain: *bon repos.* The Squire will be with you pretty early in the morning, to ask for the money you owe him."

* * * * *

With these sarcastic observations Mr. Brock departed; not by the window, as Mrs. Catherine had done, but by the door, quietly, and so into the street. And when, the next morning, the doctor came to visit his patient, he brought with him a story how, at the dead of night, Mr. Brock had roused the ostler at the stables where the Captain's horses were kept—had told him that Mrs. Catherine had poisoned the Count, and had run off with a thousand pounds; and how he and all lovers of justice ought to scour the country in pursuit of the criminal. For this end Mr. Brock mounted the Count's best horse —that very animal on which he had carried away Mrs. Catherine: and thus, on a single night, Count Maximilian had lost his mistress, his money, his horse, his corporal, and was very near losing his life.

CHAPTER IV

IN this woful plight, moneyless, wifeless, horseless, corporalless, with a gag in his mouth and a rope round his body, are we compelled to leave the gallant Galgenstein, until his friends and the progress of this history shall deliver him from his durance. Mr. Brock's adventures on the Captain's horse must likewise be pretermitted; for it is our business to follow Mrs. Catherine through the window by which she made her escape, and among the various chances that befell her.

She had one cause to congratulate herself,—that she had not her baby at her back; for the infant was safely housed under the care of a nurse, to whom the Captain was answerable. Beyond this her prospects were but dismal: no home to fly to, but a few shillings in her pocket, and a whole heap of injuries and dark revengeful thoughts in her bosom: it was a sad task to her to look either backwards or forwards. Whither was she to fly? How to live? What good chance was to befriend her? There was an angel watching over the steps of Mrs. Cat——not a good one, I think, but one of those from that unnameable place, who have their many subjects here on earth, and often are pleased to extricate them from worse perplexities.

Mrs. Cat, now, had not committed murder, but as bad as murder; and as she felt not the smallest repentance in her heart—as she had, in the course of her life and connection with the Captain, performed and gloried in a number of wicked coquetries, idlenesses, vanities, lies, fits of anger, slanders, foul abuses, and what not—she was fairly bound over to this dark angel whom we have alluded to; and he dealt with her, and aided her, as one of his own children.

I do not mean to say that, in this strait, he appeared to her in the likeness of a gentleman in black, and made her sign her name in blood to a document conveying over to him her soul, in exchange for certain conditions to be performed by him. Such diabolical bargains have always appeared to me unworthy of the astute person-age who is supposed to be one of the parties to them; and who would scarcely be fool enough to pay dearly for that which he can have in a few years for nothing. It is not, then, to be supposed that a demon of darkness appeared to Mrs. Cat, and led her into a flaming chariot, harnessed by dragons, and careering through air at the rate of a thousand leagues a minute. No such thing: the vehicle that was sent to aid her was one of a much more vulgar description.

The "Liverpool carryvan," then, which in the year 1706 used to perform the journey between London and that place in ten days, left Birmingham about an hour after Mrs. Catherine had quitted that town; and as she sat weeping on a hillside, and plunged in bitter medita-tion, the lumbering, jingling vehicle overtook her. The coachman was marching by the side of his horses, and encouraging them to maintain their pace of two miles an hour; the passengers had some of them left the vehicle, in order to walk up the hill; and the carriage had arrived at the top of it, and, meditating a brisk trot down the declivity, waited there until the lagging passengers should arrive: when Jehu, casting a good-natured glance upon Mrs. Catherine, asked the pretty maid whence she was come, and whether she would like a ride in his carriage. To the latter of which questions Mrs. Catherine replied truly yes; to the former, her answer was that she had come from Stratford: whereas, as we very well know, she had lately quitted Birmingham.

"Hast thee seen a woman pass this way, on a black horse, with a large bag of goold over the saddle?" said Jehu, preparing to mount upon the roof of his coach.

"No, indeed," said Mrs. Cat.

"Nor a trooper on another horse after her—no? Well, there be a mortal row down Birmingham way about sich a one. She have killed, they say, nine gentlemen at supper, and have strangled a German prince in bed. She have robbed him of twenty thousand guineas, and have rode away on a black horse."

"That can't be I," said Mrs. Cat, naïvely, "for I have but three shillings and a groat."

"No, it can't be thee, truly, for where's your bag of goold? and, besides, thee hast got too pretty a face to do such wicked things as to kill nine gentlemen and strangle a German prince."

"Law, coachman," said Mrs. Cat, blushing archly—"Law, coachman, *do* you think so?" The girl would have been pleased with a compliment even on her way to be hanged; and the parley ended by Mrs. Catherine stepping into the carriage, where there was room for eight people at least, and where two or three individuals had already taken their places.

For these Mrs. Catherine had in the first place to make a story, which she did; and a very glib one for a person of her years and education. Being asked whither she was bound, and how she came to be alone of a morning sitting by a road-side, she invented a neat history suitable to the occasion, which elicited much interest from her fellow-passengers: one in particular, a young man, who had caught a glimpse of her face under her hood, was very tender in his attentions to her.

But whether it was that she had been too much fatigued by the occurrences of the past day and sleepless night, or whether the little laudanum which she had drunk a few hours previously now began to act upon her, certain it is that Mrs. Cat now suddenly grew sick, feverish, and extraordinarily sleepy; and in this state she continued for many hours, to the pity of all her fellow-travellers. At length the "carryvan" reached the inn, where horses and passengers were accustomed to rest for a few hours, and to dine; and Mrs. Catherine was somewhat awakened by the stir of the passengers, and the friendly voice of the inn-servant welcoming them to dinner. The gentleman who had been smitten by her beauty now urged her very politely to descend; which, taking the protection of his arm, she accordingly did.

He made some very gallant speeches to her as she stepped out; and she must have been very much occupied by them, or rapt up in her own thoughts, or stupefied by sleep, fever, and opium, for she did not take any heed of the place into which she was going: which had she done, she would probably have preferred remaining

in the coach, dinnerless and ill. Indeed, the inn into
which she was about to make her entrance was no other
than the "Bugle," from which she set forth at the commencement of this history; and which then, as now, was
kept by her relative, the thrifty Mrs. Score. That good
landlady, seeing a lady, in a smart hood and cloak, leaning, as if faint, upon the arm of a gentleman of good
appearance, concluded them to be man and wife, and
folks of quality too; and with much discrimination, as
well as sympathy, led them through the public kitchen
to her own private parlour, or bar, where she handed
the lady an armchair, and asked what she would like to
drink. By this time and indeed at the very moment she
heard her aunt's voice, Mrs. Catherine was aware of her
situation; and when her companion retired, and the
landlady with much officiousness insisted on removing
her hood, she was quite prepared for the screech of surprise which Mrs. Score gave on dropping it, exclaiming,
"Why, law bless us, it's our Catherine!"

"I'm very ill, and tired, aunt," said Cat; "and would
give the world for a few hours' sleep."

"A few hours and welcome, my love, and a sack-
posset too. You do look sadly tired and poorly, sure
enough. Ah, Cat, Cat! you great ladies are sad rakes,
I do believe. I wager now, that with all your balls,
and carriages, and fine clothes, you are neither so happy
nor so well as when you lived with your poor old aunt,
who used to love you so." And with these gentle words,
and an embrace or two, which Mrs. Catherine wondered
at, and permitted, she was conducted to that very bed
which the Count had occupied a year previously, and undressed, and laid in it, and affectionately tucked up, by
her aunt, who marvelled at the fineness of her clothes,

as she removed them piece by piece; and when she saw
that in Mrs. Catherine's pocket there was only the sum
of three-and-four-pence, said, archly, "There was no
need of money, for the Captain took care of that."

Mrs. Cat did not undeceive her; and deceived Mrs.
Score certainly was,—for she imagined the well-dressed
gentleman who led Cat from the carriage was no other
than the Count; and, as she had heard, from time to
time, exaggerated reports of the splendour of the establishment which he kept up, she was induced to look upon
her niece with the very highest respect, and to treat her
as if she were a fine lady. " And so she *is* a fine lady,"
Mrs. Score had said months ago, when some of these
flattering stories reached her, and she had overcome her
first fury at Catherine's elopement. " The girl was very
cruel to leave me; but we must recollect that she is as
good as married to a nobleman, and must all forget and
forgive, you know."

This speech had been made to Doctor Dobbs, who was
in the habit of taking a pipe and a tankard at the
"Bugle," and it had been roundly reprobated by the
worthy divine; who told Mrs. Score that the crime of
Catherine was only the more heinous, if it had been
committed from interested motives; and protested that,
were she a princess, he would never speak to her again.
Mrs. Score thought and pronounced the Doctor's opinion to be very bigoted; indeed, she was one of those persons who have a marvellous respect for prosperity, and
a corresponding scorn for ill-fortune. When, therefore, she returned to the public room, she went graciously to the gentleman who had led Mrs. Catherine
from the carriage, and with a knowing curtsey wel-
comed him to the "Bugle;" told him that his lady would

not come to dinner, but bade her say, with her best love
to his lordship, that the ride had fatigued her, and that
she would lie in bed for an hour or two.

This speech was received with much wonder by his
lordship; who was, indeed, no other than a Liverpool
tailor going to London to learn fashions; but he only
smiled, and did not undeceive the landlady, who herself
went off, smilingly, to bustle about dinner.

The two or three hours allotted to that meal by the liberal coachmasters of those days passed away, and Mr.
Coachman, declaring that his horses were now rested
enough, and that they had twelve miles to ride, put the
steeds to, and summoned the passengers. Mrs. Score,
who had seen with much satisfaction that her niece was
really ill, and her fever more violent, and hoped to have
her for many days an inmate in her house, now came forward, and casting upon the Liverpool tailor a look of
profound but respectful melancholy, said, " My lord (for
I recollect your lordship quite well), the lady upstairs is
so ill, that it would be a sin to move her: had I not better
tell coachman to take down your lordship's trunks, and
the lady's, and make you a bed in the next room?"

Very much to her surprise, this proposition was received with a roar of laughter. "Madam," said the
person addressed, "I'm not a lord, but a tailor and
draper; and as for that young woman, before to-day I
never set eyes on her."

"*What!*" screamed out Mrs. Score. "Are not you
the Count?   Do you mean to say that you a'n't Cat's—?
Do you mean to say that you didn't order her bed, and
that you won't pay this here little bill?"   And with this
she produced a document, by which the Count's lady
was made her debtor in a sum of half-a-guinea.

These passionate words excited more and more laughter. "Pay it, my lord," said the coachman; "and then come along, for time presses." "Our respects to her ladyship," said one passenger. "Tell her my lord can't wait," said another; and with much merriment one and all quitted the hotel, entered the coach, and rattled off.

Dumb—pale with terror and rage—bill in hand, Mrs. Score had followed the company; but when the coach disappeared, her senses returned. Back she flew into the inn, overturning the ostler, not deigning to answer Dr. Dobbs (who, from behind soft tobacco-fumes, mildly asked the reason of her disturbance), and, bounding upstairs like a fury, she rushed into the room where Catherine lay.

"Well, madam!" said she, in her highest key, "do you mean that you have come into this here house to swindle me? Do you dare for to come with your airs here, and call yourself a nobleman's lady, and sleep in the best bed, when you're no better nor a common tramper? I'll thank you, ma'am, to get out, ma'am. I'll have no sick paupers in this house, ma'am. You know your way to the workhouse, ma'am, and there I'll trouble you for to go." And here Mrs. Score proceeded quickly to pull off the bedclothes; and poor Cat arose, shivering with fright and fever.

She had no spirit to answer, as she would have done the day before, when an oath from any human being would have brought half-a-dozen from her in return; or a knife, or a plate, or a leg of mutton, if such had been to her hand. She had no spirit left for such repartees; but in reply to the above words of Mrs. Score, and a great many more of the same kind—which are not necessary for our history, but which that lady uttered with inconceivable shrillness and volubility, the poor wench could say little,—only sob and shiver, and gather up the clothes again, crying, " Oh, aunt, don't speak unkind to me!   I'm very unhappy, and very ill!"

" Ill, you strumpet! ill, be hanged!   Ill is as ill does; and if you are ill, it's only what you merit.   Get out! dress yourself—tramp!   Get to the workhouse, and don't come to cheat me any more!   Dress yourself—do you hear?   Satin petticoat forsooth, and lace to her smock!"

Poor, wretched, chattering, burning, shivering, Catherine huddled on her clothes as well as she might: she seemed hardly to know or see what she was doing, and did not reply a single word to the many that the landlady let fall.   Cat tottered down the narrow stairs, and through the kitchen, and to the door; which she caught hold of, and paused awhile, and looked into Mrs. Score's face, as for one more chance.   " Get out, you nasty trull!" said that lady, sternly, with arms akimbo; and poor Catherine, with a most piteous scream and outgush of tears, let go of the door-post and staggered away into the road.

*   *   *   *   *

" Why, no—yes—no—it is poor Catherine Hall, as I live!" said somebody starting up, shoving aside Mrs. Score very rudely, and running into the road, wig off and pipe in hand.   It was honest Doctor Dobbs; and the result of his interview with Mrs. Cat was, that he gave up for ever smoking his pipe at the " Bugle;" and that she lay sick of a fever for some weeks in his house.

*   *   *   *   *

Over this part of Mrs. Cat's history we shall be as brief as possible; for, to tell the truth, nothing immoral occurred during her whole stay at the good Doctor's house; and we are not going to insult the reader by offering him silly pictures of piety, cheerfulness, good sense, and simplicity; which are milk-and-water virtues after all, and have no relish with them like a good strong vice, highly peppered. Well, to be short: Dr. Dobbs, though a profound theologian, was a very simple gentleman; and before Mrs. Cat had been a month in the house, he had learned to look upon her as one of the most injured and repentant characters in the world; and had, with Mrs. Dobbs, resolved many plans for the future welfare of the young Magdalen. " She was but sixteen, my love, recollect," said the Doctor; " she was carried off, not by her own wish either. The Count swore he would marry her; and, though she did not leave him until that monster tried to poison her, yet think what a fine Christian spirit the poor girl has shown! she forgives him as heartily—more heartily, I am sure, than I do Mrs. Score for turning her adrift in that wicked way." The reader will perceive some difference in the Doctor's statement and ours, which we assure him is the true one; but the fact is, the honest rector had had his tale from Mrs. Cat, and it was not in his nature to doubt, if she had told him a history ten times more wonderful.

The reverend gentleman and his wife then laid their heads together; and, recollecting something of John Hayes's former attachment to Mrs. Cat, thought that it might be advantageously renewed, should Hayes be still constant. Having very adroitly sounded Catherine (so adroitly, indeed, as to ask her " whether she would like to marry John Hayes? "), that young woman had replied, " No. She had loved John Hayes—he had been her early, only love; but she was fallen now, and not good enough for him." And this made the Dobbs family admire her more and more, and cast about for means to bring the marriage to pass.

Hayes was away from the village when Mrs. Cat had arrived there; but he did not fail to hear of her illness, and how her aunt had deserted her, and the good Doctor taken her in. The worthy Doctor himself met Mr. Hayes on the green; and, telling him that some repairs were wanting in his kitchen, begged him to step in and examine them. Hayes first said no, plump, and then no, gently; and then pished, and then psha'd; and then, trembling very much, went in: and there sat Mrs. Catherine, trembling very much too.

What passed between them? If your ladyship is anxious to know, think of that morning when Sir John himself popped the question. Could there be anything more stupid than the conversation which took place? Such stuff is not worth repeating: no, not when uttered by people in the very genteelest of company; as for the amorous dialogue of a carpenter and an ex-barmaid, it is worse still. Suffice it to say, that Mr. Hayes, who had had a year to recover from his passion, and had, to all appearances, quelled it, was over head and ears again the very moment he saw Mrs. Cat, and had all his work to do again.

Whether the Doctor knew what was going on, I can't say; but this matter is certain, that every evening Hayes was now in the rectory kitchen, or else walking abroad with Mrs. Catherine: and whether she ran away with him, or he with her, I shall not make it my business to inquire; but certainly at the end of three months (which must be crowded up into this one little sentence), another elopement took place in the village. "I should have prevented it, certainly," said Dr. Dobbs—whereat his wife smiled; "but the young people kept the matter a secret from me." And so he would, had he known it; but though Mrs. Dobbs had made several attempts to acquaint him with the precise hour and method of the intended elopement, he peremptorily ordered her to hold her tongue. The fact is, that the matter had been discussed by the rector's lady many times. "Young Hayes," would she say, "has a pretty little fortune and trade of his own; he is an only son, and may marry as he likes; and though not specially handsome, generous, or amiable, has an undeniable love for Cat (who, you know, must not be particular), and the sooner she marries him, I think, the better. They can't be married at our church, you know, and—" "Well," said the Doctor, "if they are married elsewhere, *I* can't help it, and know nothing about it, look you." And upon this hint the elopement took place: which, indeed, was peaceably performed early one Sunday morning about a month after; Mrs. Hall getting behind Mr. Hayes on a pillion, and all the children of the parsonage giggling behind the window-blinds to see the pair go off.

During this month Mr. Hayes had caused the banns to be published at the town of Worcester; judging rightly that in a great town they would cause no such remark as in a solitary village, and thither he conducted his lady. O ill-starred John Hayes! whither do the dark fates lead you? O foolish Dr. Dobbs, to forget that young people ought to honour their parents, and to yield to silly Mrs. Dobbs's ardent propensity for making matches!

*　　　*　　　*　　　*　　　*

The *London Gazette* of the 1st April, 1706, contains a proclamation by the Queen for putting into execution an Act of Parliament for the encouragement and increase of seamen, and for the better and speedier manning of her Majesty's fleet, which authorises all justices to issue warrants to constables, petty constables, headboroughs, and tything-men, to enter, and if need be, to break open the doors of any houses where they shall believe deserting seamen to be; and for the further increase and encouragement of the navy, to take ablebodied landsmen when seamen fail. This Act, which occupies four columns of the *Gazette,* and another of similar length and meaning for pressing men into the army, need not be quoted at length here; but caused a mighty stir throughout the kingdom at the time when it was in force.

As one has seen or heard, after the march of a great army, a number of rogues and loose characters bring up the rear; in like manner, at the tail of a great measure of State, follow many roguish personal interests, which are protected by the main body. The great measure of Reform, for instance, carried along with it much private jobbing and swindling—as could be shown were we not inclined to deal mildly with the Whigs; and this Enlistment Act, which, in order to maintain the British glories in Flanders, dealt most cruelly with the British people in England (it is not the first time that a man has been pinched at home to make a fine appearance abroad), created a great company of rascals and informers throughout the land, who lived upon it; or upon extortion from those who were subject to it, or not being subject to it were frightened into the belief that they were.

When Mr. Hayes and his lady had gone through the marriage ceremony at Worcester, the former, concluding that at such a place lodging and food might be pro-

The Interrupted Marriage

cured at a cheaper rate, looked about carefully for the meanest public-house in the town, where he might deposit his bride.

In the kitchen of this inn, a party of men were drinking; and, as Mrs. Hayes declined, with a proper sense of her superiority, to eat in company with such low fellows, the landlady showed her and her husband to an inner apartment, where they might be served in private.

The kitchen party seemed, indeed, not such as a lady would choose to join. There was one huge lanky fellow, that looked like a soldier, and had a halberd; another was habited in a sailor's costume, with a fascinating patch over one eye; and a third, who seemed the leader of the gang, was a stout man in a sailor's frock and a horseman's jack-boots, whom one might fancy, if he were anything, to be a horse-marine.

Of one of these worthies, Mrs. Hayes thought she knew the figure and voice; and she found her conjectures were true, when, all of a sudden, three people, without "with your leave" or "by your leave," burst into the room, into which she and her spouse had retired. At their head was no other than her old friend, Mr. Peter Brock; he had his sword drawn, and his finger to his lips, enjoining silence, as it were, to Mrs. Catherine. He with the patch on his eye seized incontinently on Mr. Hayes; the tall man with the halberd kept the door; two or three heroes supported the one-eyed man; who, with a loud voice, exclaimed, "Down with your arms— no resistance! you are my prisoner, in the Queen's name!"

And here, at this lock, we shall leave the whole company until the next chapter; which may possibly explain what they were.

CHAPTER V

"YOU don't sure believe these men?" said Mrs. Hayes, as soon as the first alarm caused by the irruption of Mr. Brock and his companions had subsided. "These are no magistrate's men: it is but a trick to rob you of your money, John."

"I will never give up a farthing of it!" screamed Hayes.

"Yonder fellow," continued Mrs. Catherine, "I know, for all his drawn sword and fierce looks; his name is—"

"Wood, madam, at your service!" said Mr. Brock. "I am follower to Mr. Justice Gobble, of this town: a'n't I, Tim?" said Mr. Brock to the tall halberd-man who was keeping the door.

"Yes, indeed," said Tim, archly; "we're all followers of his honour, Justice Gobble."

"Certainly!" said the one-eyed man.

"Of course!" cried the man in the nightcap.

"I suppose, madam, you're satisfied *now?*" continued Mr. Brock *a.* Wood. "You can't deny the testimony of gentlemen like these; and our commission is to apprehend all able-bodied male persons who can give no good account of themselves, and enrol them in the service of her Majesty. Look at this Mr. Hayes" (who stood trembling in his shoes). "Can there be a bolder, properer, straighter gentleman? We'll have him for a grenadier before the day's over!"

"Take heart, John—don't be frightened. Psha! I tell you I know the man," cried out Mrs. Hayes: "he is only here to extort money."

"Oh, for that matter, I *do* think I recollect the lady. Let me see? where was it? At Birmingham, I think,— ay, at Birmingham,—about the time when they tried to murder Count Gal—"

"Oh, sir!" here cried Madam Hayes, dropping her voice at once from a tone of scorn to one of gentlest entreaty, "what is it you want with my husband? I know not, indeed, if ever I saw you before. For what do you seize him? How much will you take to release him, and let us go? Name the sum; he is rich, and—"

"*Rich,* Catherine!" cried Hayes. "Rich!—O heavens! Sir, I have nothing but my hands to support me: I am a poor carpenter, sir, working under my father!"

"He can give twenty guineas to be free; I know he can!" said Mrs. Cat.

"I have but a guinea to carry me home," sighed out Hayes.

"But you have twenty at home, John," said his wife. "Give these brave gentlemen a writing to your mother, and she will pay; and you will let us free then, gentlemen—won't you?"

"When the money's paid, yes," said the leader, Mr. Brock.

"Oh, in course," echoed the tall man with the halberd. "What's a thrifling detintion, my dear?" continued he, addressing Hayes. "We'll amuse you in your absence, and drink to the health of your pretty wife here."

This promise, to do the halberdier justice, he fulfilled. He called upon the landlady to produce the desired liquor; and when Mr. Hayes flung himself at that lady's feet, demanding succour from her, and asking whether there was no law in the land—

"There's no law at the 'Three Rooks' except *this!*" said Mr. Brock in reply, holding up a horse-pistol. To which the hostess, grinning, assented, and silently went her way.

After some further solicitations, John Hayes drew out the necessary letter to his father, stating that he was pressed, and would not be set free under a sum of twenty guineas; and that it would be of no use to detain the bearer of the letter, inasmuch as the gentlemen who had possession of him vowed that they would murder him should any harm befall their comrade. As a further proof of the authenticity of the letter, a token was added: a ring that Hayes wore, and that his mother had given him.

The missives were, after some consultation, entrusted to the care of the tall halberdier, who seemed to rank as second in command of the forces that marched under Corporal Brock. This gentleman was called indifferently Ensign, Mr., or even Captain Macshane; his intimates occasionally in sport called him Nosey, from the prominence of that feature in his countenance; or Spindleshins, for the very reason which brought on the first Edward a similar nickname. Mr. Macshane then quitted Worcester, mounted on Hayes's horse; leaving all parties at the "Three Rooks" not a little anxious for his return.

This was not to be expected until the next morning; and a weary *nuit de noces* did Mr. Hayes pass. Dinner was served, and, according to promise, Mr. Brock and his two friends enjoyed the meal along with the bride and bridegroom. Punch followed, and this was taken in company; then came supper. Mr. Brock alone partook of this, the other two gentlemen preferring the society of their pipes and the landlady in the kitchen.

"It is a sorry entertainment I confess," said the ex-corporal, "and a dismal way for a gentleman to spend his bridal night; but somebody must stay with you, my dears: for who knows but you might take a fancy to scream out of window, and then there would be murder, and the deuce and all to pay? One of us must stay, and my friends love a pipe, so you must put up with my company until he can relieve guard."

The reader will not, of course, expect that three people who were to pass the night, however unwillingly, together in an inn-room, should sit there dumb and moody, and without any personal communication; on the contrary, Mr. Brock, as an old soldier, entertained his prisoners with the utmost courtesy, and did all that lay in his power, by the help of liquor and conversation, to render their durance tolerable. On the bridegroom his attentions were a good deal thrown away: Mr. Hayes consented to drink copiously, but could not be made to talk much; and, in fact, the fright of the seizure, the fate hanging over him should his parents refuse a ransom, and the tremendous outlay of money which would take place should they accede to it, weighed altogether on his mind so much as utterly to unman it.

As for Mrs. Cat, I don't think she was at all sorry in her heart to see the old Corporal: for he had been a

friend of old times—dear times to her; she had had from
him, too, and felt for him not a little kindness; and there
was really a very tender, innocent friendship subsisting
between this pair of rascals, who relished much a night's
conversation together.

The Corporal, after treating his prisoners to punch
in great quantities, proposed the amusement of cards:
over which Mr. Hayes had not been occupied more than
an hour, when he found himself so excessively sleepy as
to be persuaded to fling himself down on the bed, dressed
as he was, and there to snore away until morning.

Mrs. Catherine had no inclination for sleep; and the
Corporal, equally wakeful, plied incessantly the bottle,
and held with her a great deal of conversation. The
sleep, which was equivalent to the absence of John
Hayes, took all restraint from their talk. She explained
to Brock the circumstances of her marriage, which we
have already described; they wondered at the chance
which had brought them together at the "Three
Rooks;" nor did Brock at all hesitate to tell her at once
that his calling was quite illegal, and that his intention
was simply to extort money. The worthy Corporal had
not the slightest shame regarding his own profession,
and cut many jokes with Mrs. Cat about her late one;
her attempt to murder the Count, and her future prospects as a wife.

And here, having brought him upon the scene again,
we may as well shortly narrate some of the principal
circumstances which befell him after his sudden departure from Birmingham; and which he narrated with
much candour to Mrs. Catherine.

He rode the Captain's horse to Oxford (having exchanged his military dress for a civil costume on the

road), and at Oxford he disposed of "George of Denmark," a great bargain, to one of the heads of colleges. As soon as Mr. Brock, who took on himself the style and title of Captain Wood, had sufficiently examined the curiosities of the University, he proceeded at once to the capital: the only place for a gentleman of his fortune and figure.

Here he read, with a great deal of philosophical indifference, in the *Daily Post,* the *Courant,* the *Observator,* the *Gazette,* and the chief journals of those days, which he made a point of examining at "Button's" and "Will's," an accurate description of his person, his clothes, and the horse he rode, and a promise of fifty guineas' reward to any person who would give an account of him (so that he might be captured) to Captain Count Galgenstein at Birmingham, to Mr. Murfey at the "Golden Ball" in the Savoy, or Mr. Bates at the "Blew Anchor in Pickadilly." But Captain Wood, in an enormous full-bottomed periwig that cost him sixty pounds,[1] with high red heels to his shoes, a silver sword, and a gold snuff-box, and a large wound (obtained, he said, at the seige of Barcelona), which disfigured much of his countenance, and caused him to cover one eye, was in small danger, he thought, of being mistaken for Corporal Brock, the deserter of Cutts's; and strutted along the Mall with as grave an air as the very best nobleman who appeared there. He was generally, indeed, voted to be very good company; and as his expenses were unlimited ("A few convent candlesticks, my dear," he used to whisper, "melt into a vast number of doubloons"), he commanded as good society

---

[1] In the ingenious, contemporary history of Moll Flanders, a periwig is mentioned as costing that sum.

as he chose to ask for; and it was speedily known as a fact throughout town, that Captain Wood, who had served under his Majesty Charles III. of Spain, had carried off the diamond petticoat of our Lady of Compostella, and lived upon the proceeds of the fraud.   People were good Protestants in those days, and many a one longed to have been his partner in the pious plunder.

All surmises concerning his wealth, Captain Wood, with much discretion, encouraged. He contradicted no report, but was quite ready to confirm all; and when two different rumours were positively put to him, he used only to laugh, and say, " My dear sir, *I* don't make the stories; but I'm not called upon to deny them; and I give you fair warning, that I shall assent to every one of them; so you may believe them or not, as you please."   And so he had the reputation of being a gentleman, not only wealthy, but discreet. In truth, it was almost a pity that worthy Brock had not been a gentleman born; in which case, doubtless, he would have lived and died as became his station; for he spent his money like a gentleman, he loved women like a gentleman, he would fight like a gentleman, he gambled and got drunk like a gentleman. What did he want else? Only a matter of six descents, a little money, and an estate, to render him the equal of St. John or Harley. "Ah, those were merry days!" would Mr. Brock say,—for he loved, in a good old age, to recount the story of his London fashionable campaign;—" and when I think how near I was to become a great man, and to die perhaps a general, I can't but marvel at the wicked obstinacy of my ill-luck."

" I will tell what I did, my dear: I had lodgings in Piccadilly, as if I were a lord; I had two large periwigs,

Captain Brock Appears
at Court with My Lord
Peterborough

and three suits of laced clothes; I kept a little black
dressed out like a Turk; I walked daily in the Mall; I
dined at the politest ordinary in Covent Garden; I frequented the best of coffee-houses, and knew all the pretty
fellows of the town; I cracked a bottle with Mr. Addison,
and lent many a piece to Dick Steele (a sad debauched
rogue, my dear); and, above all, I'll tell you what I
did—the noblest stroke that sure ever a gentleman performed in my situation.

"One day, going into 'Will's,' I saw a crowd of gentlemen gathered together, and heard one of them
say, 'Captain Wood! I don't know the man; but there
was a Captain Wood in Southwell's regiment.' Egad,
it was my Lord Peterborough himself who was talking
about me! So, putting off my hat, I made a most gracious *congé* to my lord, and said I knew *him,* and rode
behind him at Barcelona on our entry into that town.

"'No doubt you did, Captain Wood,' says my lord,
taking my hand; 'and no doubt you know me: for many
more know Tom Fool, than Tom Fool knows.' And
with this, at which all of us laughed, my lord called for
a bottle, and he and I sat down and drank it together.

"Well, he was in disgrace, as you know, but he grew
mighty fond of me, and—would you believe it?—nothing would satisfy him but presenting me at Court!
Yes, to her sacred Majesty the Queen, and my Lady
Marlborough, who was in high feather. Ay, truly, the
sentinels on duty used to salute me as if I were Corporal John himself! I was in the high road to fortune.
Charley Mordaunt used to call me Jack, and drink
canary at my chambers; I used to make one at my Lord
Treasurer's levee; I had even got Mr. Army-Secretary
Walpole to take a hundred guineas in a compliment;

and he had promised me a majority: when bad luck turned, and all my fine hopes were overthrown in a twinkling.

"You see, my dear, that after we had left that gaby, Galgenstein,—ha, ha,—with a gag in his mouth, and twopence-halfpenny in his pocket, the honest Count was in the sorriest plight in the world; owing money here and there to tradesmen, a cool thousand to the Warwick-shire Squire: and all this on eighty pounds a year! Well, for a little time the tradesmen held their hands; while the jolly Count moved heaven and earth to catch hold of his dear Corporal and his dear money-bags over again, and placarded every town from London to Liverpool with descriptions of my pretty person. The bird was flown, however,—the money clean gone,—and when there was no hope of regaining it, what did the creditors do but clap my gay gentleman into Shrewsbury gaol: where I wish he had rotted, for my part.

"But no such luck for honest Peter Brock, or Captain Wood, as he was in those days. One blessed Monday I went to wait on Mr. Secretary, and he squeezed my hand and whispered to me that I was to be Major of a regiment in Virginia—the very thing: for you see, my dear, I didn't care about joining my Lord Duke in Flanders; being pretty well known to the army there. The Secretary squeezed my hand (it had a fifty-pound bill in it) and wished me joy, and called me Major, and bowed me out of his closet into the ante-room; and, as gay as may be, I went off to the ' Tilt-yard Coffee-house ' in Whitehall, which is much frequented by gentlemen of our profession, where I bragged not a little of my good luck.

"Amongst the company were several of my acquaintance, and amongst them a gentleman I did not much care to see, look you! I saw a uniform that I knew—red and yellow facings—Cutts's, my dear; and the wearer of this was no other than his Excellency Gustavus Adolphus Maximilian, whom we all know of!

"He stared me full in the face, right into my eye (t'other one was patched, you know); and after standing stock-still with his mouth open, gave a step back, and then a step forward, and then screeched out, ' It's Brock!'

"'I beg your pardon, sir,' says I; 'did you speak to me?'

"'I'll *swear* it's Brock,' cries Gal, as soon as he hears my voice, and laid hold of my cuff (a pretty bit of mechlin as ever you saw, by the way).

"'Sirrah!' says I, drawing it back, and giving my lord a little touch of the fist (just at the last button of the waistcoat, my dear,—a rare place if you wish to prevent a man from speaking too much: it sent him reeling to the other end of the room). 'Ruffian!' says I. 'Dog!' says I. 'Insolent puppy and coxcomb! what do you mean by laying your hand on me?'

"'Faith, Major, you giv him his *billyful,*' roared out a long Irish unattached ensign, that I had treated with many a glass of Nantz at the tavern. And so, indeed, I had; for the wretch could not speak for some minutes, and all the officers stood laughing at him, as he writhed and wriggled hideously.

"'Gentlemen, this is a monstrous scandal,' says one officer. 'Men of rank and honour at fists like a parcel of carters!'

"'Men of honour!' says the Count, who had fetched up his breath by this time. (I made for the door, but

Macshane held me and said, 'Major, you are not going
to shirk him, sure?' Whereupon I gripped his hand
and vowed I would have the dog's life.)

"'Men of honour!' says the Count. 'I tell you the
man is a deserter, a thief, and a swindler! He was my
corporal, and ran away with a thou—'

"'Dog, you lie!' I roared out, and made another cut
at him with my cane; but the gentlemen rushed between
us.

"'O bluthanowns!' says honest Macshane, 'the lying
scounthrel this fellow is! Gentlemen, I swear be me
honour that Captain Wood was wounded at Barcelona; and that I saw him there; and that he and I ran
away together at the battle of Almanza, and bad luck
to us.'

"You see, my dear, that these Irish have the strongest imaginations in the world; and that I had actually
persuaded poor Mac that he and I were friends in Spain.
Everybody knew Mac, who was a character in his way,
and believed him.

"'Strike a gentleman!' says I. 'I'll have your blood,
I will.'

"'This instant,' says the Count, who was boiling with
fury; 'and where you like.'

"'Montague House,' says I. 'Good,' says he. And
off we went. In good time too, for the constables came
in at the thought of such a disturbance, and wanted to
take us in charge.

"But the gentlemen present, being military men,
would not hear of this. Out came Mac's rapier, and that
of half-a-dozen others; and the constables were then
told to do their duty if they liked, or to take a crown-
piece and leave us to ourselves. Off they went; and

presently, in a couple of coaches, the Count and his
friends, I and mine, drove off to the fields behind Montague House.   Oh, that vile coffee-house! why did I
enter it?

"We came to the ground.   Honest Macshane was
my second, and much disappointed because the second
on the other side would not make a fight of it, and exchange a few passes with him; but he was an old major,
a cool old hand, as brave as steel, and no fool.   Well,
the swords are measured, Galgenstein strips off his
doublet, and I my handsome cut-velvet in like fashion.
Galgenstein flings off his hat, and I handed mine over
—the lace on it cost me twenty pounds.   I longed to be
at him, for—curse him!—I hate him, and know that he
has no chance with me at sword's-play.

"'You'll not fight in that periwig, sure?' says Macshane.   'Of course not,' says I, and took it off.

"May all barbers be roasted in flames; may all periwigs, bobwigs, scratchwigs, and Ramillies cocks, frizzle
in purgatory from this day forth to the end of time!
Mine was the ruin of me: what might I not have been
now but for that wig?

"I gave it over to Ensign Macshane, and with it went
what I had quite forgotten, the large patch which I wore
over one eye, which popped out fierce, staring, and lively
as was ever any eye in the world.

"'Come on!' says I, and made a lunge at my Count;
but he sprang back, (the dog was as active as a hare,
and knew, from old times, that I was his master with
the small-sword,) and his second, wondering, struck up
my blade.

"'I will not fight that man,' says he, looking mighty
pale.   'I swear upon my honour that his name is Peter

Brock: he was for two years my corporal, and deserted, running away with a thousand pounds of my moneys. Look at the fellow! what is the matter with his eye? why did he wear a patch over it? But stop!' says he. 'I have more proof. Hand me my pocket-book.' And from it, sure enough, he produced the infernal proclamation announcing my desertion! 'See if the fellow has a scar across his left ear' (and I can't say, my dear, but what I have: it was done by a cursed Dutchman at the Boyne). 'Tell me if he has not got C.R. in blue upon his right arm' (and there it is sure enough). 'Yonder swaggering Irishman may be his accomplice for what I know; but I will have no dealings with Mr. Brock, save with a constable for a second.'

"'This is an odd story, Captain Wood,' said the old Major, who acted for the Count.

"'A scounthrelly falsehood regarding me and my friend!' shouted out Mr. Macshane; 'and the Count shall answer for it.'

"'Stop, stop,' says the Major. 'Captain Wood is too gallant a gentleman, I am sure, not to satisfy the Count; and will show us that he has no such mark on his arm as only private soldiers put there.'

"'Captain Wood,' says I, 'will do no such thing, Major. I'll fight that scoundrel Galgenstein, or you, or any of you, like a man of honour; but I won't submit to be searched like a thief!'

"'No, in coorse,' said Macshane.

"'I must take my man off the ground,' says the Major.

"'Well, take him, sir,' says I, in a rage, 'and just let me have the pleasure of telling him that he's a coward and a liar; and that my lodgings are in Piccadilly, where, if ever he finds courage to meet me, he may hear of me!'

"'Faugh! I shpit on ye all,' cries my gallant ally Macshane. And sure enough he kept his word, or all but—suiting the action to it at any rate.

"And so we gathered up our clothes, and went back in our separate coaches, and no blood spilt.

"'And is it thrue now,' said Mr. Macshane, when we were alone—'is it thrue now, all these divvles have been saying?'

"'Ensign,' says I, 'you're a man of the world?'

"''Deed and I am, and Insign these twenty-two yeas.'

"'Perhaps you'd like a few pieces?' says I.

"'Faith and I should; for, to tell you the secred thrut, I've not tasted mate these four days.'

"'Well then, Ensign, it *is* true,' says I; 'and as for meat, you shall have some at the first cook-shop.' I bade the coach stop until he bought a plateful, which he ate in the carriage, for my time was precious. I just told him the whole story: at which he laughed, and swore that it was the best piece of *generalship* he ever heard on. When his belly was full, I took out a couple of guineas and gave them to him. Mr. Macshane began to cry at this, and kissed me, and swore he never would desert me: as, indeed, my dear, I don't think he will; for we have been the best of friends ever since, and he's the only man I ever could trust, I think.

"I don't know what put it into my head, but I had a scent of some mischief in the wind; so stopped the coach a little before I got home, and, turning into a tavern, begged Macshane to go before me to my lodging, and see if the coast was clear: which he did; and came back to me as pale as death, saying that the house was full of constables. The cursed quarrel at the Tilt-yard, had, I suppose, set the beaks upon me; and a pretty sweep they made of it. Ah, my dear! five hundreds pounds in money, five suits of laced clothes, three periwigs, besides laced shirts, swords, canes, and snuff-boxes; and all to go back to that scoundrel Count.

"It was all over with me, I saw—no more being a gentleman for me; and if I remained to be caught, only a choice between Tyburn and a file of grenadiers. My love, under such circumstances, a gentleman can't be particular, and must be prompt: the livery-stable was hard by where I used to hire my coach to go to Court, —ha! ha!—and was known as a man of substance. Thither I went immediately. 'Mr. Warmmash,' says I, 'my gallant friend here and I have a mind for a ride and a supper at Twickenham, so you must lend us a pair of your best horses.' Which he did in a twinkling, and off we rode.

"We did not go into the Park, but turned off and cantered smartly up towards Kilburn; and, when we got into the country, galloped as if the devil were at our heels. Bless you, my love, it was all done in a minute: and the Ensign and I found ourselves regular knights of the road, before we knew where we were almost. Only think of our finding you and your new husband at the 'Three Rooks!' There's not a greater fence than the landlady in all the country. It was she that put us on seizing your husband, and introduced us to the other two gentlemen, whose names I don't know any more than the dead."

*   *   *   *   *

"And what became of the horses?" said Mrs. Catherine to Mr. Brock, when his tale was finished.

"Rips, madam," said he; "mere rips. We sold them at Stourbridge fair, and got but thirteen guineas for the two."

"And—and—the Count, Max; where is he, Brock?" sighed she.

"Whew!" whistled Mr. Brock. "What, hankering after him still? My dear, he is off to Flanders with his regiment; and I make no doubt, there have been twenty Countesses of Galgenstein since your time."

"I don't believe any such thing, sir," said Mrs. Catherine, starting up very angrily.

"If you did, I suppose you'd laudanum him; wouldn't you?"

"Leave the room, fellow," said the lady. But she recollected herself speedily again; and, clasping her hands, and looking very wretched at Brock, at the ceiling, at the floor, at her husband (from whom she violently turned away her head), she began to cry piteously: to which tears the Corporal set up a gentle accompaniment of whistling, as they trickled one after another down her nose.

I don't think they were tears of repentance; but of regret for the time when she had her first love, and her fine clothes, and her white hat and blue feather. Of the two, the Corporal's whistle was much more innocent than the girl's sobbing: he was a rogue; but a good-natured old fellow, when his humour was not crossed. Surely our novel-writers make a great mistake in divesting their rascals of all gentle human qualities; they have such—and the only sad point to think of is, in all private concerns of life, abstract feelings, and dealings with friends, and so on, how dreadfully like a rascal is to an honest man. The man who murdered the Italian boy, set him first to play with his children whom he loved, and who doubtless deplored his loss.

CHAPTER VI

THE ADVENTURES OF THE AMBASSADOR, MR. MACSHANE

IF we had not been obliged to follow history in all respects, it is probable that we should have left out the last adventure of Mrs. Catherine and her husband, at the inn at Worcester, altogether; for, in truth, very little came of it, and it is not very romantic or striking. But we are bound to stick closely, above all, by THE TRUTH—the truth, though it be not particularly pleasant to read of or to tell. As anybody may read in the "Newgate Calendar," Mr. and Mrs. Hayes were taken at an inn at Worcester; were confined there; were swindled by persons who pretended to impress the bridegroom for military service. What is one to do after that? Had we been writing novels instead of authentic histories, we might have carried them anywhere else we choose: and we had a great mind to make Hayes philosophizing with Bolingbroke, like a certain Devereux; and Mrs. Catherine *maîtresse en titre* to Mr. Alexander Pope, Doctor Sacheverel, Sir John Reade the oculist, Dean Swift, or Marshal Tallard; as the very commonest romancer would under such circumstances. But alas and alas! truth must be spoken, whatever else is in the wind; and the excellent "Newgate Calendar," which contains the biographies and thanatographies of Hayes and his wife, does not say a word of their connections with any of the leading literary or military heroes of the

99

time of her Majesty Queen Anne. The "Calendar" says, in so many words, that Hayes was obliged to send to his father in Warwickshire for money to get him out of the scrape, and that the old gentleman came down to his aid. By this truth must we stick; and not for the sake of the most brilliant episode,—no, not for a bribe of twenty extra guineas per sheet, would we depart from it.

Mr. Brock's account of his adventure in London has given the reader some short notice of his friend, Mr. Macshane. Neither the wits nor the principles of that worthy Ensign were particularly firm: for drink, poverty, and a crack on the skull at the battle of Steenkirk had served to injure the former; and the Ensign was not in his best days possessed of any share of the latter. He had really, at one period, held such a rank in the army, but pawned his half-pay for drink and play; and for many years past had lived, one of the hundred thousand miracles of our city, upon nothing that anybody knew of, or of which he himself could give any account. Who has not a catalogue of these men in his list? who can tell whence comes the occasional clean shirt, who supplies the continual means of drunkenness, who wards off the daily-impending starvation? Their life is a wonder from day to day: their breakfast a wonder; their dinner a miracle; their bed an interposition of Providence. If you and I, my dear sir, want a shilling to-morrow, who will give it us? Will *our* butchers give us mutton-chops? will *our* laundresses clothe us in clean linen?—not a bone or a rag. Standing as we do (may it be ever so) somewhat removed from want,[1] is there

[1] The author, it must be remembered, has his lodgings and food provided for him by the government of his country.

one of us who does not shudder at the thought of descending into the lists to combat with it, and expect anything but to be utterly crushed in the encounter?

Not a bit of it, my dear sir.   It takes much more than you think for to starve a man.   Starvation is very little when you are used to it.   Some people I know even, who live on it quite comfortably, and make their daily bread by it.   It had been our friend Macshane's sole profession for many years; and he did not fail to draw from it such a livelihood as was sufficient, and perhaps too good, for him.   He managed to dine upon it a certain or rather uncertain number of days in the week, to sleep somewhere, and to get drunk at least three hundred times a year.   He was known to one or two noblemen who occasionally helped him with a few pieces, and whom he helped in turn—never mind how. He had other acquaintances whom he pestered undauntedly; and from whom he occasionally extracted a dinner, or a crown, or mayhap, by mistake, a gold-headed cane, which found its way to the pawnbroker's. When flush of cash, he would appear at the coffee-house; when low in funds, the deuce knows into what mystic caves and dens he slunk for food and lodging. He was perfectly ready with his sword, and when sober, or better still, a very little tipsy, was a complete master of it; in the art of boasting and lying he had hardly any equals; in shoes he stood six feet five inches; and here is his complete *signalement*.   It was a fact that he had been in Spain as a volunteer, where he had shown some gallantry, had had a brain-fever, and was sent home to starve as before.

Mr. Macshane had, however, like Mr. Conrad, the Corsair, one virtue in the midst of a thousand crimes,—

he was faithful to his employer for the time being: and a story is told of him, which may or may not be to his credit, viz., that being hired on one occasion by a certain lord to inflict a punishment upon a *roturier* who had crossed his lordship in his amours, he, Macshane, did actually refuse from the person to be belaboured, and who entreated his forbearance, a larger sum of money than the nobleman gave him for the beating; which he performed punctually, as bound in honour and friendship. This tale would the Ensign himself relate, with much self-satisfaction; and when, after the sudden flight from London, he and Brock took to their roving occupation, he cheerfully submitted to the latter as his commanding officer, called him always Major, and, bating blunders and drunkenness, was perfectly true to his leader. He had a notion—and, indeed, I don't know that it was a wrong one—that his profession was now, as before, strictly military, and according to the rules of honour. Robbing he called plundering the enemy; and hanging was, in his idea, a dastardly and cruel advantage that the latter took, and that called for the sternest reprisals.

The other gentlemen concerned were strangers to Mr. Brock, who felt little inclined to trust either of them upon such a message, or with such a large sum to bring back. They had, strange to say, a similar mistrust on their side; but Mr. Brock lugged out five guineas, which he placed in the landlady's hand as security for his comrade's return; and Ensign Macshane, being mounted on poor Hayes's own horse, set off to visit the parents of that unhappy young man. It was a gallant sight to behold our thieves' ambassador, in a faded sky-blue suit with orange facings, in a pair

of huge jack-boots unconscious of blacking, with a
mighty basket-hilted sword by his side, and a little
shabby beaver cocked over a large tow-periwig, ride out
from the inn of the "Three Rooks" on his mission to
Hayes's paternal village.

It was eighteen miles distant from Worcester; but
Mr. Macshane performed the distance in safety, and in
sobriety moreover (for such had been his instructions),
and had no difficulty in discovering the house of old
Hayes: towards which, indeed, John's horse trotted incontinently.   Mrs. Hayes, who was knitting at the
house-door, was not a little surprised at the appearance
of the well-known grey gelding, and of the stranger
mounted upon it.

Flinging himself off the steed with much agility, Mr.
Macshane, as soon as his feet reached the ground,
brought them rapidly together, in order to make a profound and elegant bow to Mrs. Hayes; and slapping
his greasy beaver against his heart, and poking his periwig almost into the nose of the old lady, demanded
whether he had the "shooprame honour of adthressing
Misthriss Hees?"

Having been answered in the affirmative, he then proceeded to ask whether there was a blackguard boy in
the house who would take "the horse to the steeble;"
whether "he could have a dthrink of small-beer or
buthermilk, being, faith, uncommon dthry;" and
whether, finally, "he could be feevored with a few minutes' private conversation with her and Mr. Hees, on
a matther of consitherable impartance?"   All these pre-
liminaries were to be complied with before Mr. Macshane would enter at all into the subject of his visit.
The horse and man were cared for; Mr. Hayes was

called in; and not a little anxious did Mrs. Hayes grow, in the meanwhile, with regard to the fate of her darling son. "Where is he? How is he? Is he dead?" said the old lady. "O yes, I'm sure he's dead!"

"Indeed, madam, and you're misteeken intirely: the young man is perfectly well in health."

"Oh, praised be heaven!"

"But mighty cast down in sperrits. To misfortunes, madam, look you, the best of us are subject; and a trifling one has fell upon your son."

And herewith Mr. Macshane produced a letter in the handwriting of young Hayes, of which we have had the good luck to procure a copy. It ran thus:—

"Honoured Father and Mother,—The bearer of this is a kind gentleman, who has left me in a great deal of trouble. Yesterday, at this towne, I fell in with some gentlemen of the queene's servas; after drinking with whom, I accepted her Majesty's mony to enliste. Repenting thereof, I did endeavour to escape; and, in so doing, had the misfortune to strike my superior officer, whereby I made myself liable to Death, according to the rules of warr. If, however, I pay twenty ginnys, all will be wel. You must give the same to the barer, els I shall be shott without fail on Tewsday morning. And so no more from your loving son,

"*From my prison at Bristol,*   "John Hayes.
   this unhappy Monday."

When Mrs. Hayes read this pathetic missive, its success with her was complete, and she was for going immediately to the cupboard, and producing the money necessary for her darling son's release. But the carpenter Hayes was much more suspicious. "I don't know you, sir," said he to the ambassador.

"Do you doubt my honour, sir?" said the Ensign, very fiercely.

"Why, sir," replied Mr. Hayes, "I know little about it one way or other, but shall take it for granted, if you will explain a little more of this business."

"I sildom condescind to explean," said Mr. Macshane, "for it's not the custom in my rank; but I'll explean anything in reason."

"Pray, will you tell me in what regiment my son is enlisted?"

"In coorse. In Colonel Wood's fut, my dear; and a gallant corps it is as any in the army."

"And you left him?"

"On me soul, only three hours ago, having rid like a horse-jockey ever since; as in the sacred cause of humanity, curse me, every man should."

As Hayes's house was seventy miles from Bristol, the old gentleman thought this was marvellous quick riding, and so cut the conversation short. "You have said quite enough, sir," said he, "to show me there is some roguery in the matter, and that the whole story is false from beginning to end."

At this abrupt charge the Ensign looked somewhat puzzled, and then spoke with much gravity. "Roguery," said he, "Misthur Hees, is a sthrong term; and which, in consideration of my friendship for your family, I shall pass over. You doubt your son's honour, as there wrote by him in black and white?"

"You have forced him to write," said Mr. Hayes.

"The sly old divvle's right," muttered Mr. Macshane, aside. "Well, sir, to make a clean breast of it, he *has* been forced to write it. The story about the enlistment is a pretty fib, if you will, from beginning to end. And what then, my dear? Do you think your son's any better off for that?"

"Oh, where is he?" screamed Mrs. Hayes, plumping down on her knees. "We *will* give him the money, won't we, John?"

"I know you will, madam, when I tell you where he is. He is in the hands of some gentlemen of my acquaintance, who are at war with the present government, and no more care about cutting a man's throat than they do a chicken's. He is a prisoner, madam, of our sword and spear. If you choose to ransom him, well and good; if not, peace be with him! for never more shall you see him."

"And how do I know you won't come back to-morrow for more money?" asked Mr. Hayes.

"Sir, you have my honour; and I'd as lieve break my neck as my word," said Mr. Macshane, gravely. "Twenty guineas is the bargain. Take ten minutes to talk of it—take it then, or leave it; it's all the same to me, my dear." And it must be said of our friend the Ensign, that he meant every word he said, and that he considered the embassy on which he had come as perfectly honourable and regular.

"And pray, what prevents us," said Mr. Hayes, starting up in a rage, "from taking hold of you, as a surety for him?"

"You wouldn't fire on a flag of truce, would ye, you dishonourable ould civilian?" replied Mr. Macshane. "Besides," says he, "there's more reasons to prevent you: the first is this," pointing to his sword; "here are two more"—and these were pistols; "and the last and the best of all is, that you might hang me and dthraw me and quarther me, and yet never see so much as the tip of your son's nose again. Look you, sir, we run mighty risks in our profession—it's not all play, I can tell you. We're obliged to be punctual, too, or it's all up with the thrade. If I promise that your son will die as sure as fate to-morrow morning, unless I return home safe, our people *must* keep my promise; or else what chance is there for me? You would be down upon me in a moment with a posse of constables, and have me swinging before Warwick gaol. Pooh, my dear! you never would sacrifice a darling boy like John Hayes, let alone his lady, for the sake of my long carcass. One or two of our gentlemen have been taken that way already, because parents and guardians would not believe them."

"*And what became of the poor children?*" said Mrs. Hayes, who began to perceive the gist of the argument, and to grow dreadfully frightened.

"Don't let's talk of them, ma'm: humanity shudthers at the thought!" And herewith Mr. Macshane drew his finger across his throat, in such a dreadful way as to make the two parents tremble. "It's the way of war, madam, look you. The service I have the honour to belong to is not paid by the Queen; and so we're obliged to make our prisoners pay, according to established military practice."

No lawyer could have argued his case better than Mr. Macshane so far; and he completely succeeded in convincing Mr. and Mrs. Hayes of the necessity of ransoming their son. Promising that the young man should be restored to them next morning, along with his beautiful lady, he courteously took leave of the old couple, and made the best of his way back to Worcester again. The elder Hayes wondered who the lady could be of whom the ambassador had spoken, for their son's elopement was altogether unknown to them; but anger or doubt about this subject was overwhelmed by their fears for their darling John's safety. Away rode the gallant Macshane with the money necessary to effect this; and it must be mentioned, as highly to his credit, that he never once thought of appropriating the sum to himself, or of deserting his comrades in any way.

His ride from Worcester had been a long one. He had left that city at noon, but before his return thither the sun had gone down; and the landscape, which had been dressed like a prodigal, in purple and gold, now appeared like a Quaker, in dusky grey; and the trees by the road-side grew black as undertakers or physicians, and, bending their solemn heads to each other, whispered ominously among themselves; and the mists hung on the common; and the cottage lights went out one by one; and the earth and heaven grew black, but for some twinkling useless stars, which freckled the ebon countenance of the latter; and the air grew colder; and about two o'clock the moon appeared, a dismal, pale-faced rake, walking solitary through the deserted sky; and about four, mayhap, the Dawn (wretched 'prentice-boy!) opened in the east the shutters of the Day:—in other words, more than a dozen hours had passed. Corporal Brock had been relieved by Mr. Redcap, the latter by Mr. Sicklop, the one-eyed gentleman; Mrs. John Hayes, in spite of her sorrows and bashfulness, had followed the example of her husband, and fallen asleep by his side—slept for many hours—and awakened still under the guardianship of Mr. Brock's troop; and all parties began anxiously to expect the return of the ambassador, Mr. Macshane.

That officer, who had performed the first part of his

journey with such distinguished prudence and success, found the night, on his journey homewards, was growing mighty cold and dark; and as he was thirsty and hungry, had money in his purse, and saw no cause to hurry, he determined to take refuge at an alehouse for the night, and to make for Worcester by dawn the next morning. He accordingly alighted at the first inn on his road, consigned his horse to the stable, and entering the kitchen, called for the best liquor in the house.

A small company was assembled at the inn, among whom Mr. Macshane took his place with a great deal of dignity; and having a considerable sum of money in his pocket, felt a mighty contempt for his society, and soon let them know the contempt he felt for them. After a third flagon of ale, he discovered that the liquor was sour, and emptied, with much spluttering and grimaces, the remainder of the beer into the fire. This process so offended the parson of the parish (who in those good old times did not disdain to take the post of honour in the chimney-nook), that he left his corner, looking wrathfully at the offender; who without any more ado instantly occupied it. It was a fine thing to hear the jingling of the twenty pieces in his pocket, the oaths which he distributed between the landlord, the guests, and the liquor—to remark the sprawl of his mighty jack-boots, before the sweep of which the timid guests edged further and further away; and the languishing leers which he cast on the landlady, as with wide-spread arms he attempted to seize upon her.

When the ostler had done his duties in the stable, he entered the inn, and whispered the landlord that "the stranger was riding John Hayes's horse:" of which fact the host soon convinced himself, and did not fail to have some suspicions of his guest. Had he not thought that times were unquiet, horses might be sold, and one man's money was as good as another's, he probably would have arrested the Ensign immediately, and so lost all the profit of the score which the latter was causing every moment to be enlarged.

In a couple of hours, with that happy facility which one may have often remarked in men of the gallant Ensign's nation, he had managed to disgust every one of the landlord's other guests, and scare them from the kitchen. Frightened by his addresses, the landlady too had taken flight; and the host was the only person left in the apartment; who there stayed for interest's sake. merely, and listened moodily to his tipsy guest's conversation. In an hour more, the whole house was awakened by a violent noise of howling, curses, and pots clattering to and fro. Forth issued Mrs. Landlady in her night-gear, out came John Ostler with his pitchfork, downstairs tumbled Mrs. Cook and one or two guests, and found the landlord and ensign on the kitchen-floor —the wig of the latter lying, much singed and emitting strange odours, in the fireplace, his face hideously distorted, and a great quantity of his natural hair in the partial occupation of the landlord; who had drawn it and the head down towards him, in order that he might have the benefit of pummelling the latter more at his ease. In revenge, the landlord was undermost, and the Ensign's arms were working up and down his face and body like the flaps of a paddle-wheel: the man of war had clearly the best of it.

The combatants were separated as soon as possible; but as soon as the excitement of the fight was over, Ensign Macshane was found to have no further powers of speech, sense, or locomotion, and was carried by his late antagonist to bed. His sword and pistols, which had been placed at his side at the commencement of the evening, were carefully put by, and his pocket visited. Twenty guineas in gold, a large knife—used, probably, for the cutting of bread-and-cheese—some crumbs of those delicacies and a paper of tobacco found in the breeches-pockets, and in the bosom of the sky-blue coat the leg of a cold fowl and half of a raw onion, constituted his whole property.

These articles were not very suspicious; but the beating which the landlord had received tended greatly to confirm his own and his wife's doubts about their guest; and it was determined to send off in the early morning to Mr. Hayes, informing him how a person had lain at their inn who had ridden thither mounted upon young Hayes's horse. Off set John Ostler at earliest dawn; but on his way he woke up Mr. Justice's clerk, and communicated his suspicions to him; and Mr. Clerk consulted with the village baker, who was up always early; and the clerk, the baker, the butcher with his cleaver, and two gentlemen who were going to work, all adjourned to the inn.

Accordingly, when Ensign Macshane was in a truckle-bed, plunged in that deep slumber which only innocence and drunkenness enjoy in this world, and charming the ears of morn by the regular and melodious music of his nose, a vile plot was laid against him; and when about seven of the clock he woke, he found, on sitting up in his bed, three gentlemen on each side of it, armed, and looking ominous. One held a constable's staff, and, albeit unprovided with a warrant, would take upon himself the responsibility of seizing Mr. Mac-

shane, and of carrying him before his worship at the
hall.

"Taranouns, man!" said the Ensign, springing up
in bed, and abruptly breaking off a loud, sonorous yawn,
with which he had opened the business of the day, "you
won't deteen a gentleman who's on life and death? I
give ye my word, an affair of honour."

"How came you by that there horse?" said the baker.

"How came you by these here fifteen guineas?" said
the landlord, in whose hands, by some process, five of
the gold pieces had disappeared.

"What is this here idolatrous string of beads?" said
the clerk.

Mr. Macshane, the fact is, was a Catholic, but did
not care to own it: for in those days his religion was not
popular. "Baids? Holy Mother of saints! give me
back them baids," said Mr. Macshane, clasping his
hands. "They were blest, I tell you, by his holiness the
po—psha! I mane they belong to a darling little daughter I had that's in heaven now: and as for the money
and the horse, I should like to know how a gentleman
is to travel in this counthry without them?"

"Why, you see, he may travel in the country to *git*
'em," here shrewdly remarked the constable; "and it's
our belief that neither horse nor money is honestly come
by. If his worship is satisfied, why so, in course, shall
we be; but there is highwaymen abroad, look you; and,
to our notion, you have very much the cut of one."

Further remonstrances or threats on the part of Mr.
Macshane were useless. Although he vowed that he
was first-cousin to the Duke of Leinster, an officer in
her Majesty's service, and the dearest friend Lord
Marlborough had, his impudent captors would not be-

lieve a word of his statement (which, further, was garnished with a tremendous number of oaths) ; and he was,
about eight o'clock, carried up to the house of Squire
Ballance, the neighbouring justice of the peace.

When the worthy magistrate asked the crime of which
the prisoner had been guilty, the captors looked somewhat puzzled for the moment; since, in truth, it could
not be shown that the Ensign had committed any crime
at all; and if he had confined himself to simple silence,
and thrown upon them the onus of proving his misde-
meanors, Justice Ballance must have let him loose, and
soundly rated his clerk and the landlord for detaining
an honest gentleman on so frivolous a charge.

But this caution was not in the Ensign's disposition;
and though his accusers produced no satisfactory charge
against him, his own words were quite enough to show
how suspicious his character was. When asked his name,
he gave it in as Captain Geraldine, on his way to Ireland,
by Bristol, on a visit to his cousin the Duke of Leinster.
He swore solemnly that his friends, the Duke of Marlborough and Lord Peterborough, under both of whom
he had served, should hear of the manner in which he
had been treated; and when the justice,—a sly old gentleman, and one that read the *Gazettes,*—asked him at
what battles he had been present, the gallant Ensign
pitched on a couple in Spain and in Flanders, which had
been fought within a week of each other, and vowed that
he had been desperately wounded at both; so that, at the
end of his examination, which had been taken down by
the clerk, he had been made to acknowledge as follows:—
Captain Geraldine, six feet four inches in height; thin,
with a very long red nose, and red hair; grey eyes, and
speaks with a strong Irish accent; is the first-cousin of

the Duke of Leinster, and in constant communication with him: does not know whether his Grace has any children; does not know whereabouts he lives in London; cannot say what sort of a looking man his Grace is: is acquainted with the Duke of Marlborough, and served in the dragoons at the battle of Ramillies; at which time he was with my Lord Peterborough before Barcelona. Borrowed the horse which he rides from a friend in London three weeks since. Peter Hobbs, ostler, swears that it was in his master's stable four days ago, and is the property of John Hayes, carpenter. Cannot account for the fifteen guineas found on him by the landlord; says they were twenty; says he won them at cards, a fortnight since, at Edinburgh; says he is riding about the country for his amusement: afterwards says he is on a matter of life and death, and going to Bristol; declared last night, in the hearing of several witnesses, that he was going to York; says he is a man of independent property, and has large estates in Ireland, and a hundred thousand pounds in the Bank of England. Has no shirt or stockings, and the coat he wears is marked " S.S." In his boots is written " Thomas Rodgers," and in his hat is the name of the " Rev. Doctor Snoffler."

Dr. Snoffler lived at Worcester, and had lately advertised in the *Hue and Cry* a number of articles taken from his house. Mr. Macshane said, in reply to this, that his hat had been changed at the inn, and he was ready to take his oath that he came thither in a gold-laced one. But this fact was disproved by the oaths of many persons who had seen him at the inn. And he was about to be imprisoned for the thefts which he had not committed (the fact about the hat being, that he had purchased it from a gentleman at the " Three Rooks " for two pints of beer) —he was about to be remanded, when, behold, Mrs. Hayes the elder made her appearance; and to her it was that the Ensign was indebted for his freedom.

Old Hayes had gone to work before the ostler arrived; but when his wife heard the lad's message, she instantly caused her pillion to be placed behind the saddle, and mounting the grey horse, urged the stable-boy to gallop as hard as ever he could to the justice's house.

She entered panting and alarmed. "Oh, what is your honour going to do to this honest gentleman?" said she. "In the name of heaven, let him go! His time is precious —he has important business—business of life and death."

"I tould the jidge so," said the Ensign, "but he refused to take my word—the sacred wurrd of honour of Captain Geraldine."

Macshane was good at a single lie, though easily flustered on an examination; and this was a very creditable stratagem to acquaint Mrs. Hayes with the name that he bore.

"What! you know Captain Geraldine?" said Mr. Ballance, who was perfectly well acquainted with the carpenter's wife.

"In coorse she does. Hasn't she known me these tin years? Are we not related? Didn't she give me the very horse which I rode, and, to make belave, tould you I'd bought in London?"

"Let her tell her own story. Are you related to Captain Geraldine, Mrs. Hayes?"

"Yes—oh, yes!"

"A very elegant connection! And you gave him the horse, did you, of your own free-will?"

"Oh, yes! of my own will—I would give him anything. Do, do, your honour, let him go! His child is dying," said the old lady, bursting into tears. " It may be dead before he gets to—before he gets there. Oh, your honour, your honour, pray, pray, don't detain him!"

The justice did not seem to understand this excessive sympathy on the part of Mrs. Hayes; nor did the father himself appear to be nearly so affected by his child's probable fate as the honest woman who interested herself for him. On the contrary when she made this passionate speech, Captain Geraldine only grinned and said, " Niver mind, my dear. If his honour will keep an honest gentleman for doing nothing, why let him—the law must settle between us; and as for the child, poor thing, the Lord deliver it! "

At this, Mrs. Hayes fell to entreating more loudly than ever; and as there was really no charge against him, Mr. Ballance was constrained to let him go.

The landlord and his friends were making off, rather confused, when Ensign Macshane called upon the former in a thundering voice to stop, and refund the five guineas which he had stolen from him. Again the host swore there were but fifteen in his pocket. But when, on the Bible, the Ensign solemnly vowed that he had twenty, and called upon Mrs. Hayes to say whether yesterday, half-an-hour before he entered the inn, she had not seen him with twenty guineas, and that lady expressed herself ready to swear that she had, Mr. Landlord looked more crestfallen than ever, and said that he had not counted the money when he took it; and though he did in his soul believe that there were only fifteen guineas, rather than be suspected of a shabby action, he would pay the five guineas out of his own pocket; which

he did, and with the Ensign's, or rather Mrs. Hayes's
own coin.

As soon as they were out of the justice's house, Mr.
Macshane, in the fulness of his gratitude, could not help
bestowing an embrace upon Mrs. Hayes.   And when
she implored him to let her ride behind him to her darling
son, he yielded with a very good grace, and off the pair
set on John Hayes's grey.

*   *   *   *   *

"Who has Nosey brought with him now?" said Mr.
Sicklop, Brock's one-eyed confederate, who, about three
hours after the above adventure, was lolling in the yard
of the "Three Rooks."   It was our Ensign, with the
mother of his captive.   They had not met with any accident in their ride.

" I shall now have the shooprame bliss," said Mr. Macshane, with much feeling, as he lifted Mrs. Hayes from
the saddle—"the shooprame bliss of intwining two
harrts that are mead for one another.   Ours, my dear, is
a dismal profession; but ah! don't moments like this
make aminds for years of pain?   This way, my dear.
Turn to your right, then to your left—mind the stip—
and the third door round the corner."

All these precautions were attended to; and after giving his concerted knock, Mr. Macshane was admitted
into an apartment, which he entered holding his gold
pieces in the one hand, and a lady by the other.

We shall not describe the meeting which took place between mother and son.   The old lady wept copiously;
the young man was really glad to see his relative, for he
deemed that his troubles were over.   Mrs. Cat bit her
lips, and stood aside, looking somewhat foolish; Mr.
Brock counted the money; and Mr. Macshane took a

large dose of strong waters, as a pleasing solace for his labours, dangers, and fatigue.

When the maternal feelings were somewhat calmed, the old lady had leisure to look about her, and really felt a kind of friendship and goodwill for the company of thieves in which she found herself. It seemed to her that they had conferred an actual favour on her, in robbing her of twenty guineas, threatening her son's life, and finally letting him go.

"Who is that droll old gentleman?" said she; and being told that it was Captain Wood, she dropped him a curtsey, and said, with much respect, "Captain, your very humble servant;" which compliment Mr. Brock acknowledged by a gracious smile and bow. "And who is this pretty young lady?" continued Mrs. Hayes.

"Why—hum—oh—mother, you must give her your blessing. She is Mrs. John Hayes." And herewith Mr. Hayes brought forward his interesting lady, to introduce her to his mamma.

The news did not at all please the old lady; who received Mrs. Catherine's embrace with a very sour face indeed. However, the mischief was done; and she was too glad to get back her son to be, on such an occasion, very angry with him. So, after a proper rebuke, she told Mrs. John Hayes that though she never approved of her son's attachment, and thought he married below his condition, yet as the evil was done, it was their duty to make the best of it; and she, for her part, would receive her into her house, and make her as comfortable there as she could.

"I wonder whether she has any more money in that house?" whispered Mr. Sicklop to Mr. Redcap; who, with the landlady, had come to the door of the room, and had been amusing themselves by the contemplation of this sentimental scene.

"What a fool that wild Hirishman was not to bleed her for more," said the landlady; "but he's a poor ignorant Papist. I'm sure my man" (this gentleman had been hanged) "wouldn't have come away with such a beggarly sum."

"Suppose we have some more out of 'em?" said Mr. Redcap. "What prevents us? We have got the old mare, and the colt too,—ha! ha! and the pair of 'em ought to be worth at least a hundred to us."

This conversation was carried on *sotto voce;* and I don't know whether Mr. Brock had any notion of the plot which was arranged by the three worthies. The landlady began it. "Which punch, madam, will you take?" says she. "You must have something for the good of the house, now you are in it."

"In coorse," said the Ensign.

"Certainly," said the other three. But the old lady said she was anxious to leave the place; and putting down a crown-piece, requested the hostess to treat the gentlemen in her absence. "Good-by, Captain," said the old lady.

"Ajew!" cried the Ensign, "and long life to you, my dear. You got me out of a scrape at the justice's yonder; and, split me! but Insign Macshane will remimber it as long as he lives."

And now Hayes and the two ladies made for the door; but the landlady placed herself against it, and Mr. Sicklop said, "No, no, my pretty madams, you ain't a-going off so cheap as that neither; you are not going out for a beggarly twenty guineas, look you,—we must have more."

Mr. Hayes starting back, and cursing his fate, fairly burst into tears; the two women screamed; and Mr. Brock looked as if the proposition both amused and had been expected by him: but not so Ensign Macshane.

"Major!" said he, clawing fiercely hold of Brock's arms.

"Ensign," said Mr. Brock, smiling.

" Arr we, or arr we not, men of honour?"

" Oh, in coorse," said Brock, laughing, and using Macshane's favourite expression.

" If we *arr* men of honour, we are bound to stick to our word; and hark ye, you dirty one-eyed scoundrel, if you don't immadiately make way for these leedies, and this lily-livered young jontleman who's crying so, the Meejor here and I will lug out and force you." And so saying, he drew his great sword and made a pass at Mr. Sicklop; which that gentleman avoided, and which caused him and his companion to retreat from the door. The landlady still kept her position at it, and with a storm of oaths against the Ensign, and against two Englishmen who ran away from a wild Hirishman, swore she would not budge a foot, and would stand there until her dying day.

" Faith, then, needs must," said the Ensign, and made a lunge at the hostess, which passed so near the wretch's throat, that she screamed, sank on her knees, and at last opened the door.

Down the stairs, then, with great state, Mr. Macshane led the elder lady, the married couple following; and having seen them to the street, took an affectionate farewell of the party, whom he vowed that he would come and see. "You can walk the eighteen miles aisy, between this and nightfall," said he.

"*Walk!*" exclaimed Mr. Hayes. "Why, haven't we got Ball, and shall ride and tie all the way?"

"Madam!" cried Macshane, in a stern voice, "honour before everything. Did you not, in the presence of his worship, vow and declare that you gave me that horse, and now d'ye talk of taking it back again? Let me tell you, madam, that such paltry thricks ill become a person of your years and respectability, and ought never to be played with Insign Timothy Macshane."

He waved his hat and strutted down the street; and Mrs. Catherine Hayes, along with her bridegroom and mother-in-law, made the best of their way homeward on foot.

CHAPTER VII

WHICH EMBRACES A PERIOD OF SEVEN YEARS

THE recovery of so considerable a portion of his property from the clutches of Brock was, as may be imagined, no trifling source of joy to that excellent young man, Count Gustavus Adolphus de Galgenstein; and he was often known to say, with much archness, and a proper feeling of gratitude to the Fate which had ordained things so, that the robbery was, in reality, one of the best things that could have happened to him: for, in event of Mr. Brock's *not* stealing the money, his Excellency the Count would have had to pay the whole to the Warwickshire Squire, who had won it from him at play. He was enabled, in the present instance, to plead his notorious poverty as an excuse; and the Warwickshire conqueror got off with nothing, except a very badly written autograph of the Count's, simply acknowledging the debt.

This point his Excellency conceded with the greatest candour; but (as, doubtless, the reader may have remarked in the course of his experience,) to owe is not quite the same thing as to pay; and from the day of his winning the money until the day of his death the Warwickshire Squire did never, by any chance, touch a single bob, tizzy, tester, moidore, maravedi, doubloon, tomaun, or rupee, of the sum which Monsieur de Galgenstein had lost to him.

That young nobleman was, as Mr. Brock hinted in the

little autobiographical sketch which we gave in a former chapter, incarcerated for a certain period, and for certain other debts, in the donjons of Shrewsbury; but he released himself from them by that noble and consolatory method of whitewashing which the law has provided for gentlemen in his oppressed condition; and he had not been a week in London, when he fell in with, and overcame, or put to flight, Captain Wood, *alias* Brock, and immediately seized upon the remainder of his property. After receiving this, the Count, with commendable discretion, disappeared from England altogether for a while; nor are we at all authorised to state that any of his debts to his tradesmen were discharged, any more than his debts of honour, as they are pleasantly called.

Having thus settled with his creditors, the gallant Count had interest enough with some of the great folk to procure for himself a post abroad, and was absent in Holland for some time. It was here that he became acquainted with the lovely Madam Silverkoop, the widow of a deceased gentleman of Leyden; and although the lady was not at that age at which tender passions are usually inspired—being sixty—and though she could not, like Mademoiselle Ninon de l'Enclos, then at Paris, boast of charms which defied the progress of time,—for Mrs. Silverkoop was as red as a boiled lobster, and as unwieldy as a porpoise; and although her mental attractions did by no means make up for her personal deficiencies,—for she was jealous, violent, vulgar, drunken, and stingy to a miracle: yet her charms had an immediate effect on Monsieur de Galgenstein; and hence, perhaps, the reader (the rogue! how well he knows the world!) will be led to conclude that the honest widow was *rich*.

Such, indeed, she was; and Count Gustavus, despising

the difference between his twenty quarterings and her twenty thousand pounds, laid the most desperate siege to her, and finished by causing her to capitulate; as I do believe, after a reasonable degree of pressing, any woman will do to any man: such, at least, has been *my* experience in the matter.

The Count then married; and it was curious to see how he—who, as we have seen in the case of Mrs. Cat, had been as great a tiger and domestic bully as any extant— now, by degrees, fell into a quiet submission towards his enormous Countess; who ordered him up and down as a lady orders her footman, who permitted him speedily not to have a will of his own, and who did not allow him a shilling of her money, without receiving for the same an accurate account.

How was it that he, the abject slave of Madam Silverkoop, had been victorious over Mrs. Cat? The first blow is, I believe, the decisive one in these cases, and the Countess had stricken it a week after their marriage;—establishing a supremacy which the Count never afterwards attempted to question.

We have alluded to his Excellency's marriage, as in duty bound, because it will be necessary to account for his appearance hereafter in a more splendid fashion than that under which he has hitherto been known to us; and just comforting the reader by the knowledge that the union, though prosperous in a worldly point of view, was, in reality, extremely unhappy, we must say no more from this time forth of the fat and legitimate Madame de Galgenstein. Our darling is Mrs. Catherine, who had formerly acted in her stead; and only in so much as the fat Countess did influence in any way the destinies of our heroine, or those wise and virtuous persons who have appeared and are to follow her to her end, shall we in any degree allow her name to figure here. It is an awful thing to get a glimpse, as one sometimes does, when the time is past, of some little, little wheel which works the whole mighty machinery of FATE, and see how our destinies turn on a minute's delay or advance, or on the turning of a street, or on somebody else's turning of a street, or on somebody else's doing of something else in Downing Street or in Timbuctoo, now or a thousand years ago. Thus, for instance, if Miss Poots, in the year 1695, had never been the lovely inmate of a Spielhaus at Amsterdam, Mr. Van Silverkoop would never have seen her; if the day had not been extraordinarily hot, the worthy merchant would never have gone thither; if he had not been fond of Rhenish wine and sugar, he never would have called for any such delicacies; if he had not called for them, Miss Ottilia Poots would never have brought them, and partaken of them; if he had not been rich, she would certainly have rejected all the advances made to her by Silverkoop; if he had not been so fond of Rhenish and sugar, he never would have died; and Mrs. Silverkoop would have been neither rich nor a widow, nor a wife to Count von Galgenstein. Nay, nor would this history have ever been written; for if Count Galgenstein had not married the rich widow, Mrs. Catherine would never have—

Oh, my dear Madam! you thought we were going to tell you. Pooh! nonsense,—no such thing! not for two or three and seventy pages or so—when perhaps, you *may* know what Mrs. Catherine never would have done.

The reader will remember, in the second chapter of these Memoirs, the announcement that Mrs. Catherine had given to the world a child, who might bear, if he

chose, the arms of Galgenstein, with the further adorn-
ment of a bar-sinister. This child had been put out to
nurse some time before its mother's elopement from the
Count; and as that nobleman was in funds at the time
(having had that success at play which we duly chroni-
cled), he paid a sum of no less than twenty guineas,
which was to be the yearly reward of the nurse into
whose charge the boy was put. The woman grew fond
of the brat; and when, after the first year, she had no
further news or remittances from father or mother, she
determined, for a while at least, to maintain the infant
at her own expense: for, when rebuked by her neighbours
on this score, she stoutly swore that no parents could ever
desert their children, and that some day or other she
should not fail to be rewarded for her trouble with this
one.

Under this strange mental hallucination poor Goody
Billings, who had five children and a husband of her own,
continued to give food and shelter to little Tom for a
period of no less than seven years; and though it must be
acknowledged that the young gentleman did not in the
slightest degree merit the kindnesses shown to him,
Goody Billings, who was of a very soft and pitiful disposition, continued to bestow them upon him: because,
she said, he was lonely and unprotected, and deserved
them more than other children who had fathers and
mothers to look after them. If, then, any difference was
made between Tom's treatment and that of her own
brood, it was considerably in favour of the former; to
whom the largest proportions of treacle were allotted
for his bread, and the handsomest supplies of hasty
pudding. Besides, to do Mrs. Billings justice, there
was a party against him; and that consisted not only
of her husband and her five children, but of every

single person in the neighbourhood who had an opportunity of seeing and becoming acquainted with Master
Tom.

A celebrated philosopher—I think Miss Edgeworth—
has broached the consolatory doctrine, that in intellect
and disposition all human beings are entirely equal, and
that circumstance and education are the causes of the
distinctions and divisions which afterwards unhappily
take place among them. Not to argue this question,
which places Jack Howard and Jack Thurtell on an
exact level,—which would have us to believe that Lord
Melbourne is by natural gifts and excellences a man as
honest, brave, and far-sighted as the Duke of Wellington,—which would make out that Lord Lyndhurst is, in
point of principle, eloquence, and political honesty, no
better than Mr. O'Connell,—not, I say, arguing this doctrine, let us simply state that Master Thomas Billings
(for, having no other, he took the name of the worthy
people who adopted him,) was in his long-coats fearfully
passionate, screaming and roaring perpetually, and
showing all the ill that he *could* show. At the age of two,
when his strength enabled him to toddle abroad, his favourite resort was the coal-hole or the dungheap: his roar-
ings had not diminished in the least, and he had added to
his former virtues two new ones,—a love of fighting and
stealing; both which amiable qualities he had many opportunities of exercising every day. He fought his little
adoptive brothers and sisters; he kicked and cuffed his
father and mother; he fought the cat, stamped upon the
kittens, was worsted in a severe battle with the hen in the
back-yard; but, in revenge, nearly beat a little sucking-
pig to death, whom he caught alone, and rambling near
his favourite haunt, the dunghill. As for stealing, he
stole the eggs, which he perforated and emptied; the

butter, which he ate with or without bread, as he could find it; the sugar, which he cunningly secreted in the leaves of a Baker's *Chronicle,* that nobody in the establishment could read; and thus from the pages of history he used to suck in all he knew—thieving and lying namely; in which, for his years, he made wonderful progress. If any followers of Miss Edgeworth and the philosophers are inclined to disbelieve this statement, or to set it down as overcharged and distorted, let them be assured that just this very picture was, of all pictures in the world, taken from nature. I, Ikey Solomons, once had a dear little brother who could steal before he could walk (and this not from encouragement,—for, if you know the world, you must know that in families of our profession the point of honour is sacred at home,—but from pure nature)—who could steal, I say, before he could walk, and lie before he could speak; and who, at four and a half years of age, having attacked my sister Rebecca on some question of lollipops, had smitten her on the elbow with a fire-shovel, apologized to us by saying simply, "—— her, I wish it had been her head!" Dear, dear Aminadab! I think of you, and laugh these philosophers to scorn. Nature made you for that career which you fulfilled: you were from your birth to your dying a scoundrel; you *couldn't* have been anything else, however your lot was cast; and blessed it was that you were born among the prigs,—for had you been of any other profession, alas! alas! what ills might you have done? As I have heard the author of "Richelieu," "Siamese Twins," &c. say, "Poëta nascitur non fit," which means that though he had tried ever so much to be a poet, it was all moonshine: in the like manner, I say, "*Roagus* nascitur non fit." We have it from nature, and so a fig for Miss Edgeworth.

In this manner, then, while his father, blessed with a wealthy wife, was leading, in a fine house, the life of a galley-slave; while his mother, married to Mr. Hayes, and made an honest woman of, as the saying is, was passing her time respectably in Warwickshire, Mr. Thomas Billings was inhabiting the same county, not cared for by either of them; but ordained by Fate to join them one day, and have a mighty influence upon the fortunes of both. For, as it has often happened to the traveller in the York or the Exeter coach to fall snugly asleep in his corner, and on awaking suddenly to find himself sixty or seventy miles from the place where Somnus first visited him: as, we say, although you sit still, Time, poor wretch, keeps perpetually running on, and so must run day and night, with never a pause or a halt of five minutes to get a drink, until his dying day; let the reader imagine that since he left Mrs. Hayes and all the other worthy personages of this history, in the last chapter, seven years have sped away; during which, all our heroes and heroines have been accomplishing their destinies.

Seven years of country carpentering, or other trading, on the part of a husband, of ceaseless scolding, violence, and discontent on the part of a wife, are not pleasant to describe: so we shall omit altogether any account of the early married life of Mr. and Mrs. John Hayes. The " Newgate Calendar " (to which excellent compilation we and the *other* popular novelists of the day can never be sufficiently grateful) states that Hayes left his house three or four times during this period, and, urged by the restless humours of his wife, tried several professions; returning, however, as he grew weary of each, to his wife and his paternal home. After a certain time his parents died, and by their demise he succeeded to a small property, and the carpentering business, which he for some time followed.

What, then, in the meanwhile, had become of Captain Wood, or Brock, and Ensign Macshane?—the only persons now to be accounted for in our catalogue. For about six months after their capture and release of Mr. Hayes, those noble gentlemen had followed, with much prudence and success, that trade which the celebrated and polite Duval, the ingenious Sheppard, the dauntless Turpin, and indeed many other heroes of our most popular novels, had pursued, or were pursuing, in their time. And so considerable were said to be Captain Wood's gains, that reports were abroad of his having somewhere a buried treasure; to which he might have added more, had not Fate suddenly cut short his career as a prig. He and the Ensign were—shame to say—transported for stealing three pewter-pots off a railing at Exeter; and not being known in the town, which they had only reached that morning, they were detained by no further charges, but simply condemned on this one. For this misdemeanor, her Majesty's Government vindictively sent them for seven years beyond the sea; and, as the fashion then was, sold the use of their bodies to Virginian planters during that space of time. It is thus, alas! that the strong are always used to deal with the weak, and many an honest fellow has been led to rue his unfortunate difference with the law.

Thus, then, we have settled all scores. The Count is in Holland with his wife; Mrs. Cat in Warwickshire along with her excellent husband; Master Thomas Billings with his adoptive parents in the same county; and the two military gentlemen watching the progress and cultivation of the tobacco and cotton plant in the New

World. All these things having passed between the acts, dingaring-a-dingaring-a-dingledingle-ding, the drop draws up, and the next act begins. By the way, the play *ends* with a drop: but that is neither here nor there.

* * * * *

> [Here, as in a theatre, the orchestra is supposed to play something melodious. The people get up, shake themselves, yawn, and settle down in their seats again. " Porter, ale, ginger-beer, cider," comes round, squeezing through the legs of the gentlemen in the pit. Nobody takes anything as usual; and lo! the curtain rises again. " 'Sh, 'shsh, 'shshshhh! Hats off! " says everybody.]

* * * * *

Mrs. Hayes had now been for six years the adored wife of Mr. Hayes, and no offspring had arisen to bless their loves and perpetuate their name. She had obtained a complete mastery over her lord and master; and having had, as far as was in that gentleman's power, every single wish gratified that she could demand, in the way of dress, treats to Coventry and Birmingham, drink, and what not—for, though a hard man, John Hayes had learned to spend his money pretty freely on himself and her—having had all her wishes gratified, it was natural that she should begin to find out some more; and the next whim she hit upon was to be restored to her child. It may be as well to state that she had never informed her husband of the existence of that phenomenon, although he was aware of his wife's former connection with the Count,—Mrs. Hayes, in their matrimonial quarrels, invariably taunting him with accounts of her former splendour and happiness, and with his own meanness of taste in condescending to take up with his Excellency's leavings.

She determined, then (but as yet had not confided her determination to her husband), she would have her boy; although in her seven years' residence within twenty miles of him she had never once thought of seeing him: and the kind reader knows that when his excellent lady determines on a thing—a shawl, or an opera-box, or a new carriage, or twenty-four singing-lessons from Tamburini, or a night at the "Eagle Tavern" City Road, or a ride in a buss to Richmond and tea and brandy-and-water at "Rose Cottage Hotel"—the reader, high or low, knows that when Mrs. Reader desires a thing, have it she will; you may just as well talk of avoiding her as of avoiding gout, bills, or grey hairs—and that you know is impossible. I, for my part, have had all three —ay, and a wife too.

I say that when a woman is resolved on a thing, happen it will: if husbands refuse, Fate will interfere (*flectere si nequeo,* &c.; but quotations are odious). And some hidden power was working in the case of Mrs. Hayes, and, for its own awful purposes, lending her its aid.

Who has not felt how he works—the dreadful, conquering Spirit of Ill? Who cannot see, in the circle of his own society, the fated and foredoomed to woe and evil? Some call the doctrine of destiny a dark creed; but, for me, I would fain try and think it a consolatory one. It is better, with all one's sins upon one's head, to deem oneself in the hands of Fate than to think—with our fierce passions and weak repentances; with our resolves so loud, so vain, so ludicrously, despicably weak

and frail; with our dim, wavering, wretched conceits
about virtue, and our irresistible propensity to wrong,—
that we are the workers of our future sorrow or happiness. If we depend on our strength, what is it against
mighty circumstance? If we look to ourselves, what
hope have we? Look back at the whole of your life,
and see how Fate has mastered you and it. Think of
your disappointments and your successes. Has *your*
striving influenced one or the other? A fit of indiges-
tion puts itself between you and honours and reputation; an apple plops on your nose, and makes you a
world's wonder and glory; a fit of poverty makes a rascal of you, who were, and are still, an honest man; clubs,
trumps, or six lucky mains at dice, make an honest man
for life of you, who ever were, will be, and are a rascal.
Who sends the illness? who causes the apple to fall?
who deprives you of your worldly goods? or who shuf-
fles the cards, and brings trumps, honour, virtue, and
prosperity back again? You call it chance; ay, and so
it is chance that when the floor gives way, and the rope
stretches tight, the poor wretch before St. Sepulchre's
clock dies. Only with us, clear-sighted mortals as we
are, we can't *see* the rope by which we hang, and know
not when or how the drop may fall.

But *revenons à nos moutons:* let us return to that
sweet lamb, Master Thomas, and the milk-white ewe,
Mrs. Cat. Seven years had passed away, and she began
to think that she should very much like to see her child
once more. It was written that she should; and you
shall hear how, soon after, without any great exertions
of hers, back he came to her.

In the month of July, in the year 1715, there came
down a road about ten miles from the city of Worcester,

two gentlemen; not mounted, Templar-like, upon one horse, but having a horse between them—a sorry bay, with a sorry saddle, and a large pack behind it; on which each by turn took a ride. Of the two, one was a man of excessive stature, with red hair, a very prominent nose, and a faded military dress; while the other, an old weather-beaten, sober-looking personage, wore the costume of a civilian—both man and dress appearing to have reached the autumnal, or seedy state. However, the pair seemed, in spite of their apparent poverty, to be passably merry. The old gentleman rode the horse; and had, in the course of their journey, ridden him two miles at least in every three. The tall one walked with immense strides by his side; and seemed, indeed, as if he could have quickly outstripped the four-footed animal, had he chosen to exert his speed, or had not affection for his comrade retained him at his stirrup.

A short time previously the horse had cast a shoe; and this the tall man on foot had gathered up, and was holding in his hand: it having been voted that the first blacksmith to whose shop they should come should be called upon to fit it again upon the bay horse.

"Do you remimber this counthry, Meejor?" said the tall man, who was looking about him very much pleased, and sucking a flower. "I think thim green cornfields is prettier looking at than the d—— tobacky out yondther, and bad luck to it!"

"I recollect the place right well, and some queer pranks we played here seven years agone," responded the gentleman addressed as Major. "You remember that man and his wife, whom we took in pawn at the 'Three Rooks?'"

"And the landlady only hung last Michaelmas?" said the tall man, parenthetically.

"Hang the landlady!—we've got all we ever would out of *her,* you know. But about the man and woman. You went after the chap's mother, and, like a jackass, as you are, let him loose. Well, the woman was that Catherine that you've often heard me talk about. I like the wench, —— her, for I almost brought her up; and she was for a year or two along with that scoundrel Galgenstein, who has been the cause of my ruin."

"The inferrnal blackguard and ruffian!" said the tall man; who, with his companion, has no doubt been recognized by the reader.

"Well, this Catherine had a child by Galgenstein; and somewhere here hard by the woman lived to whom we carried the brat to nurse. She was the wife of a blacksmith, one Billings: it won't be out of the way to get our horse shod at his house, if he is alive still, and we may learn something about the little beast. I should be glad to see the mother well enough."

"Do I remimber her?" said the Ensign. "Do I remimber whisky? Sure I do, and the snivelling sneak her husband, and the stout old lady her mother-in-law, and the dirty one-eyed ruffian who sold me the parson's hat, that had so nearly brought me into trouble. Oh but it was a rare rise we got out of them chaps, and the old landlady that's hanged too!" And here both Ensign Macshane and Major Brock, or Wood, grinned, and showed much satisfaction.

It will be necessary to explain the reason of it. We gave the British public to understand that the landlady of the "Three Rooks," at Worcester, was a notorious fence, or banker of thieves; that is, a purchaser of their merchandise.   In her hands Mr. Brock and his companion had left property to the amount of sixty or seventy pounds, which was secreted in a cunning recess in a chamber of the " Three Rooks," known only to the landlady and the gentlemen who banked with her; and in this place, Mr. Sicklop, the one-eyed man who had joined in the Hayes adventure, his comrade, and one or two of the topping prigs of the county, were free.   Mr. Sicklop had been shot dead in a night attack near Bath; the landlady had been suddenly hanged, as an accomplice in another case of robbery; and when, on their return from Virginia, our two heroes, whose hopes of livelihood depended upon it, had bent their steps towards Worcester, they were not a little frightened to hear of the cruel fate of the hostess and many of the amiable frequenters of the " Three Rooks."   All the goodly company were separated; the house was no longer an inn.   Was the money gone too?   At least it was worth while to look—which Messrs. Brock and Macshane determined to do.

The house being now a private one, Mr. Brock, with a genius that was above his station, visited its owner, with a huge portfolio under his arm, and, in the character of a painter, requested permission to take a particular sketch from a particular window. The Ensign followed with the artist's materials (consisting simply of a screw-driver and a crow-bar); and it is hardly necessary to say that, when admission was granted to them, they opened the well-known door, and to their inexpressible satisfaction discovered, not their own peculiar savings exactly, for these had been appropriated instantly on hearing of their transportation, but stores of money and goods to the amount of near three hundred pounds: to which Mr. Macshane said they had as just and honourable a right as anybody else. And so they had as just a right as anybody—except the original owners; but who was to discover them?

With this booty they set out on their journey—anywhere, for they knew not whither; and it so chanced that when their horse's shoe came off, they were within a few furlongs of the cottage of Mr. Billings, the blacksmith. As they came near, they were saluted by tremendous roars issuing from the smithy. A small boy was held across the bellows, two or three children of smaller and larger growth were holding him down, and many others of the village were gazing in at the window, while a man, half-naked, was lashing the little boy with a whip, and occasioning the cries heard by the travellers. As the horse drew up, the operator looked at the newcomers for a moment, and then proceeded incontinently with his work; belabouring the child more fiercely than ever.

When he had done, he turned round to the newcomers and asked how he could serve them? whereupon Mr. Wood (for such was the name he adopted, and by such we shall call him to the end) wittily remarked that however he might wish to serve *them,* he seemed mightily inclined to serve that young gentleman first.

"It's no joking matter," said the blacksmith: "if I don't serve him so now, he'll be worse off in his old age. He'll come to the gallows, as sure as his name is Bill— never mind what his name is." And so saying, he gave the urchin another cut; which elicited, of course, another scream.

"Oh! his name is Bill?" said Captain Wood.

"His name's *not* Bill!" said the blacksmith, sulkily. "He's no name; and no heart, neither. My wife took the brat in, seven years ago, from a beggarly French chap to nurse, and she kept him, for she was a good soul" (here his eyes began to wink), "and she's—she's gone now" (here he began fairly to blubber). "And d—— him, out of love for her, I kept him too, and the scoundrel is a liar and a thief. This blessed day, merely to vex me and my boys here, he spoke ill of her he did, and I'll—cut—his————life—out—I—will!" and with each word honest Mulciber applied a whack on the body of little Tom Billings; who, by shrill shrieks, and oaths in treble, acknowledged the receipt of the blows.

"Come, come," said Mr. Wood, "set the boy down, and the bellows a-going; my horse wants shoeing, and the poor lad has had strapping enough."

The blacksmith obeyed, and cast poor Master Thomas loose. As he staggered away and looked back at his tormentor, his countenance assumed an expression which made Mr. Wood say, grasping hold of Macshane's arm, "It's the boy, it's the boy! when his mother gave Galgenstein the laudanum, she had the self-same look with her!"

"Had she really now?" said Mr. Macshane. "And pree, Meejor, who *was* his mother?"

"Mrs. Cat, you fool!" answered Wood.

"Then, upon my secred word of honour, she's a mighty fine *kitten* anyhow, my dear. Aha!"

"They don't *drown* such kittens," said Mr. Wood, archly; and Macshane, taking the allusion, clapped his finger to his nose in token of perfect approbation of his commander's sentiment.

While the blacksmith was shoeing the horse, Mr.

Wood asked him many questions concerning the lad whom he had just been chastising, and succeeded, beyond a doubt, in establishing his identity with the child whom Catherine Hall had brought into the world seven years since. Billings told him of all the virtues of his wife, and the manifold crimes of the lad: how he stole, and fought, and lied, and swore; and though the youngest under his roof, exercised the most baneful influence over all the rest of his family. He was determined at last, he said, to put him to the parish, for he did not dare to keep him.

"He's a fine whelp, and would fetch ten pieces in Virginny," sighed the Ensign.

"Crimp, of Bristol, would give five for him," said Mr. Wood, ruminating.

"Why not take him?" said the Ensign.

"Faith, why not?" said Mr. Wood. "His keep, meanwhile, will not be sixpence a day." Then turning round to the blacksmith, "Mr. Billings," said he, "you will be surprised, perhaps, to hear that I know everything regarding that poor lad's history. His mother was an unfortunate lady of high family, now no more; his father a German nobleman, Count de Galgenstein by name."

"The very man!" said Billings: "a young, fairhaired man, who came here with the child, and a dragoon sergeant."

"Count de Galgenstein by name, who, on the point of death, recommended the infant to me."

"And did he pay you seven years' boarding?" said Mr. Billings, who was quite alive at the very idea.

"Alas, sir, not a jot! he died, sir, six hundred pounds in my debt; didn't he, Ensign?"

"Six hundred, upon my secred honour! I remember when he got into the house along with the poli—"

"Psha! what matters it?" here broke out Mr. Wood, looking fiercely at the Ensign. "Six hundred pounds he owes me: how was he to pay you? But he told me to take charge of this boy, if I found him; and found him I have, and *will* take charge of him, if you will hand him over."

"Send our Tom!" cried Billings. And when that youth appeared, scowling, and yet trembling, and prepared, as it seemed, for another castigation, his father, to his surprise, asked him if he was willing to go along with those gentlemen, or whether he would be a good lad and stay with him.

Mr. Tom replied immediately, "I won't be a good lad, and I'd rather go to —— than stay with you!"

"Will you leave your brothers and sisters?" said Billings, looking very dismal.

"Hang my brothers and sisters—I hate 'em; and, besides, I haven't got any!"

"But you had a good mother, hadn't you, Tom?"

Tom paused for a moment.

"Mother's gone," said he, "and you flog me, and I'll go with these men."

"Well, then, go thy ways," said Billings, starting up in a passion: "go thy ways for a graceless reprobate; and if this gentleman will take you, he may do so."

After some further parley, the conversation ended, and the next morning Mr. Wood's party consisted of three: a little boy being mounted upon the bay horse, in addition to the Ensign or himself; and the whole company went journeying towards Bristol.

* * * * *

We have said that Mrs. Hayes had, on a sudden, taken a fit of maternal affection, and was bent upon being restored to her child; and that benign destiny which watched over the life of this lucky lady instantly set about gratifying her wish, and, without cost to herself of coach-hire or saddle-horse, sent the young gentleman very quickly to her arms. The village in which the Hayeses dwelt was but a very few miles out of the road from Bristol; whither, on the benevolent mission above hinted at, our party of worthies were bound: and coming, towards the afternoon, in sight of the house of that very Justice Ballance who had been so nearly the ruin of Ensign Macshane, that officer narrated, for the hundredth time, and with much glee, the circumstances which had then befallen him, and the manner in which Mrs. Hayes, the elder, had come forward to his rescue.

"Suppose we go and see the old girl?" suggested Mr. Wood. "No harm can come to us now." And his comrade always assenting, they wound their way towards the village, and reached it as the evening came on. In the public-house where they rested, Wood made inquiries concerning the Hayes family; was informed of the death of the old couple, of the establishment of John Hayes and his wife in their place, and of the kind of life that these latter led together. When all these points had been imparted to him, he ruminated much: an expression of sublime triumph and exultation at length lighted up his features. "I think, Tim," said he at last, "that we can make more than five pieces of that boy."

"Oh, in coorse!" said Timothy Macshane, Esq.; who always agreed with his "Meejor."

"In coorse, you fool! and how? I'll tell you how. This Hayes is well to do in the world, and—"

"And we'll nab him again—ha, ha!" roared out Macshane. "By my secred honour, Meejor, there never was a gineral like you at a strathyjam!"

"Peace, you bellowing donkey, and don't wake the child. The man is well to do, his wife rules him, and they have no children. Now, either she will be very glad to have the boy back again, and pay for the finding of him, or else she has said nothing about him, and will pay us for being silent too: or, at any rate, Hayes himself will be ashamed at finding his wife the mother of a child a year older than his marriage, and will pay for the keeping of the brat away. There's profit, my dear, in any one of the cases, or my name's not Peter Brock."

When the Ensign understood this wondrous argument, he would fain have fallen on his knees and worshipped his friend and guide. They began operations, almost immediately, by an attack on Mrs. Hayes. On hearing, as she did in private interview with the excorporal the next morning, that her son was found, she was agitated by both of the passions which Wood attributed to her. She longed to have the boy back, and would give any reasonable sum to see him; but she dreaded exposure, and would pay equally to avoid that. How could she gain the one point and escape the other?

Mrs. Hayes hit upon an expedient which, I am given to understand, is not uncommon now-a-days. She suddenly discovered that she had a dear brother, who had been obliged to fly the country in consequence of having joined the Pretender, and had died in France, leaving behind him an only son. This boy her brother had, with his last breath, recommended to her protection, and had confided him to the charge of a brother officer who was now in the country, and would speedily make his appearance; and, to put the story beyond a doubt, Mr. Wood wrote the letter from her brother stating all these particulars, and Ensign Macshane received full instructions how to perform the part of the "brother officer." What consideration Mr. Wood received for his services, we cannot say; only it is well known that Mr. Hayes caused to be committed to gaol a young apprentice in his service, charged with having broken open a cupboard in which Mr. Hayes had forty guineas in gold and silver, and to which none but he and his wife had access.

Having made these arrangements, the Corporal and his little party decamped to a short distance, and Mrs. Catherine was left to prepare her husband for a speedy addition to his family, in the shape of this darling nephew. John Hayes received the news with anything but pleasure. He had never heard of any brother of Catherine's; she had been bred at the workhouse, and nobody ever hinted that she had relatives: but it is easy for a lady of moderate genius to invent circumstances; and with lies, tears, threats, coaxings, oaths, and other blandishments, she compelled him to submit.

Two days afterwards, as Mr. Hayes was working in his shop with his lady seated beside him, the trampling of a horse was heard in his court-yard, and a gentleman, of huge stature, descended from it, and strode into the shop. His figure was wrapped in a large cloak; but Mr. Hayes could not help fancying that he had somewhere seen his face before.

"This, I preshoom," said the gentleman, "is Misther Hayes, that I have come so many miles to see, and this is his amiable lady? I was the most intimate frind, madam, of your laminted brother, who died in King Lewis's service, and whose last touching letthers I despatched to you two days ago. I have with me a further precious token of my dear friend, Captain Hall—it is *here.*"

And so saying, the military gentleman, with one arm, removed his cloak, and stretching forward the other into Hayes's face almost, stretched likewise forward a little boy, grinning and sprawling in the air, and prevented only from falling to the ground by the hold which the Ensign kept of the waistband of his little coat and breeches.

"Isn't he a pretty boy?" said Mrs. Hayes, sidling up to her husband tenderly, and pressing one of Mr. Hayes's hands.

*   *   *   *   *

About the lad's beauty it is needless to say what the carpenter thought; but that night, and for many, many nights after, the lad stayed at Mr. Hayes's.

Catherine's Present
to Mr. Hayes

CHAPTER VIII

ENUMERATES THE ACCOMPLISHMENTS OF MASTER
THOMAS BILLINGS—INTRODUCES BROCK AS
DR. WOOD—AND ANNOUNCES THE EX-
ECUTION OF ENSIGN MACSHANE

WE are obliged, in recording this history, to follow
accurately that great authority, the "Calen-
darium Newgaticum Roagorumque Registerium," of
which every lover of literature in the present day knows
the value; and as that remarkable work totally discards
all the unities in its narratives, and reckons the life of
its heroes only by their actions, and not by periods of
time, we must follow in the wake of this mighty ark—a
humble cockboat. When it pauses, we pause; when it
runs ten knots an hour, we run with the same celerity;
and as, in order to carry the reader from the penultimate
chapter of this work unto the last chapter, we were compelled to make him leap over a gap of seven blank years,
ten years more must likewise be granted to us before we
are at liberty to resume our history.

During that period, Master Thomas Billings had
been under the especial care of his mother; and, as may be
imagined, he rather increased than diminished the accomplishments for which he had been remarkable while
under the roof of his foster-father. And with this advantage, that while at the blacksmith's, and only three
or four years of age, his virtues were necessarily appre-

ciated only in his family circle, and among those few acquaintances of his own time of life whom a youth of
three can be expected to meet in the alleys or over the
gutters of a small country hamlet,—in his mother's residence, his circle extended with his own growth, and he
began to give proofs of those powers of which in infancy
there had been only encouraging indications. Thus it
was nowise remarkable that a child of four years should
not know his letters, and should have had a great disin-
clination to learn them; but when a young man of fifteen
showed the same creditable ignorance, the same undeviating dislike, it was easy to see that he possessed much
resolution and perseverance. When it was remarked,
too, that, in case of any difference, he not only beat the
usher, but by no means disdained to torment and bully
the very smallest boys of the school, it was easy to see
that his mind was comprehensive and careful, as well as
courageous and grasping. As it was said of the Duke of
Wellington, in the Peninsula, that he had a thought for
everybody—from Lord Hill to the smallest drummer
in the army—in like manner Tom Billings bestowed *his*
attention on high and low; but in the shape of blows:
he would fight the strongest and kick the smallest, and
was always at work with one or the other. At thirteen,
when he was removed from the establishment whither
he had been sent, he was the cock of the school out of
doors, and the very last boy in. He used to let the little
boys and new-comers pass him by, and laugh; but he
always belaboured them unmercifully afterwards; and
then it was, he said, *his* turn to laugh. With such a pug-
nacious turn, Tom Billings ought to have been made a
soldier and might have died a marshal; but, by an unlucky ordinance of fate, he was made a tailor, and died

a—never mind what for the present; suffice it to say, that he was suddenly cut off at a very early period of his existence, by a disease which has exercised considerable ravages among the British youth.

By consulting the authority above mentioned, we find that Hayes did not confine himself to the profession of a carpenter, or remain long established in the country; but was induced, by the eager spirit of Mrs. Catherine most probably, to try his fortune in the metropolis; where he lived, flourished, and died. Oxford Road, Saint Giles's and Tottenham Court, were at various periods of his residence in town, inhabited by him. At one place, he carried on the business of green-grocer and small-coalman; in another, he was carpenter, undertaker, and lender of money to the poor: finally, he was a lodging-house keeper in the Oxford or Tyburn Road; but continued to exercise the last-named charitable profession.

Lending as he did upon pledges, and carrying on a pretty large trade, it was not for him, of course, to inquire into the pedigree of all the pieces of plate, the bales of cloth, swords, watches, wigs, shoebuckles, &c., that were confided by his friends to his keeping; but it is clear that his friends had the requisite confidence in him, and that he enjoyed the esteem of a class of characters who still live in history, and are admired unto this very day. The mind loves to think that, perhaps, in Mr. Hayes's back-parlour the gallant Turpin might have hob-and-nobbed with Mrs. Catherine; that here, perhaps, the noble Sheppard might have cracked his joke, or quaffed his pint of rum. Who knows but that Macheath and Paul Clifford may have crossed legs under Hayes's dinner-table? But why pause to speculate on things

that might have been? why desert reality for fond imagination, or call up from their honoured graves the
sacred dead? I know not: and yet, in sooth, I can never
pass Cumberland Gate without a sigh, as I think of the
gallant cavaliers who traversed that road in old time.
Pious priests accompanied their triumphs; their char-
iots were surrounded by hosts of glittering javelin-men.
As the slave at the car of the Roman conqueror shouted,
"Remember thou art mortal!" before the eyes of the
British warrior rode the undertaker and his coffin, telling him that he too must die! Mark well the spot! A
hundred years ago Albion Street (where comic Power
dwelt, Milesia's darling son)—Albion Street was a
desert. The square of Connaught was without its penultimate, and, strictly speaking, *naught*. The Edgware
Road was then a road, 'tis true; with tinkling waggons
passing now and then, and fragrant walls of snowy
hawthorn blossoms. The ploughman whistled over Nut-
ford Place; down the green solitudes of Sovereign
Street the merry milkmaid led the lowing kine. Here,
then, in the midst of green fields and sweet air—before
ever omnibuses were, and when Pineapple Turnpike and
Terrace were alike unknown—here stood Tyburn: and
on the road towards it, perhaps to enjoy the prospect,
stood, in the year 1725, the habitation of Mr. John
Hayes.

One fine morning in the year 1725, Mrs. Hayes, who
had been abroad in her best hat and riding-hood; Mr.
Hayes, who for a wonder had accompanied her; and
Mrs. Springatt, a lodger, who for a remuneration had
the honour of sharing Mrs. Hayes's friendship and
table: all returned, smiling and rosy, at about half-past
ten o'clock, from a walk which they had taken to Bays-

water. Many thousands of people were likewise seen flocking down the Oxford Road; and you would rather have thought, from the smartness of their appearance and the pleasure depicted in their countenances, that they were just issuing from a sermon, than quitting the ceremony which they had been to attend.

The fact is, that they had just been to see a gentleman hanged,—a cheap pleasure, which the Hayes family never denied themselves; and they returned home with a good appetite to breakfast, braced by the walk, and tickled into hunger as it were by the spectacle. I can recollect, when I was a gyp at Cambridge, that the "men" used to have breakfast-parties for the very same purpose; and the exhibition of the morning acted infallibly upon the stomach, and caused the young students to eat with much voracity.

Well, Mrs. Catherine, a handsome, well-dressed, plump, rosy woman, of three or four and thirty (and when, my dear, is a woman handsomer than at that age?) came in quite merrily from her walk, and entered the back-parlour, which looked into a pleasant yard, or garden, whereon the sun was shining very gaily; and where, at a table covered with a nice white cloth, laid out with some silver mugs, too, and knives, all with different crests and patterns, sat an old gentleman reading in an old book.

"Here we are at last, Doctor," said Mrs. Hayes, "and here's his speech." She produced the little halfpenny tract, which to this day is sold at the gallows-foot upon the death of every offender. "I've seen a many men turned off, to be sure; but I never did see one who bore it more like a man than he did."

"My dear," said the gentleman addressed as Doctor,

"he was as cool and as brave as steel, and no more minded hanging than tooth-drawing."

"It was the drink that ruined him," said Mrs. Cat.

"Drink, and bad company. I warned him, my dear, —I warned him years ago: and directly he got into Wild's gang, I knew that he had not a year to run. Ah, why, my love, will men continue such dangerous courses," continued the Doctor, with a sigh, "and jeopardy their lives for a miserable watch or a snuff-box, of which Mr. Wild takes three-fourths of the produce? But here comes the breakfast; and, egad, I am as hungry as a lad of twenty."

Inded, at this moment Mrs. Hayes's servant appeared with a smoking dish of bacon and greens; and Mr. Hayes himself ascended from the cellar (of which he kept the key), bearing with him a tolerably large jug of small-beer. To this repast the Doctor, Mrs. Springatt (the other lodger), and Mr. and Mrs. Hayes, proceeded with great alacrity. A fifth cover was laid, but not used; the company remarking that "Tom had very likely found some acquaintances at Tyburn, with whom he might choose to pass the morning."

Tom was Master Thomas Billings, now of the age of sixteen: slim, smart, five feet ten inches in height, handsome, sallow in complexion, black-eyed, and black-haired. Mr. Billings was apprentice to a tailor, of tolerable practice, who was to take him into partnership at the end of his term. It was supposed, and with reason, that Tom would not fail to make a fortune in this business; of which the present head was one Beinkleider, a German. Beinkleider was skilful in his trade (after the manner of his nation, which in breeches and metaphysics —in inexpressibles and incomprehensibles—may instruct

all Europe), but too fond of his pleasure. Some prom-
issory-notes of his had found their way into Hayes's
hands, and had given him the means not only of provid-
ing Master Billings with a cheap apprenticeship, and
a cheap partnership afterwards; but would empower
him, in one or two years after the young partner had
joined the firm, to eject the old one altogether. So that
there was every prospect that, when Mr. Billings was
twenty-one years of age, poor Beinkleider would have
to act, not as his master, but his journeyman.

Tom was a very precocious youth; was supplied by
a doting mother with plenty of pocket-money, and spent
it with a number of lively companions of both sexes, at
plays, bull-baitings, fairs, jolly parties on the river, and
such like innocent amusements. He could throw a main,
too, as well as his elders; had pinked his man, in a row
at Madam King's in the Piazza; and was much respected
at the Roundhouse.

Mr. Hayes was not very fond of this promising young
gentleman; indeed, he had the baseness to bear malice,
because, in a quarrel which occurred about two years
previously, he, Hayes, being desirous to chastise Mr.
Billings, had found himself not only quite incompetent,
but actually at the mercy of the boy; who struck
him over the head with a joint-stool, felled him to the
ground, and swore he would have his life. The Doctor,
who was then also a lodger at Mr. Hayes's, interposed,
and restored the combatants, not to friendship, but to
peace. Hayes never afterwards attempted to lift his
hand to the young man, but contented himself with
hating him profoundly. In this sentiment Mr. Billings
participated cordially; and, quite unlike Mr. Hayes,
who never dared to show his dislike, used on every oc-

casion when they met, by actions, looks, words, sneers, and curses, to let his step-father know the opinion which he had of him. Why did not Hayes discard the boy altogether? Because, if he did so, he was really afraid of his life, and because he trembled before Mrs. Hayes, his lady, as the leaf trembles before the tempest in October. His breath was not his own, but hers; his money, too, had been chiefly of her getting,—for though he was as stingy and mean as mortal man can be, and so likely to save much, he had not the genius for *getting* which Mrs. Hayes possessed. She kept his books (for she had learned to read and write by this time), she made his bargains, and she directed the operations of the poor-spirited little capitalist. When bills became due, and creditors pressed for time, then she brought Hayes's own professional merits into play. The man was as deaf and cold as a rock; never did poor tradesman gain a penny from him; never were the bailiffs delayed one single minute from their prey. The Beinkleider business, for instance, showed pretty well the genius of the two. Hayes was for closing with him at once; but his wife saw the vast profits which might be drawn out of him, and arranged the apprenticeship and the partnership before alluded to. The woman heartily scorned and spit upon her husband, who fawned upon her like a spaniel. She loved good cheer; she did not want for a certain kind of generosity. The only feeling that Hayes had for any one except himself was for his wife, whom he held in a cowardly awe and attachment: he liked drink, too, which made him chirping and merry, and accepted willingly any treats that his acquaintances might offer him; but he would suffer agonies when his wife brought or ordered from the cellar a bottle of wine.

And now for the Doctor. He was about seventy years of age. He had been much abroad; he was of a sober, cheerful aspect; he dressed handsomely and quietly in a broad hat and cassock; but saw no company except the few friends whom he met at the coffee-house. He had an income of about a hundred pounds, which he promised to leave to young Billings. He was amused with the lad, and fond of his mother, and had boarded with them for some years past. The Doctor, in fact, was our old friend Corporal Brock; the Rev. Dr. Wood now, as he had been Major Wood fifteen years back.

Any one who has read the former part of this history must have seen that we have spoken throughout with invariable respect of Mr. Brock; and that in every circumstance in which he has appeared, he has acted not only with prudence, but often with genius. The early obstacle to Mr. Brock's success was want of conduct simply. Drink, women, play—how many a brave fellow have they ruined!—had pulled Brock down as often as his merit had carried him up. When a man's passion for play has brought him to be a scoundrel, it at once ceases to be hurtful to him in a worldly point of view; he cheats, and wins. It is only for the idle and luxurious that women retain their fascinations to a very late period; and Brock's passions had been whipped out of him in Virginia; where much ill health, ill treatment, hard labour, and hard food, speedily put an end to them. He forgot there even how to drink; rum or wine made this poor declining gentleman so ill that he could indulge in them no longer; and so his three vices were cured. Had he been ambitious, there is little doubt but that Mr. Brock, on his return from transportation, might have risen in the world; but he was old and a philoso-

pher: he did not care about rising. Living was cheaper
in those days, and interest for money higher: when he
had amassed about six hundred pounds, he purchased
an annuity of seventy-two pounds, and gave out—why
should he not?—that he had the capital as well as the
interest. After leaving the Hayes family in the country, he found them again in London: he took up his
abode with them, and was attached to the mother and
the son. Do you suppose that rascals have not affections like other people? hearts, madam—ay, hearts—and
family ties which they cherish? As the Doctor lived on
with this charming family, he began to regret that he
had sunk all his money in annuities, and could not, as
he repeatedly vowed he would, leave his savings to his
adopted children.

He felt an indescribable pleasure ("*suave mari
magno,*" &c.) in watching the storms and tempests of
the Hayes *ménage*. He used to encourage Mrs. Catherine into anger when, haply, that lady's fits of calm
would last too long; he used to warm up the disputes
between wife and husband, mother and son, and enjoy
them beyond expression: they served him for daily
amusement; and he used to laugh until the tears ran
down his venerable cheeks at the accounts which young
Tom continually brought him of his pranks abroad,
among watchmen and constables, at taverns or elsewhere.

When, therefore, as the party were discussing their
bacon and cabbage, before which the Rev. Doctor with
much gravity said grace, Master Tom entered, Doctor
Wood, who had before been rather gloomy, immediately
brightened up, and made a place for Billings between
himself and Mrs. Catherine.

"How do, old cock?" said that young gentleman

familiarly. "How goes it, mother?" And so saying, he seized eagerly upon the jug of beer which Mr. Hayes had drawn, and from which the latter was about to help himself, and poured down his throat exactly one quart.

"Ah!" said Mr. Billings, drawing breath after a draught which he had learned accurately to gauge from the habit of drinking out of pewter measures which held precisely that quantity.—"Ah!" said Mr. Billings, drawing breath, and wiping his mouth with his sleeves, "this is very thin stuff, old Squaretoes; but my coppers have been red-hot since last night, and they wanted a sluicing."

"Should you like some ale, dear?" said Mrs. Hayes, that fond and judicious parent.

"A quart of brandy, Tom?" said Dr. Wood. "Your papa will run down to the cellar for it in a minute."

"I'll see him hanged first!" cried Mr. Hayes, quite frightened.

"Oh, fie, now, you unnatural father!" said the Doctor.

The very name of father used to put Mr. Hayes in a fury. "I'm not his father, thank heaven!" said he.

"No, nor nobody else's," said Tom.

Mr. Hayes only muttered "Base-born brat!"

"His father was a gentleman,—that's more than *you* ever were!" screamed Mrs. Hayes. "His father was a man of spirit; no cowardly sneak of a carpenter, Mr. Hayes! Tom has noble blood in his veins, for all he has a tailor's appearance; and if his mother had had her right, she would be now in a coach-and-six."

"I wish I could find my father," said Tom; "for I think Polly Briggs and I would look mighty well in a coach-and-six." Tom fancied that if his father was a

Count at the time of his birth, he must be a prince now; and, indeed, went among his companions by the latter august title.

" Ay, Tom, that you would," cried his mother, looking at him fondly.

"With a sword by my side, and a hat and feather, there's never a lord at St. James's would cut a finer figure."

After a little more of this talk, in which Mrs. Hayes let the company know her high opinion of her son— who, as usual, took care to show his extreme contempt for his step-father—the latter retired to his occupations; the lodger, Mrs. Springatt, who had never said a word all this time, retired to her apartment on the second floor; and, pulling out their pipes and tobacco, the old gentleman and the young one solaced themselves with half-an-hour's more talk and smoking; while the thrifty Mrs. Hayes, opposite to them, was busy with her books.

"What's in the confessions?" said Mr. Billings to Doctor Wood. "There were six of 'em besides Mac: two for sheep, four housebreakers; but nothing of consequence, I fancy."

"There's the paper," said Wood, archly. "Read for yourself, Tom."

Mr. Tom looked at the same time very fierce and very foolish; for, though he could drink, swear, and fight, as well as any lad of his inches in England, reading was not among his accomplishments. "I tell you what, Doctor," said he, "—— you! have no bantering with me,—for I'm not the man that will bear it, —— me!" and he threw a tremendous swaggering look across the table.

"I want you to learn to read, Tommy dear. Look at

your mother there over her books: she keeps them as neat as a scrivener now, and at twenty she could make never a stroke."

"Your godfather speaks for your good, child; and for me, thou knowest that I have promised thee a gold-headed cane and periwig on the first day that thou canst read me a column of the *Flying Post.*"

"Hang the periwig!" said Mr. Tom, testily. "Let my godfather read the paper himself, if he has a liking for it."

Whereupon the old gentleman put on his spectacles, and glanced over the sheet of whitey-brown paper, which, ornamented with a picture of a gallows at the top, contained the biographies of the seven unlucky individuals who had that morning suffered the penalty of the law. With the six heroes who came first in the list we have nothing to do; but have before us a copy of the paper containing the life of No. 7, and which the Doctor read with an audible voice:

" Captain Macshane

" The seventh victim to his own crimes was the famous highwayman, Captain Macshane, so well known as the Irish Fire-eater.

" The Captain came to the ground in a fine white lawn shirt and nightcap; and, being a Papist in his religion, was attended by Father O'Flaherty, Popish priest, and chaplain to the Bavarian Envoy.

" Captain Macshane was born of respectable parents, in the town of Clonakilty, in Ireland, being descended from most of the kings in that country. He had the honour of serving their Majesties King William and

Queen Mary, and her Majesty Queen Anne, in Flanders and Spain, and obtained much credit from my Lords Marlborough and Peterborough for his valour.

"But being placed on half-pay at the end of the war, Ensign Macshane took to evil courses; and, frequenting the bagnios and dice-houses, was speedily brought to ruin.

"Being at this pass, he fell in with the notorious Captain Wood, and they two together committed many atrocious robberies in the inland counties; but these being too hot to hold them, they went into the west, where they were unknown. Here, however, the day of retribution arrived; for, having stolen three pewter-pots from a public-house, they, under false names, were tried at Exeter, and transported for seven years beyond the sea. Thus it is seen that Justice never sleeps; but, sooner or later, is sure to overtake the criminal.

"On their return from Virginia, a quarrel about booty arose between these two, and Macshane killed Wood in a combat that took place between them near to the town of Bristol; but a waggon coming up, Macshane was obliged to fly without the ill-gotten wealth: so true is it, that wickedness never prospers.

"Two days afterwards, Macshane met the coach of Miss Macraw, a Scotch lady and heiress, going, for lumbago and gout, to the Bath. He at first would have robbed this lady; but such were his arts, that he induced her to marry him; and they lived together for seven years in the town of Eddenboro, in Scotland,—he passing under the name of Colonel Geraldine. The lady dying, and Macshane having expended all her wealth, he was obliged to resume his former evil courses, in order to save himself from starvation; whereupon he robbed a Scotch lord, by name the Lord of Whistlebinkie, of a mull of snuff; for which crime he was condemned to the Tolbooth prison at Eddenboro, in Scotland, and whipped many times in publick.

"These deserved punishments did not at all alter Captain Macshane's disposition; and on the 17th of February last, he stopped the Bavarian Envoy's coach on Blackheath, coming from Dover, and robbed his Excellency and his chaplain; taking from the former his money, watches, star, a fur-cloak, his sword (a very valuable one) ; and from the latter a Romish missal, out of which he was then reading, and a case-bottle."

"The Bavarian Envoy!" said Tom parenthetically. "My master, Beinkleider, was his lordship's regimental tailor in Germany, and is now making a court suit for him. It will be a matter of a hundred pounds to him, I warrant."

Dr. Wood resumed his reading. "Hum—hum! A Romish missal, out of which he was reading, and a case-bottle.

"By means of the famous Mr. Wild, this notorious criminal was brought to justice, and the case-bottle and missal have been restored to Father O'Flaherty.

"During his confinement in Newgate, Mr. Macshane could not be brought to express any contrition for his crimes, except that of having killed his commanding officer. For this Wood he pretended an excessive sorrow, and vowed that usquebaugh had been the cause of his death,—indeed, in prison he partook of no other liquor, and drunk a bottle of it on the day before his death.

"He was visited by several of the clergy and gentry in his cell; among others, by the Popish priest whom he had robbed, Father O'Flaherty, before mentioned, who attended him likewise in his last moments (if that idolatrous worship may be called attention) ; and likewise by the Father's patron, the Bavarian Ambassador, his Excellency Count Maximilian de Galgenstein."

      *   *   *   *   *

As old Wood came to these words, he paused to give them utterance.

"What! Max?" screamed Mrs. Hayes, letting her ink-bottle fall over her ledgers.

"Why, be hanged if it ben't my father!" said Mr. Billings.

"Your father, sure enough, unless there be others of his name, and unless the scoundrel is hanged," said the Doctor—sinking his voice, however, at the end of the sentence.

Mr. Billings broke his pipe in an agony of joy. "I think we'll have the coach now, mother," says he; "and I'm blessed if Polly Briggs shall not look as fine as a duchess."

"Polly Briggs is a low slut, Tom, and not fit for the likes of you, his Excellency's son. Oh, fie! You must be a gentleman now, sirrah; and I doubt whether I shan't take you away from that odious tailor's shop altogether."

To this proposition Mr. Billings objected altogether; for, besides Mrs. Briggs before alluded to, the young gentleman was much attached to his master's daughter, Mrs. Margaret Gretel, or Gretchen Beinkleider.

"No," says he. "There will be time to think of that hereafter, ma'am. If my Pa makes a man of me, why, of course, the shop may go to the deuce, for what I care; but we had better wait, look you, for something certain, before we give up such a pretty bird in the hand as this."

" He speaks like Solomon," said the Doctor.

" I always said he would be a credit to his old mother, didn't I, Brock?" cried Mrs. Cat, embracing her son very affectionately. "A credit to her; ay, I warrant, a real blessing! And dost thou want any money, Tom? for a lord's son must not go about without a few pieces in his pocket. And I tell thee, Tommy, thou must go and see his lordship; and thou shalt have a piece of brocade for a waistcoat, thou shalt; ay, and the silver-hilted sword I told thee of: but oh, Tommy, Tommy! have a care, and don't be a-drawing of it in naughty company at the gaming-houses, or at the—"

"A drawing of fiddlesticks, mother! If I go to see my father, I must have a reason for it; and instead of going with a sword in my hand, I shall take something else in it."

" The lad *is* a lad of nous," cried Dr. Wood, "although his mother does spoil him so cruelly. Look you, Madam Cat: did you not hear what he said about Beinkleider and the clothes? Tommy will just wait on the Count with his lordship's breeches. A man may learn a deal of news in the trying on of a pair of breeches."

And so it was agreed that in this manner the son should at first make his appearance before his father. Mrs. Cat gave him the piece of brocade, which, in the course of the day, was fashioned into a smart waistcoat (for Beinkleider's shop was close by, in Cavendish Square). Mrs. Gretel, with many blushes, tied a fine blue riband round his neck; and, in a pair of silk stockings, with gold buckles to his shoes, Master Billings looked a very proper young gentleman.

"And, Tommy," said his mother, blushing and hesitating, "should Max—should his lordship ask after your—want to know if your mother is alive, you can say she is, and well, and often talks of old times. And, Tommy" (after another pause), "you needn't say anything about Mr. Hayes; only say I'm quite well."

Mrs. Hayes looked at him as he marched down the street, a long, long way. Tom was proud and gay in his new costume, and was not unlike his father. As she looked, lo! Oxford Street disappeared, and she saw a green common, and a village, and a little inn. There was a soldier leading a pair of horses about on the green common; and in the inn sat a cavalier, so young, so merry, so beautiful! Oh, what slim white hands he had; and winning words, and tender, gentle blue eyes! Was it not an honour to a country lass that such a noble gentleman should look at her for a moment? Had he not some charm about him that she must needs obey when he whispered in her ear, "Come, follow me!" As she walked towards the lane that morning, how well she remembered each spot as she passed it, and the look it wore for the last time! How the smoke was rising from the pastures, how the fish were jumping and plashing in the mill-stream! There was the church, with all its windows lighted up with gold, and yonder were the reapers sweeping down the brown corn. She tried to sing as she went up the hill—what was it? She could not remember; but oh, how well she remembered the sound of the horse's hoofs, as they came quicker, quicker—nearer, nearer! How noble he looked on his great horse! Was he thinking of her, or were they all silly words which he spoke last night, merely to pass away the time and deceive poor girls with? Would he remember them, would he?

*　　　*　　　*　　　*　　　*

"Cat my dear," here cried Mr. Brock, *alias* Captain, *alias* Dr. Wood, "here's the meat a-getting cold, and I am longing for my breakfast."

As they went in he looked her hard in the face. "What, *still* at it, you silly girl? I've been watching you these five minutes, Cat; and be hanged but I think a word from Galgenstein, and you would follow him as a fly does a treacle-pot?"

They went into breakfast; but though there was a hot shoulder of mutton and onion-sauce—Mrs. Catherine's favourite dish—she never touched a morsel of it.

In the meanwhile Mr. Thomas Billings, in his new clothes which his mamma had given him, in his new riband which the fair Miss Beinkleider had tied round his neck, and having his Excellency's breeches wrapped in a silk handkerchief in his right hand, turned down in the direction of Whitehall, where the Bavarian Envoy lodged. But, before he waited on him, Mr. Billings, being excessively pleased with his personal appearance, made an early visit to Mrs. Briggs, who lived in the neighbourhood of Swallow Street; and who, after expressing herself with much enthusiasm regarding her Tommy's good looks, immediately asked him what he would stand to drink? Raspberry gin being suggested, a pint of that liquor was sent for; and so great was the confidence and intimacy subsisting between these two young people, that the reader will be glad to hear that Mrs. Polly accepted every shilling of the money which Tom Billings had received from his mamma the day before; nay, could with difficulty be prevented from seizing upon the cut-velvet breeches which he was carrying to the nobleman for whom they were made. Having paid his adieux to Mrs. Polly, Mr. Billings departed to visit his father.

CHAPTER IX

I DON'T know in all this miserable world a more miserable spectacle than that of a young fellow of five or six and forty. The British army, that nursery of valour, turns out many of the young fellows I mean: who, having flaunted in dragoon uniforms from seventeen to six-and-thirty; having bought, sold, or swapped during that period some two hundred horses; having played, say fifteen thousand games at billiards; having drunk some six thousand bottles of wine; having consumed a reasonable number of Nugee coats, split many dozen pairs of high-heeled Hoby boots, and read the newspaper and the army-list duly, retire from the service when they have attained their eighth lustre, and saunter through the world, trailing from London to Cheltenham, and from Boulogne to Paris, and from Paris to Baden, their idleness, their ill-health, and their *ennui*. "In the morning of youth," and when seen along with whole troops of their companions, these flowers look gaudy and brilliant enough; but there is no object more dismal than one of them alone, and in its autumnal or seedy state. My friend, Captain Popjoy, is one of them who has arrived at this condition, and whom everybody knows by his title of Father Pop. A kinder, simpler, more empty-headed fellow does not exist.   He is forty-seven years old, and appears a young, good-looking man of sixty.   At the time of the Army of Occupation he really was as good-looking a man as any in the Dragoons.   He now uses all sorts of stratagems to cover the bald place on his head, by combing certain thin grey side-locks over it.   He has, in revenge, a pair of enormous moustaches, which he dyes of the richest blue-black.   His nose is a good deal larger and redder than it used to be; his eyelids have grown flat and heavy; and a little pair of red, watery eyeballs float in the midst of them: it seems as if the light which was once in those sickly green pupils had extravasated into the white part of the eye.   If Pop's legs are not so firm and muscular as they used to be in those days when he took such leaps into White's buckskins, in revenge his waist is much larger.   He wears a very good coat, however, and a waistband, which he lets out after dinner. Before ladies he blushes, and is as silent as a schoolboy. He calls them "modest women."   His society is chiefly among young lads belonging to his former profession. He knows the best wine to be had at each tavern or café, and the waiters treat him with much respectful familiarity.   He knows the names of every one of them; and shouts out, "Send Markwell here!" or, "Tell Cuttriss to give us a bottle of the yellow seal!" or, "Dizzy voo, Monsure Borrel, noo donny shampang frappy," &c. He always makes the salad or the punch, and dines out three hundred days in the year: the other days you see him in a two-franc eating-house at Paris, or prowling about Rupert Street or St. Martin's Court, where you get a capital cut of meat for eightpence.   He has decent lodgings and scrupulously clean linen; his animal functions are still tolerably well preserved, his spiritual have evaporated long since; he sleeps well, has no conscience, believes himself to be a respectable fellow, and is tolerably happy on the days when he is asked out to dinner.

Poor Pop is not very high in the scale of created beings; but, if you fancy there is none lower, you are in egregious error. There was once a man who had a mysterious exhibition of an animal quite unknown to naturalists, called "the wusser." Those curious individuals who desired to see the *wusser* were introduced into an apartment where appeared before them nothing more than a little lean, shrivelled, hideous, blear-eyed, mangy pig. Every one cried out "Swindle!" and "Shame!" "Patience, gentlemen, be heasy," said the showman: "look at that there hanimal; it's a perfect phenomaly of hugliness: I engage you never see such a pig." Nobody ever had seen. "Now, gentlemen," said he, "I'll keep my promise, has per bill; and bad as that there pig is, look at this here" (he showed another). "Look at this here, and you'll see at once that it's *a wusser.*" In like manner the Popjoy breed is bad enough, but it serves only to show off the Galgenstein race; which is *wusser.*

Galgenstein had led a very gay life, as the saying is, for the last fifteen years; such a gay one, that he had lost all capacity of enjoyment by this time, and only possessed inclinations without powers of gratifying them. He had grown to be exquisitely curious and fastidious about meat and drink, for instance, and all that he wanted was an appetite. He carried about with him a French cook, who could not make him eat; a doctor, who could not make him well; a mistress, of whom he was heartily sick after two days; a priest, who had been a favourite of the exemplary Dubois, and by turns used to tickle him by the imposition of a penance, or by the repetition of a tale from the *recueil* of Nocé, or La Fare. All his appetites were wasted and worn; only some monstrosity would galvanize them into momentary action. He was in that effete state to which many noblemen of his time had arrived; who were ready to believe in ghost-raising or in gold-making, or to retire into monasteries and wear hair-shirts, or to dabble in conspiracies, or to die in love with little cook-maids of fifteen, or to pine for the smiles or at the frowns of a prince of the blood, or to go mad at the refusal of a chamberlain's key. The last gratification he remembered to have enjoyed was that of riding bare-headed in a soaking rain for three hours by the side of his Grand Duke's mistress's coach; taking the *pas* of Count Krähwinkel, who challenged him, and was run through the body for this very dispute. Galgenstein gained a rheumatic gout by it, which put him to tortures for many months; and was further gratified with the post of English Envoy. He had a fortune, he asked no salary, and could look the envoy very well. Father O'Flaherty did all the duties, and furthermore acted as a spy over the ambassador—a sinecure post; for the man had no feelings, wishes, or opinions—absolutely none.

"Upon my life, father," said this worthy man, "I care for nothing. You have been talking for an hour about the Regent's death, and the Duchess of Phalaris, and sly old Fleury, and what not; and I care just as much as if you told me that one of my Bauers at Galgenstein had killed a pig; or as if my lackey, La Rose yonder, had made love to my mistress."

"He does!" said the reverend gentleman.

"Ah, Monsieur l'Abbé!" said La Rose, who was arranging his master's enormous court periwig, "you are, hélas! wrong. Monsieur le Comte will not be angry at my saying that I wish the accusation were true."

The Count did not take the slightest notice of La Rose's wit, but continued his own complaints.

"I tell you, Abbé, I care for nothing. I lost a thousand guineas t'other night at basset; I wish to my heart I could have been vexed about it. Egad! I remember the day when to lose a hundred made me half mad for a month. Well, next day I had my revenge at dice, and threw thirteen mains. There was some delay; a call for fresh bones, I think; and would you believe it? I fell asleep with the box in my hand!"

"A desperate case, indeed," said the Abbé.

"If it had not been for Krähwinkel I should have been a dead man, that's positive. That pinking him saved me."

"I make no doubt of it," said the Abbé. "Had your Excellency not run him through, he, without a doubt, would have done the same for you."

"Psha! you mistake my words, Monsieur l'Abbé" (yawning). "I mean—what cursed chocolate!—that I was dying for want of excitement. Not that I care for dying; no, d—— me, if I do!"

"*When* you do, your Excellency means," said the Abbé, a fat, grey-haired Irishman, from the Irlandois College at Paris.

His Excellency did not laugh, nor understand jokes of any kind; he was of an undeviating stupidity, and only replied, "Sir, I mean what I say. I don't care for living: no, nor for dying either; but I can speak as well

as another, and I'll thank you not to be correcting my
phrases as if I were one of your cursed school-boys, and
not a gentleman of fortune and blood."

Herewith the Count, who had uttered four sentences
about himself (he never spoke of anything else), sunk
back on his pillows again, quite exhausted by his eloquence. The Abbé, who had a seat and a table by the
bedside, resumed the labours which had brought him
into the room in the morning, and busied himself with
papers, which occasionally he handed over to his superior
for approval.

Presently Monsieur La Rose appeared.

"Here is a person with clothes from Mr. Beinkleider's. Will your Excellency see him, or shall I bid him
leave the clothes?"

The Count was very much fatigued by this time; he
had signed three papers, and read the first half-dozen
lines of a pair of them.

"Bid the fellow come in, La Rose; and, hark ye,
give me my wig: one must show one's self to be a gentleman before these scoundrels." And he therefore
mounted a large chestnut-coloured, orange-scented
pyramid of horse-hair, which was to awe the new-
comer.

He was a lad of about seventeen, in a smart waistcoat
and a blue riband: our friend Tom Billings, indeed.
He carried under his arm the Count's destined breeches.
He did not seem in the least awed, however, by his Excellency's appearance, but looked at him with a great
degree of curiosity and boldness. In the same manner
he surveyed the chaplain, and then nodded to him with
a kind look of recognition.

"Where have I seen the lad?" said the father. "Oh,

I have it! My good friend, you were at the hanging yesterday, I think?"

Mr. Billings gave a very significant nod with his head. "I never miss," said he.

"What a young Turk! And pray, sir, do you go for pleasure, or for business?"

"Business! what do you mean by business?"

"Oh, I did not know whether you might be brought up to the trade, or your relations be undergoing the operation."

"My relations," said Mr. Billings, proudly, and staring the Count full in the face, "was not made for no such thing. I'm a tailor now, but I'm a gentleman's son: as good a man, ay, as his lordship there: for *you* a'n't his lordship—you're the Popish priest you are; and we were very near giving you a touch of a few Protestant stones, master."

The Count began to be a little amused; he was pleased to see the Abbé look alarmed, or even foolish.

"Egad, Abbé," said he, "you turn as white as a sheet."

"I don't fancy being murdered, my lord," said the Abbé, hastily; "and murdered for a good work. It was but to be useful to yonder poor Irishman, who saved me as a prisoner in Flanders, when Marlborough would have hung me up like poor Macshane himself was yesterday."

"Ah!" said the Count, bursting out with some energy, "I was thinking who the fellow could be, ever since he robbed me on the Heath. I recollect the scoundrel now: he was a second in a duel I had here in the year 6."

"Along with Major Wood, behind Montague

House," said Mr. Billings. "*I*'ve heard on it." And
here he looked more knowing than ever.

"*You!*" cried the Count, more and more surprised.
"And pray who the devil *are* you?"

"My name's Billings."

"Billings?" said the Count.

"I come out of Warwickshire," said Mr. Billings.

"Indeed!"

"I was born at Birmingham town."

"Were you, really!"

"My mother's name was Hall," continued Billings,
in a solemn voice. "I was put out to nurse along with
John Billings, a blacksmith; and my father run away.
Now do you know who I am?"

"Why, upon honour, now," said the Count, who was
amused,—"upon honour, Mr. Billings, I have not that
advantage."

"Well, then, my lord, *you're my father!*"

Mr. Billings, when he said this, came forward to the
Count with a theatrical air; and, flinging down the
breeches of which he was the bearer, held out his arms
and stared, having very little doubt but that his lordship
would forthwith spring out of bed and hug him to his
heart. A similar piece of *naïveté* many fathers of
families have, I have no doubt, remarked in their children; who, not caring for their parents a single doit,
conceive, nevertheless, that the latter are bound to show
all sorts of affection for them. His lordship did move,
but backwards towards the wall, and began pulling at
the bell-rope with an expression of the most intense
alarm.

"Keep back, sirrah!—keep back! Suppose I *am*
your father, do you want to murder me? Good heavens,

how the boy smells of gin and tobacco! Don't turn away, my lad! sit down there at a proper distance. And, La Rose, give him some eau-de-Cologne, and get a cup of coffee. Well, now, go on with your story. Egad, my dear Abbé, I think it is very likely that what the lad says is true."

"If it is a family conversation," said the Abbé, "I had better leave you."

"Oh, for heaven's sake, no! I could not stand the boy alone. Now, Mister ah!—What's-your-name? Have the goodness to tell your story."

Mr. Billings was wofully disconcerted; for his mother and he had agreed that as soon as his father saw him he would be recognized at once, and, mayhap, made heir to the estates and title; in which, being disappointed, he very sulkily went on with his narrative, and detailed many of those events with which the reader has already been made acquainted. The Count asked the boy's mother's Christian name, and being told it, his memory at once returned to him.

"What! are you little Cat's son?" said his Excellency. "By heavens, mon cher Abbé, a charming creature, but a tigress—positively a tigress. I recollect the whole affair now. She's a little, fresh, black-haired woman, a'n't she? with a sharp nose and thick eyebrows, ay? Ah! yes, yes," went on my lord, "I recollect her, I recollect her. It was at Birmingham I first met her: she was my Lady Trippet's woman, wasn't she?"

"She was no such thing," said Mr. Billings, hotly. "Her aunt kept the 'Bugle Inn' on Waltham Green, and your lordship seduced her."

"Seduced her! Oh, 'gad, so I did. Stap me, now, I did. Yes, I made her jump on my black horse, and

bore her off like—like Æneas bore away his wife from
the siege of Rome! hey, l'Abbé?"

"The events were precisely similar," said the Abbé.
"It is wonderful what a memory you have!"

"I was always remarkable for it," continued his Excellency. "Well, where was I,—at the black horse?
Yes, at the black horse. Well, I mounted her on the
black horse, and rode her *en croupe,* egad—ha, ha!—to
Birmingham; and there we billed and cooed together
like a pair of turtle-doves: yes—ha!—that we did!"

"And this, I suppose, is the end of some of the *billings?*" said the Abbé, pointing to Mr. Tom.

"Billings! what do you mean? Yes—oh—ah—a
pun, a calembourg. Fi donc, M. l'Abbé." And then,
after the wont of very stupid people, M. de Galgenstein
went on to explain to the Abbé his own pun. "Well,
but to proceed," cries he. "We lived together at Birmingham, and I was going to be married to a rich heiress,
egad! when what do you think this little Cat does? She
murders me, egad! and makes me *manquer* the marriage. Twenty thousand, I think it was; and I wanted
the money in those days. Now, wasn't she an abominable monster, that mother of yours, hey, Mr. a—What's-
your-name?"

"She served you right!" said Mr. Billings, with a
great oath, starting up out of all patience.

"Fellow!" said his Excellency, quite aghast, "do you
know to whom you speak?—to a nobleman of seventy-
eight descents; a count of the Holy Roman empire; a
representative of a sovereign? Ha, egad! Don't
stamp, fellow, if you hope for my protection."

"D—n your protection!" said Mr. Billings, in a
fury. "Curse you and your protection too! I'm a

free-born Briton, and no —— French Papist! And
any man who insults my mother—ay, or calls me feller,
had better look to himself and the two eyes in his head,
I can tell him!" And with this Mr. Billings put himself into the most approved attitude of the Cockpit, and
invited his father, the reverend gentleman, and M. La
Rose the valet, to engage with him in a pugilistic encounter. The two latter, the Abbé especially, seemed
dreadfully frightened; but the Count now looked on
with much interest; and giving utterance to a feeble
kind of chuckle, which lasted for about half a minute,
said,—

"Paws off, Pompey! You young hang-dog, you—
egad, yes, aha! 'pon honour, you're a lad of spirit;
some of your father's spunk in you, hey? I know him
by that oath. Why, sir, when I was sixteen, I used to
swear—to swear, egad, like a Thames waterman, and
exactly in this fellow's way! Buss me, my lad; no, kiss
my hand. That will do"—and he held out a very lean
yellow hand, peering from a pair of yellow ruffles. It
shook very much, and the shaking made all the rings
upon it shine only the more.

"Well," says Mr. Billings, "if you wasn't a-going to
abuse me nor mother, I don't care if I shake hands with
you. I ain't proud!"

The Abbé laughed with great glee; and that very
evening sent off to his court a most ludicrous, *spicy* description of the whole scene of meeting between this
amiable father and child; in which he said that young
Billings was the *élève favorite* of M. Kitch, Ecuyer,
le bourreau de Londres, and which made the Duke's mistress laugh so much that she vowed that the Abbé should
have a bishopric on his return: for, with such store of

wisdom, look you, my son, was the world governed in those days.

The Count and his offspring meanwhile conversed with some cordiality. The former informed the latter of all the diseases to which he was subject, his manner of curing them, his great consideration as chamberlain to the Duke of Bavaria; how he wore his court suits, and of a particular powder which he had invented for the hair; how, when he was seventeen, he had run away with a canoness, egad! who was afterwards locked up in a convent, and grew to be sixteen stone in weight; how he remembered the time when ladies did not wear patches; and how the Duchess of Marlborough boxed his ears when he was so high, because he wanted to kiss her.

All these important anecdotes took some time in the telling, and were accompanied by many profound moral remarks; such as, "I can't abide garlic, nor white-wine, stap me! nor Sauerkraut, though his Highness eats half a bushel per day. I ate it the first time at court; but when they brought it me a second time, I refused—refused, split me and grill me if I didn't! Everybody stared; his Highness looked as fierce as a Turk; and that infernal Krähwinkel (my dear, I did for him afterwards)—that cursed Krähwinkel, I say, looked as pleased as possible, and whispered to Countess Fritsch, 'Blitzchen Frau Gräfinn,' says he, 'it's all over with Galgenstein.' What did I do? I had the *entrée,* and demanded it. 'Altesse,' says I, falling on one knee, 'I ate no Kraut at dinner to-day. You remarked it: I saw your Highness remark it.'

"'I did, M. le Comte,' said his Highness, gravely.

"I had almost tears in my eyes; but it was necessary

to come to a resolution, you know. 'Sir,' said I, 'I speak with deep grief to your Highness, who are my benefactor, my friend, my father; but of this I am resolved, I WILL NEVER EAT SAUERKRAUT MORE: it don't agree with me. After being laid up for four weeks by the last dish of Sauerkraut of which I partook, I may say with confidence—*it don't* agree with me. By impairing my health, it impairs my intellect, and weakens my strength; and both I would keep for your Highness's service.'

"'Tut, tut!' said his Highness. 'Tut, tut, tut!' Those were his very words.

"'Give me my sword or my pen,' said I. 'Give me my sword or my pen, and with these Maximilian de Galgenstein is ready to serve you; but sure,—sure, a great prince will pity the weak health of a faithful subject, who does not know how to eat Sauerkraut?' His Highness was walking about the room: I was still on my knees, and stretched forward my hand to seize his coat.

"'GEHT ZUM TEUFEL, sir!' said he, in a loud voice (it means 'Go to the deuce,' my dear),—'Geht zum Teufel, and eat what you like!' With this he went out of the room abruptly; leaving in my hand one of his buttons, which I keep to this day. As soon as I was alone, amazed by his great goodness and bounty, I sobbed aloud—cried like a child" (the Count's eyes filled and winked at the very recollection), "and when I went back into the card-room, stepping up to Krähwinkel, 'Count,' says I, 'who looks foolish now?'—Hey there, La Rose, give me the diamond— Yes, that was the very pun I made, and very good it was thought. 'Krähwinkel,' says I, '*who looks foolish now?*' and from that day to this I was never at a court-day asked to eat Sauerkraut—*never*."

"Hey there, La Rose! Bring me that diamond snuff-box in the drawer of my *secrétaire;*" and the snuff-box was brought. "Look at it, my dear," said the Count, "for I saw you seemed to doubt. There is the button—the very one that came off his grace's coat."

Mr. Billings received it, and twisted it about with a stupid air. The story had quite mystified him; for he did not dare yet to think his father was a fool—his respect for the aristocracy prevented him.

When the Count's communications had ceased, which they did as soon as the story of the Sauerkraut was finished, a silence of some minutes ensued. Mr. Billings was trying to comprehend the circumstances above narrated; his lordship was exhausted; the chaplain had quitted the room directly the word Sauerkraut was mentioned—he knew what was coming. His lordship looked for some time at his son; who returned the gaze with his mouth wide open. "Well," said the Count—"well, sir? What are you sitting there for? If you have nothing to say, sir, you had better go. I had you here to amuse me—split me—and not to sit there staring!"

Mr. Billings rose in a fury.

"Hark ye, my lad," said the Count, "tell La Rose to give thee five guineas, and, ah—come again some morning. A nice, well-grown young lad," mused the Count, as Master Tommy walked wondering out of the apartment; "a pretty fellow enough, and intelligent too."

"Well, he *is* an odd fellow, my father," thought Mr. Billings, as he walked out, having received the sum offered to him. And he immediately went to call upon his friend, Polly Briggs, from whom he had separated in the morning.

What was the result of their interview is not at all necessary to the progress of this history. Having made her, however, acquainted with the particulars of his visit to his father, he went to his mother's, and related to her all that had occurred.

Poor thing, she was very differently interested in the issue of it!

CHAPTER X

ABOUT a month after the touching conversation
above related, there was given, at Marylebone Gardens, a grand concert and entertainment, at which the
celebrated Madame Aménaïde, a dancer of the theatre at
Paris, was to perform, under the patronage of several
English and foreign noblemen; among whom was his
Excellency the Bavarian Envoy. Madame Aménaïde
was, in fact, no other than the *maîtresse en titre* of the
Monsieur de Galgenstein, who had her a great bargain
from the Duke de Rohan-Chabot at Paris.

It is not our purpose to make a great and learned display here, otherwise the costumes of the company assembled at this fête might afford scope for at least half-a-
dozen pages of fine writing; and we might give, if need
were, specimens of the very songs and music sung on the
occasion. Does not the Burney collection of music, at
the British Museum, afford one an ample store of songs
from which to choose? Are there not the memoirs of
Colley Cibber? those of Mrs. Clark, the daughter of
Colley? Is there not Congreve, and Farquhar—nay,
and at a pinch, the "Dramatic Biography," or even the
Spectator, from which the observant genius might bor-

row passages, and construct pretty antiquarian fig-
ments? Leave we these trifles to meaner souls! Our
business is not with the breeches and periwigs, with the
hoops and patches, but with the divine hearts of men,
and the passions which agitate them. What need, therefore, have we to say that on this evening, after the dancing, the music, and the fireworks, Monsieur de Galgenstein felt the strange and welcome pangs of appetite,
and was picking a cold chicken, along with some other
friends, in an arbour—a cold chicken, with an accompaniment of a bottle of champagne—when he was led
to remark that a very handsome, plump little person, in
a gorgeous stiff damask gown and petticoat, was sauntering up and down the walk running opposite his sup-
ping-place, and bestowing continual glances towards
his Excellency. The lady, whoever she was, was in a
mask, such as ladies of high and low fashion wore at
public places in those days, and had a male companion.
He was a lad of only seventeen, marvellously well
dressed—indeed, no other than the Count's own son,
Mr. Thomas Billings; who had at length received from
his mother the silver-hilted sword, and the wig, which
that affectionate parent had promised to him.

In the course of the month which had elapsed since
the interview that has been described in the former chapter, Mr. Billings had several times had occasion to wait
on his father; but though he had, according to her
wishes, frequently alluded to the existence of his mother,
the Count had never at any time expressed the slightest
wish to renew his acquaintance with that lady; who, if
she had seen him, had only seen him by stealth.

The fact is, that after Billings had related to her the
particulars of his first meeting with his Excellency;

which ended, like many of the latter visits, in nothing at all; Mrs. Hayes had found some pressing business, which continually took her to Whitehall, and had been prowling from day to day about Monsieur de Galgenstein's lodgings. Four or five times in the week, as his Excellency stepped into his coach, he might have remarked, had he chosen, a woman in a black hood, who was looking most eagerly into his eyes: but those eyes had long since left off the practice of observing; and Madam Catherine's visits had so far gone for nothing.

On this night, however, inspired by gaiety and drink, the Count had been amazingly stricken by the gait and ogling of the lady in the mask. The Reverend O'Flaherty, who was with him, and had observed the figure in the black cloak, recognized, or thought he recognized, her. " It is the woman who dogs your Excellency every day," said he. " She is with that tailor lad who loves to see people hanged—your Excellency's son, I mean." And he was just about to warn the Count of a conspiracy evidently made against him, and that the son had brought, most likely, the mother to play her arts upon him—he was just about, I say, to show to the Count the folly and danger of renewing an old *liaison* with a woman such as he had described Mrs. Cat to be, when his Excellency, starting up, and interrupting his ghostly adviser at the very beginning of his sentence, said, "Egad, l'Abbé, you are right—it *is* my son, and a mighty smart-looking creature with him. Hey! Mr. What's-your-name—Tom, you rogue, don't you know your own father?" And so saying, and cocking his beaver on one side, Monsieur de Galgenstein strutted jauntily after Mr. Billings and the lady.

It was the first time that the Count had formally recognized his son.

"Tom, you rogue," stopped at this, and the Count came up. He had a white velvet suit, covered over with stars and orders, a neat modest wig and bag, and peach-coloured silk-stockings with silver clasps. The lady in the mask gave a start as his Excellency came forward. "Law, mother, don't squeege so," said Tom. The poor woman was trembling in every limb; but she had presence of mind to "squeege" Tom a great deal harder; and the latter took the hint, I suppose, and was silent.

The splendid Count came up. Ye gods, how his embroidery glittered in the lamps! What a royal exhalation of musk and bergamot came from his wig, his handkerchief, and his grand lace ruffles and frills! A broad yellow riband passed across his breast, and ended at his hip in a shining diamond cross—a diamond cross, and a diamond sword-hilt! Was anything ever seen so beautiful? And might not a poor woman tremble when such a noble creature drew near to her, and deigned, from the height of his rank and splendour, to look down upon her? As Jove came down to Semele in state, in his habits of ceremony, with all the grand cordons of his orders blazing about his imperial person—thus dazzling, magnificent, triumphant, the great Galgenstein descended towards Mrs. Catherine. Her cheeks glowed red hot under her coy velvet mask, her heart thumped against the whalebone prison of her stays. What a delicious storm of vanity was raging in her bosom! What a rush of long-pent recollections burst forth at the sound of that enchanting voice!

As you wind up a hundred-guinea chronometer with a twopenny watch-key—as by means of a dirty wooden plug you set all the waters of Versailles a-raging, and splashing, and storming—in like manner, and by like humble agents, were Mrs. Catherine's tumultuous passions set going. The Count, we have said, slipped up to his son, and merely saying, "How do, Tom?" cut the young gentleman altogether, and passing round to the lady's side, said, "Madam, 'tis a charming evening— egad it is!" She almost fainted: it was the old voice. There he was, after seventeen years, once more at her side!

Now I know what I could have done. I can turn out a quotation from Sophocles (by looking to the index) as well as another: I can throw off a bit of fine writing too, with passion, similes, and a moral at the end. What, pray, is the last sentence but one but the very finest writing? Suppose, for example, I had made Maximilian, as he stood by the side of Catherine, look up towards the clouds, and exclaim, in the words of the voluptuous Cornelius Nepos,

$$
\begin{aligned}
&\text{'Αέναοι νεφέλαι} \\
&\text{'Αρθῶμεν φανεραὶ} \\
&\text{Δροσερὰν φύσιν εὐάγητοι, κ. τ. λ.}
\end{aligned}
$$

Or suppose, again, I had said, in a style still more popular:—The Count advanced towards the maiden. They both were mute for a while; and only the beating of her heart interrupted that thrilling and passionate silence. Ah, what years of buried joys and fears, hopes and disappointments, arose from their graves in the far past, and in those brief moments flitted before the united ones! How sad was that delicious retrospect, and oh, how sweet! The tears that rolled down the cheek of

each were bubbles from the choked and moss-grown wells
of youth; the sigh that heaved each bosom had some
lurking odours in it—memories of the fragrance of boy-
hood, echoes of the hymns of the young heart!   Thus is
it ever—for these blessed recollections the soul always
has a place; and while crime perishes, and sorrow is forgotten, the beautiful alone is eternal.

"O golden legends, written in the skies!" mused De
Galgenstein, "ye shine as ye did in the olden days! *We*
change, but *ye* speak ever the same language. Gazing
in your abysmal depths, the feeble ratioci—"

　　　　*　　　*　　　*　　　*　　　*

　　　　*　　　*　　　*　　　*　　　*

There, now, are six columns[1] of the best writing to
be found in this or any other book. Galgenstein has
quoted Euripides thrice, Plato once, Lycophron nine
times, besides extracts from the Latin syntax and the
minor Greek poets. Catherine's passionate embreath-
ings are of the most fashionable order; and I call upon
the ingenious critic of the X—— newspaper to say
whether they do not possess the real impress of the giants
of the olden time—the real Platonic smack, in a word?
Not that I want in the least to show off; but it is as
well, every now and then, to show the public what one
can do.

Instead, however, of all this rant and nonsense, how
much finer is the speech that the Count really did make?
"It is a very fine evening,—egad it is!" The "egad"
did the whole business: Mrs. Cat was as much in love

---

[1] There *were* six columns, as mentioned by the accurate Mr. Solomons; but
we have withdrawn two pages and three-quarters, because, although our correspondent has been excessively eloquent, according to custom, we were anxious to come to the facts of the story.

Mr. Solomons, by sending to our office, may have the cancelled passages.—
O. Y.

with him now as ever she had been; and, gathering up all her energies, she said, "It is dreadful hot too, I think;" and with this she made a curtsey.

"Stifling, split me!" added his Excellency. "What do you say, madam, to a rest in an arbour, and a drink of something cool?"

"Sir!" said the lady, drawing back.

"Oh, a drink—a drink by all means," exclaimed Mr. Billings, who was troubled with a perpetual thirst. "Come, mo—, Mrs. Jones, I mean: you're fond of a glass of cold punch, you know; and the rum here is prime, I can tell you."

The lady in the mask consented with some difficulty to the proposal of Mr. Billings, and was led by the two gentlemen into an arbour, where she was seated between them; and some wax-candles being lighted, punch was brought.

She drank one or two glasses very eagerly, and so did her two companions; although it was evident to see, from the flushed looks of both of them, that they had little need of any such stimulus. The Count, in the midst of his champagne, it must be said, had been amazingly stricken and scandalized by the appearance of such a youth as Billings in a public place, with a lady under his arm. He was, the reader will therefore understand, in the moral stage of liquor; and when he issued out, it was not merely with the intention of examining Mr. Billings's female companion, but of administering to him some sound correction for venturing, at his early period of life, to form any such acquaintances. On joining Billings, his Excellency's first step was naturally to examine the lady. After they had been sitting for a while over their punch, he bethought him of his original purpose, and began to address a number of moral remarks to his son.

We have already given some specimens of Monsieur de Galgenstein's sober conversation; and it is hardly necessary to trouble the reader with any further reports of his speeches.   They were intolerably stupid and dull; as egotistical as his morning lecture had been, and a hundred times more rambling and prosy.   If Cat had been in the possession of her sober senses, she would have seen in five minutes that her ancient lover was a ninny, and have left him with scorn; but she was under the charm of old recollections, and the sound of that silly voice was to her magical.   As for Mr. Billings, he allowed his Excellency to continue his prattle; only frowning, yawning, cursing occasionally, but drinking continually.

So the Count descanted at length upon the enormity of young Billings's early *liaisons;* and then he told his own, in the year four, with a burgomaster's daughter at Ratisbon, when he was in the Elector of Bavaria's service—then, after Blenheim, when he had come over to the Duke of Marlborough, when a physician's wife at Bonn poisoned herself for him, &c. &c.; of a piece with the story of the canoness, which has been recorded before.   All the tales were true.   A clever, ugly man every now and then is successful with the ladies; but a handsome fool is irresistible.   Mrs. Cat listened and listened. Good heavens! she had heard all these tales before, and recollected the place and the time—how she was hemming a handkerchief for Max; who came round and kissed her, vowing that the physician's wife was nothing compared to her—how he was tired, and lying on the sofa, just come home from shooting.   How handsome he looked!   Cat thought he was only the handsomer

now; and looked more grave and thoughtful, the dear
fellow!

The garden was filled with a vast deal of company of
all kinds, and parties were passing every moment before
the arbour where our trio sat. About half-an-hour after
his Excellency had quitted his own box and party, the
Rev. Mr. O'Flaherty came discreetly round, to examine
the proceedings of his diplomatical *chef*. The lady in
the mask was listening with all her might; Mr. Billings
was drawing figures on the table with punch; and the
Count talking incessantly. The Father Confessor
listened for a moment; and then, with something re-
sembling an oath, walked away to the entry of the gardens, where his Excellency's gilt coach, with three footmen, was waiting to carry him back to London. "Get
me a chair, Joseph," said his Reverence, who infinitely
preferred a seat gratis in the coach. "That fool," muttered he, "will not move for this hour." The reverend
gentleman knew that, when the Count was on the subject of the physician's wife, his discourses were intolerably long; and took upon himself, therefore, to disap-
pear, along with the rest of the Count's party; who
procured other conveyances, and returned to their
homes.

After this quiet shadow had passed before the Count's
box, many groups of persons passed and repassed; and
among them was no other than Mrs. Polly Briggs, to
whom we have been already introduced. Mrs. Polly
was in company with one or two other ladies, and leaning on the arm of a gentleman with large shoulders and
calves, a fierce cock to his hat, and a shabby genteel air.
His name was Mr. Moffat, and his present occupation
was that of door-keeper at a gambling-house in Covent

Garden; where, though he saw many thousands pass daily under his eyes, his own salary amounted to no more than four-and-sixpence weekly,—a sum quite insufficient to maintain him in the rank which he held.

Mr. Moffat had, however, received some funds—amounting, indeed, to a matter of twelve guineas—within the last month, and was treating Mrs. Briggs very generously to the concert. It may be as well to say that every one of the twelve guineas had come out of Mrs. Polly's own pocket; who, in return, had received them from Mr. Billings. And as the reader may remember that, on the day of Tommy's first interview with his father, he had previously paid a visit to Mrs. Briggs, having under his arm a pair of breeches, which Mrs. Briggs coveted—he should now be informed that she desired these breeches, not for pin-cushions, but for Mr. Moffat, who had long been in want of a pair.

Having thus episodically narrated Mr. Moffat's history, let us state that he, his lady, and their friends, passed before the Count's arbour, joining in a melodious chorus to a song which one of the society, an actor of Betterton's, was singing:—

> " 'Tis my will, when I'm dead, that no tear shall be shed,
>   No ' Hic jacet ' be graved on my stone;
> But pour o'er my ashes a bottle of red,
>   And say a good fellow is gone,
>   My brave boys!
>   And say a good fellow is gone."

"My brave boys" was given with vast emphasis by the party; Mr. Moffat growling it in a rich bass, and Mrs. Briggs in a soaring treble. As to the notes, when quavering up to the skies, they excited various emotions among the people in the gardens. " Silence them black-guards!" shouted a barber, who was taking a pint of small beer along with his lady. " Stop that there infernal screeching!" said a couple of ladies, who were sipping ratafia in company with two pretty fellows.

"Dang it, it's Polly!" said Mr. Tom Billings, bolting out of the box, and rushing towards the sweet-voiced Mrs. Briggs. When he reached her, which he did quickly, and made his arrival known by tipping Mrs. Briggs slightly on the waist, and suddenly bouncing down before her and her friend, both of the latter drew back somewhat startled.

"Law, Mr. Billings!" says Mrs. Polly, rather coolly, "is it you? Who thought of seeing you here?"

"Who's this here young feller?" says towering Mr. Moffat, with his bass voice.

"It's Mr. Billings, cousin, a friend of mine," said Mrs. Polly, beseechingly.

"Oh, cousin, if it's a friend of yours, he should know better how to conduct himself, that's all. Har you a dancing-master, young feller, that you cut them there capers before gentlemen?" growled Mr. Moffat; who hated Mr. Billings, for the excellent reason that he lived upon him.

"Dancing-master be hanged!" said Mr. Billings, with becoming spirit: "if you call me dancing-master, I'll pull your nose."

"What!" roared Mr. Moffat, "pull my nose? *My nose!* I'll tell you what, my lad, if you durst move me, I'll cut your throat, curse me!"

"Oh, Moffy—cousin, I mean—'tis a shame to treat the poor boy so. Go away, Tommy; do go away; my cousin's in liquor," whimpered Madam Briggs, who really thought that the great doorkeeper would put his threat into execution.

"Tommy!" said Mr. Moffat, frowning horribly; "Tommy to me too?   Dog, get out of my ssss——" *sight* was the word which Mr. Moffat intended to utter; but he was interrupted; for, to the astonishment of his friends and himself, Mr. Billings did actually make a spring at the monster's nose, and caught it so firmly, that the latter could not finish his sentence.

The operation was performed with amazing celerity; and, having concluded it, Mr. Billings sprung back, and whisked from out its sheath that new silver-hilted sword which his mamma had given him.   "Now," said he, with a fierce kind of calmness, "now for the throat-cutting, cousin: I'm your man!"

How the brawl might have ended, no one can say, had the two gentlemen actually crossed swords; but Mrs. Polly, with a wonderful presence of mind, restored peace by exclaiming, "Hush, hush! the beaks, the beaks!" Upon which, with one common instinct, the whole party made a rush for the garden gates, and disappeared into the fields.   Mrs. Briggs knew her company: there was something in the very name of a constable which sent them all a-flying.

After running a reasonable time, Mr. Billings stopped.   But the great Moffat was nowhere to be seen, and Polly Briggs had likewise vanished.   Then Tom bethought him that he would go back to his mother; but, arriving at the gate of the gardens, was refused admittance, as he had not a shilling in his pocket.   "I've left," says Tommy, giving himself the airs of a gentleman, "some friends in the gardens.   I'm with his Excellency the Bavarian henvy."

"Then you had better go away with him," said the gate people.

"But I tell you I left him there, in the grand circle, with a lady; and, what's more, in the dark walk, I have left a silver-hilted sword."

"Oh, my lord, I'll go and tell him then," cried one of the porters, "if you will wait."

Mr. Billings seated himself on a post near the gate, and there consented to remain until the return of his messenger. The latter went straight to the dark walk, and found the sword, sure enough. But, instead of returning it to its owner, this discourteous knight broke the trenchant blade at the hilt; and flinging the steel away, pocketed the baser silver metal, and lurked off by the private door consecrated to the waiters and fiddlers.

In the meantime, Mr. Billings waited and waited. And what was the conversation of his worthy parents inside the garden?   I cannot say; but one of the waiters declared that he had served the great foreign Count with two bowls of rack-punch, and some biscuits, in No. 3: that in the box with him were first a young gentleman, who went away, and a lady, splendidly dressed and masked: that when the lady and his lordship were alone, she edged away to the further end of the table, and they had much talk: that at last, when his Grace had pressed her very much, she took off her mask and said, "Don't you know me now, Max?" that he cried out, "My own Catherine, thou art more beautiful than ever!" and wanted to kneel down and vow eternal love to her; but she begged him not to do so in a place where all the world would see: that then his Highness paid, and they left the gardens, the lady putting on her mask again.

When they issued from the gardens, "Ho! Joseph La Rose, my coach!" shouted his Excellency, in rather a husky voice; and the men who had been waiting came up with the carriage. A young gentleman, who was dozing on one of the posts at the entry, woke up suddenly at the blaze of the torches and the noise of the footmen. The Count gave his arm to the lady in the mask, who slipped in; and he was whispering La Rose, when the lad who had been sleeping hit his Excellency on the shoulder, and said, " I say, Count, you can give *me* a cast home too," and jumped into the coach.

When Catherine saw her son, she threw herself into his arms, and kissed him with a burst of hysterical tears; of which Mr. Billings was at a loss to understand the meaning. The Count joined them, looking not a little disconcerted; and the pair were landed at their own door, where stood Mr. Hayes, in his nightcap, ready to receive them, and astounded at the splendour of the equipage in which his wife returned to him.

CHAPTER XI

AN ingenious magazine-writer, who lived in the time of Mr. Brock and the Duke of Marlborough, compared the latter gentleman's conduct in battle, when he

> " In peaceful thought the field of death surveyed,
>   To fainting squadrons lent the timely aid;
>   Inspired repulsed battalions to engage,
>   And taught the doubtful battle where to rage " —

Mr. Joseph Addison, I say, compared the Duke of Marlborough to an angel, who is sent by Divine command to chastise a guilty people—

> " And pleased his Master's orders to perform,
>   Rides on the whirlwind, and directs the storm."

The four first of these novel lines touch off the Duke's disposition and genius to a tittle. He had a love for such scenes of strife: in the midst of them his spirit rose calm and supreme, soaring (like an angel or not, but anyway the compliment is a very pretty one) on the battle-clouds majestic, and causing to ebb or to flow the mighty tide of war.

But as this famous simile might apply with equal propriety to a bad angel as to a good one, it may in like manner be employed to illustrate small quarrels as well as great—a little family squabble, in which two or three people are engaged, as well as a vast national dispute, argued on each side by the roaring throats of five hundred angry cannon. The poet means, in fact, that the Duke of Marlborough had an immense genius for mischief.

Our friend Brock, or Wood (whose actions we love to illustrate by the very handsomest similes), possessed this genius in common with his Grace; and was never so happy, or seen to so much advantage, as when he was employed in setting people by the ears. His spirits, usually dull, then rose into the utmost gaiety and good-humour. When the doubtful battle flagged, he by his art would instantly restore it. When, for instance, Tom's repulsed battalions of rhetoric fled from his mamma's fire, a few words of apt sneer or encouragement on Wood's part would bring the fight round again; or when Mr. Hayes's fainting squadrons of abuse broke upon the stubborn squares of Tom's bristling obstinacy, it was Wood's delight to rally the former, and bring him once more to the charge. A great share had this man in making those bad people worse. Many fierce words and bad passions, many falsehoods and knaveries on Tom's part, much bitterness, scorn, and jealousy on the part of Hayes and Catherine, might be attributed to this hoary old tempter, whose joy and occupation it was to raise and direct the domestic storms and whirlwinds of the family of which he was a member. And do not let us be accused of an undue propensity to use sounding words, because we compare three scoundrels in the Tyburn Road to so many armies, and Mr. Wood to a mighty field-marshal. My dear sir, when you have well studied the world—how supremely great the meanest thing in this world is, and how infinitely mean the greatest—I am mistaken if you do not make a strange and proper jumble of the sublime and the ridiculous, the lofty and the low. I have looked at the world, for my part, and come to the conclusion that I know not which is which.

Well, then, on the night when Mrs. Hayes, as recorded by us, had been to the Marylebone Gardens, Mr. Wood had found the sincerest enjoyment in plying her husband with drink; so that, when Catherine arrived at home, Mr. Hayes came forward to meet her in a manner which showed that he was not only surly but drunk. Tom stepped out of the coach first; and Hayes asked him, with an oath, where he had been? The oath Mr. Billings sternly flung back again (with another in its company), and at the same time refused to give his stepfather any sort of answer to his query.

"The old man is drunk, mother," said he to Mrs. Hayes, as he handed that lady out of the coach (before leaving which she had to withdraw her hand rather violently from the grasp of the Count, who was inside). Hayes instantly showed the correctness of his surmise by slamming the door courageously in Tom's face, when he attempted to enter the house with his mother. And when Mrs. Catherine remonstrated, according to her wont, in a very angry and supercilious tone, Mr. Hayes replied with equal haughtiness, and a regular quarrel ensued.

People were accustomed in those days to use much more simple and expressive terms of language than are now thought polite; and it would be dangerous to give, in this present year 1840, the exact words of reproach which passed between Hayes and his wife in 1726. Mr. Wood sat near, laughing his sides out. Mr. Hayes swore that his wife should not go abroad to tea-gardens in search of vile Popish noblemen; to which Mrs. Hayes replied, that Mr. Hayes was a pitiful, lying, sneaking cur, and that she would go where she pleased. Mr. Hayes rejoined, that if she said much more he would take a stick to her. Mr. Wood whispered, "And serve her right." Mrs. Hayes thereupon swore she had stood his cowardly blows once or twice before, but that if ever he did so again, as sure as she was born, she would stab him. Mr. Wood said, "Curse me, but I like her spirit."

Mr. Hayes took another line of argument, and said, "The neighbours would talk, madam."

"Ay, that they will, no doubt," said Mr. Wood.

"Then let them," said Catherine. "What do we care about the neighbours? Didn't the neighbours talk when you sent Widow Wilkins to gaol? Didn't the neighbours talk when you levied on poor old Thomson? You didn't mind *then,* Mr. Hayes."

"Business, ma'am, is business; and if I did distrain on Thomson, and lock up Wilkins, I think you knew about it as much as I."

"I'faith, I believe you're a pair," said Mr. Wood.

"Pray, sir, keep your tongue to yourself. Your opinion isn't asked anyhow—no, nor your company wanted neither," cried Mrs. Catherine, with proper spirit.

At which remark Mr. Wood only whistled.

"I have asked this here gentleman to pass this evening along with me. We've been drinking together, ma'am."

"That we have," said Mr. Wood, looking at Mrs. Cat with the most perfect good-humour.

"I say, ma'am, that we've been a-drinking together; and when we've been a-drinking together, I say that a man is my friend. Dr. Wood is my friend, madam—the Rev. Dr. Wood. We've passed the evening in company, talking about politics, madam—politics and riddle-iddle-igion. We've not been flaunting in tea-gardens, and ogling the men."

"It's a lie!" shrieked Mrs. Hayes. "I went with Tom—you know I did: the boy wouldn't let me rest till I promised to go."

"Hang him, I hate him," said Mr. Hayes: "he's always in my way."

"He's the only friend I have in the world, and the only being I care a pin for," said Catherine.

"He's an impudent, idle, good-for-nothing scoundrel, and I hope to see him hanged!" shouted Mr. Hayes. "And pray, madam, whose carriage was that as you came home in? I warrant you paid something for the ride—Ha, ha!"

"Another lie!" screamed Cat, and clutched hold of a supper-knife. "Say it again, John Hayes, and by ——, I'll do for you."

"Do for me? Hang me," said Mr. Hayes, flourishing a stick, and perfectly pot-valiant, "do you think I care for a bastard and a—?"

He did not finish the sentence, for the woman ran at him like a savage, knife in hand. He bounded back, flinging his arms about wildly, and struck her with his staff sharply across the forehead. The woman went down instantly. A lucky blow was it for Hayes and her: it saved him from death, perhaps, and her from murder.

All this scene—a very important one of our drama—might have been described at much greater length; but, in truth, the author has a natural horror of dwelling too long upon such hideous spectacles: nor would the reader be much edified by a full and accurate knowledge of what took place. The quarrel, however, though not more violent than many that had previously taken place between Hayes and his wife was about to cause vast changes in the condition of this unhappy pair.

Hayes was at the first moment of his victory very much alarmed; he feared that he had killed the woman; and Wood started up rather anxiously too, with the same fancy. But she soon began to recover. Water was brought; her head was raised and bound up; and in a short time Mrs. Catherine gave vent to a copious fit of tears, which relieved her somewhat. These did not affect Hayes much—they rather pleased him, for he saw he had got the better; and although Cat fiercely turned upon him when he made some small attempt towards reconciliation, he did not heed her anger, but smiled and winked in a self-satisfied way at Wood. The coward was quite proud of his victory; and finding Catherine asleep, or apparently so, when he followed her to bed, speedily gave himself up to slumber too, and had some pleasant dreams to his portion.

Mr. Wood also went sniggering and happy upstairs to his chamber. The quarrel had been a real treat to him; it excited the old man—tickled him into good-humour; and he promised himself a rare continuation of the fun when Tom should be made acquainted with the circumstances of the dispute. As for his Excellency the Count, the ride from Marylebone Gardens, and a tender squeeze of the hand which Catherine permitted to him

on parting, had so inflamed the passions of the nobleman, that after sleeping for nine hours, and taking his
chocolate as usual the next morning, he actually delayed
to read the newspaper, and kept waiting a toy-shop lady
from Cornhill (with the sweetest bargain of mechlin
lace), in order to discourse to his chaplain on the charms
of Mrs. Hayes.

She, poor thing, never closed her lids, except when
she would have had Mr. Hayes imagine that she slum-
bered; but lay beside him, tossing and tumbling, with
hot eyes wide open, and heart thumping, and pulse of a
hundred and ten, and heard the heavy hours tolling;
and at last the day came peering, haggard, through the
window-curtains, and found her still wakeful and
wretched.

Mrs. Hayes had never been, as we have seen, especially fond of her lord; but now, as the day made visible
to her the sleeping figure and countenance of that gentleman, she looked at him with a contempt and loathing
such as she had never felt even in all the years of her
wedded life. Mr. Hayes was snoring profoundly: by
his bedside, on his ledger, stood a large greasy tin
candlestick, containing a lank tallow-candle, turned
down in the shaft; and in the lower part, his keys, purse,
and tobacco-pipe; his feet were huddled up in his greasy
threadbare clothes; his head and half his sallow face
muffled up in a red woollen nightcap; his beard was of
several days' growth; his mouth was wide open, and he
was snoring profoundly: on a more despicable little
creature the sun never shone. And to this sordid wretch
was Catherine united for ever. What a pretty rascal
history might be read in yonder greasy day-book, which
never left the miser!—he never read in any other. Of

what a treasure were yonder keys and purse the keepers! not a shilling they guarded but was picked from the pocket of necessity, plundered from needy wantonness, or pitilessly squeezed from starvation. "A fool, a miser, and a coward! Why was I bound to this wretch?" thought Catherine: "I, who am high-spirited and beautiful (did not *he* tell me so?) ; I who, born a beggar, have raised myself to competence, and might have mounted— who knows whither?—if cursed Fortune had not baulked me!"

As Mrs. Cat did not utter these sentiments, but only thought them, we have a right to clothe her thoughts in the genteelest possible language; and, to the best of our power, have done so. If the reader examines Mrs. Hayes's train of reasoning, he will not, we should think, fail to perceive how ingeniously she managed to fix all the wrong upon her husband, and yet to twist out some consolatory arguments for her own vanity. This perverse argumentation we have all of us, no doubt, employed in our time. How often have we,—we poets, politicians, philosophers, family-men,—found charming excuses for our own rascalities in the monstrous wickedness of the world about us; how loudly have we abused the times and our neighbours! All this devil's logic did Mrs. Catherine, lying wakeful in her bed on the night of the Marylebone fête, exert in gloomy triumph.

It must, however, be confessed, that nothing could be more just than Mrs. Hayes's sense of her husband's scoundrelism and meanness; for if we have not proved these in the course of this history, we have proved nothing. Mrs. Cat had a shrewd, observing mind; and if she wanted for proofs against Hayes, she had but to look before and about her to find them. This amiable pair

were lying in a large walnut-bed, with faded silk furniture, which had been taken from under a respectable old
invalid widow, who had become security for a prodigal
son; the room was hung round with an antique tapestry
(representing Rebecca at the Well, Bathsheba Bathing,
Judith and Holofernes, and other subjects from Holy
Writ), which had been many score times sold for fifty
pounds, and bought back by Mr. Hayes for two, in
those accommodating bargains which he made with
young gentlemen, who received fifty pounds of money
and fifty of tapestry in consideration of their hundred-
pound bills. Against this tapestry, and just cutting off
Holofernes's head, stood an enormous ominous black
clock, the spoil of some other usurious transaction. Some
chairs, and a dismal old black cabinet, completed the
furniture of this apartment: it wanted but a ghost to
render its gloom complete.

Mrs. Hayes sat up in the bed sternly regarding her
husband. There is, to be sure, a strong magnetic influence in wakeful eyes so examining a sleeping person (do
not you, as a boy, remember waking of bright summer
mornings and finding your mother looking over you? had
not the gaze of her tender eyes stolen into your senses
long before you woke, and cast over your slumbering
spirit a sweet spell of peace, and love, and fresh-spring-
ing joy?) Some such influence had Catherine's looks
upon her husband: for, as he slept under them, the man
began to writhe about uneasily, and to burrow his head
in the pillow, and to utter quick, strange moans and
cries, such as have often jarred one's ear while watching
at the bed of the feverish sleeper. It was just upon six,
and presently the clock began to utter those dismal
grinding sounds, which issue from clocks at such periods,

and which sound like the death-rattle of the departing
hour.   Then the bell struck the knell of it; and with this
Mr. Hayes awoke, and looked up, and saw Catherine
gazing at him.

Their eyes met for an instant, and Catherine turned
away, burning red, and looking as if she had been caught
in the commission of a crime.

A kind of blank terror seized upon old Hayes's soul:
a horrible icy fear, and presentiment of coming evil;
and yet the woman had but looked at him.   He thought
rapidly over the occurrences of the last night, the quarrel, and the end of it.   He had often struck her before when angry, and heaped all kinds of bitter words
upon her; but, in the morning, she bore no malice,
and the previous quarrel was forgotten, or, at least,
passed over.   Why should the last night's dispute not
have the same end?   Hayes calculated all this, and tried
to smile.

"I hope we're friends, Cat?" said he.   "You know
I was in liquor last night, and sadly put out by the loss
of that fifty pound.   They'll ruin me, dear—I know they
will."

Mrs. Hayes did not answer.

"I should like to see the country again, dear," said
he, in his most wheedling way.   "I've a mind, do you
know, to call in all our money?   It's you who've made
every farthing of it, that's sure; and it's a matter of two
thousand pound by this time.   Suppose we go into Warwickshire, Cat, and buy a farm, and live genteel.
Shouldn't you like to live a lady in your own county
again?   How they'd stare at Birmingham! hey, Cat?"

And with this Mr. Hayes made a motion, as if he
would seize his wife's hand, but she flung his back again.

"Coward!" said she, "you want liquor to give you courage, and then you've only heart enough to strike women."

"It was only in self-defence, my dear," said Hayes, whose courage was all gone. "You tried, you know, to—to—"

"To *stab* you; and I wish I had!" said Mrs. Hayes, setting her teeth, and glaring at him like a demon; and so saying she sprung out of bed. There was a great stain of blood on her pillow. "Look at it," said she. "That blood's of your shedding!" and at this Hayes fairly began to weep, so utterly downcast and frightened was the miserable man. The wretch's tears only inspired his wife with a still greater rage and loathing; she cared not so much for the blow, but she hated the man: the man to whom she was tied for ever—for ever! The bar between her and wealth, happiness, love, rank perhaps. "If I were free," thought Mrs. Hayes (the thought had been sitting at her pillow all night, and whispering ceaselessly into her ear)—"If I were free, Max would marry me; I know he would:—he said so yesterday!"

* * * * *

As if by a kind of intuition, old Wood seemed to read all this woman's thoughts; for he said that day with a sneer, that he would wager she was thinking how much better it would be to be a Count's lady than a poor miser's wife. "And faith," said he, "a Count and a chariot-and-six is better than an old skinflint with a cudgel." And then he asked her if her head was better, and supposed that she was used to beating; and cut sundry other jokes, which made the poor wretch's wounds of mind and body feel a thousand times sorer.

Tom, too, was made acquainted with the dispute, and swore his accustomed vengeance against his stepfather. Such feelings, Wood, with a dexterous malice, would never let rest; it was his joy, at first quite a disinterested one, to goad Catherine and to frighten Hayes: though, in truth, that unfortunate creature had no occasion for incitements from without to keep up the dreadful state of terror and depression into which he had fallen.

For, from the morning after the quarrel, the horrible words and looks of Catherine never left Hayes's memory; but a cold fear followed him—a dreadful prescience. He strove to overcome this fate as a coward would—to kneel to it for compassion—to coax and wheedle it into forgiveness. He was slavishly gentle to Catherine, and bore her fierce taunts with mean resignation. He trembled before young Billings, who was now established in the house (his mother said, to protect her against the violence of her husband), and suffered his brutal language and conduct without venturing to resist.

The young man and his mother lorded over the house: Hayes hardly dared to speak in their presence; seldom sat with the family except at meals; but slipped away to his chamber (he slept apart now from his wife) or passed the evening at the public-house, where he was constrained to drink—to spend some of his beloved sixpences for drink!

And, of course, the neighbours began to say, "John Hayes neglects his wife." "He tyrannizes over her, and beats her." "Always at the public-house, leaving an honest woman alone at home!"

The unfortunate wretch did *not* hate his wife. He was used to her—fond of her as much as he could be fond—sighed to be friends with her again—repeatedly would creep, whimpering, to Wood's room, when the latter was alone, and beg him to bring about a reconciliation. They *were* reconciled, as much as ever they could be. The woman looked at him, thought what she might be but for him, and scorned and loathed him with a feeling that almost amounted to insanity. What nights she lay awake, weeping and cursing herself and him! His humility and beseeching looks only made him more despicable and hateful to her.

If Hayes did not hate the mother, however, he hated the boy—hated and feared him dreadfully. He would have poisoned him if he had had the courage; but he dared not: he dared not even look at him as he sat there, the master of the house, in insolent triumph. O God! how the lad's brutal laughter rung in Hayes's ears; and how the stare of his fierce, bold black eyes pursued him! Of a truth, if Mr. Wood loved mischief, as he did, honestly and purely for mischief's sake, he had enough here. There was mean malice, and fierce scorn, and black revenge, and sinful desire, boiling up in the hearts of these wretched people, enough to content Mr. Wood's great master himself.

Hayes's business, as we have said, was nominally that of a carpenter; but since, for the last few years, he had added to it that of a lender of money, the carpenter's trade had been neglected altogether for one so much more profitable. Mrs. Hayes had exerted herself, with much benefit to her husband, in his usurious business. She was a resolute, clear-sighted, keen woman, that did not love money, but loved to be rich and push her way in the world. She would have nothing to do with the trade now, however, and told her husband to manage it himself. She felt that she was separated from him for ever, and could no more be brought to consider her interests as connected with his own.

The man was well fitted for the creeping and niggling of his dastardly trade; and gathered his moneys, and busied himself with his lawyer, and acted as his own book-keeper and clerk, not without satisfaction. His wife's speculations, when they worked in concert, used often to frighten him. He never sent out his capital without a pang, and only because he dared not question her superior judgment and will. He began now to lend no more: he could not let the money out of his sight. His sole pleasure was to creep up into his room, and count and recount it. When Billings came into the house, Hayes had taken a room next to that of Wood. It was a protection to him; for Wood would often rebuke the lad for using Hayes ill: and both Catherine and Tom treated the old man with deference.

At last—it was after he had collected a good deal of his money—Hayes began to reason with himself, " Why should I stay?—stay to be insulted by that boy, or murdered by him? He is ready for any crime." He determined to fly. He would send Catherine money every year. No—she had the furniture; let her let lodgings —that would support her. He would go, and live away, abroad in some cheap place—away from that boy and his horrible threats. The idea of freedom was agreeable to the poor wretch; and he began to wind up his affairs as quickly as he could.

Hayes would now allow no one to make his bed or enter his room; and Wood could hear him through the panels fidgeting perpetually to and fro, opening and shutting of chests, and clinking of coin. At the least sound he would start up, and would go to Billings's door and listen. Wood used to hear him creeping through the passages, and returning stealthily to his own chamber.

One day the woman and her son had been angrily taunting him in the presence of a neighbour. The neighbour retired soon; and Hayes, who had gone with him to the door, heard, on returning, the voice of Wood in the parlour. The old man laughed in his usual saturnine way, and said, "Have a care, Mrs. Cat; for if Hayes were to die suddenly, by the laws, the neighbours would accuse thee of his death."

Hayes started as if he had been shot. "He too is in the plot," thought he. "They are all leagued against me: they *will* kill me: they are only biding their time." Fear seized him, and he thought of flying that instant and leaving all; and he stole into his room and gathered his money together. But only a half of it was there: in a few weeks all would have come in. He had not the heart to go. But that night Wood heard Hayes pause at *his* door, before he went to listen at Mrs. Catherine's. "What is the man thinking of?" said Wood. "He is gathering his money together. Has he a hoard yonder unknown to us all?"

Wood thought he would watch him. There was a closet between the two rooms: Wood bored a hole in the panel, and peeped through. Hayes had a brace of pistols, and four or five little bags before him on the table. One of these he opened, and placed, one by one, five-and-twenty guineas into it. Such a sum had been due that day—Catherine spoke of it only in the morning; for the debtor's name had by chance been mentioned in the conversation. Hayes commonly kept but a few guineas in the house. For what was he amassing all these? The next day, Wood asked for change for a

twenty-pound bill. Hayes said he had but three guineas.
And when asked by Catherine where the money was that
was paid the day before, said that it was at the banker's.
" The man is going to fly," said Wood; " that is sure:
if he does, I know him—he will leave his wife without
a shilling."

He watched him for several days regularly: two or
three more bags were added to the former number.
" They are pretty things, guineas," thought Wood, " and
tell no tales, like bank-bills."   And he thought over the
days when he and Macshane used to ride abroad in
search of them.

I don't know what thoughts entered into Mr. Wood's
brain; but the next day, after seeing young Billings, to
whom he actually made a present of a guinea, that young
man, in conversing with his mother, said, " Do you know,
mother, that if you were free, and married the Count,
I should be a lord?   It's the German law, Mr. Wood
says; and you know he was in them countries with Marlborough."

" Ay, that he would," said Mr. Wood, " in Germany:
but Germany isn't England; and it's no use talking of
such things."

" Hush, child," said Mrs. Hayes, quite eagerly: " how
can *I* marry the Count?   Besides, a'n't I married, and
isn't he too great a lord for me?"

" Too great a lord?—not a whit, mother.   If it wasn't
for Hayes, I might be a lord now.   He gave me five
guineas only last week; but curse the skinflint who never
will part with a shilling."

" It's not so bad as his striking your mother, Tom.   I
had my stick up, and was ready to fell him t'other night,"
added Mr. Wood.   And herewith he smiled, and looked

steadily in Mrs. Catherine's face. She dared not look again; but she felt that the old man knew a secret that she had been trying to hide from herself. Fool! he knew it; and Hayes knew it dimly: and never, never, since that day of the gala, had it left her, sleeping or waking. When Hayes, in his fear, had proposed to sleep away from her, she started with joy: she had been afraid that she might talk in her sleep, and so let slip her horrible confession.

Old Wood knew all her history since the period of the Marylebone fête. He had wormed it out of her, day by day; he had counselled her how to act; warned her not to yield; to procure, at least, a certain provision for her son, and a handsome settlement for herself, if she determined on quitting her husband. The old man looked on the business in a proper philosophical light, told her bluntly that he saw she was bent upon going off with the Count, and bade her take precautions; else she might be left as she had been before.

Catherine denied all these charges; but she saw the Count daily, notwithstanding, and took all the measures which Wood had recommended to her. They were very prudent ones. Galgenstein grew hourly more in love: never had he felt such a flame; not in the best days of his youth; not for the fairest princess, countess, or actress, from Vienna to Paris.

At length—it was the night after he had seen Hayes counting his money-bags—old Wood spoke to Mrs. Hayes very seriously. "That husband of yours, Cat," said he, "meditates some treason; ay, and fancies we are about such. He listens nightly at your door and at mine: he is going to leave you, be sure on't; and if he leaves you, he leaves you to starve."

"I can be rich elsewhere," said Mrs. Cat.

"What, with Max?"

"Ay, with Max: and why not?" said Mrs. Hayes.

"Why not, fool! Do you recollect Birmingham? Do you think that Galgenstein, who is so tender now because he *hasn't* won you, will be faithful because he *has*? Psha, woman, men are not made so! Don't go to him until you are sure: if you were a widow now, he would marry you; but never leave yourself at his mercy: if you were to leave your husband to go to him, he would desert you in a fortnight!"

She might have been a Countess! she knew she might, but for this cursed barrier between her and her fortune. Wood knew what she was thinking of, and smiled grimly.

"Besides," he continued, "remember Tom. As sure as you leave Hayes without some security from Max, the boy's ruined: he who might be a lord, if his mother had but— Psha! never mind: that boy will go on the road, as sure as my name's Wood. He's a Turpin cock in his eye, my dear,—a regular Tyburn look. He knows too many of that sort already; and is too fond of a bottle and a girl to resist and be honest when it comes to the pinch."

"It's all true," said Mrs. Hayes. "Tom's a high mettlesome fellow, and would no more mind a ride on Hounslow Heath than he does a walk now in the Mall."

"Do you want him hanged, my dear?" said Wood.

"Ah, Doctor!"

"It *is* a pity, and that's sure," concluded Mr. Wood, knocking the ashes out of his pipe, and closing this interesting conversation. "It is a pity that that old skinflint should be in the way of both your fortunes; and he about to fling you over, too!"

Mrs. Catherine retired musing, as Mr. Billings had previously done; a sweet smile of contentment lighted up the venerable features of Doctor Wood, and he walked abroad into the streets as happy a fellow as any in London.

CHAPTER XII

TREATS OF LOVE, AND PREPARES FOR DEATH

AND to begin this chapter, we cannot do better than quote a part of a letter from M. l'Abbé O'Flaherty to Madame la Comtesse de X—— at Paris:—

"MADAM,—The little Arouet de Voltaire, who hath come 'hither to take a turn in England,' as I see by the post of this morning, hath brought me a charming pacquet from your ladyship's hands, which ought to render a reasonable man happy; but, alas! makes your slave miserable. I think of dear Paris (and something more dear than all Paris, of which, Madam, I may not venture to speak further) —I think of dear Paris, and find myself in this dismal *Vitehall,* where, when the fog clears up, I can catch a glimpse of muddy Thames, and of that fatal palace which the kings of England have been obliged to exchange for your noble castle of Saint Germains, that stand so stately by silver Seine. Truly, no bad bargain. For my part, I would give my grand ambassadorial saloons, hangings, gildings, feasts, valets, ambassadors and all, for a *bicoque* in sight of the Thuilleries' towers, or my little cell in the Irlandois.

" My last sheets have given you a pretty notion of our ambassador's public doings; now for a pretty piece of private scandal respecting that great man. Figure to yourself, Madam, his Excellency is in love; actually in love, talking day and night about a certain fair one whom he hath picked out of a gutter; who is well nigh forty years old; who was his mistress when he was in England a captain of dragoons, some sixty, seventy, or a hundred years since; who hath had a son by him, moreover, a sprightly lad, apprentice to a tailor of eminence that has the honour of making his Excellency's breeches.

" Since one fatal night when he met this fair creature at a certain place of publique resort, called Marylebone Gardens, our Cyrus hath been an altered creature. Love hath mastered this brainless ambassador, and his antics afford me food for perpetual mirth. He sits now opposite to me at a table inditing a letter to his Catherine, and copying it from—what do you think?—from the 'Grand Cyrus.' *I swear, madam, that my happiness would be to offer you this hand, as I have my heart long ago, and I beg you to bear in mind this declaration.* I have just dictated to him the above tender words; for our envoy, I need not tell you, is not strong at writing or thinking.

" The fair Catherine, I must tell you, is no less than a carpenter's wife, a well-to-do bourgeois, living at the Tyburn, or Gallows Road. She found out her ancient lover very soon after our arrival, and hath a marvellous hankering to be a Count's lady. A pretty little creature is this Madam Catherine. Billets, breakfasts, pretty walks, presents of silks and satins, pass daily between the pair; but, strange to say, the lady is as virtuous as Diana, and hath resisted all my Count's cajoleries hitherto. The poor fellow told me, with tears in his eyes, that he believed he should have carried her by storm on the very first night of their meeting, but that her son stepped into the way; and he or somebody else hath been in the way ever since. Madam will never appear alone. I believe it is this wondrous chastity of the lady that has elicited this wondrous constancy of the gentleman. She is holding out for a settlement; who knows if not for a marriage? Her husband, she says, is ailing; her lover is fool enough, and she herself conducts her negotiations, as I must honestly own, with a pretty notion of diplomacy."

*　　*　　*　　*　　*

This is the only part of the reverend gentleman's letter that directly affects this history. The rest contains some scandal concerning greater personages about the court, a great share of abuse of the Elector of Hanover, and a pretty description of a boxing-match at Mr. Figg's amphitheatre in Oxford Road, where John Wells, of Edmund Bury (as by the papers may be seen), master of the noble science of self-defence, did engage with Edward Sutton, of Gravesend, master of the said science; and the issue of the combat.

"N.B."—adds the Father, in a postscript—"Monsieur Figue gives a hat to be cudgelled for before the Master mount; and the whole of this fashionable information hath been given me by Monseigneur's son, Monsieur Billings, *garçon-tailleur,* Chevalier de Galgenstein."

Mr. Billings was, in fact, a frequent visitor at the Ambassador's house; to whose presence he, by a general order, was always admitted. As for the connection between Mrs. Catherine and her former admirer, the Abbé's history of it is perfectly correct; nor can it be

said that this wretched woman, whose tale now begins
to wear a darker hue, was, in anything but *soul,* faithless
to her husband.   But she hated him, longed to leave
him, and loved another: the end was coming quickly,
and every one of our unknowing actors and actresses
were to be implicated, more or less, in the catastrophe.

It will be seen that Mrs. Cat had followed pretty
closely the injunctions of Mr. Wood in regard to her
dealings with the Count; who grew more heart-stricken
and tender daily, as the completion of his wishes was
delayed, and his desires goaded by contradiction.   The
Abbé has quoted one portion of a letter written by him;
here is the entire performance, extracted, as the holy
father said, chiefly from the romance of the "Grand
Cyrus:"—

"*Unhappy* MAXIMILIAN *unto unjust* CATHERINA.

"MADAM,—It must needs be that I love you better than
any ever did, since, notwithstanding your injustice in
calling me perfidious, I love you no less than I did before.   On the contrary, my passion is so violent, and
your unjust accusation makes me so sensible of it, that
if you did but know the resentments of my soule, you
would confess your selfe the most cruell and unjust
woman in the world.   You shall, ere long, Madam, see
me at your feete; and as you were my first passion, so
you will be my last.

"On my knees I will tell you, at the first handsom
opportunity that the grandure of my passion can only
be equalled by your beauty; it hath driven me to such
a fatall necessity, as that I cannot hide the misery which
you have caused.   Sure, the hostil goddes have, to
plague me, ordayned that fatal marridge, by which you

are bound to one so infinitely below you in degree. Were
that bond of ill-omind Hymen cut in twayn witch
binds you, I swear, Madam, that my happiniss woulde
be to offer you this hande, as I have my harte long agoe.
And I praye you to beare in minde this declaraçion,
which I here sign with my hande, and witch I pray you
may one day be called upon to prove the truth on. Be-
leave me, Madam, that there is none in the world who
doth more honor to your vertue than myselfe, nor who
wishes your happinesse with more zeal than—MAXI-
MILIAN.

"From my lodgings in Whitehall, this 25th of February.

*" To the incomparable Catherina, these, with a scarlet satten
petticoat."*

The Count had debated about the sentence promising
marriage in event of Hayes's death; but the honest
Abbé cut these scruples very short, by saying, justly,
that, because he wrote in that manner, there was no need
for him to act so; that he had better not sign and address
the note in full; and that he presumed his Excellency
was not quite so timid as to fancy that the woman would
follow him all the way to Germany, when his diplomatic
duties would be ended; as they would soon.

The receipt of this billet caused such a flush of joy
and exultation to unhappy happy Mrs. Catherine,
that Wood did not fail to remark it, and speedily learned
the contents of the letter. Wood had no need to bid the
poor wretch guard it very carefully: it never from that
day forth left her; it was her title of nobility,—her pass
to rank, wealth, happiness. She began to look down on
her neighbours; her manner to her husband grew more

than ordinarily scornful; the poor, vain wretch longed to tell her secret, and to take her place openly in the world. She a Countess, and Tom a Count's son! She felt that she should royally become the title!

About this time—and Hayes was very much frightened at the prevalence of the rumour—it suddenly began to be bruited about in his quarter that he was going to quit the country. The story was in everybody's mouth; people used to sneer, when he turned pale, and wept, and passionately denied it. It was said, too, that Mrs. Hayes was not his wife, but his mistress—everybody had this story,—his mistress, whom he treated most cruelly, and was about to desert. The tale of the blow which had felled her to the ground was known in all quarters. When he declared that the woman tried to stab him, nobody believed him: the women said he would have been served right if she had done so. How had these stories gone abroad? "Three days more, and I *will* fly," thought Hayes; "and the world may say what it pleases."

Ay, fool, fly—away so swiftly that Fate cannot overtake thee: hide so cunningly that Death shall not find thy place of refuge!

CHAPTER XIII

THE reader, doubtless, doth now partly understand what dark acts of conspiracy are beginning to gather around Mr. Hayes; and possibly hath comprehended—

1. That if the rumour was universally credited which declared that Mrs. Catherine was only Hayes's mistress, and not his wife,

She might, if she so inclined, marry another person; and thereby not injure her fame and excite wonderment, but actually add to her reputation.

2. That if all the world did steadfastly believe that Mr. Hayes intended to desert this woman, after having cruelly maltreated her,

The direction which his journey might take would be of no consequence; and he might go to Highgate, to Edinburgh, to Constantinople, nay, down a well, and no soul would care to ask whither he had gone.

These points Mr. Hayes had not considered duly. The latter case had been put to him, and annoyed him, as we have seen; the former had actually been pressed upon him by Mrs. Hayes herself; who, in almost the only communication she had had with him since their last quarrel, had asked him, angrily, in the presence of Wood and her son, whether he had dared to utter such lies, and how it came to pass that the neighbours looked scornfully at her, and avoided her?

To this charge Mr. Hayes pleaded, very meekly, that he was not guilty; and young Billings, taking him by the collar, and clinching his fist in his face, swore a dreadful oath that he would have the life of him, if he dared abuse his mother. Mrs. Hayes then spoke of the general report abroad, that he was going to desert her; which, if he attempted to do, Mr. Billings vowed that he would follow him to Jerusalem, and have his blood. These threats, and the insolent language of young Billings, rather calmed Hayes than agitated him: he longed to be on his journey; but he began to hope that no obstacle would be placed in the way of it. For the first time since many days, he began to enjoy a feeling something akin to security, and could look with tolerable confidence towards a comfortable completion of his own schemes of treason.

These points being duly settled, we are now arrived, O public, at a point for which the author's soul hath been yearning ever since this history commenced. We are now come, O critic, to a stage of the work when this tale begins to assume an appearance so interestingly horrific, that you must have a heart of stone if you are not interested by it. O candid and discerning reader, who art sick of the hideous scenes of brutal bloodshed which have of late come forth from pens of certain eminent wits,[1] if you turn away disgusted from the book, remember that this passage hath not been written for you, or such as you, who have taste to know and hate the style in which it hath been composed; but for the public, which hath no such taste:—for the public, which can patronize four different representations of Jack Sheppard,—for the public, whom its literary providers

[1] This was written in 1840.

have gorged with blood and foul Newgate garbage,—
and to whom we poor creatures, humbly following at
the tail of our great high-priests and prophets of the
press, may, as in duty bound, offer some small gift of
our own: a little mite truly, but given with good will.
Come up, then, fair Catherine, and brave Count;—
appear gallant Brock, and faultless Billings;—hasten
hither, honest John Hayes: the former chapters are but
flowers in which we have been decking you for the sacrifice.   Ascend to the altar, ye innocent lambs, and
prepare for the final act: lo! the knife is sharpened, and
the sacrificer ready!   Stretch your throats, sweet ones,
—for the public is thirsty, and must have blood!

CHAPTER THE LAST

THAT Mr. Hayes had some notion of the attachment of Monsieur de Galgenstein for his wife is
very certain: the man could not but perceive that she was
more gaily dressed, and more frequently absent than
usual; and must have been quite aware that from the
day of the quarrel until the present period, Catherine
had never asked him for a shilling for the house expenses. He had not the heart to offer, however; nor,
in truth, did she seem to remember that money was due.

She received, in fact, many sums from the tender
Count. Tom was likewise liberally provided by the
same personage; who was, moreover, continually sending presents of various kinds to the person on whom his
affections were centred.

One of these gifts was a hamper of choice mountain-
wine, which had been some weeks in the house, and excited the longing of Mr. Hayes; who loved wine very
much. This liquor was generally drank by Wood and
Billings, who applauded it greatly; and many times,
in passing through the back-parlour, which he had to
traverse in order to reach the stair, Hayes had cast a
tender eye towards the drink; of which, had he dared,
he would have partaken.

On the 1st of March, in the year 1726, Mr. Hayes
had gathered together almost the whole sum with which he
intended to decamp; and having on that very day recov-

ered the amount of a bill which he thought almost hopeless, he returned home in tolerable good-humour; and
feeling, so near was his period of departure, something
like security.   Nobody had attempted the least violence
on him: besides, he was armed with pistols, had his
money in bills and a belt about his person, and really
reasoned with himself that there was no danger for him
to apprehend.

He entered the house about dusk, at five o'clock.   Mrs.
Hayes was absent with Mr. Billings; only Mr. Wood
was smoking, according to his wont, in the little back-
parlour; and as Mr. Hayes passed, the old gentleman
addressed him in a friendly voice, and, wondering that
he had been such a stranger, invited him to sit and take
a glass of wine.   There was a light and a foreman in the
shop; Mr. Hayes gave his injunctions to that person,
and saw no objection to Mr. Wood's invitation.

The conversation, at first a little stiff between the
two gentlemen, began speedily to grow more easy and
confidential: and so particularly bland and good-
humoured was Mr. or Doctor Wood, that his companion
was quite caught, and softened by the charm of his
manner; and the pair became as good friends as in the
former days of their intercourse.

"I wish you would come down sometimes of evenings," quoth Doctor Wood; "for, though no book-
learned man, Mr. Hayes, look you, you are a man of
the world, and I can't abide the society of boys.   There's
Tom, now, since this tiff with Mrs. Cat, the scoundrel
plays the Grand Turk here!   The pair of 'em, betwixt
them, have completely gotten the upper hand of you.
Confess that you are beaten, Master Hayes, and don't
like the boy?"

"No more I do," said Hayes; "and that's the truth on't. A man doth not like to have his wife's sins flung in his face, nor to be perpetually bullied in his own house by such a fiery sprig as that."

"Mischief, sir,—mischief only," said Wood: "'tis the fun of youth, sir, and will go off as age comes to the lad. Bad as you may think him—and he is as skittish and fierce, sure enough, as a young colt—there is good stuff in him; and though he hath, or fancies he hath, the right to abuse every one, by the Lord he will let none others do so! Last week, now, didn't he tell Mrs. Cat that you served her right in the last beating matter? and weren't they coming to knives, just as in your case? By my faith, they were. Ay, and at the 'Braund's Head,' when some fellow said that you were a bloody Bluebeard, and would murder your wife, stab me if Tom wasn't up in an instant and knocked the fellow down for abusing of you!"

The first of these stories was quite true; the second was only a charitable invention of Mr. Wood, and employed, doubtless, for the amiable purpose of bringing the old and young men together. The scheme partially succeeded; for, though Hayes was not so far mollified towards Tom as to entertain any affection for a young man whom he had cordially detested ever since he knew him, yet he felt more at ease and cheerful regarding himself: and surely not without reason. While indulging in these benevolent sentiments, Mrs. Catherine and her son arrived, and found, somewhat to their astonishment, Mr. Hayes seated in the back-parlour, as in former times; and they were invited by Mr. Wood to sit down and drink.

We have said that certain bottles of mountain-wine

were presented by the Count to Mrs. Catherine: these were, at Mr. Wood's suggestion, produced; and Hayes, who had long been coveting them, was charmed to have an opportunity to drink his fill. He forthwith began bragging of his great powers as a drinker, and vowed that he could manage eight bottles without becoming intoxicated.

Mr. Wood grinned strangely, and looked in a peculiar way at Tom Billings, who grinned too. Mrs. Cat's eyes were turned towards the ground; but her face was deadly pale.

The party began drinking. Hayes kept up his reputation as a toper, and swallowed one, two, three bottles without wincing. He grew talkative and merry, and began to sing songs and to cut jokes; at which Wood laughed hugely, and Billings after him. Mrs. Cat could not laugh; but sat silent. What ailed her? Was she thinking of the Count? She had been with Max that day, and had promised him, for the next night at ten, an interview near his lodgings at Whitehall. It was the first time that she would see him alone. They were to meet (not a very cheerful place for a love-tryst) at St. Margaret's churchyard, near Westminster Abbey. Of this, no doubt Cat was thinking; but what could she mean by whispering to Wood, " No, no! for God's sake, not to-night!"

" She means we are to have no more liquor," said Wood to Mr. Hayes; who heard this sentence, and seemed rather alarmed.

" That's it,—no more liquor," said Catherine, eagerly; " you have had enough to-night. Go to bed, and lock your door, and sleep, Mr. Hayes."

" But I say I've *not* had enough drink!" screamed

Hayes; "I'm good for five bottles more, and wager I will drink them too."

"Done, for a guinea!" said Wood.

"Done, and done!" said Billings.

"Be *you* quiet!" growled Hayes, scowling at the lad. "I will drink what I please, and ask no counsel of yours." And he muttered some more curses against young Billings, which showed what his feelings were towards his wife's son; and which the latter, for a wonder, only received with a scornful smile, and a knowing look at Wood.

Well! the five extra bottles were brought, and drank by Mr. Hayes; and seasoned by many songs from the *recueil* of Mr. Thomas D'Urfey and others. The chief part of the talk and merriment was on Hayes's part; as, indeed, was natural,—for, while he drank bottle after bottle of wine, the other two gentlemen confined themselves to small beer,—both pleading illness as an excuse for their sobriety.

And now might we depict, with much accuracy, the course of Mr. Hayes's intoxication, as it rose from the merriment of the three-bottle point to the madness of the four—from the uproarious quarrelsomeness of the sixth bottle to the sickly stupidity of the seventh; but we are desirous of bringing this tale to a conclusion, and must pretermit all consideration of a subject so curious, so instructive, and so delightful. Suffice it to say, as a matter of history, that Mr. Hayes did actually drink seven bottles of mountain-wine; and that Mr. Thomas Billings went to the "Braund's Head," in Bond Street, and purchased another, which Hayes likewise drank.

"That'll do," said Mr. Wood to young Billings; and

they led Hayes up to bed, whither, in truth, he was un-able to walk himself.

*   *   *   *   *
　　*   *   *   *

Mrs. Springatt, the lodger, came down to ask what the noise was.   " 'Tis only Tom Billings making merry with some friends from the country," answered Mrs. Hayes; whereupon Springatt retired, and the house was quiet.

*   *   *   *   *
　　*   *   *   *
*   *   *   *   *

Some scuffling and stamping was heard about eleven o'clock.

*   *   *   *   *
　　*   *   *   *
*   *   *   *   *

After they had seen Mr. Hayes to bed, Billings re-membered that he had a parcel to carry to some person in the neighbourhood of the Strand; and, as the night was remarkably fine, he and Mr. Wood agreed to walk together, and set forth accordingly.

[Here follows a description of the THAMES AT MIDNIGHT, in a fine historical style; with an account of Lambeth, Westminster, the Savoy, Baynard's Castle, Arundel House, the Temple; of Old London Bridge, with its twenty arches, " on which be houses builded, so that it seemeth rather a continuall street than a bridge; " of Bankside, and the " Globe " and the " Fortune " Theatres; of the ferries across the river, and of the pirates who infest the same,—namely, tinklermen, petermen, hebbermen, trawlermen; of the fleet of barges that lay at the Savoy steps; and of the long lines of slim wherries sleeping on the river-banks and basking and shining in the moonbeams.   A combat on the

river is described, that takes place between the crews of a tinklerman's boat and the water-bailiff's. Shouting his war-cry, " St.
Mary Overy *à la rescousse!* " the water-bailiff sprung at the
throat of the tinklerman captain. The crews of both vessels, as
if aware that the struggle of their chiefs would decide the contest,
ceased hostilities, and awaited on their respective poops the issue
of the death-shock. It was not long coming. " Yield, dog! "
said the water-bailiff. The tinklerman could not answer,—for his
throat was grasped too tight in the iron clench of the city cham-
pion; but drawing his snickersnee, he plunged it seven times in the
bailiff's chest: still the latter fell not. The death-rattle gurgled
in the throat of his opponent; his arms fell heavily to his side.
Foot to foot, each standing at the side of his boat, stood the two
brave men,—*they were both dead!* " In the name of St. Clement
Danes," said the master, " give way, my men! " and, thrusting
forward his halberd (seven feet long, richly decorated with velvet
and brass nails, and having the city arms, argent, a cross gules,
and in the first quarter a dagger displayed of the second), he
thrust the tinklerman's boat away from his own; and at once the
bodies of the captains plunged down, down, down, down in the
unfathomable waters.

After this follows another episode. Two masked ladies quarrel
at the door of a tavern overlooking the Thames: they turn out
to be Stella and Vanessa, who have followed Swift thither; who
is in the act of reading " Gulliver's Travels " to Gay, Arbuthnot,
Bolingbroke, and Pope. Two fellows are sitting shuddering
under a doorway; to one of them Tom Billings flung a sixpence.
He little knew that the names of those two young men were—
Samuel Johnson and *Richard Savage.*]

ANOTHER LAST CHAPTER

MR. HAYES did not join the family the next day; and it appears that the previous night's reconciliation was not very durable; for when Mrs. Springatt asked Wood for Hayes, Mr. Wood stated that Hayes had gone away without saying whither he was bound, or how long he might be absent. He only said, in rather a sulky tone, that he should probably pass the night at a friend's house. "For my part, I know of no friend he hath," added Mr. Wood; "and pray heaven that he may not think of deserting his poor wife, whom he hath beaten and ill-used so already!" In this prayer Mrs. Springatt joined; and so these two worthy people parted.

What business Billings was about cannot be said; but he was this night bound towards Marylebone Fields, as he was the night before for the Strand and Westminster; and, although the night was very stormy and rainy, as the previous evening had been fine, old Wood good-naturedly resolved upon accompanying him; and forth they sallied together.

Mrs. Catherine, too, had *her* business, as we have seen; but this was of a very delicate nature. At nine o'clock, she had an appointment with the Count; and faithfully, by that hour, had found her way to Saint Margaret's churchyard, near Westminster Abbey, where she awaited Monsieur de Galgenstein.

The spot was convenient, being very lonely, and at the same time close to the Count's lodgings at White-hall. His Excellency came, but somewhat after the hour; for, to say the truth, being a freethinker, he had the most firm belief in ghosts and demons, and did not care to pace a churchyard alone. He was comforted, therefore, when he saw a woman muffled in a cloak, who held out her hand to him at the gate, and said, " Is that you?" He took her hand,—it was very clammy and cold; and at her desire he bade his confidential footman, who had attended him with a torch, to retire, and leave him to himself.

The torch-bearer retired, and left them quite in dark-ness; and the pair entered the little cemetery, cautiously threading their way among the tombs. They sat down on one, underneath a tree it seemed to be; the wind was very cold, and its piteous howling was the only noise that broke the silence of the place. Catherine's teeth were chattering, for all her wraps; and when Max drew her close to him, and encircled her waist with one arm, and pressed her hand, she did not repulse him, but rather came close to him, and with her own damp fingers feebly returned his pressure.

The poor thing was very wretched and weeping. She confided to Max the cause of her grief. She was alone in the world,—alone and penniless. Her husband had left her; she had that very day received a letter from him which confirmed all that she had suspected so long. He had left her, carried away all his property, and would not return!

If we say that a selfish joy filled the breast of Mon-sieur de Galgenstein, the reader will not be astonished. A heartless libertine, he felt glad at the prospect of

Catherine's ruin; for he hoped that necessity would make her his own. He clasped the poor thing to his heart, and vowed that he would replace the husband she had lost, and that his fortune should be hers.

"Will you replace him?" said she.

"Yes, truly, in everything but the name, dear Catherine; and when he dies, I swear you shall be Countess of Galgenstein."

"Will you swear?" she cried, eagerly.

"By every thing that is most sacred: were you free now, I would" (and here he swore a terrific oath) "at once make you mine."

We have seen before that it cost Monsieur de Galgenstein nothing to make these vows. Hayes was likely, too, to live as long as Catherine—as long, at least, as the Count's connection with her; but he was caught in his own snare.

She took his hand and kissed it repeatedly, and bathed it in her tears, and pressed it to her bosom. "Max," she said, "*I am free!* Be mine, and I will love you as I have done for years and years."

Max started back. "What, is he dead?" he said.

"No, no, not dead: but he never was my husband."

He let go her hand, and, interrupting her, said sharply, "Indeed, madam, if this carpenter never was your husband, I see no cause why *I* should be. If a lady, who hath been for twenty years the mistress of a miserable country boor, cannot find it in her heart to put up with the protection of a nobleman—a sovereign's representative—she may seek a husband elsewhere!"

"I was no man's mistress except yours," sobbed Catherine, wringing her hands and sobbing wildly; "but, O heaven! I deserved this. Because I was a child, and you saw, and ruined, and left me—because, in my sorrow and repentance, I wished to repair my crime, and was touched by that man's love, and married him—because he too deceives and leaves me—because, after loving you—madly loving you for twenty years—I will not now forfeit your respect, and degrade myself by yielding to your will, you too must scorn me! It is too much—too much—O heaven!" And the wretched woman fell back almost fainting.

Max was almost frightened by this burst of sorrow on her part, and was coming forward to support her; but she motioned him away, and, taking from her bosom a letter, said, "If it were light, you could see, Max, how cruelly I have been betrayed by that man who called himself my husband. Long before he married me, he was married to another. This woman is still living, he says; and he says he leaves me for ever."

At this moment the moon, which had been hidden behind Westminster Abbey, rose above the vast black mass of that edifice, and poured a flood of silver light upon the little church of St. Margaret's, and the spot where the lovers stood. Max was at a little distance from Catherine, pacing gloomily up and down the flags. She remained at her old position at the tombstone under the tree, or pillar, as it seemed to be, as the moon got up. She was leaning against the pillar, and holding out to Max, with an arm beautifully white and rounded, the letter she had received from her husband: "Read it, Max," she said: "I asked for light, and here is heaven's own, by which you may read."

But Max did not come forward to receive it. On a sudden his face assumed a look of the most dreadful surprise and agony. He stood still, and stared with wild eyes starting from their sockets; he stared upwards, at a point seemingly above Catherine's head. At last he raised up his finger slowly, and said, " Look, Cat—*the head—the head!*" Then uttering a horrible laugh, he fell down grovelling among the stones, gibbering and writhing in a fit of epilepsy.

Catherine started forward and looked up. She had been standing against a post, not a tree—the moon was shining full on it now; and on the summit, strangely distinct, and smiling ghastly, was a livid human head.

The wretched woman fled—she dared look no more. And some hours afterwards, when, alarmed by the Count's continued absence, his confidential servant came back to seek for him in the churchyard, he was found sitting on the flags, staring full at the head, and laughing, and talking to it wildly, and nodding at it. He was taken up a hopeless idiot, and so lived for years and years; clanking the chain, and moaning under the lash, and howling through long nights when the moon peered through the bars of his solitary cell, and he buried his face in the straw.

———————

There—the murder is out! And having indulged himself in a chapter of the very finest writing, the author begs the attention of the British public towards it; humbly conceiving that it possesses some of those peculiar merits which have rendered the fine writing in other chapters of the works of other authors so famous.

Without bragging at all, let us just point out the chief claims of the above pleasing piece of composition. In the first place, it is perfectly stilted and unnatural; the dialogue and the sentiments being artfully arranged, so as to be as strong and majestic as possible. Our dear Cat is but a poor, illiterate country wench, who has come from cutting her husband's throat; and yet, see! she talks and looks like a tragedy princess, who is suffering in the most virtuous blank verse. This is the proper end of fiction, and one of the greatest triumphs that a novelist can achieve: for to make people sympathize with virtue is a vulgar trick that any common fellow can do; but it is not everybody who can take a scoundrel, and cause us to weep and whimper over him as though he were a very saint. Give a young lady of five years old a skein of silk and a brace of netting needles, and she will in a short time turn you out a decent silk purse—anybody can; but try her with a sow's ear, and see whether she can make a silk purse out of *that*. That is the work for your real great artist; and pleasant it is to see how many have succeeded in these latter days.

The subject is strictly historical, as any one may see by referring to the *Daily Post* of March 3, 1726, which contains the following paragraph:—

"Yesterday morning, early, a man's head, that by the freshness of it seemed to have been newly cut off from the body, having its own hair on, was found by the river's side, near Millbank, Westminster, and was afterwards exposed to public view in St. Margaret's churchyard, where thousands of people have seen it; but none could tell who the unhappy person was, much less who committed such a horrid and barbarous action. There are various conjectures relating to the deceased; but there being nothing certain, we omit them. The head was much hacked and mangled in the cutting off."

The head which caused such an impression upon Monsieur de Galgenstein was, indeed, once on the shoulders of Mr. John Hayes, who lost it under the following circumstances. We have seen how Mr. Hayes was induced to drink. Mr. Hayes having been encouraged in drinking the wine, and growing very merry therewith, he sang and danced about the room; but his wife, fearing the quantity he had drunk would not have the wished-for effect on him, she sent away for another bottle, of which he drank also. This effectually answered their expectations; and Mr. Hayes became thereby intoxicated, and deprived of his understanding.

He, however, made shift to get into the other room, and, throwing himself upon the bed, fell asleep; upon which Mrs. Hayes reminded them of the affair in hand, and told them that was the most proper juncture to finish the business.[1]

    *   *   *   *   *

Ring, ding, ding! the gloomy green curtain drops, the *dramatis personæ* are duly disposed of, the nimble candle-snuffers put out the lights, and the audience goeth pondering home. If the critic take the pains to ask why the author, who hath been so diffuse in describing the early and fabulous acts of Mrs. Catherine's existence, should so hurry off the catastrophe where a deal of the very finest writing might have been employed, Solomons replies that the "ordinary" narrative is far more emphatic than any composition of his own could be, with all the rhetorical graces which he might employ.

---

[1] The description of the murder and the execution of the culprits, which here follows in the original, was taken from the newspapers of the day. Coming from such a source they have, as may be imagined, no literary merit whatever. The details of the crime are simply horrible, without one touch of even that sort of romance which sometimes gives a little dignity to murder. As such they precisely suited Mr. Thackeray's purpose at the time—which was to show the real manners and customs of the Sheppards and Turpins who were then the popular heroes of fiction. But now-a-days there is no such purpose to serve, and therefore these too literal details are omitted.

Mr. Aram's trial, as taken by the penny-a-liners of those days, hath always interested him more than the lengthened and poetical report which an eminent novelist has given of the same. Mr. Turpin's adventures are more instructive and agreeable to him in the account of the Newgate Plutarch, than in the learned Ainsworth's "Biographical Dictionary." And as he believes that the professional gentlemen who are employed to invest such heroes with the rewards that their great actions merit, will go through the ceremony of the grand cordon with much more accuracy and despatch than can be shown by the most distinguished amateur; in like manner he thinks that the history of such investitures should be written by people directly concerned, and not by admiring persons without, who must be ignorant of many of the secrets of Ketchcraft. We very much doubt if Milton himself could make a description of an execution half so horrible as the simple lines in the *Daily Post* of a hundred and ten years since, that now lies before us— "herrlich wie am ersten Tag,"—as bright and clean as on the day of publication. Think of it! it has been read by Belinda at her toilet, scanned at "Button's" and "Will's," sneered at by wits, talked of in palaces and cottages, by a busy race in wigs, red heels, hoops, patches, and rags of all variety—a busy race that hath long since plunged and vanished in the unfathomable gulf towards which we march so briskly.

Where are they? "Afflavit Deus"—and they are gone! Hark! is not the same wind roaring still that shall sweep us down? and yonder stands the compositor at his types who shall put up a pretty paragraph some day to say how, "*Yesterday,* at his house in Grosvenor Square," or "At Botany Bay, universally regretted," died So-and-So. Into what profound moralities is the paragraph concerning Mrs. Catherine's burning leading us!

Ay, truly, and to that very point have we wished to come; for, having finished our delectable meal, it behoves us to say a word or two by way of grace at its conclusion, and be heartily thankful that it is over. It has been the writer's object carefully to exclude from his drama (except in two very insignificant instances— mere walking-gentlemen parts,) any characters but those of scoundrels of the very highest degree. That he has not altogether failed in the object he had in view, is evident from some newspaper critiques which he has had the good fortune to see; and which abuse the tale of "Catherine" as one of the dullest, most vulgar, and immoral works extant. It is highly gratifying to the author to find that such opinions are abroad, as they convince him that the taste for Newgate literature is on the wane, and that when the public critic has right down undisguised immorality set before him, the honest creature is shocked at it, as he should be, and can declare his indignation in good round terms of abuse. The characters of the tale *are* immoral, and no doubt of it; but the writer humbly hopes the end is not so. The public was, in our notion, dosed and poisoned by the prevailing style of literary practice, and it was necessary to administer some medicine that would produce a wholesome nausea, and afterwards bring about a more healthy habit.

And thank heaven, this effect *has* been produced in very many instances, and that the "Catherine" cathartic has acted most efficaciously. The author has been pleased at the disgust which his work has excited, and has watched with benevolent carefulness the wry faces that have been made by many of the patients who have swallowed the dose. Solomons remembers, at the establishment in Birchin Lane where he had the honour of receiving his education, there used to be administered to the boys a certain cough-medicine, which was so excessively agreeable that all the lads longed to have colds in order to partake of the remedy. Some of our popular novelists have compounded their drugs in a similar way, and made them so palatable that a public, once healthy and honest, has been well-nigh poisoned by their wares. Solomons defies any one to say the like of himself—that his doses have been as pleasant as champagne, and his pills as sweet as barley-sugar;—it has been his attempt to make vice to appear entirely vicious; and in those instances where he hath occasionally introduced something like virtue, to make the sham as evident as possible, and not allow the meanest capacity a single chance to mistake it.

And what has been the consequence? That wholesome nausea which it has been his good fortune to create wherever he has been allowed to practise in his humble circle.

Has any one thrown away a halfpennyworth of sympathy upon any person mentioned in this history? Surely no. But abler and more famous men than Solomons have taken a different plan; and it becomes every man in his vocation to cry out against such, and expose their errors as best he may.

Labouring under such ideas, Mr. Isaac Solomons, junior, produced the romance of Mrs. Cat, and confesses himself completely happy to have brought it to a conclusion. His poem may be dull—ay, and probably is. The great Blackmore, the great Dennis, the great Sprat, the great Pomfret, not to mention great men of our own time—have they not also been dull, and had pretty reputations too? Be it granted, Solomons *is* dull; but don't attack his morality; he humbly submits that, in his poem, no man shall mistake virtue for vice, no man shall allow a single sentiment of pity or admiration to enter his bosom for any character of the piece; it being, from beginning to end, a scene of unmixed rascality performed by persons who never deviate into good feeling. And, although he doth not pretend to equal the great modern authors, whom he hath mentioned, in wit or descriptive power; yet, in the point of moral, he meekly believes that he has been their superior; feeling the greatest disgust for the characters he describes, and using his humble endeavour to cause the public also to hate them.

Horsemonger Lane, January, 1840.

THE FITZ-BOODLE PAPERS

THE
FITZ-BOODLE PAPERS[1]

FITZ-BOODLE'S CONFESSIONS

PREFACE

GEORGE FITZ-BOODLE, ESQUIRE, TO OLIVER YORKE, ESQUIRE

Omnium Club, May 20, 1842

DEAR SIR,—I have always been considered the
third-best whist-player in Europe, and (though
never betting more than five pounds) have for many
years past added considerably to my yearly income by
my skill in the game, until the commencement of the
present season, when a French gentleman, Monsieur
Lalouette, was admitted to the club where I usually play.
His skill and reputation were so great, that no men of
the club were inclined to play against us two of a side;
and the consequence has been, that we have been in a
manner pitted against one another. By a strange turn
of luck (for I cannot admit the idea of his superiority),
Fortune, since the Frenchman's arrival, has been almost
constantly against me, and I have lost two-and-thirty
nights in the course of a couple of score of nights' play.
Everybody knows that I am a poor man; and so much

---

[1] The " Fitz-Boodle Papers " first appeared in *Fraser's
Magazine* for the year 1842.

has Lalouette's luck drained my finances, that only last week I was obliged to give him that famous grey cob on which you have seen me riding in the Park (I can't afford a thorough-bred, and hate a cocktail),—I was, I say, forced to give him up my cob in exchange for four ponies which I owed him.   Thus, as I never walk, being a heavy man whom nobody cares to mount, my time hangs heavily on my hands; and as I hate home, or that apology for it—a bachelor's lodgings—and as I have nothing earthly to do now until I can afford to purchase another horse, I spend my time in sauntering from one club to another, passing many rather listless hours in them before the men come in.

You will say, Why not take to backgammon, or écarté, or amuse yourself with a book? Sir (putting out of the question the fact that I do not play upon credit), I make a point never to play before candles are lighted; and as for books, I must candidly confess to you I am not a reading man.   'Twas but the other day that some one recommended me to read your Magazine after dinner, saying it contained an exceedingly witty article upon—I forget what.   I give you my honour, sir, that I took up the work at six, meaning to amuse myself till seven, when Lord Trumpington's dinner was to come off, and egad! in two minutes I fell asleep, and never woke till midnight.   Nobody ever thought of looking for me in the library, where nobody ever goes; and so ravenously hungry was I, that I was obliged to walk off to Crockford's for supper.

What is it that makes you literary persons so stupid? I have met various individuals in society who I was told were writers of books, and that sort of thing, and expecting rather to be amused by their conversation, have invariably found them dull to a degree, and as for information, without a particle of it. Sir, I actually asked one of these fellows, "What was the nick to seven?" and he stared in my face, and said he didn't know. He was hugely over-dressed in satin, rings, chains and so forth; and at the beginning of dinner was disposed to be rather talkative and pert; but my little sally silenced *him,* I promise you, and got up a good laugh at his expense too. "Leave George alone," said little Lord Cinqbars, "I warrant he'll be a match for any of you literary fellows." Cinqbars is no great wiseacre; but, indeed, it requires no great wiseacre to know *that.*

What is the simple deduction to be drawn from this truth? Why, this—that a man to be amusing and well-informed, has no need of books at all, and had much better go to the world and to men for his knowledge. There was Ulysses, now, the Greek fellow engaged in the Trojan war, as I dare say you know; well, he was the cleverest man possible, and how? From having seen men and cities, their manners noted and their realms surveyed, to be sure. So have I. I have been in every capital, and can order a dinner in every language in Europe.

My notion, then, is this. I have a great deal of spare time on my hands, and as I am told you pay a handsome sum to persons writing for you, I will furnish you occasionally with some of my views upon men and things; occasional histories of my acquaintance, which I think may amuse you; personal narratives of my own; essays, and what not. I am told that I do not spell correctly. This, of course, I don't know; but you will remember that Richelieu and Marlborough could not spell, and, egad! I am an honest man, and desire to be no better than they.

I know that it is the matter, and not the manner, which is of importance. Have the goodness, then, to let one of your understrappers correct the spelling and the grammar of my papers; and you can give him a few shillings in my name for his trouble.

Begging you to accept the assurance of my high consideration, I am, sir,

Your obedient servant,
GEORGE SAVAGE FITZ-BOODLE.

P.S.—By the way, I have said in my letter that I found *all* literary persons vulgar and dull. Permit me to contradict this with regard to yourself. I met you once at Blackwall, I think it was, and really did not remark anything offensive in your accent or appearance.

―――――――

BEFORE commencing the series of moral disquisitions, &c. which I intend, the reader may as well know who I am, and what my past course of life has been. To say that I am a Fitz-Boodle is to say at once that I am a gentleman. Our family has held the estate of Boodle ever since the reign of Henry II.; and it is out of no ill will to my elder brother, or unnatural desire for his death, but only because the estate is a very good one, that I wish heartily it was mine: I would say as much of Chatsworth or Eaton Hall.

I am not, in the first place, what is called a ladies' man, having contracted an irrepressible habit of smoking after dinner, which has obliged me to give up a great deal of the dear creatures' society; nor can I go much

to country-houses for the same reason. Say what they
will, ladies do not like you to smoke in their bed-rooms;
their silly little noses scent out the odour upon the chintz,
weeks after you have left them. Sir John has been
caught coming to bed particularly merry and redolent
of cigar-smoke; young George, from Eton, was absolutely found in the little green-house puffing an Havannah; and when discovered, they both lay the blame upon
Fitz-Boodle. "It was Mr. Fitz-Boodle, mamma," says
George, "who offered me the cigar, and I did not like
to refuse him." "That rascal Fitz seduced us, my
dear," says Sir John, "and kept us laughing until past
midnight." Her ladyship instantly sets me down as a
person to be avoided. "George," whispers she to her
boy, "promise me, on your honour, when you go to town,
not to know that man." And when she enters the break-
fast-room for prayers, the first greeting is a peculiar
expression of countenance, and inhaling of breath, by
which my lady indicates the presence of some exceedingly disagreeable odour in the room. She makes you
the faintest of curtsies, and regards you, if not with a
"flashing eye," as in the novels, at least with a "distended nostril." During the whole of the service, her
heart is filled with the blackest gall towards you; and
she is thinking about the best means of getting you out
of the house.

What is this smoking that it should be considered a
crime? I believe in my heart that women are jealous
of it, as of a rival. They speak of it as of some secret,
awful vice that seizes upon a man, and makes him a
pariah from genteel society. I would lay a guinea that
many a lady who has just been kind enough to read the
above lines lays down the book, after this confession of

mine that I am a smoker, and says, "Oh, the vulgar wretch!" and passes on to something else.

The fact is, that the cigar *is* a rival to the ladies, and their conqueror too. In the chief pipe-smoking nations they are kept in subjection. While the chief, Little White Belt, smokes, the women are silent in his wigwam; while Mahomet Ben Jawbrahim causes volumes of odorous incense of Latakia to play round his beard, the women of the harem do not disturb his meditations, but only add to the delight of them by tinkling on a dulcimer and dancing before him. When Professor Strumpff of Göttingen takes down No. 13 from the wall, with a picture of Beatrice Cenci upon it, and which holds a pound of canaster, the Frau Professorin knows that for two hours Hermann is engaged, and takes up her stockings and knits in quiet. The constitution of French society has been quite changed within the last twelve years: an ancient and respectable dynasty has been overthrown; an aristocracy which Napoleon could never master has disappeared: and from what cause? I do not hesitate to say,—*from the habit of smoking*. Ask any man whether, five years before the revolution of July, if you wanted a cigar at Paris, they did not bring you a roll of tobacco with a straw in it? Now, the whole city smokes; society is changed; and be sure of this, ladies, a similar combat is going on in this country at present between cigar-smoking and you. Do you suppose you will conquer? Look over the wide world, and see that your adversary has overcome it. Germany has been puffing for threescore years; France smokes to a man. Do you think you can keep the enemy out of England? Psha! look at his progress. Ask the clubhouses, Have they smoking-rooms, or not? Are they not obliged to yield to the general want of the age, in spite of the resistance of the old women on the committees? I, for my part, do not despair to see a bishop lolling out of the "Athenæum" with a cheroot in his mouth, or, at any rate, a pipe stuck in his shovel-hat.

But as in all great causes and in promulgating new and illustrious theories, their first propounders and exponents are generally the victims of their enthusiasm, of course the first preachers of smoking have been martyrs, too; and George Fitz-Boodle is one. The first gas-man was ruined; the inventor of steam-engine printing became a pauper. I began to smoke in days when the task was one of some danger, and paid the penalty of my crime. I was flogged most fiercely for my first cigar; for, being asked to dine one Sunday evening with a half-pay colonel of dragoons (the gallant, simple, humorous Shortcut—heaven bless him!—I have had many a guinea from him who had so few), he insisted upon my smoking in his room at the "Salopian," and the consequence was, that I became so violently ill as to be reported intoxicated upon my return to Slaughter-House School, where I was a boarder, and I was whipped the next morning for my peccadillo. At Christ Church, one of our tutors was the celebrated lamented Otto Rose, who would have been a bishop under the present Government, had not an immoderate indulgence in water-gruel cut short his elegant and useful career. He was a good man, a pretty scholar and poet (the episode upon the discovery of eau-de-Cologne, in his prize-poem on "The Rhine," was considered a masterpiece of art, though I am not much of a judge myself upon such matters), and he was as remarkable for his fondness for a tuft as for his nervous antipathy to tobacco. As ill-luck would have it, my rooms (in Tom Quad) were exactly under his; and I was grown by this time to be a confirmed smoker. I was a baronet's son (we are of James's the First's creation), and I do believe our tutor could have pardoned any crime in the world but this. He had seen me in a tandem, and at that moment was seized with a violent fit of sneezing— (sternutatory paroxysm he called it) —at the conclusion of which I was a mile down the Woodstock Road. He had seen me in pink, as we used to call it, swaggering in the open sunshine across a grass-plat in the court; but spied out opportunely a servitor, one Todhunter by name, who was going to morning chapel with his shoestring untied, and forthwith sprung towards that unfortunate person, to set him an imposition. Everything, in fact, but tobacco he could forgive. Why did cursed fortune bring him into the rooms over mine? The odour of the cigars made his gentle spirit quite furious; and one luckless morning, when I was standing before my " oak," and chanced to puff a great *bouffée* of Varinas into his face, he forgot his respect for my family altogether (I was the second son, and my brother a sickly creature *then,*—he is now sixteen stone in weight, and has a half-score of children) ; gave me a severe lecture, to which I replied rather hotly, as was my wont. And then came demand for an apology; refusal on my part; appeal to the dean; convocation; and rustication of George Savage Fitz-Boodle.

My father had taken a second wife (of the noble house of Flintskinner), and Lady Fitz-Boodle detested smoking, as a woman of her high principles should. She had an entire mastery over the worthy old gentleman, and thought I was a sort of demon of wickedness. The old man went to his grave with some similar notion,—heaven help him! and left me but the wretched twelve thousand pounds secured to me on my poor mother's property.

In the army, my luck was much the same. I joined the —th Lancers, Lieut.-Col. Lord Martingale, in the year 1817. I only did duty with the regiment for three months. We were quartered at Cork, where I found the Irish doodheen and tobacco the pleasantest smoking possible; and was found by his lordship, one day upon stable duty, smoking the shortest, dearest little dumpy clay-pipe in the world.

"Cornet Fitz-Boodle," said my lord, in a towering passion, "from what blackguard did you get that pipe?"

I omit the oaths which garnished invariably his lordship's conversation.

"I got it, my lord," said I, "from one Terence Mullins, a jingle-driver, with a packet of his peculiar tobacco. You sometimes smoke Turkish, I believe; do try this. Isn't it good?" And in the simplest way in the world I puffed a volume into his face. "I see you like it," said I, so coolly, that the men—and I do believe the horses—burst out laughing.

He started back—choking almost, and recovered himself only to vent such a storm of oaths and curses that I was compelled to request Capt. Rawdon (the captain on duty) to take note of his lordship's words; and unluckily could not help adding a question which settled my business. "You were good enough," I said, "to ask me, my lord, from what blackguard I got my pipe; might I ask from what blackguard you learned your language?"

This was quite enough. Had I said, "From what *gentleman* did your lordship learn your language?" the point would have been quite as good, and my Lord Martingale would have suffered in my place: as it was, I was so strongly recommended to sell out by his Royal Highness the Commander-in-Chief, that, being of a good-natured disposition, never knowing how to refuse a friend, I at once threw up my hopes of military distinction and retired into civil life.

My lord was kind enough to meet me afterwards in a field in the Glanmire Road, where he put a ball into my leg.   This I returned to him some years later with about twenty-three others—black ones—when he came to be balloted for at a club of which I have the honour to be a member.

Thus by the indulgence of a simple and harmless propensity,—of a propensity which can inflict an injury upon no person or thing except the coat and the person of him who indulges in it,—of a custom honoured and observed in almost all the nations of the world,—of a custom which, far from leading a man into any wickedness or dissipation to which youth is subject, on the contrary, begets only benevolent silence and thoughtful good-humoured observation—I found at the age of twenty all my prospects in life destroyed.   I cared not for woman in those days: the calm smoker has a sweet companion in his pipe.   I did not drink immoderately of wine; for though a friend to trifling potations, to excessively strong drinks tobacco is abhorrent.   I never thought of gambling, for the lover of the pipe has no need of such excitement; but I was considered a monster of dissipation in my family, and bade fair to come to ruin.

"Look at George," my mother-in-law said to the genteel and correct young Flintskinners.   "He entered the world with every prospect in life, and see in what an abyss of degradation his fatal habits have plunged him! At school he was flogged and disgraced, he was disgraced and rusticated at the university, he was disgraced and expelled from the army! He might have had the living of Boodle " (her ladyship gave it to one of her nephews), "but he would not take his degree; his papa would have purchased him a troop—nay, a lieutenant-colonelcy some day, but for his fatal excesses. And now as long as my dear husband will listen to the voice of a wife who adores him—never, never shall he spend a shilling upon so worthless a young man. He has a small income from his mother (I cannot but think that the first Lady Fitz-Boodle was a weak and misguided person); let him live upon his mean pittance as he can, and I heartily pray we may not hear of him in gaol!"

My brother, after he came to the estate, married the ninth daughter of our neighbour, Sir John Spreadeagle; and Boodle Hall has seen a new little Fitz-Boodle with every succeeding spring. The dowager retired to Scotland with a large jointure and a wondrous heap of savings. Lady Fitz is a good creature, but she thinks me something diabolical, trembles when she sees me, and gathers all her children about her, rushes into the nursery whenever I pay that little seminary a visit, and actually slapped poor little Frank's ears one day when I was teaching him to ride upon the back of a Newfoundland dog.

"George," said my brother to me the last time I paid him a visit at the old hall, "don't be angry, my dear fellow, but Maria is in a—hum—in a delicate situation, expecting her—hum "—(the eleventh) —"and do you know you frighten her? It was but yesterday you met her in the rookery—you were smoking that enormous German pipe—and when she came in she had an hysterical seizure, and Drench says that in her situation it's dangerous.   And I say, George, if you go to town you'll find a couple of hundred at your banker's."   And with this the poor fellow shook me by the hand, and called for a fresh bottle of claret.

Afterwards he told me, with many hesitations, that my room at Boodle Hall had been made into a second nursery.   I see my sister-in-law in London twice or thrice in the season, and the little people, who have almost forgotten to call me uncle George.

It's hard, too, for I am a lonely man after all, and my heart yearns to them.   The other day I smuggled a couple of them into my chambers, and had a little feast of cream and strawberries to welcome them.   But it had like to have cost the nursery-maid (a Swiss girl that Fitz-Boodle hired somewhere in his travels) her place.   My step-mamma, who happened to be in town, came flying down in her chariot, pounced upon the poor thing and the children in the midst of the entertainment; and when I asked her, with rather a bad grace to be sure, to take a chair and a share of the feast—

"Mr. Fitz-Boodle," said she, "I am not accustomed to sit down in a place that smells of tobacco like an ale-house—an ale-house inhabited by a *serpent,* sir!   A *serpent!*—do you understand me?—who carries his poison into his brother's own house, and purshues his eenfamous designs before his brother's own children.   Put on Miss Maria's bonnet this instant.   Mamsell, ontondyvoo?   *Metty le bonny à mamsell.*   And I shall take care, Mamsell, that you return to Switzerland to-morrow.

I've no doubt you are a relation of Courvoisier—*oui! oui! Courvoisier, vous comprenny*—and you shall certainly be sent back to your friends."

With this speech, and with the children and their maid sobbing before her, my lady retired; but for once my sister-in-law was on my side, not liking the meddlement of the elder lady.

I know, then, that from indulging in that simple habit of smoking, I have gained among the ladies a dreadful reputation. I see that they look coolly upon me, and darkly at their husbands when they arrive at home in my company. Men, I observe, in consequence, ask me to dine much oftener at the club, or the "Star and Garter" at Richmond, or at "Lovegrove's," than in their own houses; and with this sort of arrangement I am fain to acquiesce; for, as I said before, I am of an easy temper, and can at any rate take my cigar-case out after dinner at Blackwall, when my lady or the duchess is not by. I know, of course, the best *men* in town; and as for ladies' society, not having it (for I will have none of your pseudo-ladies, such as sometimes honour bachelors' parties,—actresses, couturières, opera-dancers, and so forth) —as for ladies' society, I say, I cry pish! 'tis not worth the trouble of the complimenting, and the bother of pumps and black silk stockings.

Let any man remember what ladies' society was when he had an opportunity of seeing them among themselves, as What-d'ye-call'im does in the Thesmophoria— (I beg pardon, I was on the verge of a classical allusion, which I abominate) —I mean at that period of his life when the intellect is pretty acute, though the body is small— namely, when a young gentleman is about eleven years of age, dining at his father's table during the holidays, and is requested by his papa to quit the dinner-table when the ladies retire from it.

Corbleu! I recollect their whole talk as well as if it had been whispered but yesterday; and can see, after a long dinner, the yellow summer sun throwing long shadows over the lawn before the dining-room windows, and my poor mother and her company of ladies sailing away to the music-room in old Boodle Hall. The Countess Dawdley was the great lady in our county, a portly lady who used to love crimson satin in those days, and birds-of-paradise. She was flaxen-haired, and the Regent once said she resembled one of King Charles's beauties.

When Sir John Todcaster used to begin his famous story of the exciseman (I shall not tell it here, for very good reasons), my poor mother used to turn to Lady Dawdley, and give that mystic signal at which all females rise from their chairs. Tufthunt, the curate, would spring from his seat, and be sure to be the first to open the door for the retreating ladies; and my brother Tom and I, though remaining stoutly in our places, were speedily ejected from them by the governor's invariable remark, "Tom and George, if you have had *quite* enough of wine, you had better go and join your mamma." Yonder she marches, heaven bless her! through the old oak hall (how long the shadows of the antlers are on the wainscot, and the armour of Rollo Fitz-Boodle looks in the sunset as if it were emblazoned with rubies)—yonder she marches, stately and tall, in her invariable pearl-coloured tabinet, followed by Lady Dawdley, blazing like a flamingo; next comes Lady Emily Tufthunt (she was Lady Emily Flintskinner), who will not for all the world take precedence of rich, vulgar, kind, good-humoured Mrs. *Colonel* Grogwater, as she would be called, with a yellow little husband from Madras, who first taught me to drink sangaree. He was a new arrival in our county, but paid nobly to the hounds, and occupied hospitably a house which was always famous for its hospitality—Sievely Hall (poor Bob Cullender ran through seven thousand a year before he was thirty years old). Once when I was a lad, Colonel Grogwater gave me two gold mohurs out of his desk for whist-markers, and I'm sorry to say I ran up from Eton and sold them both for seventy-three shillings at a shop in Cornhill. But to return to the ladies, who are all this while kept waiting in the hall, and to their usual conversation after dinner.

Can any man forget how miserably flat it was? Five matrons sit on sofas, and talk in a subdued voice:—

First Lady (mysteriously).—" My dear Lady Dawdley, do tell me about poor Susan Tuckett."

Second Lady.—" All three children are perfectly well, and I assure you as fine babies as I ever saw in my life. I made her give them Daffy's Elixir the first day; and it was the greatest mercy that I had some of Frederick's baby-clothes by me; for you know I had provided Susan with sets for one only, and really—"

Third Lady.—" Of course one couldn't; and for my part I think your ladyship is a great deal too kind to these people. A little gardener's boy dressed in Lord Dawdley's frocks indeed! I recollect that one at his christening had the sweetest lace in the world!"

Fourth Lady.—" What do you think of this, ma'am—Lady Emily, I mean? I have just had it from Howell and James:—guipure, they call it. Isn't it an odd name for lace? And they charge me, upon my conscience, four guineas a yard!"

Third Lady.—" My mother, when she came to Flint-skinner, had lace upon her robe that cost sixty guineas a yard, ma'am! 'Twas sent from Malines direct by our relation, the Count d'Araignay."

Fourth Lady (*aside*).—" I thought she would not let the evening pass without talking of her Malines lace and her Count d'Araignay. Odious people! they don't spare their backs, but they pinch their—"

Here Tom upsets a coffee-cup over his white jean trousers, and another young gentleman bursts into a laugh, saying, " By Jove, that's a good 'un!"

" George, my dear," says mamma, " had not you and your young friend better go into the garden? But mind, no fruit, or Dr. Glauber must be called in again immediately!" And we all go, and in ten minutes I and my brother are fighting in the stables.

If, instead of listening to the matrons and their discourse, we had taken the opportunity of attending to the conversation of the Misses, we should have heard matter not a whit more interesting.

First Miss.—" They were all three in blue crape; you never saw anything so odious. And I know for a certainty that they wore those dresses at Muddlebury, at the archery-ball, and I dare say they had them in town."

Second Miss.—" Don't you think Jemima decidedly crooked? And those fair complexions, they freckle so, that really Miss Blanche ought to be called Miss Brown."

Third Miss.—" He, he, he!"

Fourth Miss.—" Don't you think Blanche is a pretty name?"

First Miss.—"La! do you think so, dear? Why, it's my second name!"

Second Miss.—"Then I'm sure Captain Travers thinks it a *beautiful* name!"

Third Miss.—"He, he, he!"

Fourth Miss.—"What was he telling you at dinner that seemed to interest you so?"

First Miss.—"O law, nothing!—that is, yes! Charles—that is,—Captain Travers, is a sweet poet, and was reciting to me some lines that he had composed upon a faded violet:—

> " ' The odour from the flower is gone,
>   That like thy—'

like thy something, I forget what it was; but his lines are sweet, and so original too! I wish that horrid Sir John Todcaster had not begun his story of the exciseman, for Lady Fitz-Boodle always quits the table when he begins."

Third Miss.—"Do you like those tufts that gentlemen wear sometimes on their chins?"

Second Miss.—"Nonsense, Mary!"

Third Miss.—"Well, I only asked, Jane. Frank thinks, you know, that he shall very soon have one, and puts bear's-grease on his chin every night."

Second Miss.—"Mary, nonsense!"

Third Miss.—"Well, only ask him. You know he came to our dressing-room last night and took the pomatum away; and he says that when boys go to Oxford they always—"

First Miss.—"O heavens! have you heard the news about the Lancers? Charles—that is, Captain Travers, told it me!"

Second Miss.—"Law! they won't go away before the ball, I hope!"

First Miss.—"No, but on the 15th they are to shave their moustaches!   He says that Lord Tufto is in a perfect fury about it!"

Second Miss.—"And poor George Beardmore, too!" &c.

Here Tom upsets the coffee over his trousers, and the conversations end.   I can recollect a dozen such, and ask any man of sense whether such talk amuses him?

Try again to speak to a young lady while you are dancing—what we call in this country—a quadrille. What nonsense do you invariably give and receive in return!   No, I am a woman-scorner, and don't care to own it.   I hate young ladies!   Have I not been in love with several, and has any one of them ever treated me decently?   I hate married women!   Do they not hate me? and, simply because I smoke, try to draw their husbands away from my society?   I hate dowagers!   Have I not cause?   Does not every dowager in London point to George Fitz-Boodle as to a dissolute wretch among whom young and old should avoid?

And yet do not imagine that I have not loved.   I have, and madly, many, many times!   I am but eight-and-thirty,[1] not past the age of passion, and may very likely end by running off with an heiress—or a cook-maid (for who knows what strange freaks Love may choose to play in his own particular person? and I hold a man to be a mean creature who calculates about checking any such sacred impulse as lawful love)—I say, though despising the sex in general for their conduct to me, I know of particular persons belonging to it who

---

[1] He is five-and-forty, if he is a day old.—O. Y.

are worthy of all respect and esteem, and as such I beg
leave to point out the particular young lady who is
perusing these lines. Do not, dear madam, then imagine that if I knew you I should be disposed to sneer at
you. Ah, no! Fitz-Boodle's bosom has tenderer sentiments than from his way of life you would fancy, and
stern by rule is only too soft by practice. Shall I
whisper to you the story of one or two of my attach-
ments? All terminating fatally (not in death, but in
disappointment, which, as it occurred, I used to imagine
a thousand times more bitter than death, but from which
one recovers somehow more readily than from the other-
named complaint)—all, I say, terminating wretchedly
to myself, as if some fatality pursued my desire to become a domestic character.

My first love—no, let us pass *that* over. Sweet one!
thy name shall profane no hireling page. Sweet, sweet
memory! Ah, ladies, those delicate hearts of yours have,
too, felt the throb. And between the last *ob* in the word
throb and the words now written, I have passed a delicious period of perhaps an hour, perhaps a minute, I know
not how long, thinking of that holy first love and of her
who inspired it. How clearly every single incident of the
passion is remembered by me! and yet 'twas long, long
since. I was but a child then—a child at school—and,
if the truth must be told, L—ra R–ggl–s (I would
not write her whole name to be made one of the
Marquess of Hertford's executors) was a woman full
thirteen years older than myself; at the period of which
I write she must have been at least five-and-twenty.
She and her mother used to sell tarts, hard-bake, lollipops, and other such simple comestibles, on Wednesdays
and Saturdays (half-holidays), at a private school where

I received the first rudiments of a classical education.   I used to go and sit before her tray for hours, but I do not think the poor girl ever supposed any motive led me so constantly to her little stall beyond a vulgar longing for her tarts and her ginger-beer.   Yes, even at that early period my actions were misrepresented, and the fatality which has oppressed my whole life began to show itself, ——the purest passion was misinterpreted by her and my school-fellows, and they thought I was actuated by simple gluttony.   They nicknamed me Alicompayne.

Well, be it so.   Laugh at early passion ye who will; a high-born boy madly in love with a lowly ginger-beer girl!   She married afterwards, took the name of Latter, and now keeps with her old husband a turnpike, through which I often ride; but I can recollect her bright and rosy of a sunny summer afternoon, her red cheeks shaded by a battered straw bonnet, her tarts and ginger-beer upon a neat white cloth before her, mending blue worsted stockings until the young gentlemen should interrupt her by coming to buy.

Many persons will call this description low; I do not envy them their gentility, and have always observed through life (as, to be sure, every other *gentleman* has observed as well as myself) that it is your *parvenu* who stickles most for what he calls the genteel, and has the most squeamish abhorrence for what is frank and natural.   Let us pass at once, however, as all the world must be pleased, to a recital of an affair which occurred in the very best circles of society, as they are called, viz. my next unfortunate attachment.

It did not occur for several years after that simple and platonic passion just described: for though they may talk of youth as the season of romance, it has always appeared to me that there are no beings in the world so entirely unromantic and selfish as certain young English gentlemen from the age of fifteen to twenty. The oldest Lovelace about town is scarcely more hard-hearted and scornful than they; they ape all sorts of selfishness and *rouerie:* they aim at excelling at cricket, at billiards, at rowing, and drinking, and set more store by a red coat and a neat pair of top-boots than by any other glory. A young fellow staggers into college-chapel of a morning, and communicates to all his friends that he was "*so cut* last night," with the greatest possible pride. He makes a joke of having sisters and a kind mother at home who loves him; and if he speaks of his father, it is with a knowing sneer to say that he has a tailor's and a horse-dealer's bill that will surprise "the old governor." He would be ashamed of being in love. I, in common with my kind, had these affectations, and my perpetual custom of smoking added not a little to my reputation as an accomplished *roué*. What came of this custom in the army and at college, the reader has already heard. Alas! in life it went no better with me, and many pretty chances I had went off in that accursed smoke.

After quitting the army in the abrupt manner stated, I passed some short time at home, and was tolerated by my mother-in-law, because I had formed an attachment to a young lady of good connections and with a considerable fortune, which was really very nearly becoming mine. Mary M'Alister was the only daughter of Colonel M'Alister, late of the Blues, and Lady Susan his wife. Her ladyship was no more; and, indeed, of no family compared to ours (which has refused a peerage any time these two hundred years); but being an earl's

daughter and a Scotchwoman, Lady Emily Fitz-Boodle did not fail to consider her highly.   Lady Susan
was daughter of the late Admiral Earl of Marlingspike
and Baron Plumduff.   The Colonel, Miss M'Alister's
father, had a good estate, of which his daughter was
the heiress, and as I fished her out of the water upon
a pleasure-party, and swam with her to shore, we became naturally intimate, and Colonel M'Alister forgot, on account of the service rendered to him, the dreadful reputation for profligacy which I enjoyed in the
county.

Well, to cut a long story short, which is told here
merely for the moral at the end of it, I should have been
Fitz-Boodle M'Alister at this minute most probably,
and master of four thousand a year, but for the fatal
cigar-box.   I bear Mary no malice in saying that she
was a high-spirited little girl, loving, before all things,
her own way; nay, perhaps I do not, from long habit
and indulgence in tobacco-smoking, appreciate the delicacy of female organizations, which were oftentimes
most painfully affected by it.   She was a keen-sighted
little person, and soon found that the world had belied
poor George Fitz-Boodle; who, instead of being the
cunning monster people supposed him to be, was a simple, reckless, good-humoured, honest fellow, marvellously addicted to smoking, idleness, and telling the
truth.   She called me Orson, and I was happy enough
on the 14th February, in the year 18— (it's of no consequence), to send her such a pretty little copy of verses
about Orson and Valentine, in which the rude habits of
the savage man were shown to be overcome by the polished graces of his kind and brilliant conqueror, that she
was fairly overcome, and said to me, "George Fitz-

Boodle, if you give up smoking for a year I will marry you."

I swore I would, of course, and went home and flung four pounds of Hudson's cigars, two meerschaum pipes that had cost me ten guineas at the establishment of Mr. Gattie at Oxford, a tobacco-bag that Lady Fitz-Boodle had given me *before* her marriage with my father (it was the only present that I ever had from her or any member of the Flintskinner family), and some choice packets of Varinas and Syrian, into the lake in Boodle Park. The weapon amongst them all which I most regretted was—will it be believed?—the little black doodheen which had been the cause of the quarrel between Lord Martingale and me. However, it went along with the others. I would not allow my groom to have so much as a cigar, lest I should be tempted hereafter; and the consequence was that a few days after many fat carps and tenches in the lake (I must confess 'twas no bigger than a pond) nibbled at the tobacco, and came floating on their backs on the top of the water quite intoxicated. My conversion made some noise in the county, being emphasized as it were by this fact of the fish. I can't tell you with what pangs I kept my resolution; but keep it I did for some time.

With so much beauty and wealth, Mary M'Alister had of course many suitors, and among them was the young Lord Dawdley, whose mamma has previously been described in her gown of red satin. As I used to thrash Dawdley at school, I thrashed him in after-life in love; he put up with his disappointment pretty well, and came after a while and shook hands with me, telling me of the bets that there were in the county, where the whole story was known, for and against me. For the fact is, as I must own, that Mary M'Alister, the queer-est, frankest of women, made no secret of the agree-ment, or the cause of it.

"I did not care a penny for Orson," she said, "but he would go on writing me such dear pretty verses that at last I couldn't help saying yes.   But if he breaks his promise to me, I declare, upon my honour, I'll break mine, and nobody's heart will be broken either."

This was the perfect fact, as I must confess, and I declare that it was only because she amused me and de-lighted me, and provoked me, and made me laugh very much, and because, no doubt, she was very rich, that I had any attachment for her.

"For heaven's sake, George," my father said to me, as I quitted home to follow my beloved to London, "remember that you are a younger brother and have a lovely girl and four thousand a year within a year's reach of you.   Smoke as much as you like, my boy, after marriage," added the old gentleman, knowingly (as if *he,* honest soul, after his second marriage, dared drink an extra pint of wine without my lady's permis-sion!) "but eschew the tobacco-shops till then."

I went to London resolving to act upon the paternal advice, and oh! how I longed for the day when I should be married, vowing in my secret soul that I would light a cigar as I walked out of St. George's, Hanover Square.

Well, I came to London, and so carefully avoided smoking that I would not even go into Hudson's shop to pay his bill, and as smoking was not the fashion then among young men as (thank heaven!) it is now, I had not many temptations from my friends' examples in my clubs or elsewhere; only little Dawdley began to smoke, as if to spite me. He had never done so before, but confessed—the rascal!—that he enjoyed a cigar now, if it were but to mortify me. But I took to other and more dangerous excitements, and upon the nights when not in attendance upon Mary M'Alister, might be found in very dangerous proximity to a polished mahogany table, round which claret-bottles circulated a great deal too often, or worse still, to a table covered with green cloth and ornamented with a couple of wax-candles and a couple of packs of cards, and four gentlemen playing the enticing game of whist. Likewise, I came to carry a snuff-box, and to consume in secret huge quantities of rappee.

For ladies' society I was even then disinclined, hating and despising small-talk, and dancing, and hot routs, and vulgar scrambles for suppers. I never could understand the pleasure of acting the part of lacquey to a dowager, and standing behind her chair, or bustling through the crowd for her carriage. I always found an opera too long by two acts, and have repeatedly fallen asleep in the presence of Mary M'Alister herself, sitting at the back of the box shaded by the huge beret of her old aunt, Lady Betty Plumduff; and many a time has Dawdley, with Miss M'Alister on his arm, wakened me up at the close of the entertainment in time to offer my hand to Lady Betty, and lead the ladies to their carriage. If I attended her occasionally to any ball or party of pleasure, I went, it must be confessed, with clumsy, ill-disguised ill-humour. Good heavens! have I often and often thought in the midst of a song, or the very thick of a ball-room, can people prefer this to a book and a sofa, and a dear, dear cigar-box, from thy stores, O charming Mariana Woodville! Deprived of my favourite plant, I grew sick in mind and body, moody, sarcastic, and discontented.

Such a state of things could not long continue, nor could Miss M'Alister continue to have much attachment for such a sullen, ill-conditioned creature as I then was. She used to make me wild with her wit and her sarcasm, nor have I ever possessed the readiness to parry or reply to those fine points of woman's wit, and she treated me the more mercilessly as she saw that I could not resist her.

Well, the polite reader must remember a great fête that was given at B—— House, some years back, in honour of his Highness the Hereditary Prince of Kalbsbraten-Pumpernickel, who was then in London on a visit to his illustrious relatives. It was a fancy ball, and the poems of Scott being at that time all the fashion, Mary was to appear in the character of the "Lady of the Lake," old M'Alister making a very tall and severe-looking harper; Dawdley, a most insignificant Fitzjames; and your humble servant a stalwart manly Roderick Dhu. We were to meet at B—— House at twelve o'clock, and as I had no fancy to drive through the town in my cab dressed in a kilt and philibeg, I agreed to take a seat in Dawdley's carriage, and to dress at his house in Mayfair. At eleven I left a very pleasant bachelors' party, growling to quit them and the honest, jovial claret-bottle, in order to scrape and cut papers like a harlequin from the theatre. When I arrived at Dawdley's, I mounted to a dressing-room, and began to array myself in my cursed costume.

The art of costuming was by no means so well understood in those days as it has been since, and mine was

out of all correctness. I was made to sport an enormous plume of black ostrich-feathers, such as never was
worn by any Highland chief, and had a huge tiger-skin
sporran to dangle like an apron before innumerable
yards of plaid petticoat.   The tartan cloak was outrageously hot and voluminous; it was the dog-days, and
all these things I was condemned to wear in the midst
of a crowd of a thousand people!

Dawdley sent up word, as I was dressing, that his
dress had not arrived, and he took my cab and drove off
in a rage to his tailor.

There was no hurry, I thought, to make a fool of myself; so having put on a pair of plaid trews, and very
neat pumps with shoe-buckles, my courage failed me as
to the rest of the dress, and taking down one of his
dressing-gowns, I went downstairs to the study, to wait
until he should arrive.

The windows of the pretty room were open, and a
snug sofa, with innumerable cushions, drawn towards
one of them.   A great tranquil moon was staring into
the chamber, in which stood, amidst books and all sorts
of bachelor's lumber, a silver tray with a couple of tall
Venice glasses, and a bottle of Maraschino bound with
straw.   I can see now the twinkle of the liquor in the
moonshine, as I poured it into the glass; and I swallowed two or three little cups of it, for my spirits were
downcast.   Close to the tray of Maraschino stood—
must I say it?—a box, a mere box of cedar, bound
rudely together with pink paper, branded with the name
of "Hudson" on the side, and bearing on the cover the
arms of Spain.   I thought I would just take up the box
and look in it.

Ah heaven! there they were—a hundred and fifty of

them, in calm, comfortable rows: lovingly side by side they lay, with the great moon shining down upon them —thin at the tip, full in the waist, elegantly round and full, a little spot here and there shining upon them— beauty-spots upon the cheek of Sylvia. The house was quite quiet. Dawdley always smoked in his room;—I had not smoked for four months and eleven days.

*　　　*　　　*　　　*　　　*

When Lord Dawdley came into the study, he did not make any remarks; and oh, how easy my heart felt! He was dressed in his green and boots, after Westall's picture, correctly.

"It's time to be off, George," said he; "they told me you were dressed long ago. Come up, my man, and get ready."

I rushed up into the dressing-room, and madly dashed my head and arms into a pool of eau-de-Cologne. I drank, I believe, a tumblerful of it. I called for my clothes, and, strange to say, they were gone. My servant brought them, however, saying that he had put them away—making some stupid excuse. I put them on, not heeding them much, for I was half tipsy with the excitement of the ci—— of the smo—— of what had taken place in Dawdley's study, and with the Maraschino and the eau-de-Cologne I had drunk.

"What a fine odour of lavender-water!" said Dawdley, as we rode in the carriage.

I put my head out of the window and shrieked out a laugh; but made no other reply.

"What's the joke, George?" said Dawdley. "Did I say anything witty?"

"No," cried I, yelling still more wildly; "nothing more witty than usual."

"Don't be severe, George," said he, with a mortified air; and we drove on to B—— House.

*   *   *   *   *

There must have been something strange and wild in my appearance, and those awful black plumes, as I passed through the crowd; for I observed people looking and making a strange nasal noise (it is called sniffing, and I have no other more delicate term for it), and making way as I pushed on. But I moved forward very fiercely, for the wine, the Maraschino, the eau-de-Cologne, and the—the excitement had rendered me almost wild; and at length I arrived at the place where my lovely Lady of the Lake and her Harper stood. How beautiful she looked,—all eyes were upon her as she stood blushing. When she saw me, however, her countenance assumed an appearance of alarm. "Good heavens, George!" she said, stretching her hand to me, "what makes you look so wild and pale?" I advanced, and was going to take her hand, when she dropped it with a scream.

"Ah—ah—ah!" she said. "Mr. Fitz-Boodle, you've been smoking!"

There was an immense laugh from four hundred people round about us, and the scoundrelly Dawdley joined in the yell. I rushed furiously out, and, as I passed, hurtled over the fat Hereditary Prince of Kalbsbraten-Pumpernickel.

"Es riecht hier ungeheuer stark von Tabak!" I heard his Highness say, as I madly flung myself through the aides-de-camp.

The next day Mary M'Alister, in a note full of the most odious good sense and sarcasm, reminded me of our agreement; said that she was quite convinced that we were not by any means fitted for one another, and begged me to consider myself henceforth quite free. The little wretch had the impertinence to send me a dozen boxes of cigars, which, she said, would console me for my lost love; as she was perfectly certain that I was not mercenary, and that I loved tobacco better than any woman in the world.

I believe she was right, though I have never to this day been able to pardon the scoundrelly stratagem by which Dawdley robbed me of a wife and won one himself. As I was lying on his sofa, looking at the moon and lost in a thousand happy contemplations, Lord Dawdley, returning from the tailor's, saw me smoking at my leisure. On entering his dressing-room, a horrible treacherous thought struck him. " I must not betray my friend," said he; " but in love all is fair, and he shall betray himself." There were my tartans, my cursed feathers, my tiger-skin sporran, upon the sofa.

He called up my groom; he made the rascal put on all my clothes, and, giving him a guinea and four cigars, bade him lock himself into the little pantry and smoke them *without taking the clothes off*. John did so, and was very ill in consequence, and so when I came to B—— House, my clothes were redolent of tobacco, and I lost lovely Mary M'Alister.

I am godfather to one of Lady Dawdley's boys, and hers is the only house where I am allowed to smoke unmolested; but I have never been able to admire Dawdley, a sly, *sournois,* spiritless, lily-livered fellow, that took his name off all his clubs the year he married.

DOROTHEA

BEYOND sparring and cricket, I do not recollect I learned anything useful at Slaughter-House School, where I was educated (according to an old family tradition, which sends particular generations of gentlemen to particular schools in the kingdom; and such is the force of habit, that though I hate the place, I shall send my own son thither too, should I marry any day). I say I learned little that was useful at Slaughter-House, and nothing that was ornamental. I would as soon have thought of learning to dance as of learning to climb chimneys. Up to the age of seventeen, as I have shown, I had a great contempt for the female race, and when age brought with it warmer and juster sentiments, where was I?—I could no more dance nor prattle to a young girl than a young bear could. I have seen the ugliest little low-bred wretches carrying off young and lovely creatures, twirling with them in waltzes, whispering between their glossy curls in quadrilles, simpering with perfect equanimity, and cutting *pas* in that abominable " cavalier seul," until my soul grew sick with fury. In a word, I determined to learn to dance.

But such things are hard to be acquired late in life, when the bones and habits of a man are formed. Look at a man in a hunting-field who has not been taught to ride as a boy. All the pluck and courage in the world will not make the man of him that I am, or as any man who has had the advantages of early education in the field.

In the same way with dancing. Though I went to work with immense energy, both in Brewer Street, Golden Square (with an advertising fellow), and afterwards with old Coulon at Paris, I never was able to be *easy* in dancing; and though little Coulon instructed me in a smile, it was a cursed forced one, that looked like the grin of a person in extreme agony. I once caught sight of it in a glass, and have hardly ever smiled since.

Most young men about London have gone through that strange secret ordeal of the dancing-school. I am given to understand that young snobs from attorneys' offices, banks, shops, and the like, make not the least mystery of their proceedings in the saltatory line, but trip gaily, with pumps in hand, to some dancing-place about Soho, waltz and quadrille it with Miss Green-grocer or Miss Butcher, and fancy they have had rather a pleasant evening. There is one house in Dover Street, where, behind a dirty curtain, such figures may be seen hopping every night, to a perpetual fiddling; and I have stood sometimes wondering in the street, with about six blackguard boys wondering too, at the strange contortions of the figures jumping up and down to the mysterious squeaking of the kit. Have they no shame *ces gens?* are such degrading initiations to be held in public? No, the snob may, but the man of refined mind never can submit to show himself in public labouring at the apprenticeship of this most absurd art. It is owing, perhaps, to this modesty, and the fact that I had no sisters at home, that I have never thoroughly been able to dance; for though I always arrive at the end of a quadrille (and thank heaven for it too!) and though, I be-

lieve, I make no mistake in particular, yet I solemnly
confess I have never been able thoroughly to comprehend the mysteries of it, or what I have been about from
the beginning to the end of the dance.   I always look
at the lady opposite, and do as she does: if *she* did not
know how to dance, *par hasard,* it would be all up.   But
if they can't do anything else, women can dance: let
us give them that praise at least.

In London, then, for a considerable time, I used to
get up at eight o'clock in the morning, and pass an hour
alone with Mr. Wilkinson, of the Theatres Royal, in
Golden Square;—an hour alone.   It was "one, two,
three; one, two, three—now jump—right foot more
out, Mr. Smith; and if you *could* try and look a little
more cheerful; your partner, sir, would like you hall the
better."   Wilkinson called me Smith, for the fact is,
I did not tell him my real name, nor (thank heaven!)
does he know it to this day.

I never breathed a word of my doings to any soul
among my friends; once a pack of them met me in the
strange neighbourhood, when, I am ashamed to say, I
muttered something about a "little French milliner,"
and walked off, looking as knowing as I could.

In Paris, two Cambridge-men and myself, who happened to be staying at a boarding-house together,
agreed to go to Coulon, a little creature of four feet
high with a pigtail.   His room was hung round with
glasses.   He made us take off our coats, and dance each
before a mirror.   Once he was standing before us playing on his kit—the sight of the little master and the
pupil was so supremely ridiculous, that I burst into a
yell of laughter, which so offended the old man that he
walked away abruptly, and begged me not to repeat

my visits.   Nor did I.   I was just getting into waltzing then, but determined to drop waltzing, and content
myself with quadrilling for the rest of my days.

This was all very well in France and England; but in
Germany what was I to do?   What did Hercules do
when Omphale captivated him?   What did Rinaldo do
when Armida fixed upon him her twinkling eyes?   Nay,
to cut all historical instances short, by going at once to
the earliest, what did Adam do when Eve tempted him?
He yielded and became her slave; and so I do heartily
trust every honest man will yield until the end of the
world—he has no heart who will not.   When I was in
Germany, I say, I began to learn to *waltz*.   The reader
from this will no doubt expect that some new love-
adventures befell me—nor will his gentle heart be
disappointed.   Two deep and tremendous incidents
occurred which shall be notified on the present occasion.

The reader, perhaps, remembers the brief appearance
of his Highness the Duke of Kalbsbraten-Pumpernickel at B—— House, in the first part of my Memoirs,
at that unlucky period of my life when the Duke was
led to remark the odour about my clothes, which lost me
the hand of Mary M'Alister.   I somehow found myself
in his Highness's territories, of which any body may
read a description in the *Almanach de Gotha*.   His
Highness's father, as is well known, married Emilia
Kunegunda Thomasina Charleria Emanuela Louisa
Georgina, Princess of Saxe-Pumpernickel, and a cousin
of his Highness the Duke.   Thus the two principalities
were united under one happy sovereign in the person of
Philibert Sigismund Emanuel Maria, the reigning
Duke, who has received from his country (on account
of the celebrated pump. which he erected in the market-

place of Kalbsbraten) the well-merited appellation of the Magnificent. The allegory which the statues round about the pump represent, is of a very mysterious and complicated sort. Minerva is observed leading up Ceres to a river-god, who has his arms round the neck of Pomona; while Mars (in a full-bottomed wig) is driven away by Peace, under whose mantle two lovely children, representing the Duke's two provinces, repose. The celebrated Speck is, as need scarcely be said, the author of this piece; and of other magnificent edifices in the Residenz, such as the guard-room, the skittle-hall (*Grossherzoglich Kalbsbratenpumpernickelisch Schkittelspielsaal*), &c., and the superb sentry-boxes before the Grand-Ducal Palace. He is Knight Grand Cross of the Ancient Kartoffel Order, as, indeed, is almost every one else in his Highness's dominions.

The town of Kalbsbraten contains a population of two thousand inhabitants, and a palace which would accommodate about six times that number. The principality sends three and a half men to the German Confederation, who are commanded by a General (Excellency), two Major-Generals, and sixty-four officers of lower grades; all noble, all knights of the Order, and almost all chamberlains to his Highness the Grand Duke. An excellent band of eighty performers is the admiration of the surrounding country, and leads the Grand-Ducal troops to battle in time of war. Only three of the contingent of soldiers returned from the Battle of Waterloo, where they won much honour; the remainder was cut to pieces on that glorious day.

There is a chamber of representatives (which, however, nothing can induce to sit), home and foreign ministers, residents from neighbouring courts, law presidents, town councils, &c., all the adjuncts of a big or little government. The court has its chamberlains and marshals, the Grand Duchess her noble ladies in waiting, and blushing maids of honour. Thou wert one, Dorothea! Dost remember the poor young Engländer? We parted in anger; but I think—I think thou hast not forgotten him.

The way in which I have Dorothea von Speck present to my mind is this: not as I first saw her in the garden— for her hair was in bandeaux then, and a large Leghorn hat with a deep riband covered half her fair face,— not in a mourning-dress, which, by the way, was none of the newest nor the best made—but as I saw her afterwards at a ball at the pleasant splendid little court, where she moved the most beautiful of the beauties of Kalbsbraten. The grand saloon of the palace is lighted —the Grand Duke and his officers, the Duchess and her ladies, have passed through. I, in my uniform of the —th, and a number of young fellows (who are evidently admiring my legs and envying my *distingué* appearance), are waiting round the entrance-door, where a huge Heyduke is standing, and announcing the titles of the guests as they arrive.

"HERR OBERHOF- UND BAU-INSPEKTOR VON SPECK!" shouts the Heyduke; and the little Inspector comes in. His lady is on his arm—huge, in towering plumes, and her favourite costume of light blue. Fair women always dress in light blue or light green; and Frau von Speck is very fair and stout.

But who comes behind her? Lieber Himmel! It is Dorothea! Did earth, among all the flowers which have sprung from its bosom, produce ever one more beautiful? She was none of your heavenly beauties, I tell you. She had nothing ethereal about her. No, sir;

she was of the earth earthy, and must have weighed ten
stone four or five, if she weighed an ounce. She had
none of your Chinese feet, nor waspy, unhealthy waists,
which those may admire who will. No: Dora's foot was
a good stout one; you could see her ankle (if her robe
was short enough) without the aid of a microscope; and
that envious little, sour, skinny Amalia von Mangel-
würzel used to hold up her four fingers and say (the two
girls were most intimate friends of course), "Dear
Dorothea's vaist is so much dicker as dis." And so I
have no doubt it was.

But what then? Goethe sings in one of his divine
epigrams:—

" Epicures vaunting their taste, entitle me vulgar and savage,
  Give them their Brussels-sprouts, but I am contented with
     cabbage."

I hate your little women—that is, when I am in love with
a tall one; and who would not have loved Dorothea?

Fancy her, then, if you please, about five feet four
inches high—fancy her in the family colour of light
blue, a little scarf covering the most brilliant shoulders
in the world; and a pair of gloves clinging close round an
arm that may, perhaps, be somewhat too large now, but
that Juno might have envied then. After the fashion of
young ladies on the continent, she wears no jewels or
gimcracks: her only ornament is a wreath of vine-leaves
in her hair, with little clusters of artificial grapes. Down
on her shoulders falls her brown hair, in rich liberal
clusters; all that health, and good-humour, and beauty
can do for her face, kind nature has done for hers. Her
eyes are frank, sparkling, and kind. As for her cheeks,

what paint-box or dictionary contains pigments or words
to describe their red? They say she opens her mouth and
smiles always to show the dimples in her cheeks. Psha!
she smiles because she is happy, and kind, and good-
humoured, and not because her teeth are little pearls.

All the young fellows crowd up to ask her to dance,
and, taking from her waist a little mother-of-pearl re-
membrancer, she notes them down. Old Schnabel for
the polonaise; Klingensphor, first waltz; Haarbart, second waltz; Count Hornpieper (the Danish envoy),
third; and so on. I have said why *I* could not ask her
to waltz, and I turned away with a pang, and played
écarté with Colonel Trumpenpack all night.

In thus introducing this lovely creature in her ball-
costume, I have been somewhat premature, and had best
go back to the beginning of the history of my acquaintance with her.

Dorothea, then, was the daughter of the celebrated
Speck before mentioned. It is one of the oldest names
in Germany, where her father's and mother's houses,
those of Speck and Eyer, are loved wherever they are
known. Unlike his warlike progenitor, Lorenzo von
Speck, Dorothea's father, had early shown himself a
passionate admirer of art; had quitted home to study
architecture in Italy, and had become celebrated
throughout Europe, and been appointed Oberhofarchi-
tect and Kunst- und Bau-inspektor of the united principalities. They are but four miles wide, and his genius
has consequently but little room to play. What art can
do, however, he does. The palace is frequently whitewashed under his eyes; the theatre painted occasionally;
the noble public buildings erected, of which I have already made mention.

I had come to Kalbsbraten, scarce knowing whither I went; and having, in about ten minutes, seen the curiosities of the place (I did not care to see the King's palace, for chairs and tables have no great charm for me), I had ordered horses, and wanted to get on I cared not whither, when Fate threw Dorothea in my way. I was yawning back to the hotel through the palace-garden, a *valet-de-place* at my side, when I saw a young lady seated under a tree reading a novel, her mamma on the same bench (a fat woman in light blue) knitting a stocking, and two officers, choked in their stays, with various orders on their spinach-coloured coats, standing by in first attitudes: the one was caressing the fat-lady-in-blue's little dog; the other was twirling his own moustache, which was already as nearly as possible curled into his own eye.

I don't know how it is, but I hate to see men evidently intimate with nice-looking women, and on good terms with themselves. There's something annoying in their cursed complacency—their evident sunshiny happiness. I've no woman to make sunshine for *me;* and yet my heart tells me that not one, but several such suns, would do good to my system.

"Who are those pert-looking officers," says I, peevishly, to the guide, "who are talking to those vulgar-looking women?"

"The big one, with the epaulets, is Major von Schnabel; the little one, with the pale face, is Stiefel von Klingenspohr."

"And the big blue woman?"

"The Grand-Ducal Pumpernickelian-court-architectress and Upper-Palace-and-building-inspectress Von Speck, born V. Eyer," replied the guide. "Your well-born honour has seen the pump in the market-place; that is the work of the great Von Speck."

" And yonder young person? "

" Mr. Court-architect's daughter; the Fräulein Doro-thea."

*   *   *   *   *

Dorothea looked up from her novel here, and turned her face towards the stranger who was passing, and then blushing turned it down again. Schnabel looked at me with a scowl, Klingenspohr with a simper, the dog with a yelp, the fat lady in blue just gave one glance, and seemed, I thought, rather well pleased. " Silence, Lischen!" said she to the dog. "Go on, darling Dor-othea," she added, to her daughter, who continued her novel.

Her voice was a little tremulous, but very low and rich. For some reason or other, on getting back to the inn, I countermanded the horses, and said I would stay for the night.

I not only stayed that night, but many, many afterwards; and as for the manner in which I became acquainted with the Speck family, why it was a good joke against me at the time, and I did not like then to have it known; but now it may as well come out at once. Speck, as everybody knows, lives in the market-place, opposite his grand work of art, the town pump, or foun-tain. I bought a large sheet of paper, and having a knack at drawing, sat down, with the greatest gravity, before the pump, and sketched it for several hours. I knew it would bring out old Speck to see. At first he contented himself by flattening his nose against the win-dow-glasses of his study, and looking what the Eng-länder was about. Then he put on his grey cap with the huge green shade, and sauntered to the door: then he walked round me, and formed one of a band of street-idlers who were looking on: then at last he could restrain himself no more, but, pulling off his cap, with a low bow, began to discourse upon arts, and architecture in particular.

"It is curious," says he, "that you have taken the same view of which a print has been engraved."

"That *is* extraordinary," says I (though it wasn't, for I had traced my drawing at a window off the very print in question). I added that I was, like all the world, immensely struck with the beauty of the edifice; heard of it at Rome, where it was considered to be superior to any of the celebrated fountains of that capital of the fine arts; finally, that unless perhaps the celebrated fountain of Aldgate in London might compare with it, Kalbsbraten building, *except* in that case, was incomparable.

This speech I addressed in French, of which the worthy Hofarchitect understood somewhat, and continuing to reply in German, our conversation grew pretty close. It is singular that I can talk to a man and pay him compliments with the utmost gravity, whereas, to a woman, I at once lose all self-possession, and have never said a pretty thing in my life.

My operations on old Speck were so conducted, that in a quarter of an hour I had elicited from him an invitation to go over the town with him, and see its architectural beauties. So we walked through the huge half-furnished chambers of the palace, we panted up the copper pinnacle of the church-tower, we went to see the Museum and Gymnasium, and coming back into the market-place again, what could the Hofarchitect do but

offer me a glass of wine and a seat in his house? He
introduced me to his Gattinn, his Leocadia (the fat
woman in blue), "as a young world-observer, and
worthy art-friend, a young scion of British Adel, who
had come to refresh himself at the Urquellen of his
race, and see his brethren of the great family of Hermann."

I saw instantly that the old fellow was of a romantic
turn, from this rodomontade to his lady: nor was she a
whit less so; nor was Dorothea less sentimental than her
mamma. She knew everything regarding the literature
of Albion, as she was pleased to call it; and asked me
news of all the famous writers there. I told her that
Miss Edgeworth was one of the loveliest young beauties at our court; I described to her Lady Morgan,
herself as beautiful as the wild Irish girl she drew; I
promised to give her a signature of Mrs. Hemans (which
I wrote for her that very evening) ; and described a fox-
hunt, at which I had seen Thomas Moore and Samuel
Rogers, Esquires; and a boxing-match, in which the
athletic author of "Pelham" was pitched against the
hardy mountain bard, Wordsworth. You see my education was not neglected, for though I have never read
the works of the above-named ladies and gentlemen, yet
I knew their names well enough.

Time passed away. I, perhaps, was never so brilliant
in conversation as when excited by the Asmanshauser
and the brilliant eyes of Dorothea that day. She and her
parents had dined at their usual heathen hour; but I
was, I don't care to own it, so smitten, that for the first
time in my life I did not even miss the meal, and talked
on until six o'clock, when tea was served. Madame
Speck said they always drank it; and so placing a tea-

spoonful of bohea in a cauldron of water, she placidly handed out this decoction, which we took with cakes and tartines. I leave you to imagine how disgusted Kling-enspohr and Schnabel looked when they stepped in as usual that evening to make their party of whist with the Speck family! Down they were obliged to sit; and the lovely Dorothea, for that night, declined to play altogether, and—sat on the sofa by me.

What we talked about, who shall tell? I would not, for my part, break the secret of one of those delicious conversations, of which I and every man in his time have held so many. You begin, very probably, about the weather—'tis a common subject, but what sentiments the genius of Love can fling into it! I have often, for my part, said to the girl of my heart for the time being, "It's a fine day," or, "It's a rainy morning!" in a way that has brought tears to her eyes. Something beats in your heart, and twangle! a corresponding string thrills and echoes in hers. You offer her anything—her knit-ting-needles, a slice of bread-and-butter—what causes the grateful blush with which she accepts the one or the other? Why, she sees your heart handed over to her upon the needles, and the bread-and-butter is to her a sandwich with love inside it. If you say to your grand-mother, "Ma'am, it's a fine day," or what not, she would find in the words no other meaning than their outward and visible one; but say so to the girl you love, and she understands a thousand mystic meanings in them. Thus, in a word, though Dorothea and I did not, prob-ably, on the first night of our meeting, talk of anything more than the weather, or trumps, or some subjects which to such listeners as Schnabel and Klingenspohr and others might appear quite ordinary, yet to *us* they had a different signification, of which Love alone held the key.

Without further ado then, after the occurrences of that evening, I determined on staying at Kalbsbraten, and presenting my card the next day to the Hof-Marshal, requesting to have the honour of being presented to his Highness the Prince, at one of whose court-balls my Dorothea appeared as I have described her.

It was summer when I first arrived at Kalbsbraten. The little court was removed to Siegmundslust, his Highness's country-seat: no balls were taking place, and, in consequence, I held my own with Dorothea pretty well. I treated her admirer, Lieutenant Klingenspohr, with perfect scorn, had a manifest advantage over Major Schnabel, and used somehow to meet the fair one every day, walking in company with her mamma in the palace garden, or sitting under the acacias, with Belotte in her mother's lap, and the favourite romance beside her. Dear, dear Dorothea! what a number of novels she must have read in her time! She confesses to me that she had been in love with Uncas, with Saint Preux, with Ivanhoe, and with hosts of German heroes of romance; and when I asked her if she, whose heart was so tender towards imaginary youths, had never had a preference for any one of her living adorers, she only looked, and blushed, and sighed, and said nothing.

You see I had got on as well as man could do, until the confounded court season and the balls began, and then—why, then came my usual luck.

Waltzing is a part of a German girl's life. With the best will in the world—which, I doubt not, she entertains for me, for I never put the matter of marriage directly to her—Dorothea could not go to balls and not waltz. It was madness to me to see her whirling round the room with officers, *attachés,* prim little chamberlains with gold keys and embroidered coats, her hair floating in the wind, her hand reposing upon the abominable little dancer's epaulet, her good-humoured face lighted up with still greater satisfaction. I saw that I must learn to waltz too, and took my measures accordingly.

The leader of the ballet at the Kalbsbraten theatre in my time was Springbock, from Vienna. He had been a regular Zephyr once, 'twas said, in his younger days; and though he is now fifteen stone weight, I can, *hélas!* recommend him conscientiously as a master; and I determined to take some lessons from him in the art which I had neglected so foolishly in early life.

It may be said, without vanity, that I was an apt pupil, and in the course of half-a-dozen lessons I had arrived at very considerable agility in the waltzing line, and could twirl round the room with him at such a pace as made the old gentleman pant again, and hardly left him breath enough to puff out a compliment to his pupil. I may say, that in a single week I became an expert waltzer; but as I wished, when I came out publicly in that character, to be quite sure of myself, and as I had hitherto practised not with a lady, but with a very fat old man, it was agreed that he should bring a lady of his acquaintance to perfect me, and accordingly, at my eighth lesson, Madame Springbock herself came to the dancing-room, and the old Zephyr performed on the violin.

If any man ventures the least sneer with regard to this lady, or dares to insinuate anything disrespectful to her or myself, I say at once that he is an impudent calumniator. Madame Springbock is old enough to be my grandmother, and as ugly a woman as I ever saw; but, though old, she was *passionnée pour la danse,* and not having (on account, doubtless, of her age and unprepossessing appearance) many opportunities of indulging in her favourite pastime, made up for lost time by immense activity whenever she could get a partner. In vain, at the end of the hour, would Springbock exclaim, "Amalia, my soul's blessing, the time is up!" "Play on, dear Alphonso!" would the old lady exclaim, whisking me round: and though I had not the least pleasure in such a homely partner, yet for the sake of perfecting myself, I waltzed and waltzed with her, until we were both half dead with fatigue.

At the end of three weeks I could waltz as well as any man in Germany.

At the end of four weeks there was a grand ball at court in honour of H. H. the Prince of Dummerland and his Princess, and *then* I determined I would come out in public. I dressed myself with unusual care and splendour. My hair was curled and my moustache dyed to a nicety; and of the four hundred gentlemen present, if the girls of Kalbsbraten *did* select one who wore an English hussar uniform, why should I disguise the fact? In spite of my silence, the news had somehow got abroad, as news will in such small towns,—Herr von Fitz-Boodle was coming out in a waltz that evening. His Highness the Duke even made an allusion to the circumstance. When on this eventful night, I went, as usual, and made him my bow in the presentation, "Vous, monsieur," said he—"vous qui êtes si jeune, devez aimer la danse." I blushed as red as my trousers, and bowing, went away.

I stepped up to Dorothea. Heavens! how beautiful

she looked! and how archly she smiled as, with a thumping heart, I asked her hand for a *waltz!* She took out her little mother-of-pearl dancing-book, she wrote down my name with her pencil: we were engaged for the fourth waltz, and till then I left her to other partners.

Who says that his first waltz is not a nervous moment? I vow I was more excited than by any duel I ever fought. I would not dance any contre-danse or galop. I repeatedly went to the buffet and got glasses of punch (dear simple Germany! 'tis with rum-punch and eggflip thy children strengthen themselves for the dance!) I went into the ball-room and looked—the couples bounded before me, the music clashed and rung in my ears—all was fiery, feverish, indistinct. The gleaming white columns, the polished oaken floors in which the innumerable tapers were reflected—all together swam before my eyes, and I was in a pitch of madness almost when the fourth waltz at length came. *"Will you dance with your sword on?"* said the sweetest voice in the world. I blushed, and stammered, and trembled, as I laid down that weapon and my cap, and hark! the music began!

Oh, how my hand trembled as I placed it round the waist of Dorothea! With my left hand I took her right —did she squeeze it? I think she did—to this day I think she did. Away we went! we tripped over the polished oak floor like two young fairies. "Courage, monsieur," said she, with her sweet smile. Then it was "Très bien, monsieur." Then I heard the voices humming and buzzing about. "Il danse bien, l'Anglais." "Ma foi, oui," says another. On we went, twirling and twisting, and turning and whirling; couple after couple dropped panting off. Little Klingenspohr himself was obliged to give in. All eyes were upon us—we were going round *alone*. Dorothea was almost exhausted, when

*   *   *   *   *

I have been sitting for two hours since I marked the asterisks, thinking—thinking. I have committed crimes in my life—who hasn't? But talk of remorse, what remorse is there like *that* which rushes up in a flood to my brain sometimes when I am alone, and causes me to blush when I'm a-bed in the dark?

I fell, sir, on that infernal slippery floor. Down we came like shot; we rolled over and over in the midst of the ball-room, the music going ten miles an hour, 800 pairs of eyes fixed upon us, a cursed shriek of laughter bursting out from all sides. Heavens! how clear I heard it, as we went on rolling and rolling! "My child! my Dorothea!" shrieked out Madame Speck, rushing forward, and as soon as she had breath to do so, Dorothea of course screamed too; then she fainted, then she was disentangled from out my spurs, and borne off by a bevy of tittering women. "Clumsy brute!" said Madame Speck, turning her fat back upon me. I remained upon my *séant,* wild, ghastly, looking about. It was all up with me—I knew it was. I wished I could have died there, and I wish so still.

Klingenspohr married her, that is the long and short; but before that event I placed a sabre-cut across the young scoundrel's nose, which destroyed *his* beauty for ever.

O Dorothea! you can't forgive me—you oughtn't to forgive me; but I love you madly still.

My next flame was Ottilia: but let us keep her for another number; my feelings overpower me at present.

OTTILIA

CHAPTER I

THE ALBUM—THE MEDITERRANEAN HEATH

TRAVELLING some little time back in a wild part of Connemara, where I had been for fishing and seal-shooting, I had the good luck to get admission to the château of a hospitable Irish gentleman, and to procure some news of my once dear Ottilia.

Yes, of no other than Ottilia v. Schlippenschlopp, the Muse of Kalbsbraten-Pumpernickel, the friendly little town far away in Sachsenland,—where old Speck built the town pump, where Klingenspohr was slashed across the nose,—where Dorothea rolled over and over in that horrible waltz with Fitz-Boo— Psha!—away with the recollection: but wasn't it strange to get news of Ottilia in the wildest corner of Ireland, where I never should have thought to hear her gentle name? Walking on that very Urrisbeg Mountain under whose shadow I heard Ottilia's name, Mackay, the learned author of the "Flora Patlandica," discovered the Mediterranean heath,—such a flower as I have often plucked on the sides of Vesuvius, and as Proserpine, no doubt, amused herself in gathering as she strayed in the fields of Enna. Here it is—the self-same flower, peering out at the Atlantic from Roundstone Bay; here, too, in this wild lonely place, nestles the fragrant memory of my Ottilia!

In a word, after a day on Ballylynch Lake (where, with a brown fly and a single hair, I killed fourteen salmon, the smallest twenty-nine pounds weight, the largest somewhere about five stone ten), my young friend Blake Bodkin Lynch Browne (a fine lad who has made his continental tour) and I adjourned, after dinner, to the young gentleman's private room, for the purpose of smoking a certain cigar; which is never more pleasant than after a hard day's sport, or a day spent in-doors, or after a good dinner, or a bad one, or at night when you are tired, or in the morning when you are fresh, or of a cold winter's day, or of a scorching summer's afternoon, or at any other moment you choose to fix upon.

What should I see in Blake's room but a rack of pipes, such as are to be found in almost all the bachelors' rooms in Germany, and amongst them was a porcelain pipe-head bearing the image of the Kalbsbraten pump! There it was: the old spout, the old familiar allegory of Mars, Bacchus, Apollo virorum, and the rest, that I had so often looked at from Hofarchitect Speck's window, as I sat there by the side of Dorothea. The old gentleman had given me one of these very pipes; for he had hundreds of them painted, wherewith he used to gratify almost every stranger who came into his native town.

Any old place with which I have once been familiar (as, perhaps, I have before stated in these " Confessions "—but never mind that) is in some sort dear to me: and were I Lord Shootingcastle or Colonel Popland, I think after a residence of six months there I should love the Fleet Prison. As I saw the old familiar pipe, I took it down, and crammed it with Cavendish tobacco, and lay down on a sofa, and puffed away for an hour well-nigh, thinking of old, old times.

"You're very entertaining to-night, Fitz," says young Blake, who had made several tumblers of punch for me, which I had gulped down without saying a word. "Don't ye think ye'd be more easy in bed than snorting and sighing there on my sofa, and groaning fit to make me go hang myself?"

"I am thinking, Blake," says I, "about Pumpernickel, where old Speck gave you this pipe."

"'Deed he did," replies the young man; "and did ye know the old Bar'n?"

"I did," said I. "My friend, I have been by the banks of the Bendemeer. Tell me, are the nightingales still singing there, and do the roses still bloom?"

"The *hwhat?*" cries Blake. "What the divvle, Fitz, are you growling about? Bendemeer Lake's in Westmoreland, as I preshume; and as for roses and nightingales, I give ye my word it's Greek ye're talking to me." And Greek it very possibly was, for my young friend, though as good across country as any man in his county, has not the fine feeling and tender perception of beauty which may be found elsewhere, dear madam.

"Tell me about Speck, Blake, and Kalbsbraten, and Dorothea, and Klingenspohr her husband."

"He with the cut across the nose, is it?" cries Blake. "I know him well, and his old wife."

"His old what, sir!" cries Fitz-Boodle, jumping up from his seat. "Klingenspohr's wife old!—Is he married again?—Is Dorothea, then, d-d-dead?"

"Dead!—no more dead than you are, only I take her to be five-and-thirty. And when a woman has had nine children, you know, she looks none the younger; and I

can tell ye, that when she trod on my corruns at a ball
at the Grand Juke's, I felt something heavier than a
feather on my foot."

"Madame de Klingenspohr, then," replied I, hesitating somewhat, "has grown rather—rather st-st-out?"
I could hardly get out the *out,* and trembled I don't
know why as I asked the question.

"Stout, begad!—she weighs fourteen stone, saddle
and bridle. That's right, down goes my pipe; flop!
crash falls the tumbler into the fender! Break away,
my boy, and remember, whoever breaks a glass here pays
a dozen."

The fact was, that the announcement of Dorothea's
changed condition caused no small disturbance within
me, and I expressed it in the abrupt manner mentioned
by young Blake.

Roused thus from my reverie, I questioned the young
fellow about his residence at Kalbsbraten, which has
been always since the war a favourite place for our
young gentry, and heard with some satisfaction that
Potzdorff was married to the Behrenstein, Haarbart
had left the dragoons, the Crown Prince had broken
with the—but mum! of what interest are all these
details to the reader, who has never been at friendly little
Kalbsbraten?

Presently Lynch reaches me down one of the three
books that formed his library (the "Racing Calendar"
and a book of fishing-flies making up the remainder of
the set). "And there's my album," says he. "You'll
find plenty of hands in it that you'll recognize, as you
are an old Pumpernickelaner." And so I did, in truth:
it was a little book after the fashion of German albums,
in which good simple little ledger every friend or
acquaintance of the owner inscribes a poem or stanza

from some favourite poet or philosopher with the transcriber's own name, as thus:—

> " To the true house-friend, and beloved Irelandish youth.
>> " ' *Sera nunquam est ad bonos mores via.*'
>>> WACKERBART, Professor at the
>> Grand-Ducal Kalbsbraten-Pumpernickelisch Gymnasium."

Another writes,—

> " ' *Wander on roses and forget me not.*'
>> AMALIA V. NACHTMUTZE,
>> GEB. V. SCHLAFROCK,"

with a flourish, and the picture mayhap of a rose. Let the reader imagine some hundreds of these interesting inscriptions, and he will have an idea of the book.

Turning over the leaves I came presently on *Dorothea's* hand. There it was, the little neat, pretty handwriting, the dear old up-and-down-strokes that I had not looked at for many a long year,—the Mediterranean heath, which grew on the sunniest banks of Fitz-Boodle's existence, and here found, dear, dear little sprig! in rude Galwagian bog-lands.

"Look at the other side of the page," says Lynch, rather sarcastically (for I don't care to confess that I kissed the name of "Dorothea v. Klingenspohr, born v. Speck" written under an extremely feeble passage of verse). "Look at the other side of the paper!"

I did, and what do you think I saw?

I saw the writing of five of the little Klingenspohrs, who have all sprung up since my time.

*   *   *   *   *

"Ha! ha! haw!" screamed the impertinent young Irishman, and the story was all over Connemara and Joyce's Country in a day after.

CHAPTER II

OTTILIA IN PARTICULAR

SOME kind critic who peruses these writings will, doubtless, have the goodness to point out that the simile of the Mediterranean heath is applied to two personages in this chapter—to Ottilia and Dorothea, and say, Psha! the fellow is but a poor unimaginative creature not to be able to find a simile apiece at least for the girls; how much better would *we* have done the business!

Well, it is a very pretty simile. The girls were rivals, were beautiful, I loved them both,—which should have the sprig of heath? Mr. Cruikshank (who has taken to serious painting) is getting ready for the exhibition a fine piece, representing Fitz-Boodle on the Urrisbeg Mountain, county Galway, Ireland, with a sprig of heath in his hand, hesitating, like Paris, on which of the beauties he should bestow it. In the background is a certain animal between two bundles of hay; but that I take to represent the critic, puzzled to which of my young beauties to assign the choice.

If Dorothea had been as rich as Miss Coutts, and had come to me the next day after the accident at the ball and said, "George, will you marry me?" it must not be supposed I would have done any such thing. *That* dream had vanished for ever: rage and pride took the place of love; and the only chance I had of recovering from my dreadful discomfiture was by bearing it

bravely, and trying, if possible, to awaken a little compassion in my favour. I limped home (arranging my
scheme with great presence of mind as I actually sat
spinning there on the ground) — I limped home, sent for
Pflastersticken, the court-surgeon, and addressed him
to the following effect: "Pflastersticken," says I,
"there has been an accident at court of which you will
hear. You will send in leeches, pills, and the deuce
knows what, and you will say that I have dislocated
my leg: for some days you will state that I am in
considerable danger. You are a good fellow and a
man of courage I know, for which very reason you can
appreciate those qualities in another; so mind, if you
breathe a word of my secret, either you or I must lose a
life."

Away went the surgeon, and the next day all Kalbsbraten knew that I was on the point of death: I had been
delirious all night, had had eighty leeches, besides I
don't know how much medicine; but the Kalsbrateners
knew to a scruple. Whenever anybody was ill, this little
kind society knew what medicines were prescribed.
Everybody in the town knew what everybody had for
dinner. If Madame Rumpel had her satin dyed ever so
quietly, the whole society was on the *qui vive;* if Countess Pultuski sent to Berlin for a new set of teeth, not a
person in Kalbsbraten but what was ready to compliment her as she put them on; if Potzdorff paid his
tailor's bill, or Muffinstein bought a piece of black wax
for his moustaches, it was the talk of the little city.
And so, of course, was my accident. In their sorrow for
my misfortune, Dorothea's was quite forgotten, and
those eighty leeches saved me. I became interesting; I
had cards left at my door; and I kept my room for a

fortnight, during which time I read every one of M. Kotzebue's plays.

At the end of that period I was convalescent, though still a little lame. I called at old Speck's house and apologized for my clumsiness, with the most admirable coolness; I appeared at court, and stated calmly that I did not intend to dance any more; and when Klingenspohr grinned, I told that young gentleman such a piece of my mind as led to his wearing a large sticking-plaster patch on his nose: which was split as neatly down the middle as you would split an orange at dessert. In a word, what man could do to repair my defeat, I did.

There is but one thing now of which I am ashamed—of those killing epigrams which I wrote (*mon Dieu!* must I own it?—but even the fury of my anger proves the extent of my love!) against the Speck family. They were handed about in confidence at court, and made a frightful sensation:

"*Is it possible?*

"There happened at Schloss P–mp–rn–ckel,
    A strange mishap our sides to tickle,
        And set the people in a roar;—
    A strange caprice of Fortune fickle:
I never thought at Pumpernickel
        To see a SPECK *upon the floor!* "

"*La Perfide Albion; or, a Caution to Waltzers.*

    " ' Come to the dance,' the Briton said,
        And forward D–r–th–a led,
            Fair, fresh, and three-and-twenty!
        Ah, girls, beware of Britons red!
        What wonder that it *turned her head?*
        SAT VERBUM SAPIENTI."

> " *Reasons for not Marrying.*
>
> " ' The lovely Miss S.
> Will surely say " yes,"
> You've only to ask and try ; '
> ' That subject we'll quit,'
> Says Georgy the wit,
> ' *I've a much better* SPEC *in my eye!* ' "

This last epigram especially was voted so killing that it flew like wildfire; and I know for a fact that our Chargé-d'Affaires at Kalbsbraten sent a courier express with it to the Foreign Office in England, whence, through our amiable Foreign Secretary, Lord P-l-m-rston, it made its way into every fashionable circle: nay, I have reason to believe caused a smile on the cheek of R-y-lty itself. Now that Time has taken away the sting of these epigrams, there can be no harm in giving them; and 'twas well enough then to endeavour to hide under the lash of wit the bitter pangs of humiliation: but my heart bleeds now to think that I should have ever brought a tear on the gentle cheek of Dorothea.

Not content with this—with humiliating her by satire, and with wounding her accepted lover across the nose— I determined to carry my revenge still farther, and to fall in love with somebody else. This person was Ottilia v. Schlippenschlopp.

Otho Sigismund Freyherr von Schlippenschlopp, Knight Grand Cross of the Ducal Order of the Two-Necked Swan of Pumpernickel, of the Porc-et-Siflet of Kalbsbraten, Commander of the George and Blue-Boar of Dummerland, Excellency, and High Chancellor of the United Duchies, lived in the second floor of a house in the Schwapsgasse; where, with his private income and

his revenues as Chancellor, amounting together to some
300*l.* per annum, he maintained such a state as very few
other officers of the Grand-Ducal Crown could exhibit.
The Baron is married to Maria Antoinetta, a Countess
of the house of Kartoffelstadt, branches of which have
taken root all over Germany. He has no sons, and but
one daughter, the Fräulein OTTILIA.

The Chancellor is a worthy old gentleman, too fat
and wheezy to preside at the Privy Council, fond of his
pipe, his ease, and his rubber. His lady is a very tall and
pale Roman-nosed Countess, who looks as gentle as Mrs.
Robert Roy, where, in the novel, she is for putting
Baillie Nicol Jarvie into the lake, and who keeps the
honest Chancellor in the greatest order. The Fräulein
Ottilia had not arrived at Kalbsbraten when the little
affair between me and Dorothea was going on; or rather
had only just come in for the conclusion of it, being presented for the first time that year at the ball where I—
where I met with my accident.

At the time when the Countess was young, it was not
the fashion in her country to educate the young ladies
so highly as since they have been educated; and provided
they could waltz, sew, and make puddings, they were
thought to be decently bred; being seldom called upon
for algebra or Sanscrit in the discharge of the honest
duties of their lives. But Fräulein Ottilia was of the
modern school in this respect, and came back from her
pension at Strasburg speaking all the languages, dab-
bling in all the sciences: an historian, a poet,—a blue
of the ultramarinest sort, in a word. What a difference
there was, for instance, between poor, simple Dorothea's
love of novel-reading and the profound encyclopædic
learning of Ottilia!

Before the latter arrived from Strasburg (where she had been under the care of her aunt the canoness, Countess Ottilia of Kartoffelstadt, to whom I here beg to offer my humblest respects), Dorothea had passed for a *bel esprit* in the little court circle, and her little simple stock of accomplishments had amused us all very well. She used to sing "Herz, mein Herz" and "T'en souviens-tu," in a decent manner (*once,* before heaven, I thought her singing better than Grisi's), and then she had a little album in which she drew flowers, and used to embroider slippers wonderfully, and was very merry at a game of loto or forfeits, and had a hundred small *agrémens de société* which rendered her an acceptable member of it.

But when Ottilia arrived, poor Dolly's reputation was crushed in a month. The former wrote poems both in French and German; she painted landscapes and portraits in real oil; and she twanged off a rattling piece of Liszt or Kalkbrenner in such a brilliant way, that Dora scarcely dared to touch the instrument after her, or venture, after Ottilia had trilled and gurgled through "Una voce," or "Di piacer" (Rossini was in fashion then), to lift up her little modest pipe in a ballad. What was the use of the poor thing going to sit in the park, where so many of the young officers used ever to gather round her? Whirr! Ottilia went by galloping on a chestnut mare with a groom after her, and presently all the young fellows who could buy or hire horseflesh were prancing in her train.

When they met, Ottilia would bounce towards her soul's darling, and put her hands round her waist, and call her by a thousand affectionate names, and then talk of her as only ladies or authors can talk of one another.

How tenderly she would hint at Dora's little imperfections of education!—how cleverly she would insinuate that the poor girl had no wit! and, thank God, no more she had. The fact is, that do what I will I see I'm in love with her still, and would be if she had fifty children; but my passion blinded me *then,* and every arrow that fiery Ottilia discharged I marked with savage joy. Dolly, thank heaven, didn't mind the wit much; she was too simple for that. But still the recurrence of it would leave in her heart a vague, indefinite feeling of pain, and somehow she began to understand that her empire was passing away, and that her dear friend hated her like poison; and so she married Klingenspohr. I have written myself almost into a reconciliation with the silly fellow; for the truth is, he has been a good, honest husband to her, and she has children, and makes puddings, and is happy.

Ottilia was pale and delicate. She wore her glistening black hair in bands, and dressed in vapoury white muslin. She sang her own words to her harp, and they commonly insinuated that she was alone in the world,— that she suffered some inexpressible and mysterious heart-pangs, the lot of all finer geniuses,—that though she lived and moved in the world she was not of it,— that she was of a consumptive tendency and might look for a premature interment. She even had fixed on the spot where she should lie: the violets grew there, she said, the river went moaning by; the grey willow whispered sadly over her head, and her heart pined to be at rest. "Mother," she would say, turning to her parent, "promise me—promise me to lay me in that spot when the parting hour has come!" At which Madame de Schlippenschlopp would shriek, and grasp her in her arms; and at which, I confess, I would myself blubber like a child.   She had six darling friends at school, and every courier from Kalbsbraten carried off whole reams of her letter-paper.

In Kalbsbraten, as in every other German town, there are a vast number of literary characters, of whom our young friend quickly became the chief.   They set up a literary journal, which appeared once a week, upon light-blue or primrose paper, and which, in compliment to the lovely Ottilia's maternal name, was called the *Kartoffelnkranz.*   Here are a couple of her ballads extracted from the *Kranz,* and by far the most cheerful specimen of her style.   For in her songs she never would willingly let off the heroines without a suicide or a consumption.   She never would hear of such a thing as a happy marriage, and had an appetite for grief quite amazing in so young a person.   As for her dying and desiring to be buried under the willow-tree, of which the first ballad is the subject, though I believed the story then, I have at present some doubts about it.   For, since the publication of my Memoirs, I have been thrown much into the society of literary persons (who admire my style hugely), and egad! though some of them are dismal enough in their works, I find them in their persons the least sentimental class that ever a gentleman fell in with.

" THE WILLOW-TREE

" Know ye the willow-tree
   Whose grey leaves quiver,
Whispering gloomily
   To yon pale river?
Lady, at even-tide
   Wander not near it:
They say its branches hide
   A sad, lost spirit!

" Once to the willow-tree
   A maid came fearful,
Pale seemed her cheek to be,
   Her blue eye tearful;
Soon as she saw the tree,
   Her step moved fleeter.
No one was there—ah me!
   No one to meet her!

" Quick beat her heart to hear
    The far bell's chime
Toll from the chapel-tower
    The trysting time:
But the red sun went down
    In golden flame,
And though she looked round,
    Yet no one came!

" Presently came the night,
    Sadly to greet her,—
Moon in her silver light,
    Stars in their glitter.
Then sank the moon away
    Under the billow,
Still wept the maid alone—
    There by the willow!

" Through the long darkness,
    By the stream rolling,
Hour after hour went on
    Tolling and tolling.

Long was the darkness,
    Lonely and stilly;
Shrill came the night-wind,
    Piercing and chilly.

" Shrill blew the morning breeze,
    Biting and cold,
Bleak peers the grey dawn
    Over the wold.
Bleak over moor and stream
    Looks the grey dawn,
Grey, with dishevelled hair,
Still stands the willow there—
    THE MAID IS GONE!

  " *Domine, Domine!*
      Sing we a litany,—
Sing for poor maiden-hearts
    broken and weary;
    Domine, Domine!
      Sing we a litany,
Wail we and weep we a wild
    Miserere! "

One of the chief beauties of this ballad (for the translation of which I received some well-merited compliments) is the delicate way in which the suicide of the poor young woman under the willow-tree is hinted at; for that she threw herself into the water and became one among the lilies of the stream, is as clear as a pikestaff. Her suicide is committed some time in the darkness, when the slow hours move on tolling and tolling, and is hinted at darkly as befits the time and the deed.

But that unromantic brute, Van Cutsem, the Dutch Chargé-d'Affaires, sent to the *Kartoffelnkranz* of the week after a conclusion of the ballad, which shows what a poor creature he must be. His pretext for writing it was, he said, because he could not bear such melancholy endings to poems and young women, and therefore he submitted the following lines:—

I

" Long by the willow-trees
   Vainly they sought her,
Wild rang the mother's screams
   O'er the grey water:
' Where is my lovely one?
   Where is my daughter?

II

" ' Rouse thee, Sir Constable—
   Rouse thee and look;
Fisherman, bring your net,
   Boatman, your hook.
Beat in the lily-beds,
   Dive in the brook!'

III

" Vainly the constable
   Shouted and called her;
Vainly the fisherman
   Beat the green alder;
Vainly he flung the net,
   Never it hauled her!

IV

" Mother, beside the fire
   Sat, her nightcap in;
Father, in easy-chair,
   Gloomily napping;
When at the window-sill
   Came a light tapping!

V

" And a pale countenance
   Looked through the case-
     ment.
Loud beat the mother's heart,
   Sick with amazement;
And at the vision, which
   Came to surprise her,
Shrieked in an agony—
   ' Lor '! it's Elizar!'

VI

" Yes, 'twas Elizabeth—
   Yes, 'twas their girl;
Pale was her cheek, and her
   Hair out of curl.
' Mother!' the loving one,
   Blushing, exclaimed,
' Let not your innocent
   Lizzy be blamed.

VII

" ' Yesterday, going to aunt
   Jones's to tea,
Mother, dear mother, I
   Forgot the door-key!
And as the night was cold,
   And the way steep,
Mrs. Jones kept me to
   Breakfast and sleep.'

VIII

" Whether her Pa and Ma
Fully believed her,
That we shall never know:
Stern they received her;
And for the work of that
Cruel, though short,
night,
Sent her to bed without
Tea for a fortnight.

IX

" MORAL

" *Hey diddle diddlety,*
Cat and the Fiddlety,
Maidens of England, take
caution by she!
Let love and suicide
Never tempt you aside,
And always remember to take
the door-key! "

Some people laughed at this parody, and even preferred it to the original; but for myself I have no patience with the individual who can turn the finest sentiments of our nature into ridicule, and make everything
sacred a subject of scorn. The next ballad is less
gloomy than that of the willow-tree, and in it the lovely
writer expresses her longing for what has charmed us
all, and, as it were, squeezes the whole spirit of the fairy
tale into a few stanzas:—

" FAIRY DAYS

" Beside the old hall-fire—upon my nurse's knee,
Of happy fairy days—what tales were told to me!
I thought the world was once—all peopled with princesses,
And my heart would beat to hear—their loves and their dis-
tresses;
And many a quiet night,—in slumber sweet and deep,
The pretty fairy people—would visit me in sleep.

" I saw them in my dreams—come flying east and west,
With wondrous fairy gifts—the new-born babe they bless'd;
One has brought a jewel—and one a crown of gold,
And once has brought a curse—but she is wrinkled and old.

The gentle queen turns pale—to hear those words of sin,
But the king he only laughs—and bids the dance begin.

" The babe has grown to be—the fairest of the land
And rides the forest green—a hawk upon her hand.
An ambling palfrey white—a golden robe and crown;
I've seen her in my dreams—riding up and down;
And heard the ogre laugh—as she fell into his snare,
At the little tender creature—who wept and tore her hair!

" But ever when it seemed—her need was at the sorest
A prince in shining mail—comes prancing through the forest.
A waving ostrich-plume—a buckler burnished bright;
I've seen him in my dreams—good sooth! a gallant knight.
His lips are coral red—beneath a dark moustache;
See how he waves his hand—and how his blue eyes flash!

" ' Come forth, thou Paynim knight!'—he shouts in accents
    clear.
The giant and the maid—both tremble his voice to hear.
Saint Mary guard him well!—he draws his falchion keen,
The giant and the knight—are fighting on the green.
I see them in my dreams—his blade gives stroke on stroke,
The giant pants and reels—and tumbles like an oak!

" With what a blushing grace—he falls upon his knee
And takes the lady's hand—and whispers, ' You are free!'
Ah! happy childish tales—of knight and faërie!
I waken from my dreams—but there's ne'er a knight for me;
I waken from my dreams—and wish that I could be
A child by the old hall-fire—upon my nurse's knee."

Indeed, Ottilia looked like a fairy herself: pale, small,
slim, and airy. You could not see her face, as it were,
for her eyes, which were so wild, and so tender, and

shone so that they would have dazzled an eagle, much more a poor goose of a Fitz-Boodle. In the theatre, when she sat on the opposite side of the house, those big eyes used to pursue me as I sat pretending to listen to the "Zauberflöte," or to "Don Carlos," or "Egmont," and at the tender passages, especially, they would have such a winning, weeping, imploring look with them as flesh and blood could not bear.

Shall I tell how I became a poet for the dear girl's sake? 'Tis surely unnecessary after the reader has perused the above versions of her poems. Shall I tell what wild follies I committed in prose as well as in verse? how I used to watch under her window of icy evenings, and with chilblainy fingers sing serenades to her on the guitar? Shall I tell how, in a sledging-party, I had the happiness to drive her, and of the delightful privilege which is, on these occasions, accorded to the driver?

Any reader who has spent a winter in Germany perhaps knows it. A large party of a score or more of sledges is formed. Away they go to some pleasure-house that has been previously fixed upon, where a ball and collation are prepared, and where each man, as his partner descends, has the delicious privilege of saluting her. O heavens and earth! I may grow to be a thousand years old, but I can never forget the rapture of that salute.

"The keen air has given me an appetite," said the dear angel, as we entered the supper-room; and to say the truth, fairy as she was, she made a remarkably good meal—consuming a couple of basins of white soup, several kinds of German sausages, some Westphalia ham, some white puddings, an anchovy-salad made with corn-

ichons and onions, sweets innumerable, and a considerable quantity of old Steinwein and rum-punch afterwards.   Then she got up and danced as brisk as a fairy;
in which operation I of course did not follow her, but
had the honour, at the close of the evening's amusement,
once more to have her by my side in the sledge, as we
swept in the moonlight over the snow.

Kalbsbraten is a very hospitable place as far as tea-
parties are concerned, but I never was in one where dinners were so scarce.   At the palace they occurred twice
or thrice in a month; but on these occasions spinsters
were not invited, and I seldom had the opportunity of
seeing my Ottilia except at evening-parties.

Nor are these, if the truth must be told, very much to
my taste.   Dancing I have forsworn, whist is too severe
a study for me, and I do not like to play écarté with old
ladies, who are sure to cheat you in the course of an
evening's play.

But to have an occasional glance at Ottilia was
enough; and many and many a napoleon did I lose to
her mamma, Madame de Schlippenschlopp, for the blest
privilege of looking at her daughter.   Many is the tea-
party I went to, shivering into cold clothes after dinner
(which is my abomination) in order to have one little
look at the lady of my soul.

At these parties there were generally refreshments of
a nature more substantial than mere tea—punch, both
milk and rum, hot wine, *consommé,* and a peculiar and
exceedingly disagreeable sandwich made of a mixture
of cold white puddings and garlic, of which I have forgotten the name, and always detested the savour.

Gradually a conviction came upon me that Ottilia *ate
a great deal.*

I do not dislike to see a woman eat comfortably.   I even think that an agreeable woman ought to be *friande,* and should love certain little dishes and knickknacks.   I know that though at dinner they commonly take nothing, they have had roast-mutton with the children at two, and laugh at their pretensions to starvation.

No! a woman who eats a grain of rice, like Amina in the "Arabian Nights," is absurd and unnatural; but there is a *modus in rebus:* there is no reason why she should be a ghoul, a monster, an ogress, a horrid gormandiseress—faugh!

It was, then, with a rage amounting almost to agony, that I found Ottilia ate too much at every meal.   She was always eating, and always eating too much.   If I went there in the morning, there was the horrid familiar odour of those oniony sandwiches; if in the afternoon, dinner had been just removed, and I was choked by reeking reminiscences of roast-meat.   Tea we have spoken of.   She gobbled up more cakes than any six people present; then came the supper and the sandwiches again, and the egg-flip and the horrible rum-punch.

She was as thin as ever—paler if possible than ever: —but, by heavens! *her nose began to grow red!*

Mon Dieu! how I used to watch and watch it!   Some days it was purple, some days had more of the vermilion —I could take an affidavit that after a heavy night's supper it was more swollen, more red than before.

I recollect one night when we were playing a round game (I had been looking at her nose very eagerly and sadly for some time), she of herself brought up the conversation about eating, and confessed that she had five meals a day.

"That accounts for it!" says I, flinging down the cards, and springing up and rushing like a madman out

of the room. I rushed away into the night, and wrestled with my passion. "What! Marry," said I, "a woman who eats meat twenty-one times in a week, besides breakfast and tea? Marry a sarcophagus, a cannibal, a butcher's shop?—Away!" I strove and strove. I drank, I groaned, I wrestled and fought with my love —but it overcame me: one look of those eyes brought me to her feet again. I yielded myself up like a slave; I fawned and whined for her; I thought her nose was not so *very* red.

Things came to this pitch that I sounded his Highness's Minister to know whether he would give me service in the Duchy; I thought of purchasing an estate there. I was given to understand that I should get a chamberlain's key and some post of honour did I choose to remain, and I even wrote home to my brother Tom in England, hinting a change in my condition.

At this juncture the town of Hamburg sent his Highness the Grand Duke (*àpropos* of a commercial union which was pending between the two States) a singular present: no less than a certain number of barrels of oysters, which are considered extreme luxuries in Germany, especially in the inland parts of the country, where they are almost unknown.

In honour of the oysters and the new commercial treaty (which arrived in *fourgons* despatched for the purpose), his Highness announced a grand supper and ball, and invited all the quality of all the principalities round about. It was a splendid affair: the grand saloon brilliant with hundreds of uniforms and brilliant toilettes—not the least beautiful among them, I need not say, was Ottilia.

At midnight the supper-rooms were thrown open, and we formed into little parties of six, each having a table, nobly served with plate, a lacquey in attendance, and a gratifying ice-pail or two of champagne to *égayer* the supper. It was no small cost to serve five hundred people on silver, and the repast was certainly a princely and magnificent one.

I had, of course, arranged with Mademoiselle de Schlippenschlopp. Captains Frumpel and Fridelberger of the Duke's Guard, Mesdames de Butterbrod and Bopp, formed our little party.

The first course, of course, consisted of *the oysters.* Ottilia's eyes gleamed with double brilliancy as the lacquey opened them. There were nine apiece for us—how well I recollect the number!

I never was much of an oyster-eater, nor can I relish them *in naturalibus* as some do, but require a quantity of sauces, lemons, cayenne peppers, bread and butter, and so forth, to render them palatable.

By the time I had made my preparations, Ottilia, the Captains, and the two ladies, had well-nigh finished theirs. Indeed Ottilia had gobbled up all hers, and there were only my nine left in the dish.

I took one—IT WAS BAD. The scent of it was enough, —they were all bad. Ottilia had eaten nine bad oysters.

I put down the horrid shell. Her eyes glistened more and more; she could not take them off the tray.

"Dear Herr George," she said, "*will you give me your oysters?*"

*   *   *   *   *
*   *   *   *   *

She had them all down—before—I could say—Jack—Robinson!

*   *   *   *   *

I left Kalbsbraten that night, and have never been there since.

FITZ-BOODLE'S PROFESSIONS

BEING APPEALS TO THE UNEMPLOYED YOUNGER SONS OF THE NOBILITY

FIRST PROFESSION

THE fair and honest proposition in which I offered to communicate privately with parents and guardians, relative to two new and lucrative professions which I had discovered, has, I find from the publisher, elicited not one single inquiry from those personages, who I can't but think are very little careful of their children's welfare to allow such a chance to be thrown away. It is not for myself I speak, as my conscience proudly tells me; for though I actually gave up Ascot in order to be in the way should any father of a family be inclined to treat with me regarding my discoveries, yet I am grieved, not on my own account, but on theirs, and for the wretched penny-wise policy that has held them back.

That they must feel an interest in my announcement is unquestionable. Look at the way in which the public prints of all parties have noticed my appearance in the character of a literary man! Putting aside my personal narrative, look at the offer I made to the nation,—a choice of no less than two new professions! Suppose I had invented as many new kinds of butcher's-meat; does any one pretend that the world, tired as it is of the perpetual recurrence of beef, mutton, veal, cold beef, cold veal, cold mutton, hashed ditto, would not have jumped eagerly at the delightful intelligence that their old, stale, stupid meals were about to be varied at last?

Of course people would have come forward. I should have had deputations from Mr. Gibletts and the fashionable butchers of this world; petitions would have poured in from Whitechapel salesmen; the speculators panting to know the discovery; the cautious with stock in hand eager to bribe me to silence and prevent the certain depreciation of the goods which they already possessed. I should have dealt with them, not greedily or rapaciously, but on honest principles of fair barter. "Gentlemen," I should have said, or rather, "Gents"— which affectionate diminutive is, I am given to understand, at present much in use among commercial persons—"Gents, my researches, my genius, or my good fortune, have brought me to the valuable discovery about which you are come to treat. Will you purchase it outright, or will you give the discoverer an honest share of the profits resulting from your speculation? My position in the world puts *me* out of the power of executing the vast plan I have formed, but 'twill be a certain fortune to him who engages in it; and why should not I, too, participate in that fortune?"

Such would have been my manner of dealing with the world, too, with regard to my discovery of the new professions. Does not the world want new professions? Are there not thousands of well-educated men panting, struggling, pushing, starving, in the old ones? Grim tenants of chambers looking out for attorneys who never come?—wretched physicians practising the stale joke of being called out of church until people no longer think fit even to laugh or to pity? Are there not hoary-headed midshipmen, antique ensigns growing mouldy upon fifty years' half-pay? Nay, are there not men who would pay anything to be employed rather than re-main idle? But such is the glut of professionals, the horrible cut-throat competition among them, that there is no chance for one in a thousand, be he ever so willing, or brave, or clever: in the great ocean of life he makes a few strokes, and puffs, and sputters, and sinks, and the innumerable waves overwhelm him and he is heard of no more.

Walking to my banker's t'other day—and I pledge my sacred honour this story is true—I met a young fel-low whom I had known *attaché* to an embassy abroad, a young man of tolerable parts, unwearied patience, with some fortune too, and, moreover, allied to a noble Whig family, whose interest had procured him his ap-pointment to the legation at Krähwinkel, where I knew him. He remained for ten years a diplomatic charac-ter; he was the working-man of the legation: he sent over the most diffuse translations of the German papers for the use of the Foreign Secretary: he signed pass-ports with most astonishing ardour; he exiled himself for ten long years in a wretched German town, dancing attendance at court-balls and paying no end of money for uniforms. And for what? At the end of the ten years—during which period of labour he never received a single shilling from the Government which employed him (rascally spendthrift of a Government, *va!*),—he was offered the paid *attachéship* to the court of H. M. the King of the Mosquito Islands, and refused that ap-pointment a week before the Whig Ministry retired. Then he knew that there was no further chance for him,

and incontinently quitted the diplomatic service for ever,
and I have no doubt will sell his uniform a bargain.
The Government had *him* a bargain certainly; nor is he
by any means the first person who has been sold at that
price.

Well, my worthy friend met me in the street and informed me of these facts with a smiling countenance,—
which I thought a masterpiece of diplomacy. Fortune
had been labouring and kicking him for ten whole years,
and here he was grinning in my face: could Monsieur
de Talleyrand have acted better? "I have given up diplomacy," said Protocol, quite simply and good-hu-
mouredly, "for between you and me, my good fellow,
it's a very slow profession; sure perhaps, but slow. But
though I gained no actual pecuniary remuneration in
the service, I have learned all the languages in Europe,
which will be invaluable to me in my new profession—
the mercantile one—in which directly I looked out for a
post I found one."

"What! and a good pay?" said I.

"Why, no; that's absurd, you know. No young
men, strangers to business, are paid much to speak of.
Besides, I don't look to a paltry clerk's pay. Some day,
when thoroughly acquainted with the business (I shall
learn it in about seven years), I shall go into a good
house with my capital and become junior partner."

"And meanwhile?"

"Meanwhile I conduct the foreign correspondence
of the eminent house of Jam, Ram, and Johnson; and
very heavy it is, I can tell you. From nine till six every
day, except foreign post days, and then from nine till
eleven. Dirty dark court to sit in; snobs to talk to,—
great change, as you may fancy."

"And you do all this for nothing?"

"I do it to learn the business." And so saying Protocol gave me a knowing nod and went his way.

Good heavens! I thought, and is this a true story? Are there hundreds of young men in a similar situation at the present day, giving away the best years of their youth for the sake of a mere windy hope of something in old age, and dying before they come to the goal? In seven years he hopes to have a business, and then to have the pleasure of risking his money? He will be admitted into some great house as a particular favour, and three months after the house will fail. Has it not happened to a thousand of our acquaintance? I thought I would run after him and tell him about the new professions that I have invented.

"Oh! ay! those you wrote about in *Fraser's Magazine.* Egad! George, Necessity makes strange fellows of us all. Who would ever have thought of you *spelling,* much more writing?"

"Never mind that. Will you, if I tell you of a new profession that, with a little cleverness and instruction from me, you may bring to a most successful end—will you, I say, make me a fair return?"

"My dear creature," replied young Protocol, "what nonsense you talk! I saw that very humbug in the Magazine. You say you have made a great discovery —very good; you puff your discovery—very right; you ask money for it—nothing can be more reasonable; and then you say that you intend to make your discovery public in the next number of the Magazine. Do you think I will be such a fool as to give you money for a thing which I can have next month for nothing? Good-by, George my boy; the *next* discovery you make I'll tell you how to get a better price for it." And with this the fellow walked off, looking supremely knowing and clever.

This tale of the person I have called Protocol is not told without a purpose, you may be sure. In the first place, it shows what are the reasons that nobody has made application to me concerning the new professions, namely, because I have passed my word to make them known in this Magazine, which persons may have for the purchasing, stealing, borrowing, or hiring, and, therefore, they will never think of applying personally to me. And, secondly, his story proves also my assertion, viz. that all professions are most cruelly crowded at present, and that men will make the most absurd outlay and sacrifices for the smallest chance of success at some future period. Well, then, I will be a benefactor to my race, if I cannot be to one single member of it, whom I love better than most men. What I have discovered I will make known; there shall be no shilly-shallying work here, no circumlocution, no bottle-conjuring business. But oh! I wish for all our sakes that I had had an opportunity to impart the secret to one or two persons only; for, after all, but one or two can live in the manner I would suggest. And when the discovery is made known, I am sure ten thousand will try. The rascals! I can see their brass-plates gleaming over scores of doors. Competition will ruin my professions, as it has all others.

It must be premised that the two professions are intended for gentlemen, and gentlemen only—men of birth and education. No others could support the parts which they will be called upon to play.

And, likewise, it must be honestly confessed that these

professions have, to a certain degree, been exercised before. Do not cry out at this and say it is no discovery! I say it *is* a discovery. It is a discovery if I show you— a gentleman—a profession which you may exercise without derogation, or loss of standing, with certain profit, nay, possibly with honour, and of which, until the reading of this present page, you never thought but as of a calling beneath your rank and quite below your reach. Sir, I do not mean to say that I create a profession. I cannot create gold; but if, when discovered, I find the means of putting it in your pocket, do I or do I not deserve credit?

I see you sneer contemptuously when I mention to you the word AUCTIONEER. "Is this all," you say, "that this fellow brags and prates about? An auctioneer forsooth! he might as well have 'invented' chimney-sweeping?"

No such thing. A little boy of seven, be he ever so low of birth, can do this as well as you. Do you suppose that little stolen Master Montague made a better sweeper than the lowest-bred chummy that yearly commemorates his release? No, sir. And he might have been ever so much a genius or a gentleman, and not have been able to make his trade respectable.

But all such trades as can be rendered decent the aristocracy has adopted one by one. At first they followed the profession of arms, flouting all others as unworthy, and thinking it ungentlemanlike to know how to read or write. They did not go into the church in very early days, till the money to be got from the church was strong enough to tempt them. It is but of later years that they have condescended to go to the bar, and since the same time only that we see some of them following trades.

I know an English lord's son who is, or was, a wine-
merchant (he may have been a bankrupt for what I
know).   As for bankers, several partners in banking-
houses have four balls to their coronets, and I have no
doubt that another sort of banking, viz. that practised
by gentlemen who lend small sums of money upon deposited securities, will be one day followed by the noble
order, so that they may have four balls on their coronets
and carriages, and three in front of their shops.

Yes, the nobles come peoplewards as the people, on
the other hand, rise and mingle with the nobles.   With
the *plebs,* of course, Fitz-Boodle, in whose veins flows
the blood of a thousand kings, can have nothing to do;
but, watching the progress of the world, 'tis impossible
to deny that the good old days of our race are passed
away.   We want money still as much as ever we did;
but we cannot go down from our castles with horse and
sword and waylay fat merchants—no, no, confounded
new policemen and the assize-courts prevent that.
Younger brothers cannot be pages to noble houses, as
of old they were, serving gentle dames without disgrace,
handing my lord's rose-water to wash, or holding his stirrup as he mounted for the chase.   A page, forsooth!   A
pretty figure would George Fitz-Boodle or any other
man of fashion cut, in a jacket covered with sugar-
loafed buttons, and handing in penny-post notes on a
silver tray.   The *plebs* have robbed us of *that* trade
among others: nor, I confess, do I much grudge them
their *trouvaille.*   Neither can we collect together a few
scores of free lances, like honest Hugh Calverly in the
Black Prince's time, or brave Harry Butler of Wallen-
stein's dragoons, and serve this or that prince, Peter the
Cruel or Henry of Trastamare, Gustavus or the Em-

peror, at our leisure; or, in default of service, fight and rob on our own gallant account, as the good gentlemen of old did. Alas! no. In South America or Texas, perhaps, a man might have a chance that way; but in the ancient world no man can fight except in the king's service (and a mighty bad service that is too), and the lowest European sovereign, were it Baldomero Espartero himself, would think nothing of seizing the best-born condottiere that ever drew sword, and shooting him down like the vulgarest deserter.

What, then, is to be done? We must discover fresh fields of enterprise—of peaceable and commercial enterprise in a peaceful and commercial age. I say, then, that the auctioneer's pulpit has never yet been ascended by a scion of the aristocracy, and am prepared to prove that they might scale it, and do so with dignity and profit.

For the auctioneer's pulpit is just the peculiar place where a man of social refinement, of elegant wit, of polite perceptions, can bring his wit, his eloquence, his taste, and his experience of life, most delightfully into play. It is not like the bar, where the better and higher qualities of a man of fashion find no room for exercise. In defending John Jorrocks in an action of trespass, for cutting down a stick in Sam Snooks's field, what powers of mind do you require?—powers of mind, that is, which Mr. Serjeant Snorter, a butcher's son with a great loud voice, a sizar at Cambridge, a wrangler, and so forth, does not possess as well as yourself? Snorter has never been in decent society in his life. He thinks the bar-mess the most fashionable assemblage in Europe, and the jokes of "grand day" the *ne plus ultra* of wit. Snorter lives near Russell Square, eats beef and York-

shire-pudding, is a judge of port-wine, is in all social
respects your inferior.   Well, it is ten to one but in the
case of Snooks *v.* Jorrocks, before mentioned, he will be
a better advocate than you; he knows the law of the case
entirely, and better probably than you.   He can speak
long, loud, to the point, grammatically—more grammatically than you, no doubt, will condescend to do.   In
the case of Snooks *v.* Jorrocks he is all that can be desired.   And so about dry disputes, respecting real property, he knows the law; and, beyond this, has no more
need to be a gentleman than my body-servant has—who,
by the way, from constant intercourse with the best
society, *is* almost a gentleman.   But this is apart from
the question.

Now, in the matter of auctioneering, this, I apprehend, is not the case, and I assert that a high-bred gentleman, with good powers of mind and speech, must,
in such a profession, make a fortune.   I do not mean in
all auctioneering matters.   I do not mean that such a
person should be called upon to sell the good-will of a
public-house, or discourse about the value of the beer-
barrels, or bars with pewter fittings, or the beauty of a
trade doing a stroke of so many hogsheads a week.   I
do not ask a gentleman to go down and sell pigs,
ploughs, and cart-horses, at Stoke Pogis; or to enlarge
at the Auction-Rooms, Wapping, upon the beauty of
the "Lively Sally" schooner.   These articles of com-
merce or use can be better appreciated by persons in a
different rank of life to his.

But there are a thousand cases in which a gentleman
only can do justice to the sale of objects which the necessity or convenience of the genteel world may require to
change hands.   All articles properly called of taste

should be put under his charge.   Pictures,—he is a travelled man, has seen and judged the best galleries of Europe, and can speak of them as a common person cannot.
For, mark you, you must have the confidence of your
society, you must be able to be familiar with them, to
plant a happy *mot* in a graceful manner, to appeal to
my lord or the duchess in such a modest, easy, pleasant
way as that her grace should not be hurt by your allusion to her—nay, amused (like the rest of the company)
by the manner in which it was done.

What is more disgusting that the familiarity of a
snob?   What more loathsome than the swaggering
quackery of some present holders of the hammer?
There was a late sale, for instance, which made some
noise in the world (I mean the late Lord Gimcrack's, at
Dilberry Hill).   Ah! what an opportunity was lost
there!   I declare solemnly that I believe, but for the
absurd quackery and braggadocio of the advertisements, much more money would have been bid; people
were kept away by the vulgar trumpeting of the auctioneer, and could not help thinking the things were
worthless that were so outrageously lauded.

They say that sort of Bartholomew-fair advocacy (in
which people are invited to an entertainment by the
medium of a hoarse yelling beef-eater, twenty-four
drums, and a jack-pudding turning head over heels) is
absolutely necessary to excite the public attention.
What an error!   I say that the refined individual so ac-
costed is more likely to close his ears, and, shuddering,
run away from the booth.   Poor Horace Waddle-
poodle! to think that thy gentle accumulation of brica-
brac should have passed away in such a manner! by
means of a man who brings down a butterfly with a

blunderbuss, and talks of a pin's head through a speaking-trumpet! Why, the auctioneer's very voice was enough to crack the Sèvres porcelain and blow the lace into annihilation. Let it be remembered that I speak of the gentleman in his public character merely, meaning to insinuate nothing more than I would by stating that Lord Brougham speaks with a northern accent, or that the voice of Mr. Sheil is sometimes unpleasantly shrill.

Now the character I have formed to myself of a great auctioneer is this. I fancy him a man of first-rate and irreproachable birth and fashion. I fancy his person so agreeable that it must be a pleasure for ladies to behold and tailors to dress it. As a private man he must move in the very best society, which will flock round his pulpit when he mounts it in his public calling. It will be a privilege for vulgar people to attend the hall where he lectures; and they will consider it an honour to be allowed to pay their money for articles the value of which is stamped by his high recommendation. Nor can such a person be a mere fribble; nor can any loose hanger-on of fashion imagine he may assume the character. The gentleman auctioneer must be an artist above all, adoring his profession; and adoring it, what must he not know? He must have a good knowledge of the history and language of all nations; not the knowledge of the mere critical scholar, but of the lively and elegant man of the world. He will not commit the gross blunders of pronunciation that untravelled Englishmen perpetrate; he will not degrade his subject by coarse eulogy, or sicken his audience with vulgar banter. He will know where to apply praise and wit properly; he will have the tact only acquired in good society, and know where a joke is in place, and how far a compliment may go. He will not outrageously and indiscriminately laud all objects committed to his charge, for he knows the value of praise; that diamonds, could we have them by the bushel, would be used as coals; that, above all, he has a character of sincerity to support; that he is not merely the advocate of the person who employs him, but that the public is his client too, who honours him and confides in him. Ask him to sell a copy of Raffaelle for an original; a trumpery modern Brussels counterfeit for real old Mechlin; some common French forged crockery for the old delightful, delicate, Dresden china; and he will quit you with scorn, or order his servant to show you the door of his study.

Study, by the way,—no, "study" is a vulgar word; every word is vulgar which a man uses to give the world an exaggerated notion of himself or his condition. When the wretched bagman, brought up to give evidence before Judge Coltman, was asked what his trade was, and replied that "he represented the house of Dobson and Hobson," he showed himself to be a vulgar, mean-souled wretch, and was most properly reprimanded by his lordship. To be a bagman is to be humble, but not of necessity vulgar. Pomposity is vulgar, to ape a higher rank than your own is vulgar, for an ensign of militia to call himself captain is vulgar, or for a bagman to style himself the "representative" of Dobson and Hobson. The honest auctioneer, then, will not call his room his study; but his "private room," or his office, or whatever may be the phrase commonly used among auctioneers.

He will not for the same reason call himself (as once in a momentary feeling of pride and enthusiasm for the profession I thought he should)—he will not call himself an "advocate," but an auctioneer. There is no need to attempt to awe people by big titles: let each man bear his own name without shame. And a very gentlemanlike and agreeable, though exceptional position (for it is clear that there cannot be more than two of the class,) may the auctioneer occupy.

He must not sacrifice his honesty, then, either for his own sake or his clients', in any way, nor tell fibs about himself or them. He is by no means called upon to draw the long bow in their behalf; all that his office obliges him to do—and let us hope his disposition will lead him to do it also—is to take a favourable, kindly, philanthropic view of the world; to say what can fairly be said by a good-natured and ingenious man in praise of any article for which he is desirous to awaken public sympathy. And how readily and pleasantly may this be done! I will take upon myself, for instance, to write an eulogium upon So-and-So's last novel, which shall be every word of it true; and which work, though to some discontented spirits it might appear dull, may be shown to be really amusing and instructive,—nay, *is* amusing and instructive,—to those who have the art of discovering where those precious qualities lie.

An auctioneer should have the organ of truth large; of imagination and comparison, considerable; of wit, great; of benevolence, excessively large.

And how happy might such a man be, and cause others to be! He should go through the world laughing, merry, observant, kind-hearted. He should love everything in the world, because his profession regards everything. With books of lighter literature (for I do not recommend the genteel auctioneer to meddle with heavy

antiquarian and philological works) he should be elegantly conversant, being able to give a neat history of
the author, a pretty sparkling kind criticism of the work,
and an appropriate eulogium upon the binding, which
would make those people read who never read before;
or buy, at least, which is his first consideration.   Of pictures we have already spoken.   Of china, of jewellery,
of gold-headed canes, valuable arms, picturesque an-
tiquities, with what eloquent *entrainement* might he not
speak!   He feels every one of these things in his heart.
He has all the tastes of the fashionable world.   Dr.
Meyrick cannot be more enthusiastic about an old suit
of armour than he; Sir Harris Nicolas not more eloquent regarding the gallant times in which it was worn,
and the brave histories connected with it.   He takes up
a pearl necklace with as much delight as any beauty who
was sighing to wear it round her own snowy throat, and
hugs a china monster with as much joy as the oldest
duchess could do.   Nor must he affect these things; he
must feel them.   He is a glass in which all the tastes
of fashion are reflected.   He must be every one of the
characters to whom he addresses himself—a genteel
Goethe or Shakspeare, a fashionable world-spirit.

How can a man be all this and not be a gentleman;
and not have had an education in the midst of the best
company—an insight into the most delicate feelings,
and wants, and usages?   The pulpit oratory of such a
man would be invaluable; people would flock to listen to
him from far and near.   He might out of a single teacup
cause streams of world-philosophy to flow, which would
be drunk in by grateful thousands; and draw out of an
old pincushion points of wit, morals, and experience,
that would make a nation wise.

Look round, examine THE ANNALS OF AUCTIONS, as Mr. Robins remarks, and (with every respect for him and his brethren) say, is there in the profession SUCH A MAN? Do we want such a man? Is such a man likely or not likely to make an immense fortune? Can we get such a man except out of the very best society, and among the most favoured there?

Everybody answers "No!" I knew you would answer no. And now, gentlemen who have laughed at my pretension to discover a profession, say, have I not? I have laid my finger upon the spot where the social deficit exists. I have shown that we labour under a want; and when the world wants, do we not know that a man will step forth to fill the vacant space that Fate has left for him? Pass we now to the—

SECOND PROFESSION

THIS profession, too, is a great, lofty, and exceptional one, and discovered by me considering these things, and deeply musing upon the necessities of society. Nor let honourable gentlemen imagine that I am enabled to offer them in this profession, more than any other, a promise of what is called future glory, deathless fame, and so forth. All that I say is, that I can put young men in the way of making a comfortable livelihood, and leaving behind them, not a name, but what is better, a decent maintenance to their children. Fitz-Boodle is as good a name as any in England. General Fitz-Boodle, who, in Marlborough's time, and in conjunction with the famous Van Slaap, beat the French in the famous action of Vischzouchee, near Mardyk, in Holland, on the 14th of February, 1709, is promised an immortality upon his tomb in Westminster Abbey; but he died of apoplexy, deucedly in debt, two years afterwards: and what after that is the use of a name?

No, no; the age of chivalry is past. Take the twenty-four first men who come into the club, and ask who they are, and how they made their money? There's Woolsey-Sackville: his father was Lord Chancellor, and sat on the woolsack, whence he took his title; his grandfather dealt in coal-sacks, and not in wool-sacks, —small coal-sacks, dribbling out little supplies of black diamonds to the poor.   Yonder comes Frank Leveson, in a huge broad-brimmed hat, his shirt-cuffs turned up to his elbows.   Leveson is as gentlemanly a fellow as the world contains, and if he has a fault, is perhaps too finikin.   Well, you fancy him related to the Sutherland family: nor, indeed, does honest Frank deny it; but *entre nous,* my good sir, his father was an attorney, and his grandfather a bailiff in Chancery Lane, bearing a name still older than that of Leveson, namely, Levy. So it is that this confounded equality grows and grows, and has laid the good old nobility by the heels.   Look at that venerable Sir Charles Kitely, of Kitely Park: he is interested about the Ashantees, and is just come from Exeter Hall.   Kitely discounted bills in the City in the year 1787, and gained his baronetcy by a loan to the French princes.   All these points of history are perfectly well known; and do you fancy the world cares? Psha!   Profession is no disgrace to a man: be what you like, provided you succeed.   If Mr. Fauntleroy could come to life with a million of money, you and I would dine with him: you know we would; for why should we be better than our neighbours?

Put, then, out of your head the idea that this or that profession is unworthy of you: take any that may bring you profit, and thank him that puts you in the way of being rich.

The profession I would urge (upon a person duly qualified to undertake it) has, I confess, at the first glance, something ridiculous about it; and will not appear to young ladies so romantic as the calling of a gallant soldier, blazing with glory, gold lace, and vermilion coats; or a dear delightful clergyman, with a sweet blue eye, and a pocket-handkerchief scented charmingly with

lavender-water.   The profession I allude to *will,* I own,
be to young women disagreeable, to sober men trivial,
to great stupid moralists unworthy.

But mark my words for it, that in the religious world
(I have once or twice, by mistake no doubt, had the
honour of dining in "serious" houses, and can vouch
for the fact that the dinners there are of excellent quality) — in the serious world, in the great mercantile world,
among the legal community (notorious feeders), in
every house in town (except some half-dozen which can
afford to do without such aid), the man I propose might
speedily render himself indispensable.

Does the reader now begin to take?   Have I hinted
enough for him that he may see with eagle glance the
immense beauty of the profession I am about to unfold
to him?   We have all seen Gunter and Chevet; Fre-
goso, on the Puerta del Sol (a relation of the ex-Minis-
ter Calomarde), is a good purveyor enough for the benighted olla-eaters of Madrid; nor have I any fault to
find with Guimard, a Frenchman, who has lately set up
in the Toledo, at Naples, where he furnishes people with
decent food.   It has given me pleasure, too, in walking
about London — in the Strand, in Oxford Street, and
elsewhere, to see fournisseurs and comestible-merchants
newly set up.   Messrs. Morell have excellent articles in
their warehouses; Fortnum and Mason are known to
most of my readers.

But what is not known, what is wanted, what is lan-
guished for in England is *a dinner-master,* — a gentleman who is not a provider of meat or wine, like the
parties before named, who can have no earthly interest
in the price of truffled turkeys or dry champagne beyond that legitimate interest which he may feel for his

client, and which leads him to see that the latter is not
cheated by his tradesmen.   For the dinner-giver is almost naturally an ignorant man.   How in mercy's
name can Mr. Serjeant Snorter, who is all day at Westminster, or in chambers, know possibly the mysteries,
the delicacy, of dinner-giving?   How can Alderman
Pogson know anything beyond the fact that venison is
good with currant-jelly, and that he likes lots of green
fat with his turtle?   Snorter knows law, Pogson is acquainted with the state of the tallow-market; but what
should he know of eating, like you and me, who have
given up our time to it?   (I say *me* only familiarly, for
I have only reached so far in the science as to know that
I know nothing.)   But men there are, gifted individuals, who have spent years of deep thought—not merely
intervals of labour, but hours of study every day—over
the gormandizing science,—who, like alchemists, have
let their fortunes go, guinea by guinea, into the all-
devouring pot,—who, ruined as they sometimes are,
never get a guinea by chance but they will have a plate
of pease in May with it, or a little feast of ortolans, or
a piece of Glo'ster salmon, or one more flask from their
favourite claret-bin.

It is not the ruined gastronomist that I would advise
a person to select as his *table-master;* for the opportunities of peculation would be too great in a position of
such confidence—such complete abandonment of one
man to another.   A ruined man would be making bargains with the tradesmen.   They would offer to cash
bills for him, or send him opportune presents of wine,
which he could convert into money, or bribe him in one
way or another.   Let this be done, and the profession
of table-master is ruined.   Snorter and Pogson may

almost as well order their own dinners, as be at the mercy of a "gastronomic agent" whose faith is not beyond all question.

A vulgar mind, in reply to these remarks regarding the gastronomic ignorance of Snorter and Pogson, might say, "True, these gentlemen know nothing of household economy, being occupied with other more important business elsewhere. But what are their wives about? Lady Pogson in Harley Street has nothing earthly to do but to mind her poodle, and her mantua-maker's and housekeeper's bills. Mrs. Snorter in Bedford Place, when she has taken her drive in the Park with the young ladies, may surely have time to attend to her husband's guests and preside over the preparations of his kitchen, as she does worthily at his hospitable mahogany." To this I answer, that a man who expects a woman to understand the philosophy of dinner-giving, shows the strongest evidence of a low mind. He is unjust towards that lovely and delicate creature, woman, to suppose that she heartily understands and cares for what she eats and drinks. No: taken as a rule, women have no real appetites. They are children in the gormandizing way; loving sugar, sops, tarts, trifles, apricot-creams, and such gewgaws. They would take a sip of Malmsey, and would drink currant-wine just as happily, if that accursed liquor were presented to them by the butler. Did you ever know a woman who could lay her fair hand upon her gentle heart and say on her conscience that she preferred dry sillery to sparkling champagne? Such a phenomenon does not exist. They are not made for eating and drinking; or, if they make a pretence to it, become downright odious. Nor can they, I am sure, witness the preparations of a really

great repast without a certain jealousy.   They grudge
spending money (ask guards, coachmen, inn-waiters,
whether this be not the case).   They will give their
all, heaven bless them! to serve a son, a grandson, or a
dear relative, but they have not the heart to pay for
small things magnificently.   They are jealous of good
dinners, and no wonder.   I have shown in a former discourse how they are jealous of smoking, and other personal enjoyments of the male.   I say, then, that Lady
Pogson or Mrs. Snorter can never conduct their husbands' table properly.   Fancy either of them consenting
to allow a calf to be stewed down into gravy for one
dish, or a dozen hares to be sacrificed to a single *purée*
of game, or the best Madeira to be used for a sauce, or
half-a-dozen of champagne to boil a ham in.   They will
be for bringing a bottle of Marsala in place of the old
particular, or for having the ham cooked in water.   But
of these matters—of kitchen philosophy—I have no
practical or theoretic knowledge; and must beg pardon if, only understanding the goodness of a dish when
cooked, I may have unconsciously made some blunder
regarding the preparation.

Let it, then, be set down as an axiom, without further
trouble of demonstration, that a woman is a bad din-
ner-caterer; either too great and simple for it, or too
mean—I don't know which it is; and gentlemen,
according as they admire or contemn the sex, may
settle that matter their own way.   In brief, the mental constitution of lovely woman is such that she cannot give a great dinner.   It must be done by a man.
It can't be done by an ordinary man, because he does
not understand it.   Vain fool! and he sends off to
the pastrycook in Great Russell Street or Baker Street,

he lays on a couple of extra waiters (green-grocers in the neighbourhood), he makes a great pother with his butler in the cellar, and fancies he has done the business.

Bon Dieu! Who has not been at those dinners?—those monstrous exhibitions of the pastrycook's art? Who does not know those made dishes with the universal sauce to each: fricandeaux, sweet-breads, damp dumpy cutlets, &c., seasoned with the compound of grease, onions, bad port-wine, cayenne pepper, curry-powder (Warren's blacking, for what I know, but the taste is always the same) —there they lie in the old corner dishes, the poor wiry Moselle and sparkling Burgundy in the ice-coolers, and the old story of white and brown soup, turbot, little smelts, boiled turkey, saddle-of-mutton, and so forth?" "Try a little of that fricandeau," says Mrs. Snorter, with a kind smile. "You'll find it, I think, very nice." Be sure it has come in a green tray from Great Russell Street. "Mr. Fitz-Boodle, you have been in Germany," cries Snorter, knowingly; "taste the hock, and tell me what you think of *that.*"

How should he know better, poor benighted creature; or she, dear good soul that she is? If they would have a leg-of-mutton and an apple-pudding, and a glass of sherry and port (or simple brandy-and-water called by its own name) after dinner, all would be very well; but they must shine, they must dine as their neighbours. There is no difference in the style of dinners in London; people with five hundred a year treat you exactly as those of five thousand. They *will* have their Moselle or hock, their fatal side-dishes brought in the green trays from the pastrycook's.

Well, there is no harm done; not as regards the dinner-givers at least, though the dinner-eaters may have to suffer somewhat; it only shows that the former are hospitably inclined, and wish to do the very best in their power,—good honest fellows! If they do wrong, how can they help it? they know no better.

And now, is it not as clear as the sun at noon-day, that A WANT exists in London for a superintendent of the table—a gastronomic agent—a dinner-master, as I have called him before? A man of such a profession would be a metropolitan benefit; hundreds of thousands of people of the respectable sort, people in white waistcoats, would thank him daily. Calculate how many dinners are given in the City of London, and calculate the numbers of benedictions that "the Agency" might win.

And as no doubt the observant man of the world has remarked that the freeborn Englishman of the respectable class is, of all others, the most slavish and truckling to a lord; that there is no fly-blown peer but he is pleased to have him at his table, proud beyond measure to call him by his surname (without the lordly prefix); and that those lords whom he does not know, he yet (the freeborn Englishman) takes care to have their pedigrees and ages by heart from his world-bible, the "Peerage:" as this is an indisputable fact, and as it is in this particular class of Britons that our agent must look to find clients, I need not say it is necessary that the agent should be as high-born as possible, and that he should be able to tack, if possible, an honourable or some other handle to his respectable name. He must have it on his professional card—

$$\boxed{\begin{array}{c} \text{The Honourable George Gormand Gobbleton,} \\ \textit{Apician Chambers, Pall Mall.} \end{array}}$$

Or,

$$\boxed{\begin{array}{c} \text{Sir Augustus Carver Cramley Cramley,} \\ \textit{Amphitryonic Council Office, Swallow Street.} \end{array}}$$

or, in some such neat way, Gothic letters on a large handsome crockeryware card, with possibly a gilt coat-of-arms and supporters, or the blood-red hand of baronetcy duly displayed. Depend on it plenty of guineas will fall in it, and that Gobbleton's supporters will support him comfortably enough.

For this profession is not like that of the auctioneer, which I take to be a far more noble one, because more varied and more truthful; but in the Agency case, a little humbug at least is necessary. A man cannot be a successful agent by the mere force of his simple merit or genius in eating and drinking. He must of necessity impose upon the vulgar to a certain degree. He must be of that rank which will lead them naturally to respect him, otherwise they might be led to jeer at his profession; but let a noble exercise it, and bless your soul, all the " Court Guide " is dumb!

He will then give out in a manly and somewhat pompous address what has before been mentioned, namely, that he has seen the fatal way in which the hospitality of

England has been perverted hitherto, *accaparé*'d by a few cooks with green trays. (He must use a good deal of French in his language, for that is considered very gentlemanlike by vulgar people.) He will take a set of chambers in Carlton Gardens, which will be richly though severely furnished, and the door of which will be opened by a French valet (he *must* be a Frenchman, remember), who will say, on letting Mr. Snorter or Sir Benjamin Pogson in, that "*Milor* is at home." Pogson will then be shown into a library furnished with massive book-cases, containing all the works on cookery and wines (the titles of them) in all the known languages in the world. Any books, of course, will do, as you will have them handsomely bound, and keep them under plate-glass. On a side-table will be little sample-bottles of wines, a few truffles on a white porcelain saucer, a prodigious strawberry or two, perhaps, at the time when such fruit costs much money. On the library will be busts marked Ude, Carême, Béchamel, in marble (never mind what heads, of course); and, perhaps, on the clock should be a figure of the Prince of Condé's cook killing himself because the fish had not arrived in time: there may be a wreath of *immortelles* on the figure to give it a more decidedly Frenchified air. The walls will be of a dark rich paper, hung round with neat gilt frames, containing plans of *menus* of various great dinners, those of Cambacères, Napoleon, Louis XIV., Louis XVIII., Heliogabalus if you like, each signed by the respective cook.

After the stranger has looked about him at these things, which he does not understand in the least, especially the truffles, which look like dirty potatoes, you will make your appearance, dressed in a dark dress, with one handsome enormous gold chain, and one large diamond ring; a gold snuff-box, of course, which you will thrust into the visitor's paw before saying a word. You will be yourself a portly grave man, with your hair a little bald and grey. In fact, in this, as in all other professions, you had best try to look as like Canning as you can.

When Pogson has done sneezing with the snuff, you will say to him, "Take a *fauteuil*. I have the honour of addressing Sir Benjamin Pogson, I believe?" And then you will explain to him your system.

This, of course, must vary with every person you address. But let us lay down a few of the heads of a plan which may be useful, or may be modified infinitely, or may be cast aside altogether, just as circumstances dictate. After all *I* am not going to turn gastronomic agent, and speak only for the benefit perhaps of the very person who is reading this:—

"SYNOPSIS OF THE GASTRONOMIC AGENCY OF THE HONOURABLE GEORGE GOBBLETON

"THE Gastronomic Agent having traversed Europe, and dined with the best society of the world, has been led naturally, as a patriot, to turn his thoughts homeward, and cannot but deplore the lamentable ignorance regarding gastronomy displayed in a country for which Nature has done almost everything.

"But it is ever singularly thus. Inherent ignorance belongs to man; and The Agent, in his Continental travels, has always remarked, that the countries most fertile in themselves were invariably worse tilled than those more barren. The Italians and the Spaniards leave their fields to Nature, as we leave our vegetables, fish and meat. And, heavens! what richness do we fling away,—

what dormant qualities in our dishes do we disregard,—
what glorious gastronomic crops (if The Agent may be
permitted the expression)—what glorious gastronomic
crops do we sacrifice, allowing our goodly meats and
fishes to lie fallow! 'Chance,' it is said by an ingenious
historian, who, having been long a secretary in the East
India House, must certainly have had access to the best
information upon Eastern matters—'Chance,' it is said
by Mr. Charles Lamb, 'which burnt down a Chinaman's
house, with a litter of sucking-pigs that were unable to
escape from the interior, discovered to the world the ex-
cellence of roast-pig.' Gunpowder, we know, was invented by a similar fortuity." [The reader will observe
that my style in the supposed character of a Gastronomic Agent is purposely pompous and loud.] "So, 'tis
said, was printing,—so glass.—We should have drunk
our wine poisoned with the villainous odour of the bora-
chio, had not some Eastern merchants, lighting their
fires in the Desert, marked the strange composition
which now glitters on our sideboards, and holds the
costly produce of our vines.

"We have spoken of the natural riches of a country.
Let the reader think but for one moment of the gastronomic wealth of our country of England, and he will be
lost in thankful amazement as he watches the astonishing riches poured out upon us from Nature's bounteous
cornucopia! Look at our fisheries!—the trout and
salmon tossing in our brawling streams; the white and
full-breasted turbot struggling in the mariner's net; the
purple lobster lured by hopes of greed into his basket-
prison, which he quits only for the red ordeal of the pot.
Look at whitebait, great heavens!—look at whitebait,
and a thousand frisking, glittering, silvery things be-

sides, which the nymphs of our native streams bear kindly
to the deities of our kitchens—our kitchens such as they
are.

"And though it may be said that other countries produce the freckle-backed salmon and the dark broad-shoul-
dered turbot; though trout frequent many a stream beside those of England, and lobsters sprawl on other
sands than ours; yet, let it be remembered, that our native country possesses these altogether, while other lands
only know them separately; that, above all, whitebait is
peculiarly our country's—our city's own! Blessings and
eternal praises be on it, and, of course, on brown bread
and butter! And the Briton should further remember,
with honest pride and thankfulness, the situation of his
capital, of London: the lordly turtle floats from the sea
into the stream, and from the stream to the city; the
rapid fleets of all the world *se donnent rendezvous* in
the docks of our silvery Thames; the produce of our
coasts and provincial cities, east and west, is borne to us
on the swift lines of lightning railroads. In a word—
and no man but one who, like The Agent, has travelled
Europe over, can appreciate the gift—there is no city on
earth's surface so well supplied with fish as London!

"With respect to our meats, all praise is supereroga-
tory. Ask the wretched hunter of *chevreuil,* the poor
devourer of *rehbraten,* what they think of the noble English haunch, that, after bounding in the Park of Knole
or Windsor, exposes its magnificent flank upon some
broad silver platter at our tables? It is enough to say of
foreign venison, that *they are obliged to lard it.* Away!
ours is the palm of roast; whether of the crisp mutton
that crops the thymy herbage of our downs, or the noble
ox who revels on lush Althorpian oil-cakes. What game

is like to ours? Mans excels us in poultry, 'tis true; but
'tis only in merry England that the partridge has a fla-
vour, that the turkey can almost *se passer de truffes,*
that the jolly juicy goose can be eaten as he deserves.

" Our vegetables, moreover, surpass all comment; Art
(by the means of glass) has wrung fruit out of the
bosom of Nature, such as she grants to no other clime.
And if we have no vineyards on our hills, we have gold
to purchase their best produce. Nature, and enterprise
that masters Nature, have done everything for our land.

" But, with all these prodigious riches in our power,
is it not painful to reflect how absurdly we employ them?
Can we say that we are in the habit of dining well? Alas,
no! and The Agent, roaming o'er foreign lands, and
seeing how, with small means and great ingenuity and
perseverance, great ends were effected, comes back sadly
to his own country, whose wealth he sees absurdly
wasted, whose energies are misdirected, and whose vast
capabilities are allowed to lie idle. * * *" [Here
should follow what I have only hinted at previously, a
vivid and terrible picture of the degradation of our table.] " * * * Oh, for a master spirit, to give an im-
petus to the land, to see its great power directed in the
right way, and its wealth not squandered or hidden, but
nobly put out to interest and spent!

" The Agent dares not hope to win that proud station
—to be the destroyer of a barbarous system wallowing
in abusive prodigality—to become a dietetic reformer—
the Luther of the table.

" But convinced of the wrongs which exist, he will do
his humble endeavour to set them right, and to those who
know that they are ignorant (and this is a vast step to
knowledge) he offers his counsels, his active co-opera-

tion, his frank and kindly sympathy.   The Agent's
qualifications are these:—

"1. He is of one of the best families in England; and
has in himself, or through his ancestors, been accustomed
to good living for centuries.   In the reign of Henry V.,
his maternal great-great-grandfather, Roger de Go-
bylton" [*the name may be varied, of course, or the
king's reign, or the dish invented*], "was the first who
discovered the method of roasting a peacock whole, with
his tail-feathers displayed; and the dish was served to
the two kings at Rouen.   Sir Walter Cramley, in Elizabeth's reign, produced before her Majesty, when at Kill-
ingworth Castle, mackerel with the famous *gooseberry
sauce,* &c.

"2. He has, through life, devoted himself to no other
study than that of the table: and has visited to that end
the courts of all the monarchs of Europe: taking the re-
ceipts of the cooks, with whom he lives on terms of intimate friendship, often at enormous expense to himself.

"3. He has the same acquaintance with all the vin-
tages of the Continent; having passed the autumn of
1811 (the comet year) on the great Weinberg of Johan-
nisberg; being employed similarly at Bordeaux, in 1834;
at Oporto, in 1820; and at Xeres de la Frontera, with his
excellent friends, Duff, Gordon and Co., the year after.
He travelled to India and back in company with fourteen pipes of Madeira (on board of the ' Samuel Snob '
East Indiaman, Captain Scuttler), and spent the vin-
tage season in the island, with unlimited powers of observation granted to him by the great houses there.

"4. He has attended Mr. Groves of Charing Cross,
and Mr. Giblett of Bond Street, in a course of purchases
of fish and meat; and is able at a glance to recognize the

age of mutton, the primeness of beef, the firmness and freshness of fish of all kinds.

"5. He has visited the parks, the grouse-manors, and the principal gardens of England, in a similar professional point of view."

The Agent then, through his subordinates, engages to provide gentlemen who are about to give dinner-parties—

"1. With cooks to dress the dinners; a list of which gentlemen he has by him, and will recommend none who are not worthy of the strictest confidence.

"2. With a *menu* for the table, according to the price which the Amphitryon chooses to incur.

"3. He will, through correspondences with the various fournisseurs of the metropolis, provide them with viands, fruit, wine, &c., sending to Paris, if need be, where he has a regular correspondence with Messrs. Chevet.

"4. He has a list of dexterous table-waiters (all answering to the name of John for fear of mistakes, the butler's name to be settled according to pleasure), and would strongly recommend that the servants of the house should be locked in the back-kitchen or servants' hall during the time the dinner takes place.

"5. He will receive and examine all the accounts of the fournisseurs,—of course pledging his honour as a gentleman not to receive one shilling of paltry gratification from the tradesmen he employs, but to see that the bills are more moderate, and their goods of better quality, than they would provide to any person of less experience than himself.

"6. His fee for superintending a dinner will be five

guineas: and The Agent entreats his clients to trust *entirely* to him and his subordinates for the arrangement of the repast,—*not to think* of inserting dishes of their own invention, or producing wine from their own cellars, as he engages to have it brought in the best order, and fit for immediate drinking. Should the Amphitryon, however, desire some particular dish or wine, he must consult The Agent, in the first case by writing, in the second, by sending a sample to The Agent's chambers. For it is manifest that the whole complexion of a dinner may be altered by the insertion of a single dish; and, therefore, parties will do well to mention their wishes on the first interview with The Agent. He cannot be called upon to recompose his bill of fare, except at great risk to the *ensemble* of the dinner and enormous inconvenience to himself.

"7. The Agent will be at home for consultation from ten o'clock until two—earlier, if gentlemen who are engaged at early hours in the City desire to have an interview: and be it remembered, that a *personal interview* is always the best: for it is greatly necessary to know not only the number but the character of the guests whom the Amphitryon proposes to entertain,—whether they are fond of any particular wine or dish, what is their state of health, rank, style, profession, &c.

"8. At two o'clock, he will commence his rounds; for as the metropolis is wide, it is clear that he must be early in the field in some districts. From 2 to 3 he will be in Russell Square and the neighbourhood; 3 to 3¾, Harley Street, Portland Place, Cavendish Square, and the environs; 3¾ to 4¼, Portman Square, Gloucester Place, Baker Street, &c.; 4¼ to 5, the new district about Hyde Park Terrace; 5 to 5¾, St. John's Wood and the Regent's Park. He will be in Grosvenor Square by 6, and in Belgrave Square, Pimlico, and its vicinity, by 7. Parties there are requested not to dine until 8 o'clock; and The Agent, once for all, peremptorily announces that he will NOT go to the palace, where it is utterly impossible to serve a good dinner."

"TO TRADESMEN

"EVERY Monday evening during the season the Gastronomic Agent proposes to give a series of trial-dinners, to which the principal gourmands of the metropolis, and a few of The Agent's most respectable clients, will be invited. Covers will be laid for *ten* at nine o'clock precisely. And as The Agent does not propose to exact a single shilling of profit from their bills, and as his recommendation will be of infinite value to them, the tradesmen he employs will furnish the weekly dinner gratis. Cooks will attend (who have acknowledged characters) upon the same terms. To save trouble, a book will be kept where butchers, poulterers, fishmongers, &c. may inscribe their names in order, taking it by turns to supply the trial-table. Wine-merchants will naturally compete every week promiscuously, sending what they consider their best samples, and leaving with the hall-porter tickets of the prices. Confectionery to be done out of the house. Fruiterers, market-men, as butchers and poulterers. The Agent's *maître-d'hôtel* will give a receipt to each individual for the articles he produces; and let all remember that The Agent is a *very keen judge,* and woe betide those who serve him or his clients ill!

"GEORGE GORMAND GOBBLETON.

"*Carlton Gardens, June* 10, 1842."

Here I have sketched out the heads of such an address as I conceive a gastronomic agent might put forth; and appeal pretty confidently to the British public regarding its merits and my own discovery. If this be not a profession—a new one—a feasible one—a lucrative one,—I don't know what is. Say that a man attends but fifteen dinners daily, that is seventy-five guineas, or five hundred and fifty pounds weekly, or fourteen thousand three hundred pounds for a season of six months: and how many of our younger sons have such a capital even? Let, then, some unemployed gentleman with the requisite qualifications come forward. It will not be necessary that he should have done all that is stated in the prospectus; but, at any rate, let him *say* he has: there can't be much harm in an innocent fib of that sort; for the gastronomic agent must be a sort of dinner-pope, whose opinions cannot be supposed to err.

And as he really will be an excellent judge of eating and drinking, and will bring his whole mind to bear upon the question, and will speedily acquire an experience which no person out of the profession can possibly have; and as, moreover, he will be an honourable man, not practising upon his client in any way, or demanding sixpence beyond his just fee, the world will gain vastly by the coming forward of such a person,—gain in good dinners, and absolutely save money: for what is five guineas for a dinner of sixteen? The sum may be *gaspillé* by a cook-wench, or by one of those abominable before-named pastrycooks with their green trays.

If any man take up the business, he will invite me, of course, to the Monday dinners. Or does ingratitude go so far as that a man should forget the author of his good fortune? I believe it does. Turn we away from the sickening theme!

And now, having concluded my professions, how shall I express my obligations to the discriminating press of this country for the unanimous applause which hailed my first appearance? It is the more wonderful, as I pledge my sacred word, I never wrote a document before much longer than a laundress's bill, or the acceptance of an invitation to dinner. But enough of this egotism: thanks for praise conferred sound like vanity; gratitude is hard to speak of, and at present it swells the full heart of

GEORGE SAVAGE FITZ-BOODLE.

TALES

TALES

THE PROFESSOR

A TALE OF SENTIMENT

"Why, then, the World's mine oyster."

CHAPTER I

I HAVE often remarked that, among other ornaments and curiosities, Hackney contains more ladies'
schools than are to be found in almost any other village,
or indeed city, in Europe. In every green rustic lane,
to every tall old-fashioned house there is an iron gate, an
ensign of blue and gold, and a large brass plate, pro-
claiming that a ladies' seminary is established upon the
premises. On one of these plates is written— (or rather
was,—for the pathetic occurrence which I have to relate
took place many years ago) —on one of these plates, I
say, was engraven the following inscription:—

"BULGARIA HOUSE

Seminary for Young Ladies from three to twenty

BY THE MISSES PIDGE

(Please wipe your shoes.)"

The Misses Pidge took a limited number of young
ladies (as limited, in fact, or as large as the public
chose), and instructed them in those branches of elegant

349

and useful learning which make the British female so superior to all other shes. The younger ones learned the principles of back-stitch, cross-stitch, bob-stitch, Doctor Watts's Hymns, and " In my Cottage near a Wood." The elder pupils diverged at once from stitching and samplers: they played like Thalberg, and pirouetted like Taglioni; they learned geography, geology, mythology, entomology, modern history, and simple equations (Miss Z. Pidge) ; they obtained a complete knowledge of the French, German, and Italian tongues, not including English, taught by Miss Pidge; Poonah painting and tambour (Miss E. Pidge) ; Brice's questions and elocution (Miss F. Pidge) ; and, to crown all, dancing and gymnastics (which had a very flourishing look in the Pidge prospectus, and were printed in German text), DANCING and GYMNASTICS, we say, by Professor DAN-DOLO. The names of other professors and assistants followed in modester type.

Although the Signor's name was decidedly foreign, so English was his appearance, and so entirely did he disguise his accent, that it was impossible to tell of what place he was a native, if not of London, and of the very heart of it; for he had caught completely the peculiarities which distinguish the so-called Cockney part of the City, and obliterated his *h*'s and doubled his *v*'s, as if he had been for all his life in the neighbourhood of Bow bells. Signor Dandolo was a stout gentleman of five feet nine, with amazing expanse of mouth, chest, and whiskers, which latter were of a red hue.

I cannot tell how this individual first received an introduction to the academy of the Misses Pidge, and established himself there. Rumours say that Miss Zela Pidge at a Hackney ball first met him, and thus the

intimacy arose: but, since the circumstances took place
which I am about to relate, that young lady declares
that *she* was not the person who brought him to Bulgaria House,—nothing but the infatuation and entreat-
ies of Mrs. Alderman Grampus could ever have induced
her to receive him. The reader will gather from this,
that Dandolo's after-conduct at Miss Pidge's was not
satisfactory, nor was it; and may every mistress of such
an establishment remember that confidence can be sometimes misplaced; that friendship is frequently but another name for villainy.

But to our story. The stalwart and active Dandolo
delighted for some time the young ladies at Miss Pidge's
by the agility which he displayed in the dance, as well
as the strength and manliness of his form, as exhibited
in the new amusement which he taught. In a very short
time, Miss Binx, a stout young lady of seventeen, who
had never until his appearance walked half a mile without puffing like an apoplectic Lord Mayor, could dance
the cachuca, swarm up a pole with the agility of a cat,
and hold out a chair for three minutes without winking.
Miss Jacobs could very nearly climb through a ladder
(Jacob's ladder, he profanely called it); and Miss Bole
ring such changes upon the dumb-bells as might have
been heard at Edmonton, if the bells could have spoken.
But the most promising pupil of Professor Dandolo,
as indeed the fairest young creature in the establishment
of Bulgaria House, was Miss Adeliza Grampus, daughter of the alderman whose name we have mentioned.
The pride of her mother, the idol of her opulent father,
Adeliza Grampus was in her nineteenth year. Eyes
have often been described; but it would require bluer ink
than ours to depict the orbs of Adeliza. The snow when

it first falls in Cheapside is not whiter than her neck,—
when it has been for some days upon the ground, tram-
pled by dustmen and jarvies, trodden down by sweeps
and gentlemen going to business, not blacker than her
hair. Slim as the Monument on Fish Street Hill, her
form was slender and tall: but it is needless to recapitu-
late her charms, and difficult indeed to describe them.
Let the reader think of his first love, and fancy Adeliza.
Dandolo, who was employed to instruct her, saw her, and
fancied her too, as many a fellow of his inflammable
temperament would have done in his place.

There are few situations in life which can be so im-
proved by an enterprising mind as that of a dancing-
master,—I mean in a tender or amatory point of view.
The dancing-master has over the back, the hands, the
feet and shoulders of his pupils an absolute command;
and, being by nature endowed with so much authority,
can speedily spread his way from the limbs to the rest
of the body, and to the mind inclusive. *"Toes a little
more out, Miss Adeliza,"* cries he, with the tenderest air
in the world: "back a *little* more straight," and he gently
seizes her hand, he raises it considerably above the level
of her ear, he places the tips of his left-hand fingers
gently upon the young lady's spine, and in this seducing
attitude gazes tenderly into her eyes! I say that no
woman at any age can stand this attitude and this look,
especially when darted from such eyes as those of Dandolo. On the two first occasions when the adventurer
attempted this audacious manœuvre, his victim blushed
only, and trembled; on the third, she dropped her full
eyelids and turned ghastly pale. "A glass of water,"
cried Adeliza, "or I faint." The dancing-master has-
tened eagerly away to procure the desired beverage, and,

as he put it to her lips, whispered thrillingly in her ear, "Thine, thine for ever, Adeliza!"

Miss Grampus sank back in the arms of Miss Binx, but not before her raptured lover saw her eyes turning towards the ceiling, and her clammy lips whispering the name of "Dandolo."

When Madame Schroeder, in the opera of "Fidelio," cries, "Nichts, nichts, mein Florestan," it is as nothing compared to the tenderness with which Miss Grampus uttered that soft name.

"Dandolo!" would she repeat to her confidante, Miss Binx; "the name was beautiful and glorious in the olden days; five hundred years since, a myriad of voices shouted it in Venice, when one who bore it came forward to wed the sea—the doge's bride! the blue Adriatic! the boundless and eternal main! The frightened Turk shrank palsied at the sound; it was louder than the loudest of the cannon, or the stormy screaming of the tempest! Dandolo! How many brave hearts beat to hear that name! how many bright swords flashed forth at that resistless war cry! Oh, Binx!" would Adeliza continue, fondly pressing the arm of that young lady, "is it not passing strange that one of that mighty ducal race should have lived to this day, and lived to love *me?* But I, too," Adeliza would add archly, "am, as you know, a daughter of the sea."

The fact was, that the father of Miss Adeliza Grampus was a shell-fishmonger, which induced the young lady to describe herself as a daughter of Ocean. She received her romantic name from her mother, after reading Miss Swipes's celebrated novel of "Toby of Warsaw;" and had been fed from her youth upwards with so much similar literary ware, that her little mind had gone distracted. Her father had sent her from home at fifteen, because she had fallen in love with the young man who opened natives in the shop, and had vowed to slay herself with the oyster-knife; at Miss Pidge's her sentiment had not deserted her; she knew all Miss Landon by heart, had a lock of Mr. Thomas Moore's hair or wig, and read more novels and poetry than ever. And thus the red-haired dancing-master became in her eyes a Venetian nobleman, with whom it was her pride and pleasure to fall in love.

Being a parlour-boarder at Miss Pidge's seminary (a privilege which was acquired by paying five annual guineas extra), Miss Grampus was permitted certain liberties which were not accorded to scholars of the ordinary description. She and Miss Binx occasionally strolled into the village by themselves; they visited the library unattended; they went upon little messages for the Misses Pidge; they walked to church alone, either before or after the long row of young virgins who streamed out on every Sabbath day from between the filigree iron railings of Bulgaria House. It is my painful duty to state, that on several of these exclusive walks they were followed, or met, by the insidious and attentive teacher of gymnastics.

Soon Miss Binx would lag behind, and—shall I own it?—would make up for the lost society of her female friend by the company of a man, a friend of the professor, mysterious and agreeable as himself. May the mistresses of all the establishments for young ladies in this kingdom, or queendom rather, peruse this, and reflect how dangerous it is for young ladies of any age—ay, even for parlour-boarders—to go out alone! In the present instance Miss Grampus enjoyed a more than

ordinary liberty, it is true: when the elder Miss Pidge
would remonstrate, Miss Zela would anxiously yield
to her request; and why?—the reason may be gathered
from the following conversation which passed between
the infatuated girl and the wily *maître-de-danse.*

"How, Roderick," would Adeliza say, "how, in the
days of our first acquaintance, did it chance that you
always addressed yourself to that odious Zela Pidge,
and never deigned to breathe a syllable to me?"

"My lips didn't speak to you, Addly" (for to such
a pitch of familiarity had they arrived), "but my heyes
did."

Adeliza was not astonished by the peculiarity of his
pronunciation, for, to say truth, it was that commonly
adopted in her native home and circle. "And mine,"
said she, tenderly, "they followed when yours were not
fixed upon them, for *then* I dared not look upwards.
And though all on account of Miss Pidge you could not
hear the accents of my voice, you might have heard the
beatings of my heart!"

"I did, I did," gasped Roderick; "I 'eard them haud-
ibly. I never spoke to you then, for I feared to waken
that foul fiend sispicion. I wished to henter your seminary, to be continually near you, to make you love me;
therefore I wooed the easy and foolish Miss Pidge,
therefore I took upon me the disguise of—ha! ha!—
of a dancing-master." (And the young man's countenance assumed a grim and demoniac smile.) "Yes;
I degraded my name and my birthright—I wore these
ignoble trappings, and all for the love of thee, my
Adeliza!" Here Signor Dandolo would have knelt
down, but the road was muddy; and, his trousers being
of nankeen, his gallant purpose was frustrated.

But the story must out, for the conversation above narrated has betrayed to the intelligent reader a considerable part of it. The fact is, as we have said, that Miss Zela Pidge, dancing at the Hackney assembly, was introduced to this man; that he had no profession—no means even of subsistence; that he saw enough of this lady to be aware that he could make her useful to his purpose; and he who had been, we believe it in our conscience, no better than a travelling mountebank or harlequin, appeared at Bulgaria House in the character of a professor of gymnastics. The governess, in the first instance, entertained for him just such a *penchant* as the pupil afterwards felt: the latter discovered the weakness of her mistress, and hence arose Miss Pidge's indulgence, and Miss Grampus's fatal passion.

"Mysterious being!" continued Adeliza, resuming the conversation which has been broken by the above explanatory hints, "how did I learn to love thee? Who art thou?—what dire fate has brought thee hither in this lowly guise to win the heart of Adeliza?"

"Hadeliza," cried he, "you say well; *I am not what I seem.* I cannot tell thee what I am; a tale of horror, of crime, forbids the dreadful confession! But dark as I am, and wretched, nay, wicked and desperate, I love thee, Hadeliza—love thee with the rapturous devotion of purer days—the tenderness of happier times! I am sad now, and fallen, lady; suffice it that I once was happy, ay, respectable."

Adeliza's cheek grew deadly pale, her step faltered, and she would have fallen to the ground, had she not been restrained by the strong arm of her lover. "I know not," said she, as she clung timidly to his neck,—

> " I know not, I hask not, if guilt's in that art,
>   I know that I love thee, whatever thou hart."

"*Gilt* in my heart," said Dandolo, " gilt in the heart of Roderick? No, never!" and he drew her towards him, and on her bonnet, her veil, her gloves, nay, on her very cheeks, he imprinted a thousand maddening kisses. "But say, my sweet one," continued he, "who art *thou?* I know you as yet only by your lovely baptismal name, and your other name of Grampus."

Adeliza looked down and blushed. "My parents are lowly," she said.

"But how, then, came you at such a seminary?" said he; "twenty pound a quarter, extras and washing not included."

"They are humble, but wealthy."

"Ha! who is your father?"

"An alderman of yon metropolis."

"An alderman! and what is his profession?"

"I blush to tell: he is—*an oystermonger.*"

"AN OYSTERMONGER!" screamed Roderick, in the largest capitals. "Ha! ha! ha! this is too much!" and he dropped Adeliza's hand, and never spoke to her during the rest of her walk. They moved moodily on for some time, Miss Binx and the other young man marching astonished in the rear. At length they came within sight of the seminary. "Here is Bulgaria House," cried the maiden steadily; "Roderick, we must part!" The effort was too much for her; she flung herself hysterically into his arms.

But, oh horror! a scream was heard from Miss Binx, who was seen scuttling at double-quick time towards the school-house. Her young man had bolted completely;

and close at the side of the lovely though imprudent couple stood the angry—and justly angry—Miss Zela Pidge!

"Oh, Ferdinand," said she, "is it thus you deceive me! Did I bring you to Bulgaria House for this?—did I give you money to buy clothes for this, that you should go by false names, and make love to that saucy, slammerkin, sentimental Miss Grampus? Ferdinand, Ferdinand," cried she, "is this true? can I credit my eyes?"

"D—— your eyes!" said the Signor, angrily, as he darted at her a withering look, and retired down the street. His curses might be heard long after he had passed. He never appeared more at Bulgaria House, for he received his dismissal the next day.

That night all the front windows of the Miss Pidges' seminary were smashed to shivers.

* * * * *

On the following Thursday, *two* places were taken in the coach to town. On the back seat sat the usher; on the front, the wasted and miserable Adeliza Grampus.

* * * * *

CHAPTER II

But the matter did not end here. Miss Grampus's departure elicited from her a disclosure of several circumstances which, we must say, in no degree increased the reputation of Miss Zela Pidge. The discoveries which she made were so awkward, the tale of crime and licentiousness revealed by her so deeply injurious to the character of the establishment, that the pupils emigrated from it in scores. Miss Binx retired to her friends at Wandsworth, Miss Jacobs to her relations in Houndsditch, and other young ladies, not mentioned in this history, to other and more moral schools; so that absolutely, at the end of a single half-year, such had been the scandal of the story, the Misses Pidge were left with only two pupils—Miss Dibble, the articled young lady, and Miss Bole, the grocer's daughter, who came in exchange for tea, candles, and other requisites supplied to the establishment by her father.

"I knew it! I knew it!" cried Zela, passionately, as she trod the echoing and melancholy schoolroom; "he told me that none ever prospered who loved him—that every flower was blighted upon which he shone! Ferdinand! Ferdinand! you have caused ruin there!" (pointing to the empty cupboards and forms); "but what is that to the blacker ruin *here*?" and the poor creature slapped her heart, and the big tears rolled down her chin, and so into her tucker.

A very few weeks after this, the plate on Bulgaria House was removed for ever. That mansion is now designated " Moscow Hall, by Mr. Swishtail and assist-ants: "—the bankrupt and fugitive Misses Pidge have fled, Heaven knows whither! for the steamers to Boulogne cost more than five shillings in those days.

Alderman Grampus, as may be imagined, did not receive his daughter with any extraordinary degree of courtesy. "He was as grumpy," Mrs. G. remarked, "on the occasion as a sow with the measles." But had he not reason? A lovely daughter who had neglected her education, forgotten her morals for the second time, and fallen almost a prey to villains! Miss Grampus for some months was kept in close confinement, nor ever suffered to stir, except occasionally to Bunhill Row for air, and to church for devotion. Still, though she knew him to be false,—though she knew that under a differ-ent, perhaps a prettier name, he had offered the same vows to another—she could not but think of Roderick.

That *professor* (as well—too well—he may be called!) knew too well her father's name and reputation to ex-perience any difficulty in finding his abode. It was, as every City man knows, in Cheapside; and thither Dan-dolo constantly bent his steps; but though he marched unceasingly about the mansion, he never (mysteriously) would pass it. He watched Adeliza walking, he fol-lowed her to church; and many and many a time as she jostled out at the gate of the Artillery-ground or the beadle-flanked portal of Bow, a tender hand would meet hers, an active foot would press upon hers, a billet dis-creetly delivered was as adroitly seized, to hide in the recesses of her pocket-handkerchief or to nestle in the fragrance of her bosom! Love! Love! how ingenious

thou art! thou canst make a ladder of a silken thread,
or a weapon of a straw; thou peerest like sunlight into
a dungeon; thou scalest, like forlorn hope, a castle wall;
the keep is taken!—the foeman has fled!—the banner of
love floats triumphantly over the corpses of the slain![1]

Thus, though denied the comfort of personal intercourse, Adeliza and her lover maintained a frequent and
tender correspondence. Nine times at least in a week,
she, by bribing her maid-servant, managed to convey
letters to the professor, to which he at rarer intervals,
though with equal warmth, replied.

" Why," said the young lady in the course of this correspondence, " why when I cast my eyes upon my Roderick, do I
see him so wofully changed in outward guise? He wears not the
dress which formerly adorned him. Is he poor?—is he in disguise?—do debts oppress him, or traitors track him for his blood?
Oh that my arms might shield him!—Oh that my purse might aid
him! It is the fondest wish of   "ADELIZA G.

" P.S.—Aware of your fondness for shell-fish, Susan will leave
a barrel of oysters at the Swan with Two Necks, directed to you,
as per desire.   "AD. G.

" P.S.—Are you partial to kippered salmon? The girl brings
three pounds of it wrapped in a silken handkerchief. 'Tis marked
with the hair of   " ADELIZA.

" P.S.—I break open my note to say that you will find in it a
small pot of anchovy paste: may it prove acceptable. Heigho! I
would that I could accompany it.   " A. G."

It may be imagined, from the text of this note, that
Adeliza had profited not a little by the perusal of Miss

---

[1] We cannot explain this last passage; but it is so beautiful that the reader
will pardon the omission of sense, which the author certainly could have put
in if he liked.

Swipes's novels; and it also gives a pretty clear notion of the conditon of her lover. When that gentleman was a professor at Bulgaria House, his costume had strictly accorded with his pretensions. He wore a black German coat loaded with frogs and silk trimming, a white broad-brimmed beaver, hessians, and nankeen tights. His costume at present was singularly changed for the worse; a rough brown frock-coat dangled down to the calves of his brawny legs, where likewise ended a pair of greasy shepherd's-plaid trousers; a dubious red waist-coat, a blue or bird's-eye neckerchief, and bluchers (or half-boots), remarkable for thickness and for mud, completed his attire. But he looked superior to his fortune; he wore his grey hat very much on one ear; he incessantly tugged at his smoky shirt-collar, and walked jingling the halfpence (when he had any) in his pocket. He was, in fact, no better than an adventurer, and the innocent Adeliza was his prey.

Though the professor read the first part of this letter with hope and pleasure, it may be supposed that the three postscripts were still more welcome to him—in fact, he literally did what is often done in novels, he *devoured* them; and Adeliza, on receiving a note from him the next day, after she had eagerly broken the seal, and with panting bosom and flashing eye glanced over the contents—Adeliza, we say, was not altogether pleased when she read the following:—

" Your goodness, dearest, passes belief; but never did poor fellow need it more than your miserable faithful Roderick. Yes! I *am* poor—I *am* tracked by hell-hounds—I *am* changed in looks, and dress, and happiness—in all but love for thee!

" Hear my tale! I come of a noble Italian family—the noblest, ay, in Venice. We were free once, and rich, and happy; but the

Prussian autograph has planted his banner on our towers—the talents of his haughty heagle have seized our wealth, and consigned most of our race to dungeons. I am not a prisoner, only an exile. A mother, a bed-ridden grandmother, and five darling sisters escaped with me from Venice, and now share my poverty and my home. But I have wrestled with misfortune in vain; I have struggled with want, till want has overcome me. Adeliza, I WANT BREAD!

" The kippered salmon was very good, the anchovies admirable. But, oh, my love! how thirsty they make those who have no means of slaking thirst! My poor grandmother lies delirious in her bed, and cries in vain for drink. Alas! our water is cut off; I have none to give her. The oysters was capital. Bless thee, bless thee! angel of bounty! Have you any more sich, and a few srimps? My sisters are *very* fond of them.

" Half-a-crown would oblige. But thou art too good to me already, and I blush to ask thee for more. Adieu, Adeliza.

" The wretched but faithful

" RODERICK FERDINAND

"(38th Count of Dandolo).

" BELL YARD: *June—.*"

A shade of dissatisfaction, we say, clouded Adeliza's fair features as she perused this note; and yet there was nothing in it which the tenderest lover might not write. But the shrimps, the half-crown, the horrid picture of squalid poverty presented by the Count, sickened her young heart; the innate delicacy of the woman revolted at the thought of all this misery.

But better thoughts succeeded: her breast heaved as she read and re-read the singular passage concerning the Prussian autograph, who had planted his standard at Venice. "I knew it!" she cried, "I knew it!—he is of noble race! Oh, Roderick, I will perish, but I will help thee!"

Alas! she was not well enough acquainted with history to perceive that the Prussian autograph had nothing to do with Venice, and had forgotten altogether that she herself had coined the story which this adventurer returned to her.

But a difficulty presented itself to Adeliza's mind. Her lover asked for money—where was she to find it? The next day the till of the shop was empty, and a weeping apprentice dragged before the Lord Mayor. It is true that no signs of the money were found upon him; it is true that he protested his innocence; but he was dismissed the alderman's service, and passed a month at Bridewell because Adeliza Grampus had a needy lover.

" Dearest," she wrote, " will three-and-twenty and sevenpence suffice? 'Tis all I have: take it, and with it the fondest wishes of your Adeliza.

" A sudden thought! Our apprentice is dismissed. My father dines abroad; I shall be in the retail establishment all the night, *alone.*   " A. G."

No sooner had the professor received this note than his mind was made up. " I will see her," he said; " I will enter that accursed shop." He did, and *to his ruin.*

*   *   *   *   *

That night Mrs. Grampus and her daughter took possession of the bar or counter, in the place which Adeliza called the retail establishment, and which is commonly denominated the shop. Mrs. Grampus herself operated with the oyster-knife, and served the Milton morsels to the customers. Age had not diminished her skill, nor had wealth rendered her too proud to re-

sume at need a profession which she had followed in
early days. Adeliza flew gracefully to and fro with
the rolls, the vinegar-bottle with perforated cork, and
the little pats of butter. A little boy ran backwards
and forwards to the "Blue Lion" over the way, for the
pots of porter, or for the brandy and water, which some
gentlemen take after the play.

Midnight arrived. Miss Grampus was looking
through the window, and contrasting the gleaming gas
which shone upon the ruby lobsters with the calm moon
which lightened up the Poultry, and threw a halo round
the Royal Exchange. She was lost in maiden medita-
tion, when her eye fell upon a pane of glass in her own
window: squeezed against this, flat and white, was the
nose of a man!—that man was Roderick Dandolo! He
seemed to be gazing at the lobsters more intensely than
at Adeliza; he had his hands in his pockets, and was
whistling "Jim Crow." [1]

Miss Grampus felt sick with joy: she staggered to the
counter, and almost fainted. The professor concluded
his melody, and entered at once into the shop. He pretended to have no knowledge of Miss Grampus, but
aborded the two ladies with easy elegance and irresistible
good-humour.

"Good evening, ma'am," said he, bowing profoundly
to the *elder* lady. "What a precious hot evening *to* be
sure!—hot, ma'am, and hungry, as they say. I could
not resist them lobsters, 'specially when I saw the lady
behind 'em."

At this gallant speech Mrs. Grampus blushed, or
looked as if she would blush, and said—

---

[1] I know this is an anachronism; but I only mean that he was performing
one of the popular melodies of the time.—M. A. T.

"Law, sir!"

"Law, indeed, ma'am," playfully continued the professor: "you're a precious deal better than law—you're *divinity*, ma'am; and this, I presume, is your sister?"

He pointed to Adeliza as he spoke, who, pale and mute, stood fainting against a heap of ginger-beer bottles. The old lady was quite won by this stale compliment.

"My daughter, sir," she said. "Addly, lay a cloth for the gentleman. Do you take hoysters, sir, hor lobsters? Both is very fine."

"Why, ma'am," said he, "to say truth, I have come forty miles since dinner, and don't care if I have a little of both. I'll begin, if you please, with that there (Lord bless its claws, they're as red as your lips!) and we'll astonish a few of the natives afterwards, *by* your leave."

Mrs. Grampus was delighted with the manners and the appetite of the stranger. She proceeded forthwith to bisect the lobster, while the professor, in a *dégagé* manner, his cane over his shoulder, and a cheerful whistle upon his lips, entered the little parlour, and took possession of a box and a table.

He was no sooner seated than, from a scuffle, a giggle, and a smack, Mrs. Grampus was induced to suspect that something went wrong in the oyster-room.

"Hadeliza!" cried she: and that young woman returned blushing now like a rose, who had been as pale before as a lily.

Mrs. G. herself took in the lobster, bidding her daughter sternly to stay in the shop. She approached the stranger with an angry air, and laid the lobster before him.

"For shame, sir!" said she solemnly; but all of a sudden she began to giggle like her daughter, and her speech ended with an *"Have done now!"*

We were not behind the curtain, and cannot of course say what took place; but it is evident that the professor was a general lover of the sex.

Mrs. Grampus returned to the shop, rubbing her lips with her fat arms, and restored to perfect good-humour. The little errand-boy was despatched over the way for a bottle of Guinness and a glass of brandy and water.

"HOT WITH!" shouted a manly voice from the eating-room, and Adeliza was pained to think that in her presence her lover could eat so well.

He ate indeed as if he had never eaten before: here is the bill as written by Mrs. Grampus herself.

	£.	s.	d.
" Two lobsters at 3s. 6d.		7	0
Salit		1	3
2 Bottils Doubling Stott		2	4
11 Doz. Best natifs		7	4
14 Pads of Botter		1	2
4 Glasses B. & W.		4	0
Bredd (love & $\frac{1}{2}$)		1	2
Brakitch of tumler		1	6
	1	5	9

" *To Samuel Grampus,*
    " *At the Mermaid in Cheapside.*

" Shell-fish in all varieties.   N.B.—A great saving in taking a quantity."

"A saving in *taking a quantity,*" said the stranger archly.   "Why, ma'am, you ought to let me off *very cheap;*" and the professor, the potboy, Adeliza, and her mamma, grinned equally at this pleasantry.

"However, never mind the pay, missis," continued he; "we an't a-going to quarrel about *that*. Hadd another glass of brandy and water to the bill, and bring it me, when it shall be as I am now."

"Law, sir," simpered Mrs. Grampus, "how's that?"

"*Reseated,* ma'am, to be sure," replied he, as he sank back upon the table. The old lady went laughing away, pleased with her merry and facetious customer; the little boy picked up the oyster-shells, of which a mighty pyramid was formed at the professor's feet.

"Here, Sammy," cried out shrill Mrs. Grampus from the shop, "go over to the 'Blue Lion' and get the gentleman his glass: but no, you are better where you are, pickin' up them shells. Go you, Hadeliza; it is but across the way."

Adeliza went with a very bad grace; she had hoped to exchange at least a few words with him her soul adored; and her mother's jealousy prevented the completion of her wish.

She had scarcely gone when Mr. Grampus entered from his dinner-party. But, though fond of pleasure, he was equally faithful to business; without a word he hung up his brass-buttoned coat, put on his hairy cap, and stuck his sleeves through his apron.

As Mrs. Grampus was tying it (an office which this faithful lady regularly performed) he asked her what business had occurred during his absence.

"Not so bad," said she; "two pound ten to-night, besides one pound eight to receive," and she handed Mr. Grampus the bill.

"How many are there on 'em?" said that gentleman smiling, as his eye gladly glanced over the items of the account.

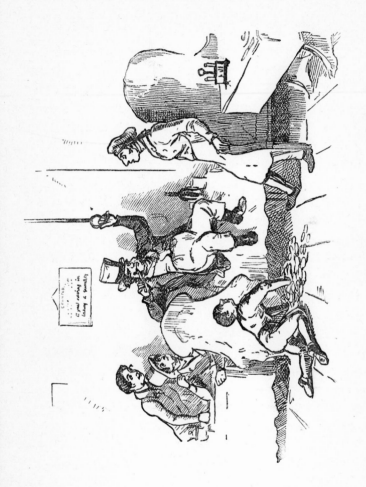

Mr. Dando Declares His
Name and Quality

" Why, that's the best of all: how many do you think? "

" If four did it," said Mr. Grampus, " they wouldn't have done badly neither."

"What do you think of *one?*" cried Mrs. G. laughing, " and he an't done yet. Haddy is gone to fetch him another glass of brandy and water."

Mr. Grampus looked very much alarmed. " Only one, and you say he an't paid? "

" No," said the lady.

Mr. Grampus seized the bill, and rushed wildly into the dining-room; the little boy was picking up the oyster-shells still, there were so many of them; the professor was seated on the table, laughing as if drunk, and picking his teeth with his fork.

Grampus, shaking in every joint, held out the bill: a horrid thought crossed him; he had seen that face before!

The professor kicked sneeringly into the air the idle piece of paper, and swung his legs recklessly to and fro.

"What a flat you are," shouted he, in a voice of thunder, " to think I'm a-goin' to pay! Pay! I never pay— I'm Dando! "

The people in the other boxes crowded forward to see the celebrated stranger; the little boy grinned as he dropped two hundred and forty-four oyster-shells, and Mr. Grampus rushed madly into his front shop, shrieking for a watchman.

As he ran, he stumbled over something on the floor—a woman and a glass of brandy and water lay there extended. Like Tarquinia reversed, Elijah Grampus was trampling over the lifeless body of Adeliza.

Why enlarge upon the miserable theme? The confiding girl, in returning with the grog from the " Blue Lion," had arrived at the shop only in time to hear the

fatal name of DANDO. She saw him, tipsy and triumphant, bestriding the festal table, and yelling with horrid
laughter! The truth flashed upon her—she fell!

Lost to worldly cares in contemplating the sorrows
of their idolised child, her parents forgot all else beside. Mrs. G. held the vinegar-cruet to her nostrils;
her husband brought the soda-water fountain to play
upon her; it restored her to life but not to sense.
When Adeliza Grampus rose from that trance she was
a MANIAC!

But what became of *the deceiver?* The gormandising
ruffian, the lying renegade, the fiend in human shape, escaped in the midst of this scene of desolation. He
walked unconcerned through the shop, his hat cocked on
one side as before, swaggering as before, whistling as
before: far in the moonlight might you see his figure;
long, long in the night-silence rang his demoniac melody
of "Jim Crow"!

*   *   *   *   *

When Samuel the boy cleaned out the shop in the
morning, and made the inventory of the goods, a silver
fork, a plated ditto, a dish, and a pewter-pot were found
to be wanting. Ingenuity will not be long in guessing
the name of *the thief.*

Gentles, my tale is told. If it may have deterred one
soul from vice, my end is fully answered: if it may have
taught to schoolmistresses carefulness, to pupils circum-
spection, to youth the folly of sickly sentiment, the pain
of bitter deception; to manhood, the crime, the *meanness*
of gluttony, the vice which it occasions, and the wicked
passions it fosters; if these, or any of these, have been
taught by the above tale, the writer seeks for no other
reward.

Note.—Please send the proceeds as requested per letter; the bearer being directed not to give up the manuscript without.

(*First published in* 1841 *in a volume entitled " Comic Tales and Sketches," edited and illustrated by Mr. Michael Angelo Titmarsh.*)

MISS LÖWE

MINNA LÖWE was the daughter of Moses Löwe, banker at Bonn. I passed through the town last year, fifteen years after the events I am about to relate, and heard that Moses was imprisoned for forgery and fraudulent bankruptcy. He merited the punishment which the merciful Prussian law inflicted on him.

Minna was the most beautiful creature that my eyes ever lighted on. Sneer not, ye Christian maidens; but the fact was so. I saw her for the first time seated at a window covered with golden vine-leaves, with grapes just turning to purple, and tendrils twisting in the most fantastical arabesques. The leaves cast a pretty chequered shadow over her sweet face, and the simple, thin, white muslin gown in which she was dressed. She had bare white arms, and a blue ribbon confined her little waist. She was knitting, as all German women do, whether of the Jewish sort or otherwise; and in the shadow of the room sat her sister Emma, a powerful woman with a powerful voice. Emma was at the piano, singing, "Herz, mein Herz, warum so trau-au-rig,"— singing much out of tune.

I had come to change one of Coutts's circulars at Löwe's bank, and was looking for the door of the caisse.

"Links, mein Herr!" said Minna Löwe, making the gentlest inclination with her pretty little head; and blushing ever so little, and raising up tenderly a pair of heavy blue eyes, and then dropping them again, over-come by the sight of the stranger. And no wonder; I was a sight worth contemplating then,—I had golden hair which fell gracefully over my shoulders, and a slim waist (where are you now, slim waist and golden hair?), and a pair of brown mustachios that curled gracefully under a firm Roman nose, and a tuft to my chin that could not but vanquish *any* woman. "Links, mein Herr," said lovely Minna Löwe.

That little word *links* dropped upon my wounded soul like balm. There is nothing in *links;* it is not a pretty word. Minna Löwe simply told me to turn to the left, when I was debating between that side and its opposite, in order to find the cash-room door. Any other person might have said *links* (or *rechts* for that matter), and would not have made the slightest impression upon me; but Minna's full red lips, as they let slip the monosyl-lable, wore a smile so tender, and uttered it with such in-conceivable sweetness, that I was overcome at once. "Sweet bell! I could have said, tinkle that dulcet note for ever,—links, clinks, linx! I love the chime. It soothes and blesses me." All this I could have said, and much more, had I had my senses about me, and had I been a proficient in the German language; but I could not speak, both from ignorance and emotion. I blushed, stuttered, took off my cap, made an immensely foolish bow, and began forthwith fumbling at the door-handle.

The reason why I have introduced the name of this siren is to show that if tobacco in a former unlucky instance [1] has proved my enemy, in the present case it

[1] See "The Fitz-Boodle Papers."

was my firmest friend. I, the descendant of the Norman Fitz-Boodle, the relative of kings and emperors, might, but for tobacco, have married the daughter of Moses Löwe, the Jew forger and convict of Bonn. I would have done it; for I hold the man a slave who calculates in love, and who thinks about prudence when his heart is in question. Men marry their cookmaids and the world looks down upon them. *Ne sit ancillæ amor pudori!* I exclaim with a notorious poet, if you heartily and entirely love your cookmaid, you are a fool and a coward not to wed her. What more can you want than to have your heart filled up? Can a duchess do more? You talk of the difference of rank and the decencies of society. Away, sir! love is divine, and knows not your paltry worldly calculations. It is not love you worship, O heartless silly calculator! it is the interest of thirty thousand pounds in the Three per Cents, and the blessing of a genteel mother-in-law in Harley Street, and the ineffable joy of snug dinners, and the butler behind your chair. Fool! love is eternal, butlers and mothers-in-law are perishable: you have but the enjoyment of your Three per Cents for forty years; and *then,* what do they avail you? But if you believe that she whom you choose, and to whom your heart clings, is to be your soul's companion, not now merely, but for *ever and ever;* then what a paltry item of money or time has deterred you from your happiness, what a miserable penny-wise economist you have been!

And here, if, as a man of the world, I might be allowed to give advice to fathers and mothers of families, it would be this: young men fall in love with people of a lower rank, and they are not strong enough to resist the dread of disinheritance, or of the world's scorn, or of

the cursed tyrant gentility, and dare not marry the woman
they love above all. But, if prudence is strong, passion
is strong too, and principle is not, and women (Heaven
keep them!) are weak. We all know what happens then.
Prudent papas and mammas say, "George will sow his
wild oats soon, he will be tired of that odious woman
one day, and we'll get a good marriage for him: meanwhile it is best to hush the matter up and pretend to
know nothing about it." But suppose George does the
only honest thing in his power, and marries the woman
he loves above all; *then* what a cry you have from parents
and guardians, what shrieks from aunts and sisters,
what excommunications and disinheriting! "What a
weak fool George is!" say his male friends in the clubs;
and no hand of sympathy is held out to poor *Mrs.*
George, who is never forgiven, but shunned like a
plague, and sneered at by a relentless pharisaical world
until death sets her free. As long as she is *unmarried,*
avoid her if you will; but as soon as she is married, go!
be kind to her, and comfort her, and pardon and forget
if you can! And lest some charitable people should
declare that I am setting up here an apology for vice,
let me here, and by the way of precaution, flatly contradict them, and declare that I only would offer a *plea
for marriage.*

But where has Minna Löwe been left during this
page of disquisition? Gazing through a sunny cluster
of vine-leaves upon a young and handsome stranger,
of noble face and exquisite proportions, who was trying
to find the door of her father's bank. That entrance
being through her amiable directions discovered, I entered and found Messrs. Moses and Solomon Löwe in
the counting-house, Herr Solomon being the son of

Moses, and head-clerk or partner in the business. That I was cheated in my little matter of exchange stands to reason. A Jew banker (or such as I have had the honour to know) cannot forego the privilege of cheating; no, if it be but for a shilling. What do I say,—a shilling?—a penny! He will cheat you, in the first place, in the exchanging your note; he will then cheat you in giving gold for your silver; and though very likely he will invite you to a splendid repast afterwards that shall have cost him a score of thalers to procure, he will have had the satisfaction of robbing you of your *groschen,* as no doubt he would rob his own father or son.

Herr Moses Löwe must have been a very sharp Israelite, indeed, to rob Herr Solomon, or *vice versâ.* The poor fellows are both in prison for a matter of forgery, as I heard last year when passing through Bonn; and I confess it was not without a little palpitation of the heart (it is a sausage-merchant's now) that I went and took one look at the house where I had at first beheld the bright eyes of Minna Löwe.

For let them say as they will, that woman whom a man has once loved *cannot* be the same to him as another. Whenever one of my passions comes into a room, my cheeks flush,—my knees tremble,—I look at her with pleased tenderness and (for the objects of my adoration do not once in forty times know their good fortune) with melancholy secret wonder. There they are, the same women, and yet not the same; it is the same nose and eyes, if you will, but not the same looks; the same voice, but not the same sweet words as of old. The figure moves, and looks and talks to you; you know how dear and how different its speech and actions once were; 'tis the hall with all the lights put out and the garlands dead (as I have said in one of my poems). Did you ever have a pocket-book that once contained five thousand pounds? Did you ever look at that pocket-book with the money lying in it? Do you remember how you respected and admired that pocket-book, investing it with a secret awe, imagining it had a superiority to other pocket-books? I have such a pocket-book; I keep it now, and often look at it rather tenderly. It cannot be as other portfolios to me. I remember that it once held five thousand pounds.

Thus it is with love. I have empty pocket-books scattered all over Europe of this kind; and I always go and look at them just for a moment, and the spirit flies back to days gone by; kind eyes look at me as of yore, and echoes of old gentle voices fall tenderly upon the ear. Away! to the true heart the past *never* is past; and some day when Death has cleared our dull faculties, and past and future shall be rolled into one, we shall . . .

Well, you were quite right, my good sir, to interrupt me; I can't help it, I am too apt to grow sentimental, and always on the most absurd pretexts. I never know when the fit will come on me, or *à propos* of what. I never was so jolly in my whole life as one day coming home from a funeral; and once went to a masked ball at Paris, the gaiety of which made me so profoundly miserable, that, egad! I wept like Xerxes (wasn't that the fellow's name?), and was sick—sick at heart. This premised, permit me, my friend, to indulge in sentiment *à propos* of Minna Löwe; for three weeks, at least, I adored the wench, and could give any person curious that way a complete psychological history of the passion's rise, progress, and decay;—decay, indeed, why do I say decay? A man does not "decay" when he tumbles down a well, he drowns there; so is love choked sometimes by abrupt conclusions, falls down wells, and, oh, the dismal truth at the bottom of them!

"If, my lord," said Herr Moses, counting out the gold fredericks to me, "you intend to shtay in our town, I hope my daughtersh and I vill have shometimesh de pleashure of your high vell-born shoshiety?"

"The town is a most delightful one, Mr. Löwe," answered I. "I am myself an Oxford man, and exceedingly interested about—ahem—about the Byzantine historians, of which I see the University is producing an edition; and I shall make I think a considerable stay." Heaven bless us! 'twas Miss Minna's eyes that had done the business. But for them I should have slept at Coblentz that very night; where, by the way, the Hôtel de la Poste is one of the very best inns in Europe.

A friend had accompanied me to Bonn,—a jolly dragoon, who was quite versed in the German language, having spent some time in the Austrian service before he joined us; or in the "Awthtwian thervith," as he would call it, with a double distilled gentility of accent very difficult to be acquired out of Regent Street. We had quarrelled already thrice on the passage from England —viz. at Rotterdam, at Cologne, and once here; so that when he said he intended to go to Mayence, I at once proclaimed that I intended to stay where I was; and with Miss Minna Löwe's image in my heart, went out and selected lodgings for myself as near as possible to her father's house. Wilder said I might go to—any place I liked; he remained in his quarters at the hotel, as I found a couple of days afterwards, when I saw the fellow smoking at the gateway in the company of a score of Prussian officers, with whom he had made acquaintance.

I for my part have never been famous for that habit of extemporaneous friendship-making which some lucky fellows possess. Like most of my countrymen, when I enter a room I always take care to look about with an air as if I heartily despised everyone, and wanted to know what the d—l they did there! Among foreigners I feel this especially; for the truth is, right or wrong, I can't help despising the rogues, and feeling manifestly my own superiority. In consequence of this amiable quality, then (in this particular instance of my life), I gave up the *table-d'hôte* dinner at the " Star " as something low and ungentlemanlike, made a point of staring and not answering when people spoke to me, and thus I have no doubt impressed all the world with a sense of my dignity. Instead of dining at the public place, then, I took my repasts alone; though, as Wilder said with some justice, though with a good deal too much *laisser-aller* of tongue, " You gweat fool, if it'th only becauth you want to be thilent, why don't you thtill dine with uth? You'll get a wegular good dinner inthtead of a bad one; and ath for *thpeaking* to you, depend on it every man in the room will thee you hanged futht!"

" Pray allow me to dine in my own way, Wilder," says I, in the most dignified way.

" Dine and be d—d!" said the lieutenant, and so I lived solitary and had my own way.

I proposed to take some German lessons; and for this purpose asked the banker, Mr. Löwe, to introduce me to a master. He procured one, a gentleman of his own persuasion; and, further, had the kindness to say that his clerk, Mr. Hirsch, should come and sit with me every morning and perfect me in the tongue; so that, with the master I had and the society I kept, I might acquire a very decent German pronunciation.

This Hirsch was a little Albino of a creature with pinkish eyes, white hair, flame-coloured whiskers, and earrings. His eyes jutted out enormously from his countenance; as did his two large swollen red lips, which had the true Israelitish coarseness. He was always, after a short time, in and out of my apartments. He brought a dozen messages and ran as many errands for me in the course of the day. My way of addressing him was, "Hirsch, you scoundrel, get my boots!" "Hirsch, my Levite, brush my coat for me!" "Run, you stag of Israel, and put this letter in the post!" and with many similar compliments. The little rascal was, to do him justice, as willing as possible, never minded by what name I called him, and, above all,—came from Minna. He was not the rose; no, indeed, nor anything like it; but, as the poet says, "he had lived beside it;" and was there in all Sharon such a rose as Minna Löwe?

If I did not write with a moral purpose, and because my unfortunate example may act wholesomely upon other young men of fashion, and induce them to learn wisdom, I should not say a single syllable about Minna Löwe, nor all the blunders I committed, nor the humiliation I suffered. There is about a young Englishman of twenty a degree of easy self-confidence, hardly possessed even by a Frenchman. The latter swaggers and bullies about his superiority, taking all opportunities to shriek it into your ears, and to proclaim the infinite merits of himself and his nation; but, upon my word, the bragging of the Frenchman is not so conceited or intolerable as that calm, silent, contemptuous conceit of us

young Britons, who think our superiority so well established that it is really not worth arguing upon, and who
take upon us to despise thoroughly the whole world
through which we pass. We are hated on the Continent,
they say, and no wonder. If any other nation were to
attempt to domineer over us as we do over Europe, we
would hate them as heartily and furiously as many a
Frenchman and Italian does us.

Now when I went abroad I fancied myself one of the
finest fellows under the sun. I patronised a banker's
dinners as if I did him honour in eating them; I took my
place before grave professors and celebrated men, and
talked vapid nonsense to them in infamous French,
laughing heartily in return at their own manner of pronouncing that language. I set down as a point beyond
question that their customs were inferior to our own,
and would not in the least scruple, in a calm way, to let
my opinion be known. What an agreeable young fellow
I must have been!

With these opinions, and my pleasant way of expressing them, I would sit for hours by the side of lovely
Minna Löwe, ridiculing with much of that elegant satire
for which the English are remarkable, every one of the
customs of the country,—the dinners, with the absurd un-
English pudding in the very midst of them; the dresses
of the men, with their braided coats and great seal-rings.
As for little Hirsch, he formed the constant subject of
my raillery with Mademoiselle Minna; and I gave it as
my fixed opinion, that he was only fit to sell sealing-wax
and oranges to the coaches in Piccadilly.

"O fous afez tant d'esprit, fous autres jeunes Anglais," would she say; and I said, "Oui, nous avons beaucoup d'esprit, beaucoup plus que les Allemands," with the

utmost simplicity; and then would half close my eyes, and give her a look that I thought must kill her.

Shall I tell the result of our conversation? In conversation 1, Minna asked me if I did not think the tea remarkably good, with which she and her sister treated me. She said it came overland from China, that her papa's correspondent at Petersburg forwarded it to them, and that no such tea was to be had in Germany. On this I seriously believed the tea to be excellent; and next morning at breakfast little Hirsch walked smirking into my room, with a parcel of six pounds of Congo, for which I had the honour of paying eighteen Prussian thalers, being two pounds fourteen shillings of our money.

The next time I called, Herr Moses insisted on regaling me with a glass of Cyprus wine. His brother Löwe of Constantinople was the only person in the world who possessed this precious liquor. Four days afterwards Löwe came to know how I liked the Cyprus wine which I had ordered, and would I like another dozen? On saying that I had not ordered any, that I did not like sweet wine, he answered, "*Pardon!*" it had been in my cellar three days, and he would send some excellent Médoc at a moderate price, and would take no refusal. A basket of Médoc came that very night in my absence, with a bill directed to the "High Well-born Count von Fitz-Boodle." This excessive desire of the Löwe family to serve me made me relax my importunities somewhat. "Ah!" says Minna, with a sigh, the next time I saw her, "have we offended you, Herr George? You don't come to see us any more now!"

"I'll come to-morrow," says I; and she gave me a look and a smile which, oh!—"I am a fool, I know I am!" as the honourable member for Montrose said t'other day.

And was not Samson ditto? Was not Hercules another? Next day she was seated at the vine-leaves as I entered the court. She smiled, and then retreated. She had been on the look-out for me, I knew she had. She held out her little hand to me as I came into the room. Oh, how soft it was and how round! and with a little apricot-coloured glove that—that I have to this day! I had been arranging a little compliment as I came along, something quite new and killing. I had only the heart to say, "Es ist sehr warm."

"Oh, Herr George!" says she; "*Lieber* Herr George; what a progress have you made in German! You speak it like a native!"

But somehow I preferred to continue the conversation in French; and it was made up, as I am bound to say, of remarks equally brilliant and appropriate with that one above given. When old Löwe came in I was winding a skein of silk, seated in an enticing attitude, gazing with all my soul at Delilah, who held down her beautiful eyes.

That day they did not sell me any bargains at all; and the next found me, you may be very sure, in the same parlour again, where, in his *schlafrock,* the old Israelite was smoking his pipe.

"Get away, papa," said Minna, "English lords can't bear smoke. I'm sure Herr George dislikes it."

"Indeed I smoke occasionally myself," answered your humble servant.

"Get his lordship a pipe, Minna, my soul's darling!" exclaimed the banker.

"Oh yes! the beautiful long Turkish one," cried Minna, springing up, and presently returned, bearing a long cherry-stick covered with a scarlet and gold cloth, at one end an enamelled amber mouthpiece, a gilded pipe at the other. In she came dancing, wand in hand, and looking like a fairy!

"Stop!" she said; "I must light it for Herr George." (By Jupiter! there was a way that girl had of pronouncing my name, "George," which I never heard equalled before or since.) And accordingly, bidding her sister get fire, she put herself in the prettiest attitude ever seen: with one little foot put forward, and her head thrown back, and a little hand holding the pipe-stick between finger and thumb, and a pair of red lips kissing the amber mouthpiece with the sweetest smile ever mortal saw. Her sister, giggling, lighted the tobacco, and presently you saw issuing from between those beautiful, smiling, red lips of Minna's a little curling, graceful white smoke which rose soaring up to the ceiling. I swear, I felt quite faint with the fragrance of it.

When the pipe was lighted, she brought it to me with quite as pretty an attitude and a glance that—Psha! I gave old Moses Löwe fourteen pounds sterling for that pipe that very evening; and as for the mouthpiece, I would not part with it away from me, but I wrapped it up in a glove that I took from the table, and put both into my breast-pocket; and next morning when Charley Wilder burst suddenly into my room, he found me sitting up in bed in a green silk nightcap, a little apricot-coloured glove lying on the counterpane before me, your humble servant employed in mumbling the mouthpiece as if it were a bit of barley-sugar.

He stopped, stared, burst into a shriek of laughter, and made a rush at the glove on the counterpane; but in a fury I sent a large single-volumed Tom Moore (I am not a poetical man, but I must confess I was reading some passages in "Lalla Rookh" that I found applicable to my situation) — I sent, I say, a Tom Moore at his head, which, luckily, missed him; and to which he responded by seizing a bolster and thumping me outrageously. It was lucky that he was a good-natured fellow, and had only resorted to that harmless weapon, for I was in such a fury that I certainly would have murdered him at the least insult.

I did not murder him then; but if he peached a single word upon the subject, I swore I would, and Wilder knew I was a man of my word. He was not unaware of my *tendre* for Minna Löwe, and was for passing some of his delicate light-dragoon jokes upon it and her; but these, too, I sternly cut short.

"Why, cuth me, if I don't think you want to mawwy her!" blurted out Wilder.

"Well, sir," said I, "and suppose I do?"

"What! mawwy the daughter of that thwindling old clotheman? I tell you what, Fitth-Boodle, they alwayth thaid you were mad in the weg'ment, and, run me thwough, if I don't think you are."

"The man," says I, "sir, who would address Mademoiselle Löwe in any but an honourable way is a scoundrel; and the man who says a word against her character is a liar!"

After a little further parley (which Wilder would not have continued but that he wanted to borrow money of me), that gentleman retired, declaring that "I wath ath thulky ath a bear with a thaw head," and left me to my apricot-coloured glove and my amber mouthpiece.

Wilder's assertion that I was going to act up to opinions which I had always professed, and to marry Minna Löwe, certainly astounded me, and gave me occasion for thought. Marry the daughter of a Jew banker! I, George Fitz-Boodle! That would never do; not unless she had a million to her fortune, at least, and it was not probable that a humble dealer at Bonn could give her so much. But, marry her or not, I could not refrain from the sweet pleasure of falling in love with her, and shut my eyes to the morrow that I might properly enjoy the day. Shortly after Wilder's departure, little Hirsch paid his almost daily visit to me. I determined—and wondered that I had never thought of the scheme before —sagely to sound him regarding Minna's fortune, and to make use of him as my letter and message-carrier.

"Ah, Hirsch! my lion of Judah!" says I, "you have brought me the pipe-stick, have you?"

"Yes, my lord, and seven pounds of the tobacco you said you liked. 'Tis real Syrian, and a great bargain you get it, I promise."

"Egad!" replied I, affecting an air of much careless ingenuousness. "Do you know, Hirsch, my boy, that the youngest of the Miss Löwes—Miss Anna, I think you call her—"

"Minna," said Hirsch, with a grin.

"Well, Minna—Minna, Hirsch, is a devilish fine girl; upon my soul now, she is."

"Do you really think so?" says Hirsch.

"'Pon my honour, I do. And yesterday, when she was lighting the pipe-stick, she looked so confoundedly handsome that I—I quite fell in love with her; really I did."

"Ho! Vell, you do our people great honour, I'm sure," answered Hirsch.

"Father a warm man?"

"Varm! How do you mean varm?"

"Why, *rich.* We call a rich man *warm* in England; only you don't understand the language. How much will he give his daughter?"

"Oh! very little. Not a veek of your income, my lord," said Hirsch.

"Pooh, pooh! You always talk of me as if I'm rich; but I tell you I am poor—exceedingly poor."

"Go away vid you!" said Hirsch, incredulously. *"You* poor!" I vish I had a year of your income; that I do" (and I have no doubt he did, or of the revenue of anyone else). "I'd be a rich man, and have de best house in Bonn."

"Are you so very poor yourself, Hirsch, that you talk in this way?" asked I.

To which the young Israelite replied, that he had not one dollar to rub against another; that Mr. Löwe was a close man; and finally (upon my pressing the point, like a cunning dog as I was!), that he would do anything to earn a little money.

"Hirsch," said I, like a wicked young reprobate and Don Juan, "will you carry a letter to Miss Minna Löwe?"

Now there was no earthly reason why I should have made a twopenny postman of Mr. Hirsch. I might with just as much ease have given Minna the letter myself. I saw her daily and for hours, and it would be hard if I could not find her for a minute alone, or at least slip a note into her glove or pocket-handkerchief, if secret the note must be. But, I don't mind owning it, I was as ignorant of any love-making which requires mystery as any bishop on the bench, and pitched upon Hirsch, as it were, because in comedies and romances that I had read the hero has always a go-between—a valet or humble follower—who performs the intrigue of the piece. So I asked Hirsch the above question, "Would he carry a letter to Miss Minna Löwe?"

"Give it me," said he, with a grin.

But the deuce of it was, it wasn't written. Rosina, in the opera, has hers ready in her pocket, and says "Eccolo quà" when Figaro makes the same request, so I told Hirsch that I would get it ready. And a very hard task I found it too, in sitting down to compose the document. It shall be in verse, thought I, for Minna understands some English; but there is no rhyme to Minna, as everybody knows, except a Cockney, who might make "thinner, dinner, winner," &c. answer to it. And as for Löwe, it is just as bad. Then it became, as I thought, my painful duty to send her a note in French; and in French finally it was composed, and I blush now when I think of the nonsense and bad grammar it contained—the conceit above all. The easy vulgar assurance of victory with which I, a raw lad from the stupidest country in Europe, assailed one of the most beautiful women in the world!

Hirsch took the letter, and to bribe the fellow to silence, I agreed to purchase a great hideous amethyst brooch, which he had offered me a dozen times for sale, and which I had always refused till now. He said it had been graciously received, but as all the family were present in the evening when I called, of course no allusion could be made to the note; but I thought Minna looked particularly kind, as I sat and lost a couple of fredericks at *écarté* to a very stout Israelite lady, Madame Löwe, junior, the wife of Monsieur Solomon Löwe. I think it was on this night, or the next, that I was induced to purchase a bale of remarkably fine lawn for shirts, for old Löwe had everything to sell, as is not uncommon with men of his profession and persuasion; and had I expressed a fancy for a coffin or a hod of mortar, I have no doubt Hirsch would have had it at my door next morning.

I went on sending letters to Minna, copying them out of a useful little work called " Le Petit Sécrétaire Français," and easily adapting them to circumstances, by altering a phrase here and there. Day and night I used to dangle about the house. It was provoking, to be sure, that Minna was never alone now; her sister or Madame Solomon was always with her, and as they naturally spoke German, of which language I knew but few words, my evenings were passed in sighing, ogling, and saying nothing. I must have been a very charming companion. One evening was pretty much like another. Four or five times in the week old Löwe would drop in and sell me a bargain. Berlin-iron chains and trinkets for my family at home, Naples soap, a case of *eau de Cologne;* a beautiful dressing-gown lined with fur for the winter; a rifle, one of the famous Frankfort make; a complete collection of the German classics; and finally, to my awful disgust, a set of the Byzantine historians.

I must tell you that, although my banking friend had furnished me with half a stone of Syrian tobacco from his brother at Constantinople, and though the most beautiful lips in the world had first taught me to smoke it, I discovered, after a few pipes of the weed, that it was not so much to my taste as that grown in the West Indies; and as his Havannah cigars were also not to my liking, I was compelled, not without some scruples of conscience at my infidelity, to procure my smoking supplies elsewhere.

And now I come to the fatal part of my story.

Wilder, who was likewise an amateur of the weed, once came to my lodgings in the company of a tobacconist whom he patronised, and who brought several boxes and samples for inspection. Herr Rohr, which was the gentleman's name, sat down with us. His wares were very good, and—must I own it?—I thought it would be a very clever and prudent thing on my part to exchange some of my rare Syrian against his canaster and Havannahs. I vaunted the quality of the goods to him, and, going into the inner room, returned with a packet of the real Syrian. Herr Rohr looked at the parcel rather contemptuously, I thought.

" I have plenty of these goods in my shop," said he.

" Why, you don't thay tho," says Wilder, with a grin; " ith the weal wegular Thywian. My friend Fitth-Boodle got it from hith bankerth, and no mithtake!"

" Was it from Mr. Löwe?" says Rohr, with another provoking sneer.

" Exactly. His brother Israel sent it from Constantinople."

" Bah!" says Rohr. " I sold this very tobacco, seven pounds of it, at fourteen groschen a pound, to Miss Minna Löwe and little Mr. Hirsch, who came express to my shop for it. Here's my seal," says Mr. Rohr. And sure enough he produced, from a very fat and dirty forefinger, a seal, which bore the engraving on the packet.

" You sold that to Miss Minna Löwe?" groaned poor George Fitz-Boodle.

" Yes, and she bated me down half a gros in the price. Heaven help you, sir! she *always* makes the bargains for her father. There's something so pretty about her that we can't resist her."

" And do you thell *wineth,* too,—Thypwuth and Médoc, hay?" continued the brute Wilder, enjoying the joke.

"No," answered Mr. Rohr, with another confounded sneer. "He makes those himself; but I *have* some very fine Médoc and Greek wine, if his high well-born lordship would like a few dozen. Shall I send a panier?"

"*Leave the room,* sir!" here shouted I, in a voice of uncontrollable ferocity, and looked so wildly that little Rohr rushed away in a fright, and Wilder burst into one of his demoniacal laughs again.

"Don't you thee, my good fwiend," continued he, "how wegularly thethe people have been doing you? I tell you their chawacterth are known all over the town. There'th not a thtudent in the place but can give you a hithtory of the family. Löwe ith an infarnal old uthuwer, and hith daughterth wegular mantwapth. At the Thtar, where I dine with the officerth of the garrithon, you and Minna are a thtandard joke. Captain Heerpauk wath caught himthelf for near thix weekth! young Von Twommel wath wemoved by hith fwiendth; old Colonel Blitz wath at one time tho nearly gone in love with the elder, that he would have had a divorth from hith lady. Among the thtudentth the mania hath been jutht the thame. Whenever one wath worth plucking, Löwe uthed to have him to hith houthe and wob him, until at latht the wathcal'th chawacter became tho well known, that the thtudentth in a body have detherted him, and you will find that not one of them will dance with hith daughterth, handthome ath they are. Go down to Godesberg to-night and thee."

"I *am* going," answered I; "the young ladies asked me to drive down in their carriage;" and I flung myself back on the sofa, and puffed away volumes of smoke, and tossed and tumbled the live-long day, with a horrible conviction that something of what Wilder had told me might be true, and with a vow to sacrifice, at least, one of the officers who had been laughing at me.

There they were, the scoundrels! in their cursed tight frock-coats and hay-coloured mustachios, twirling round in the waltzes with the citizens' daughters, when, according to promise, I arrived with the Israelitish ladies at the garden at Godesberg, where dancing is carried on twice or thrice in a week. There were the students, with their long pipes, and little caps, and long hair, tippling at the tables under the leaves, or dancing that absurd waltz which has always been the object of my contempt. The fact is, I am not a dancing man.

Students and officers, I thought, every eye was looking at me, as I entered the garden with Miss Minna Löwe on my arm. Wilder tells me that I looked blue with rage, and as if I should cut the throat of any man I met.

We had driven down in old Löwe's landau, the old gentleman himself acting as coachman, with Mr. Hirsch in his best clothes by his side. In the carriage came Madame Solomon, in yellow satin; Miss Löwe, in light green (it is astonishing how persons of a light complexion will wear this detestable colour) ; Miss Minna was in white muslin, with a pair of black knit gloves on her beautiful arms, a pink riband round her delicate waist, and a pink scarf on her shoulders, for in those days— and the fashion exists still somewhat on the Rhine—it was the custom of ladies to dress themselves in what we call an evening costume for dinner-time; and so was the lovely Minna attired. As I sat by her on the back seat, I did not say one single word, I confess, but looked unutterable things, and forgot in her beauty all the sus-

picions of the morning. I hadn't asked her to waltz—
for, the fact is, I didn't know how to waltz, and so only
begged her hand for a quadrille.

We entered thus Mr. Blintzner's garden as I have
described, the men staring at us, the lovely Minna on my
arm. I ordered refreshments for the party; and we sat
at a table near the boarded place where the people were
dancing. No one came up to ask Minna to waltz, and I
confess I was not sorry for it—for I own to that dog-in-
the-manger jealousy which is common to love—no one
came but poor little Hirsch, who had been absent to get
sandwiches for the ladies, and came up making his bow
just as I was asking Minna whether she would give no
response to my letters. She looked surprised,—looked
at Hirsch who looked at me, and laying his hand (rather
familiarly) upon my arm, put the other paw to his great
red blubber lips, as if enjoining silence; and, without a
word, carries off Minna, and began twisting her round
in the waltz.

The little brute had assumed his best clothes for the
occasion. He had a white hat and a pair of white gloves;
a green satin stock, with profuse studs of jewels in his
shirt; a yellow waistcoat, with one of pink Cashmere
underneath; very short nankeen trousers, and striped
silk stockings; and a swallow-tailed, short-waisted, light-
brown coat, with brass buttons; the tails whirled in the
wind as he and his partner spun round to a very quick
waltz,—not without agility, I confess, on the little scoundrel's part,—and oh, with what incomparable grace
on Minna's! The other waltzers cleared away, doubtless to look at her performance; but though such a rep-
tile was below my jealousy, I felt that I should have preferred to the same music to kick the little beast round

the circle rather than see his hand encircling such a waist as that.

They only made one or two turns, however, and came back. Minna was blushing very red, and very much agitated.

"Will you take one turn, Fräulein Emma?" said the active Hirsch; and after a little to-do on the part of the elder sister, she got up, and advanced to the dancing place.

What was my surprise when the people again cleared off, and left the pair to perform alone! Hirsch and his partner enjoyed their waltz, however, and returned, looking as ill-humoured as possible. The band struck up presently a quadrille tune. I would not receive any of Minna's excuses. She did not wish to dance; she was faint,—she had no *vis-à-vis*. "Hirsch," said I, with much courtesy, "take out Madame Solomon, and come and dance." We advanced,—big Mrs. Solomon and Hirsch, Minna and I,—Miss Emma remaining with her papa over the Rhine wine and sandwiches.

There were at least twenty couple, who were mustering to make a quadrille when we advanced. Minna blushed scarlet, and I felt her trembling on my arm; no doubt 'twas from joy at dancing with the fashionable young Englander. Hirsch, with a low bow and scrape, led Madame Solomon opposite us, and put himself in the fifth position. It *was* rather disgusting, certainly, for George Savage Fitz-Boodle to be dancing *vis-à-vis* with such an animal as that!

Mr. Hirsch clapped his hands with a knowing air, to begin. I looked up from Minna (what I had been whispering to her must not be concealed—in fact, I had said so previously, *es ist sehr warm;* but I said it with an accent that must have gone to her heart),—

when I say I looked up from her lovely face, I found that every one of the other couples had retired, and that we four were left to dance the quadrille by ourselves!

Yes, by heavens! it was so! Minna, from being scarlet, turned ghastly pale, and would have fallen back had I not encircled her with my arm. "I'm ill," said she; "let me go back to my father." "You *must dance,*" said I, and held up my clenched fist at Hirsch, who I thought would have moved off too; on which the little fellow was compelled to stop. And so we four went through the quadrille.

The first figure seemed to me to last a hundred thousand years. I don't know how it was that Minna did not fall down and faint; but gathering courage all of a sudden, and throwing a quick fierce look round about her, as if in defiance, and a frown which made my little angel for a moment look like a little demon, she went through the dance with as much gracefulness as a duchess. As for me,—at first the whole air seemed to be peopled with grinning faces, and I moved about almost choked with rage and passion. Then gradually the film of fury wore off, and I became wonderfully calm,—nay, had the leisure to look at Monsieur Hirsch, who performed all the steps with wonderful accuracy; and at every one of the faces round about—officers, students, and citizens. None of the gentlemen, probably, liked my face,—for theirs wore, as I looked at them, a very grave and demure expression. But as Minna was dancing, I heard a voice behind her cry, sneeringly, "Brava!" I turned quickly round, and caught the speaker. He turned very red, and so betrayed himself. Our eyes met—it was a settled thing. There was no need of any further arrangement, and it was then, as I have said, that the film cleared off; and I have to thank Captain Heerpauk for getting through the quadrille without an apoplexy.

"Did you hear that—that voice, Herr George?" said Miss Minna, looking beseechingly in my face, and trembling on my arm, as I led her back to her father. Poor soul! I saw it all at once. She loved me,—I knew she did, and trembled lest I should run into any danger. I stuttered, stammered, vowed I did not hear it; at the same time swearing inwardly an oath of the largest dimensions, that I would cut the throat whence that "Brava" issued. I left my lady for a moment, and finding Wilder, pointed out the man to him.

"Oh, Heerpauk," says he. "What do you want with him?"

"Charley," says I, with much heroism and ferocity, "*I want to shoot him;* just tell him so." And when, on demurring, I swore I would go and pull the Captain's nose on the ground, Wilder agreed to settle the business for me; and I returned to our party.

It was quite clear that we could not stay longer in the gardens. Löwe's carriage was not to come for an hour yet; for the banker would not expend money in stabling his horses at the inn, and had accordingly sent them back to Bonn. What should we do? There is a ruined castle at Godesberg, which looks down upon the fair green plain of the Rhine, where Mr. Blintzner's house stands (and let the reader be thankful that I don't give a description of scenery here): there is, I say, a castle at Godesberg. "Explorons le shatto," says I; which elegant French Hirsch translated; and this suggestion was adopted by the five Israelites, to the fairest of whom I offered my arm. The lovely Minna took it, and away we went; Wilder, who was standing at the gate, giving me a nod, to say all was right. I saw him presently strolling up the hill after me, with a Prussian officer, with whom he was talking. Old Löwe was with his daughter, and as the old banker was infirm, the pair walked but slowly. Monsieur Hirsch had given his arm to Madame Solomon. She was a fat woman; the consequence was that Minna and I were soon considerably ahead of the rest of the party, and were ascending the hill alone. I said several things to her, such as only lovers say. "Com il fay bo issy," says I, in the most insinuating way. No answer. "Es ist etwas kalt," even I continued, admirably varying my phrase. She did not speak; she was agitated by the events of the evening, and no wonder.

That fair round arm resting on mine,—that lovely creature walking by my side in the calm moonlight,— the silver Rhine flashing before us, with Drachenfels and the Seven Mountains rising clear in the distance,— the music of the dance coming up to us from the plain below,—the path winding every now and then into the darkest foliage, and at the next moment giving us rich views of the moonlit river and plain below,—could any man but feel the influence of a scene so exquisitely lovely?

"Minna," says I, as she wouldn't speak,—"Minna, I love you; you have known it long, long ago, I know you have. Nay, do not withdraw your hand; your heart has spoken for me. Be mine then!" and taking her hand, I kissed it rapturously, and should have proceeded to her cheek, no doubt, when—she gave me a swinging box on the ear, started back, and incontinently fell a-screaming as loudly as any woman ever did.

"Minna, Minna!" I heard the voice of that cursed Hirsch shouting. "Minna, *meine Gattin!*" and he rushed up the hill; and Minna flung herself in his arms, crying, "Lorenzo, my husband, save me!"

The Löwe family, Wilder, and his friend, came skurrying up the hill at the same time; and we formed what in the theatres is called a tableau.

"You coward!" says Minna, her eyes flashing fire, "who could see a woman insulted, and never defend her!"

"You coward!" roared Hirsch; "coward as well as profligate! You communicated to me your lawless love for this angel,—to me her affianced husband; and you had the audacity to send her letters, not one of which, so help me Heaven, has been received. Yes, you will laugh at Jews,—will you, you brutal Englishman? You will insult our people,—will you, you stupid islander? Psha! I spit upon you!" and here Monsieur Hirsch snapped his fingers in my face, holding Minna at the same time round the waist, who thus became the little monster's buckler.

*   *   *   *   *

They presently walked away, and left me in a pleasant condition. I was actually going to fight a duel on the morrow for the sake of this fury, and it appeared that she had flung me off for cowardice. I had allowed myself to be swindled by her father, and insulted by her filthy little bridegroom, and for what? All the consolation I got from Wilder was,—"I told you tho, my boy, but you wouldn't lithn, you gweat thtoopid blundewing ignowamuth; and now I shall have to thee you shot and buwied to-mowow; and I dare thay you won't even remember me in your will. Captain Schläger," continued he, presenting me to his companion, "Mr. Fitz-Boodle; the Captain acts for Heerpauk in the morning, and we were just talking matters over, when Webecca yonder quied out, and we found her in the armth of Bwian de Bois-Guilbert here."

Captain Schläger was a little social good-humoured man, with a mustachio of straw and silver mixed, and a brilliant purple sabre-cut across a rose-coloured nose. He had the iron cross at his buttonhole, and looked, as he was, a fierce little fighter. But he was too kind-hearted to allow of two boys needlessly cutting each other's throats; and much to the disappointment of Wilder, doubtless, who had been my second in the Martingale affair, and enjoyed no better sport, he said, in English, laughing, "Vell, make your mint easy, my goot young man, I tink you af got into enough sgrabes about dis tam Shewess; and dat you and Heerpauk haf no need to blow each other's brains off."

"Ath for Fitth apologithing," burst out Wilder, "that'th out of the quethtion. He gave the challenge, you know; and how the *dooth* ith he to apologithe now?"

"He gave the challenge, and you took it, and you are de greatest fool of de two. I say the two young men shall not fight;" and then the honest Captain entered into a history of the worthy family of Israel, which would have saved me at least fifty pounds had I known it sooner. It did not differ in substance from what Rohr and Wilder had both told me in the morning. The venerable Löwe was a great thief and extortioner; the daughters were employed as decoy-ducks, in the first place, for the University and the garrison, and afterwards for young strangers, such as my wise self, who visited the place. There was some very sad story about the elder Miss Löwe and a tutor from Saint John's College, Cambridge, who came to Bonn on a reading tour; but I am not at liberty to set down here the particulars. And with regard to Minna, there was a still more dismal history. A fine handsome young student, the pride of the University, had first ruined himself through the offices of the father, and then shot himself for love of the daughter; from which time the whole town had put the family into Coventry; nor had they appeared for two years in public until upon the present occasion with me. As for Monsieur Hirsch, he did not care. He was of a rich Frankfort family of the people, serving his apprenticeship with Löwe, a cousin, and the destined husband of the younger daughter. He traded as much as he could on his own account, and would run upon any errand, and buy or sell anything for a consideration. And so, instead of fighting Captain Heerpauk, I agreed, willingly enough, to go back to the hotel at Godesberg, and shake hands with that officer. The reconciliation, or, rather, the acquaintance between us, was effected over a bottle of wine, at Mr. Blintzner's hotel; and we rode comfortably back in a drosky together to Bonn, where the friendship was still more closely cemented by a supper. At the close of the repast, Heerpauk made a speech on England, fatherland, and German truth and love, and kindly saluted me with a kiss, which is at any lady's service who peruses this little narrative.

As for Mr. Hirsch, it must be confessed, to my shame, that the next morning a gentleman having the air of an old clothesman off duty presented me with an envelope, containing six letters of my composition addressed to Miss Minna Löwe (among them was a little poem in English, which has since called tears from the eyes of more than one lovely girl); and, furthermore, a letter from himself, in which he, Baron Hirsch, of Hirschenwald (the scoundrel, like my friend Wilder, purchased his title in the "Awthtwian Thervith")—in which he, I say, Baron Hirsch, of Hirschenwald, challenges me for insulting Miss Minna Löwe, or demands an apology.

This, I said, Mr. Hirsch might have whenever he chose to come and fetch it, pointing to a horsewhip which lay in a corner; but that he must come early, as I proposed to quit Bonn the next morning. The Baron's friend, hearing this, asked whether I would like some remarkably fine cigars for my excursion, which he could give me a great bargain. He was then shown to the door by my body-servant; nor did Hirsch von Hirschenwald come for the apology.

Twice every year, however, I get a letter from him, dated Frankfort, and proposing to make me a present of a splendid palace in Austria or Bohemia, or 200,000 florins, should I prefer money. I saw his lady at Frankfort only last year, in a front box at the theatre, loaded with diamonds, and at least sixteen stone in weight.

Ah! Minna, Minna! thou mayest grow to be as ugly as sin, and as fat as Daniel Lambert, but I have the amber mouthpiece still, and swear that the prettiest lips in Jewry have kissed it!

[The MS. here concludes with a rude design of a young lady smoking a pipe.]

("*Fitz-Boodle's Confessions,*" *Fraser's Magazine,* October 1842.)

BLUEBEARD'S GHOST

FOR some time after the fatal accident which deprived her of her husband, Mrs. Bluebeard was, as may be imagined, in a state of profound grief.

There was not a widow in all the country who went to such an expense for black bombazeen. She had her beautiful hair confined in crimped caps, and her weepers came over her elbows. Of course she saw no company except her sister Anne (whose company was anything but pleasant to the widow) ; as for her brothers, their odious mess-table manners had always been disagreeable to her. What did she care for jokes about the major, or scandal concerning the Scotch surgeon of the regiment? If they drank their wine out of black bottles or crystal, what did it matter to her? Their stories of the stable, the parade, and the last run with the hounds, were perfectly odious to her; besides, she could not bear their impertinent mustachios and filthy habit of smoking cigars.

They were always wild vulgar young men at the best; but *now*, oh! their presence to her delicate soul was horror! How could she bear to look on them after what had occurred? She thought of the best of husbands, ruthlessly cut down by their cruel heavy cavalry sabres; the kind friend, the generous landlord, the spotless justice of peace, in whose family differences these rude cornets of dragoons had dared to interfere, whose venerable blue hairs they had dragged down with sorrow to the grave!

She put up a most splendid monument to her departed

lord over the family vault of the Bluebeards. The rector, Doctor Sly, who had been Mr. Bluebeard's tutor at
college, wrote an epitaph in the most pompous yet
pathetic Latin:—" Siste, viator! mœrens conjux, heu!
quanto minus est cum reliquis versari quam tui memi-
nisse;" in a word, everything that is usually said in epi-
taphs. A bust of the departed saint, with Virtue
mourning over it, stood over the epitaph, surrounded by
medallions of his wives, and one of these medallions had
as yet no name in it, nor (the epitaph said) could the
widow ever be consoled until her own name was inscribed
there. "For then I shall be with him. In cœlo quies,"
she would say, throwing up her fine eyes to heaven, and
quoting the enormous words of the hatchment which was
put up in the church and over Bluebeard's Hall, where
the butler, the housekeeper, the footman, the housemaid,
and scullions, were all in the profoundest mourning.
The keeper went out to shoot birds in a crape band; nay,
the very scarecrows in the orchard and fruit-garden were
ordered to be dressed in black.

Sister Anne was the only person who refused to wear
black. Mrs. Bluebeard would have parted with her, but
she had no other female relative. Her father, it may be
remembered by readers of the former part of her Memoirs, had married again; and the mother-in-law and
Mrs. Bluebeard, as usual, hated each other furiously.
Mrs. Shacabac had come to the Hall on a visit of condo-
lence; but the widow was so rude to her on the second
day of the visit that the stepmother quitted the house in
a fury. As for the Bluebeards, of course *they* hated the
widow. Had not Mr. Bluebeard settled every shilling
upon her? and, having no children by his former mar-
riages, her property, as I leave you to fancy, was pretty

handsome.   So sister Anne was the only female relative
whom Mrs. Bluebeard would keep near her, and, as we
all know, a woman *must* have a female relative under any
circumstances of pain, or pleasure, or profit—when she
is married, or when she is in a delicate situation.   But let
us continue our story.

"I will never wear mourning for that odious wretch,
sister!" Anne would cry.

"I will trouble you, Miss Anne, not to use such words
in my presence regarding the best of husbands, or to quit
the room at once!" the widow would answer.

"I'm sure it's no great pleasure to sit in it.   I wonder
you don't make use of the closet, sister, where the *other*
Mrs. Bluebeards are."

"Impertinence! they were all embalmed by Monsieur
Gannal.   How dare you report the monstrous calumnies
regarding the best of men?   Take down the family Bible
and read what my blessed saint says of his wives—read it
written in his own hand:—

"'*Friday, June* 20.—Married my beloved wife, Anna Maria
Scrogginsia.

"'*Saturday, August* 1.—A bereaved husband has scarcely
strength to write down in this chronicle that the dearest of wives,
Anna Maria Scrogginsia, expired this day of sore throat.'

"There! can anything be more convincing than that?
Read again:—

"'*Tuesday, Sept.* 1.—This day I led to the hymeneal altar
my soul's blessing, Louisa Matilda Hopkinson.   May this angel
supply the place of her I have lost!

"'*Wednesday, October* 5.—Oh, heavens! pity the distraction
of a wretch who is obliged to record the ruin of his dearest hopes

and affections! This day my adored Louisa Matilda Hopkinson gave up the ghost! A complaint of the head and shoulders was the sudden cause of the event which has rendered the unhappy subscriber the most miserable of men.

"'BLUEBEARD.'.

"Every one of the women are calendared in this delightful, this pathetic, this truly virtuous and tender way; and can you suppose that a man who wrote such sentiments could be a *murderer,* miss?"

"Do you mean to say that he did not *kill* them, then?" said Anne.

"Gracious goodness, Anne, kill them! they died all as naturally as I hope you will. My blessed husband was an angel of goodness and kindness to them. Was it *his* fault that the doctors could not cure their maladies? No, that it wasn't! and when they died the inconsolable husband had their bodies embalmed, in order that on this side of the grave he might never part from them."

"And why did he take you up in the tower, pray? and why did you send me in such a hurry to the leads? and why did he sharpen his long knife, and roar out to you to COME DOWN?"

"Merely to punish me for my curiosity—the dear, good, kind, excellent creature!" sobbed the widow, overpowered with affectionate recollections of her lord's attentions to her.

"I wish," said sister Anne, sulkily, "that I had not been in such a hurry in summoning my brothers."

"Ah!" screamed Mrs. Bluebeard, with a harrowing scream, "don't—don't recall that horrid fatal day, miss! If you had not misled your brothers, my poor dear darling Bluebeard would still be in life, still—still the soul's joy of his bereaved Fatima!"

Whether it is that all wives adore husbands when the latter are no more, or whether it is that Fatima's version of the story is really the correct one, and that the common impression against Bluebeard is an odious prejudice, and that he no more murdered his wives than you and I have, remains yet to be proved, and, indeed, does not much matter for the understanding of the rest of Mrs. B.'s adventures. And though people will say that Bluebeard's settlement of his whole fortune on his wife, in event of survivorship, was a mere act of absurd mystification, seeing that he was fully determined to cut her head off after the honeymoon, yet the best test of his real intentions is the profound grief which the widow manifested for his death, and the fact that he left her mighty well to do in the world.

If anyone were to leave you or me a fortune, my dear friend, would we be too anxious to rake up the how and the why? Pooh! pooh! we would take it and make no bones about it, and Mrs. Bluebeard did likewise. Her husband's family, it is true, argued the point with her, and said, " Madam, you must perceive that Mr. Bluebeard never intended the fortune for you, as it was his fixed intention to chop off your head! it is clear that he meant to leave his money to his blood relations, therefore you ought in equity to hand it over." But she sent them all off with a flea in their ears, as the saying is, and said, " Your argument may be a very good one, but I will, if you please, keep the money." And she ordered the mourning as we have before shown, and indulged in grief, and exalted everywhere the character of the deceased. If anyone would but leave me a fortune, what a funeral and what a character I would give him!

Bluebeard Hall is situated, as we all very well know,

in a remote country district, and, although a fine residence, is remarkably gloomy and lonely. To the widow's susceptible mind, after the death of her darling husband, the place became intolerable. The walk, the lawn, the fountain, the green glades of park over which frisked the dappled deer, all—all recalled the memory of her beloved. It was but yesterday that, as they roamed through the park in the calm summer evening, her Bluebeard pointed out to the keeper the fat buck he was to kill. "Ah!" said the widow, with tears in her fine eyes, "the artless stag was shot down, the haunch was cut and roasted, the jelly had been prepared from the currant-bushes in the garden that he loved, but my Bluebeard never ate of the venison! Look, Anne sweet, pass we the old oak hall; 'tis hung with trophies won by him in the chase, with pictures of the noble race of Bluebeard! Look! by the fireplace there is the gig-whip, his riding-whip, the spud with which you know he used to dig the weeds out of the terrace-walk; in that drawer are his spurs, his whistle, his visiting-cards, with his dear dear name engraven upon them! There are the bits of string that he used to cut off the parcels and keep because string was always useful; his button-hook, and there is the peg on which he used to hang his h—h—*hat!*"

Uncontrollable emotions, bursts of passionate tears, would follow these tender reminiscences of the widow; and the long and short of the matter was, that she was determined to give up Bluebeard Hall and live elsewhere; her love for the memory of the deceased, she said, rendered the place too wretched.

Of course an envious and sneering world said that she was tired of the country and wanted to marry again; but she little heeded its taunts, and Anne, who hated her stepmother and could not live at home, was fain to accompany her sister to the town where the Bluebeards have had for many years a very large, genteel, old-fashioned house. So she went to the town-house, where they lived and quarrelled pretty much as usual; and though Anne often threatened to leave her and go to a boarding-house, of which there were plenty in the place, yet after all to live with her sister, and drive out in the carriage with the footman and coachman in mourning, and the lozenge on the panels, with the Bluebeard and Shacabac arms quartered on it, was far more respectable, and so the lovely sisters continued to dwell together.

For a lady under Mrs. Bluebeard's circumstances, the town-house had other and peculiar advantages. Besides being an exceedingly spacious and dismal brick building, with a dismal iron railing in front, and long dismal thin windows with little panes of glass, it looked out into the churchyard where, time out of mind, between two yew-trees, one of which is cut into the form of a peacock, while the other represents a dumb-waiter—it looked into the churchyard where the monument of the late Bluebeard was placed over the family vault. It was the first thing the widow saw from her bedroom window in the morning, and 'twas sweet to watch at night from the parlour the pallid moonlight lighting up the bust of the departed, and Virtue throwing great black shadows athwart it. Polyanthuses, rhododendra, ranunculuses, and other flowers with the largest names and of the most delightful odours, were planted within the little iron railing that enclosed the last resting-place of the Bluebeards; and the beadle was instructed to half-kill any little boys who might be caught plucking these sweet testimonies of a wife's affection.

Over the sideboard in the dining-room hung a full-length of Mr. Bluebeard, by Ticklegill, R.A., in a militia uniform, frowning down upon the knives and forks and silver trays. Over the mantelpiece he was represented in a hunting costume on his favourite horse; there was a sticking-plaster silhouette of him in the widow's bed-room, and a miniature in the drawing-room, where he was drawn in a gown of black and gold, holding a gold-tas-selled trencher-cap with one hand, and with the other pointing to a diagram of Pons Asinorum. This likeness was taken when he was a fellow-commoner at Saint John's College, Cambridge, and before the growth of that blue beard which was the ornament of his manhood, and a part of which now formed a beautiful blue neck-chain for his bereaved wife.

Sister Anne said the town-house was even more dismal than the country-house, for there was pure air at the Hall, and it was pleasanter to look out on a park than on a churchyard, however fine the monuments might be. But the widow said she was a light-minded hussy, and persisted as usual in her lamentations and mourning. The only male whom she would admit within her doors was the parson of the parish, who read sermons to her; and, as his reverence was at least seventy years old, Anne, though she might be ever so much minded to fall in love, had no opportunity to indulge her inclination; and the townspeople, scandalous as they might be, could not find a word to say against the *liaison* of the venerable man and the heart-stricken widow.

All other company she resolutely refused. When the

players were in the town, the poor manager, who came to beg her to bespeak a comedy, was thrust out of the gates by the big butler. Though there were balls, card-parties, and assemblies, Widow Bluebeard would never subscribe to one of them; and even the officers, those all-conquering heroes who make such ravages in ladies' hearts, and to whom all ladies' doors are commonly open, could never get an entry into the widow's house. Captain Whiskerfield strutted for three weeks up and down before her house, and had not the least effect upon her. Captain O'Grady (of an Irish regiment) attempted to bribe the servants, and one night actually scaled the garden wall; but all that he got was his foot in a man-trap, not to mention being dreadfully scarified by the broken glass; and so *he* never made love any more. Finally, Captain Blackbeard, whose whiskers vied in magnitude with those of the deceased Bluebeard himself, although he attended church regularly every week—he who had not darkened the doors of a church for ten years before —even Captain Blackbeard got nothing by his piety; and the widow never once took her eyes off her book to look at him. The barracks were in despair; and Captain Whiskerfield's tailor, who had supplied him with new clothes in order to win the widow's heart, ended by clapping the Captain into gaol.

His reverence the parson highly applauded the widow's conduct to the officers; but, being himself rather of a social turn, and fond of a good dinner and a bottle, he represented to the lovely mourner that she should endeavour to divert her grief by a little respectable society, and recommended that she should from time to time entertain a few grave and sober persons whom he would present to her. As Doctor Sly had an unbounded

influence over the fair mourner, she acceded to his desires; and accordingly he introduced to her house some
of the most venerable and worthy of his acquaintance,
—all married people, however, so that the widow should
not take the least alarm.

It happened that the Doctor had a nephew, who was
a lawyer in London, and this gentleman came dutifully
in the long vacation to pay a visit to his reverend uncle.
" He is none of your roystering dashing young fellows,"
said his reverence; " he is the delight of his mamma and
sisters; he never drinks anything stronger than tea; he
never missed church thrice a Sunday for these twenty
years; and I hope, my dear and amiable madam, that
you will not object to receive this pattern of young
men for the sake of your most devoted friend, his
uncle."

The widow consented to receive Mr. Sly. He was
not a handsome man certainly. "But what does that
matter?" said the Doctor; "he is *good,* and virtue is
better than all the beauty of all the dragoons in the
Queen's service."

Mr. Sly came there to dinner, and he came to tea; and
he drove out with the widow in the carriage with the
lozenge on it; and at church he handed the psalm-book;
and, in short, he paid her every attention which could be
expected from so polite a young gentleman.

At this the town began to talk, as people in towns will.
" The Doctor kept all bachelors out of the widow's
house," said they, " in order that that ugly nephew of his
may have the field entirely to himself." These speeches
were of course heard by sister Anne, and the little minx
was not a little glad to take advantage of them, in order
to induce her sister to see some more cheerful company.

The fact is, the young hussy loved a dance or a game at cards much more than a humdrum conversation over a tea-table; and so she plied her sister day and night with hints as to the propriety of opening her house, receiving the gentry of the county, and spending her fortune.

To this point the widow at length, though with many sighs and vast unwillingness, acceded; and she went so far as to order a very becoming half-mourning, in which all the world declared she looked charming. " I carry," said she, "my blessed Bluebeard in my heart,—*that* is in the deepest mourning for him, and when the heart grieves there is no need of outward show."

So she issued cards for a little quiet tea and supper, and several of the best families in the town and neighbourhood attended her entertainment. It was followed by another and another; and at last Captain Blackbeard was actually introduced, though, of course, he came in plain clothes.

Doctor Sly and his nephew never could abide the Captain. "They had heard some queer stories," they said, " about proceedings in barracks. Who was it that drank three bottles at a sitting? who had a mare that ran for the plate? and why was it that Dolly Coddlins left the town so suddenly?" Mr. Sly turned up the whites of his eyes as his uncle asked these questions, and sighed for the wickedness of the world. But for all that he was delighted, especially at the anger which the widow manifested when the Dolly Coddlins affair was hinted at. She was furious, and vowed she would never see the wretch again. The lawyer and his uncle were charmed. O short-sighted lawyer and parson, do you think Mrs. Bluebeard would have been so angry if she had not been jealous?—do you think she would have been jealous if she had not—had not what? She protested that she no more cared for the Captain than she did for one of her footmen; but the next time he called she would not condescend to say a word to him.

"My dearest Miss Anne," said the Captain, as he met her in Sir Roger de Coverley (she was herself dancing with Ensign Trippet), "what is the matter with your lovely sister?"

"Dolly Coddlins is the matter," said Miss Anne. "Mr. Sly has told all;" and she was down the middle in a twinkling.

The Captain blushed so at this monstrous insinuation that anyone could see how incorrect it was. He made innumerable blunders in the dance, and was all the time casting such ferocious glances at Mr. Sly (who did not dance, but sate by the widow and ate ices), that his partner thought he was mad, and that Mr. Sly became very uneasy.

When the dance was over, he came to pay his respects to the widow, and, in so doing, somehow trod so violently on Mr. Sly's foot that that gentleman screamed with pain, and presently went home. But though he was gone the widow was not a whit more gracious to Captain Blackbeard. She requested Mr. Trippet to order her carriage that night, and went home without uttering one single word to Captain Blackbeard.

The next morning, and with a face of preternatural longitude, the Reverend Doctor Sly paid a visit to the widow. "The wickedness and bloodthirstiness of the world," said he, "increase every day. O my dear madam, what monsters do we meet in it—what wretches, what assassins, are allowed to go abroad! Would you believe it, that this morning, as my nephew was taking his peaceful morning meal, one of the ruffians from the barracks presented himself with a challenge from Captain Blackbeard?"

"Is he hurt?" screamed the widow.

"No, my dear friend, my dear Frederick is not hurt. And oh, what a joy it will be to him to think you have that tender solicitude for his welfare!"

"You know I have always had the highest respect for him," said the widow; who, when she screamed, was in truth thinking of somebody else. But the Doctor did not choose to interpret her thoughts in that way, and gave all the benefit of them to his nephew.

"That anxiety, dearest madam, which you express for him emboldens me, encourages me, authorises me, to press a point on you which I am sure must have entered your thoughts ere now. The dear youth in whom you have shown such an interest lives but for you! Yes, fair lady, start not at hearing that his sole affections are yours; and with what pride shall I carry to him back the news that he is not indifferent to you!"

"Are they going to fight?" continued the lady, in a breathless state of alarm. "For Heaven's sake, dearest Doctor, prevent the horrid horrid meeting. Send for a magistrate's warrant; do anything; but do not suffer those misguided young men to cut each other's throats!"

"Fairest lady, I fly!" said the Doctor, and went back to lunch quite delighted with the evident partiality Mrs. Bluebeard showed for his nephew. And Mrs. Bluebeard, not content with exhorting him to prevent the duel, rushed to Mr. Pound, the magistrate, informed

him of the facts, got out warrants against both Mr. Sly
and the Captain, and would have put them into execution; but it was discovered that the former gentleman
had abruptly left town, so that the constable could not
lay hold of him.

It somehow, however, came to be generally known
that the widow Bluebeard had declared herself in favour
of Mr. Sly, the lawyer; that she had fainted when told
her lover was about to fight a duel; finally, that she had
accepted him, and would marry him as soon as the quarrel between him and the Captain was settled. Doctor
Sly, when applied to, hummed and ha'd, and would give
no direct answer; but he denied nothing, and looked so
knowing, that all the world was certain of the fact; and
the county paper next week stated:—

"We understand that the lovely and wealthy Mrs. Bl—b—rd
is about once more to enter the bands of wedlock with our distinguished townsman, Frederick S—y, Esquire, of the Middle Temple, London. The learned gentleman left town in consequence
of a dispute with a gallant son of Mars which was likely to have
led to warlike results, had not a magistrate's warrant intervened,
when the Captain was bound over to keep the peace."

In fact, as soon as the Captain was so bound over, Mr.
Sly came back, stating that he had quitted the town not
to avoid a duel,—far from it, but to keep out of the way
of the magistrates, and give the Captain every facility.
He had taken out no warrant; *he* had been perfectly
ready to meet the Captain; if others had been more prudent, it was not his fault. So he held up his head, and
cocked his hat with the most determined air; and all the
lawyers' clerks in the place were quite proud of their
hero.

As for Captain Blackbeard, his rage and indignation may be imagined; a wife robbed from him, his honour put in question by an odious, lanky, squinting lawyer! He fell ill of a fever incontinently; and the surgeon was obliged to take a quantity of blood from him, ten times the amount of which he swore he would have out of the veins of the atrocious Sly.

The announcement in the *Mercury,* however, filled the widow with almost equal indignation. "The widow of the gallant Bluebeard," she said, "marry an odious wretch who lives in dingy chambers in the Middle Temple! Send for Doctor Sly." The Doctor came; she rated him soundly, asked him how he dared set abroad such calumnies concerning her; ordered him to send his nephew back to London at once; and, as he valued her esteem, as he valued the next presentation to a fat living which lay in her gift, to contradict everywhere, and in the fullest terms, the wicked report concerning her.

"My dearest madam," said the Doctor, pulling his longest face, "you shall be obeyed. The poor lad shall be acquainted with the fatal change in your sentiments!"

"Change in my sentiments, Doctor Sly!"

"With the destruction of his hopes, rather let me say; and Heaven grant that the dear boy have strength to bear up against the misfortune which comes so suddenly upon him!"

The next day sister Anne came with a face full of care to Mrs. Bluebeard. "Oh that unhappy lover of yours!" said she.

"Is the Captain unwell?" exclaimed the widow.

"No, it is the other," answered sister Anne. "Poor, poor Mr. Sly! He made a will leaving you all, except five pounds a year to his laundress: he made his will, locked his door, took heart-rending leave of his uncle at night, and this morning was found hanging at his bed-post when Sambo, the black servant, took him up his water to shave. ' Let me be buried,' he said, ' with the pincushion she gave me and the locket containing her hair.' *Did* you give him a pincushion, sister? *did* you give him a locket with your hair?"

"It was only silver-gilt!" sobbed the widow; "and now, oh heavens! I have killed him!" The heart-rend-ing nature of her sobs may be imagined; but they were abruptly interrupted by her sister.

"Killed him?—no such thing! Sambo cut him down when he was as black in the face as the honest negro himself. He came down to breakfast, and I leave you to fancy what a touching meeting took place between the nephew and uncle."

"So much love!" thought the widow. "What a pity he squints so! If he would but get his eyes put straight, I might perhaps—" She did not finish the sentence: ladies often leave this sort of sentence in a sweet con-fusion.

But hearing some news regarding Captain Blackbeard, whose illness and blood-letting were described to her most pathetically, as well as accurately, by the Scotch surgeon of the regiment, her feelings of compassion to-wards the lawyer cooled somewhat; and when Doctor Sly called to know if she would condescend to meet the unhappy youth, she said, in rather a *distrait* manner, that she wished him every happiness; that she had the highest regard and respect for him; that she besought him not to think any more of committing the dreadful crime which would have made her unhappy for ever; *but* that she thought, for the sake of both parties, they had better not meet until Mr. Sly's feelings had grown somewhat more calm.

"Poor fellow! poor fellow!" said the Doctor, "may he be enabled to bear his frightful calamity! I have taken away his razors from him, and Sambo, my man, never lets him out of his sight."

The next day Mrs. Bluebeard thought of sending a friendly message to Dr. Sly's, asking for news of the health of his nephew; but, as she was giving her orders on that subject to John Thomas the footman, it happened that the Captain arrived, and so Thomas was sent downstairs again. And the Captain looked so delightfully interesting with his arm in a sling, and his beautiful black whiskers curling round a face which was paler than usual, that at the end of two hours the widow forgot the message altogether, and, indeed, I believe, asked the Captain whether he would not stop and dine. Ensign Trippet came, too, and the party was very pleasant; and the military gentlemen laughed hugely at the idea of the lawyer having been cut off the bed-post by the black servant, and were so witty on the subject, that the widow ended by half believing that the bed-post and hanging scheme on the part of Mr. Sly was only a feint —a trick to win her heart. Though this, to be sure, was not agreed to by the lady without a pang, for *entre nous,* to hang oneself for a lady is no small compliment to her attractions, and, perhaps, Mrs. Bluebeard was rather disappointed at the notion that the hanging was not a *bonâ-fide* strangulation.

However, presently her nerves were excited again; and she was consoled or horrified, as the case may be (the reader must settle the point according to his ideas and

knowledge of womankind)—she was at any rate dreadfully excited by the receipt of a billet in the well-known
clerk-like hand of Mr. Sly. It ran thus:—

" I saw you through your dining-room windows. You were
hobnobbing with Captain Blackbeard. You looked rosy and well.
You smiled. You drank off the champagne at a single draught.

" I can bear it no more. Live on, smile on, and be happy. My
ghost shall repine, perhaps, at your happiness with another—but
in life I should go mad were I to witness it.

" It is best that I should be gone.

" When you receive this, tell my uncle to drag the fish-pond at
the end of Bachelor's Acre. His black servant Sambo accompa-
nies me, it is true. But Sambo shall perish with me should his
obstinacy venture to restrain me from my purpose. I know
the poor fellow's honesty well, but I also know my own despair.

" Sambo will leave a wife and seven children. Be kind to those
orphan mulattoes for the sake of

" FREDERICK."

The widow gave a dreadful shriek, and interrupted
the two Captains, who were each just in the act of swallowing a bumper of claret. " Fly—fly—save him," she
screamed; " save him, monsters, ere it is too late!
Drowned!—Frederick!—Bachelor's Wa——" Syn-
cope took place, and the rest of the sentence was interrupted.

Deucedly disappointed at being obliged to give up
their wine, the two heroes seized their cocked-hats, and
went towards the spot which the widow in her wild exclamations of despair had sufficiently designated.

Trippet was for running to the fish-pond at the rate
of ten miles an hour. " Take it easy, my good fellow,"
said Captain Blackbeard; " running is unwholesome
after dinner. And if that squinting scoundrel of a

lawyer *does* drown himself, I shan't sleep any the worse."
So the two gentlemen walked leisurely on towards the
Bachelor's Walk; and, indeed, seeing on their way
thither Major Macabaw looking out of the window at
his quarters and smoking a cigar, they went upstairs to
consult the Major, as also a bottle of Schiedam he had.

"They come not!" said the widow, when restored to
herself. "Oh heavens! grant that Frederick is safe!
Sister Anne, go up to the leads and look if anybody is
coming." And up accordingly to the garrets sister Anne
mounted. "Do you see anybody coming, sister Anne?"

"I see Dr. Drench's little boy," said sister Anne; "he
is leaving a pill and draught at Miss Molly Grub's."

"Dearest sister Anne, don't you see anyone coming?"
shouted the widow once again.

"I see a flock of dust,—no! a cloud of sheep. Pshaw!
I see the London coach coming in. There are three out-
sides, and the guard has flung a parcel to Mrs. Jenkins's
maid."

"Distraction! Look once more, sister Anne."

"I see a crowd—a shutter—a shutter with a man on it
—a beadle—forty little boys—Gracious goodness! what
can it be?" and downstairs tumbled sister Anne, and was
looking out of the parlour-window by her sister's side,
when the crowd she had perceived from the garret
passed close by them.

At the head walked the beadle, slashing about at the
little boys.

Two score of these followed and surrounded

A SHUTTER carried by four men.

On the shutter lay *Frederick!* He was ghastly pale;
his hair was draggled over his face; his clothes stuck
tight to him on account of the wet; streams of water

gurgled down the shutter sides. But he was not dead! He turned one eye round towards the window where Mrs. Bluebeard sat, and gave her a look which she never could forget.

Sambo brought up the rear of the procession. He was quite wet through; and, if anything would have put his hair out of curl, his ducking would have done so. But, as he was not a gentleman, he was allowed to walk home on foot, and, as he passed the widow's window, he gave her one dreadful glance with his goggling black eyes, and moved on pointing with his hands to the shutter.

John Thomas the footman was instantly despatched to Doctor Sly's to have news of the patient. There was no shilly-shallying now. He came back in half an hour to say that Mr. Frederick flung himself into Bachelor's Acre fishpond with Sambo, had been dragged out with difficulty, had been put to bed, and had a pint of white wine whey, and was pretty comfortable. "Thank Heaven!" said the widow, and gave John Thomas a seven-shilling piece, and sat down with a lightened heart to tea. "What a heart!" said she to sister Anne. "And, oh, what a pity it is that he squints!"

Here the two Captains arrived. They had not been to the Bachelor's Walk; they had remained at Major Macabaw's consulting the Schiedam. They had made up their minds what to say. "Hang the fellow! he will never have the pluck to drown himself," said Captain Blackbeard. "Let us argue on that, as we may safely."

"My sweet lady," said he, accordingly, "we have had the pond dragged. No Mr. Sly. And the fisherman who keeps the punt assures us that he has not been there all day."

"Audacious falsehood!" said the widow, her eyes flashing fire. "Go, heartless man! who dares to trifle thus with the feelings of a respectable and unprotected woman. Go, sir, you're only fit for the love of a—Dolly—Coddlins!" She pronounced the *Coddlins* with a withering sarcasm that struck the Captain aghast; and sailing out of the room, she left her tea untasted, and did not wish either of the military gentlemen good-night.

But, gentles, an ye know the delicate fibre of woman's heart, ye will not in very sooth believe that such events as those we have described—such tempests of passion—fierce winds of woe—blinding lightnings of tremendous joy and tremendous grief—could pass over one frail flower and leave it all unscathed. No! Grief kills as joy doth. Doth not the scorching sun nip the rose-bud as well as the bitter wind? As Mrs. Sigourney sweetly sings—

> " Ah! the heart is a soft and a delicate thing;
> Ah! the heart is a lute with a thrilling string;
> A spirit that floats on a gossamer's wing!"

Such was Fatima's heart. In a word, the preceding events had a powerful effect upon her nervous system, and she was ordered much quiet and sal-volatile by her skilful medical attendant, Doctor Glauber.

To be so ardently, passionately loved as she was, to know that Frederick had twice plunged into death from attachment to her, was to awaken in her bosom " a thrilling string" indeed! Could she witness such attachment, and not be touched by it? She *was* touched by it —she was influenced by the virtues, by the passion, by the misfortunes of Frederick; but then he was so abominably ugly that she could not—she could not consent to become his bride!

She told Doctor Sly so. "I respect and esteem your nephew," said she; "but my resolve is made. I will continue faithful to that blessed saint, whose monument is ever before my eyes" (she pointed to the churchyard as she spoke). "Leave this poor tortured heart in quiet. It has already suffered more than most hearts could bear. I will repose under the shadow of that tomb until I am called to rest within it—to rest by the side of my Bluebeard!"

The ranunculuses, rhododendra, and polyanthuses, which ornamented that mausoleum, had somehow been suffered to run greatly to seed during the last few months, and it was with no slight self-accusation that she acknowledged this fact on visiting the "garden of the grave," as she called it; and she scolded the beadle soundly for neglecting his duty towards it. He promised obedience for the future, dug out all the weeds that were creeping round the family vault, and (having charge of the key) entered that awful place, and swept and dusted the melancholy contents of the tomb.

Next morning the widow came down to breakfast looking very pale. She had passed a bad night; she had had awful dreams; she had heard a voice call her thrice at midnight. "Pooh! my dear; it's only nervousness," said sceptical sister Anne.

Here John Thomas the footman entered, and said the beadle was in the hall, looking in a very strange way. He had been about the house since daybreak, and insisted on seeing Mrs. Bluebeard. "Let him enter," said that lady, prepared for some great mystery. The beadle came; he was pale as death; his hair was dishevelled, and his cocked-hat out of order. "What have you to say?" said the lady trembling.

Before beginning, he fell down on his knees.

"Yesterday," said he, "according to your ladyship's orders, I dug up the flower-beds of the family vault— dusted the vault and the—the coffins" (added he, trembling) "inside. Me and John Sexton did it together, and polished up the plate quite beautiful."

"For Heaven's sake, don't allude to it," cried the widow, turning pale.

"Well, my lady, I locked the door, came away, and found in my hurry—for I wanted to beat two little boys what was playing at marbles on Alderman Paunch's monyment—I found, my lady, I'd forgot my cane. I couldn't get John Sexton to go back with me till this morning, and I didn't like to go alone, and so we went this morning, and what do you think I found? I found his honour's coffin turned round, and the cane broke in two. Here's the cane!"

"Ah!" screamed the widow, "take it away—take it away!"

"Well, what does this prove," said sister Anne, "but that somebody moved the coffin and broke the cane?"

"Somebody! *who's somebody?*" said the beadle, staring round about him. And all of a sudden he started back with a tremendous roar, that made the ladies scream, and all the glasses on the sideboard jingle, and cried, "*That's the man!*"

He pointed to the portrait of Bluebeard, which stood over the jingling glasses on the sideboard. "That's the man I saw last night walking round the vault, as I'm a living sinner. I saw him a-walking round and round, and, when I went up to speak to him, I'm blessed if he didn't go in at the iron gate, which opened afore him like—like winking, and then in at the vault door, which I'd double-locked, my lady, and bolted inside, I'll take my oath on it!"

"Perhaps you had given him the key?" suggested sister Anne.

"It's never been out of my pocket. Here it is," cried the beadle, "I'll have no more to do with it;" and he flung down the ponderous key, amidst another scream from widow Bluebeard.

"At what hour did you see him?" gasped she.

"At twelve o'clock, of course."

"It must have been at that very hour," said she, "I heard the voice."

"What voice?" said Anne.

"A voice that called 'Fatima! Fatima! Fatima!' three times as plain as ever voice did."

"It didn't speak to me," said the beadle; "it only nodded its head and wagged its head and beard."

"W—w—was it a *bl—ue beard?*" said the widow.

"Powder-blue, ma'am, as I've a soul to save!"

Doctor Drench was of course instantly sent for. But what are the medicaments of the apothecary in a case where the grave gives up its dead? Doctor Sly arrived, and he offered ghostly—ah! too ghostly—consolation. He said he believed in them. His own grandmother had appeared to his grandfather several times before he married again. He could not doubt that supernatural agencies were possible, even frequent.

"Suppose he were to appear to me alone," ejaculated the widow, "I should die of fright."

The Doctor looked particularly arch. "The best way in these cases, my dear madam," said he—"the best way for unprotected ladies is to get a husband. I never heard of a first husband's ghost appearing to a woman and her second husband in my life. In all history there is no account of one."

"Ah! why should I be afraid of seeing my Bluebeard again?" said the widow; and the Doctor retired quite pleased, for the lady was evidently thinking of a second husband.

"The Captain would be a better protector for me certainly than Mr. Sly," thought the lady, with a sigh; "but Mr. Sly will certainly kill himself, and will the Captain be a match for two ghosts? Sly will kill himself; but ah! the Captain won't;" and the widow thought with pangs of bitter mortification of Dolly Coddlins. How, how should these distracting circumstances be brought to an end?

She retired to rest that night not without a tremor—to bed, but not to sleep. At midnight a voice was heard in her room crying "Fatima! Fatima! Fatima!" in awful accents. The doors banged to and fro, the bells began to ring, the maids went up and down stairs skurrying and screaming, and gave warning in a body. John Thomas, as pale as death, declared that he found Bluebeard's yeomanry sword, that hung in the hall, drawn and on the ground; and the sticking-plaster miniature in Mr. Bluebeard's bedroom was found turned topsy-turvy!

"It is some trick," said the obstinate and incredulous sister Anne. "To-night I will come and sleep with you, sister;" and the night came, and the sisters retired together.

'Twas a wild night. The wind howling without went crashing through the old trees of the old rookery round about the old church. The long bedroom windows went thump—thumping; the moon could be seen through them lighting up the graves with their ghastly shadows; the yew-tree, cut into the shape of a bird, looked particularly dreadful, and bent and swayed as if it would peck something off that other yew-tree which was of the shape of a dumb-waiter. The bells at midnight began to ring as usual, the doors clapped, jingle—jingle down came a suit of armour in the hall, and a voice came and cried, "Fatima! Fatima! Fatima! look, look, look! the tomb, the tomb, the tomb!"

She looked. The vault door was open; and there in the moonlight stood Bluebeard, exactly as he was represented in the picture in his yeomanry dress, his face frightfully pale and his great blue beard curling over his chest, as awful as Mr. Muntz's.

Sister Anne saw the vision as well as Fatima. We shall spare the account of their terrors and screams. Strange to say, John Thomas, who slept in the attic above his mistress's bedroom, declared he was on the watch all night and had seen nothing in the churchyard, and heard no sort of voices in the house.

And now the question came, What could the ghost want by appearing? "Is there anything," exclaimed the unhappy and perplexed Fatima, "that he would have me do? It is well to say 'now, now, now,' and to show himself; but what is it that makes my blessed husband so uneasy in his grave?" And all parties consulted agreed that it was a very sensible question.

John Thomas the footman, whose excessive terror at the appearance of the ghost had procured him his mistress's confidence, advised Mr. Screw, the butler, who communicated with Mrs. Baggs, the housekeeper, who condescended to impart her observations to Mrs. Bustle, the lady's-maid—John Thomas, I say, decidedly advised that my lady should consult a cunning man. There was such a man in town; he had prophesied who should marry his (John Thomas's) cousin; he had cured Farmer Horn's cattle, which were evidently bewitched; he could raise ghosts, and make them speak, and he therefore was the very person to be consulted in the present juncture.

"What nonsense is this you have been talking to the maids, John Thomas, about the conjurer who lives in—in—"

"In Hangman's Lane, ma'am, where the old gibbet used to stand," replied John, who was bringing in the muffins. "It's no nonsense, my lady. Every word as that man says comes true, and he knows everything."

"I desire you will not frighten the girls in the servants' hall with any of those silly stories," said the widow; and the meaning of this speech may, of course, at once be guessed. It was that the widow meant to consult the conjurer that very night. Sister Anne said that she would never, under such circumstances, desert her dear Fatima. John Thomas was summoned to attend the ladies with a dark lantern, and forth they set on their perilous visit to the conjurer at his dreadful abode in Hangman's Lane.

*   *   *   *   *

What took place at that frightful interview has never been entirely known. But there was no disturbance in the house on the night after. The bells slept quietly, the doors did not bang in the least, twelve o'clock struck and no ghost appeared in the churchyard, and the whole family had a quiet night. The widow attributed this to a sprig of rosemary which the wizard gave her, and a horseshoe which she flung into the garden round the family vault, and which would keep *any* ghost quiet.

It happened the next day that, going to her milliner's, sister Anne met a gentleman who has been before mentioned in this story, Ensign Trippet by name; and, indeed, if the truth must be known it somehow happened that she met the Ensign somewhere every day of the week.

"What news of the ghost, my dearest Miss Shacabac?" said he (you may guess on what terms the two young people were by the manner in which Mr. Trippet addressed the lady); "has Bluebeard's ghost frightened your sister into any more fits, or set the bells a-ringing?"

Sister Anne, with a very grave air, told him that he must not joke on so awful a subject; that the ghost had been laid for a while; that a cunning man had told her sister things so wonderful that *any* man must believe in them; that, among other things, he had shown to Fatima her future husband.

"Had," said the Ensign, "he black whiskers and a red coat?"

"No," answered Anne, with a sigh, "he had red whiskers and a black coat."

"It can't be that rascal Sly!" cried the Ensign. But Anne only sighed more deeply, and would not answer yes or no. "You may tell the poor Captain," she said, "there is no hope for him, and all he has left is to hang himself."

"He shall cut the throat of Sly first, though," replied Mr. Trippet, fiercely. But Anne said things were not decided as yet. Fatima was exceedingly restive and unwilling to acquiesce in the idea of being married to Mr. Sly; she had asked for further authority. The wizard said he could bring her own husband from the grave to point out her second bridegroom, who shall be, can be, must be, no other than Frederick Sly.

"It's a trick," said the Ensign. But Anne was too much frightened by the preceding evening's occurrences to say so. "To-night," she said, "the grave will tell all." And she left Ensign Trippet in a very solemn and affecting way.

*   *   *   *   *

At midnight three figures were seen to issue from widow Bluebeard's house and pass through the churchyard turnstile and so away among the graves.

"To call up a ghost is bad enough," said the wizard; "to make him speak is awful. I recommend you, ma'am, to beware, for such curiosity has been fatal to many. There was one Arabian necromancer of my acquaintance who tried to make a ghost speak, and was torn in pieces on the spot. There was another person who *did* hear a ghost speak certainly, but came away from the interview deaf and dumb. There was another—"

"Never mind," says Mrs. Bluebeard, all her old curiosity aroused, "see him and hear him I will. Haven't I seen him and heard him, too, already? When he's audible *and* visible, *then's* the time."

"But when you heard him," said the necromancer, "he was invisible, and when you saw him he was inaudible; so make up your mind what you will ask him, for ghosts will stand no shilly-shallying. I knew a stuttering man who was flung down by a ghost, and—"

"I *have* made up my mind," said Fatima, interrupting him.

"To ask him what husband you shall take," whispered Anne.

Fatima only turned red, and sister Anne squeezed her hand; they passed into the graveyard in silence.

There was no moon; the night was pitch-dark. They threaded their way through the graves, stumbling over them here and there. An owl was toowhooing from the church tower, a dog was howling somewhere, a cock began to crow, as they will sometimes at twelve o'clock at night.

"Make haste," said the wizard. "Decide whether you will go on or not."

"Let us go back, sister," said Anne.

"I *will* go on," said Fatima. "I should die if I gave it up, I feel I should."

"Here's the gate; kneel down," said the wizard. The women knelt down.

"Will you see your first husband or your second husband?"

"I will see Bluebeard first," said the widow; "I shall know then whether this be a mockery, or you have the power you pretend to."

At this the wizard uttered an incantation, so frightful and of such incomprehensible words, that it is impossible for any mortal to repeat them. And at the end of what seemed to be a versicle of his chant he called "Bluebeard!" There was no noise but the moaning of the wind in the trees, and toowhooing of the owl in the tower.

At the end of the second verse he paused again and called "Bluebeard!" The cock began to crow, the dog began to howl, a watchman in the town began to cry out the hour, and there came from the vault within a hollow groan, and a dreadful voice said, "Who wants me?"

Kneeling in front of the tomb, the necromancer began the third verse: as he spoke, the former phenomena were still to be remarked. As he continued, a number of ghosts rose from their graves and advanced round the kneeling figures in a circle. As he concluded, with a loud bang the door of the vault flew open, and there in blue light stood Bluebeard in his blue uniform, waving his blue sword and flashing his blue eyes round about!

" Speak now, or you are lost," said the necromancer to Fatima. But, for the first time in her life, she had not a word to say. Sister Anne, too, was dumb with terror. And, as the awful figure advanced towards them as they were kneeling, the sister thought all was over with them, and Fatima once more had occasion to repent her fatal curiosity.

The figure advanced, saying, in dreadful accents, " Fatima! Fatima! Fatima! wherefore am I called from my grave?" when all of a sudden down dropped his sword, down the ghost of Bluebeard went on his knees, and, clasping his hands together, roared out, "Mercy, mercy!" as loud as man could roar.

Six other ghosts stood round the kneeling group. " Why do you call me from the tomb?" said the first; " Who dares disturb my grave? " said the second; " Seize him and away with him!" cried the third. " Murder, mercy!" still roared the ghost of Bluebeard, as the white-robed spirits advanced and caught hold of him.

" It's only Tom Trippet," said a voice at Anne's ear.

" And your very humble servant," said a voice well known to Mrs. Bluebeard; and they helped the ladies to rise, while the other ghosts seized Bluebeard. The necromancer took to his heels and got off; he was found to be no other than Mr. Claptrap, the manager of the theatre.

It was some time before the ghost of Bluebeard could recover from the fainting fit into which he had been plunged when seized by the opposition ghosts in white; and while they were ducking him at the pump his blue beard came off, and he was discovered to be—who do you think? Why Mr. Sly, to be sure; and it appears that John Thomas the footman had lent him the uniform, and had clapped the doors, and rung the bells, and spoken down the chimney; and it was Mr. Claptrap who gave Mr. Sly the blue fire and the theatre gong, and he went to London next morning by the coach; and, as it was discovered that the story concerning Miss Coddlins was a shameful calumny, why, of course, the widow married Captain Blackbeard. Doctor Sly married them, and has always declared that he knew nothing of his nephew's doings, and wondered that he has not tried to commit suicide since his last disappointment.

Mr. and Mrs. Trippet are likewise living happily together, and this, I am given to understand, is the ultimate fate of a family in whom we were all very much interested in early life.

You will say that the story is not probable. Psha! Isn't it written in a book? and is it a whit less probable than the first part of the tale?

(*Fraser's Magazine*, October 1843.)